# STOLEN VALOR

## A CARSON BRAND NOVEL

Craig Rainey

Craig Rainey Publishing

AUSTIN, TEXAS

**Craig Rainey/Craig Rainey Publishing**
**Austin, Texas**
https://stolenvalornovel.com
https://craigrainey.com

Cover Artwork by CreativeParamita.com

**Stolen Valor/ Craig Rainey**. -- 1st ed.
ISBN: 978-1-7339867-0-0

# Reviews

For Mom and Dad.  It is your love and guidance which I still treasure and am proud to have received.

Under the loftiest monuments sleeps the dust of murder.

— ROBERT G. INGERSOLL

# Acknowledgements

When one decides to pursue as personal an endeavor as writing a novel, the process impacts nearly everyone around you. That which defined you before is slow to change, no matter how ardently you crave redefinition. An author's first book is remarkable but not as impressive as the second. One of my favorite books, The Writer's Art, by James J. Kilpatrick, contains a reference which I revisit frequently to remind myself of who I am and what I want to become. 'Someone who writes a book is an Author. Someone who writes several books is a writer.' A writer I must be.

As I wrote at the start of this page, this process impacts nearly everyone around you. Because of that imposition I must apologize to all those dear people I love and who love me in return. I apologize for monopolizing conversations with my uncontrolled excitement for those most recently written pages of my latest book. I am sorry for the confusion which ensued when I expected to be thought a serious writer, although my body of work did not support my desire. I heartily apologize to my dear Alexandra, who was integral to my process as a sounding board for ideas, and guinea pig to my prose.

I must thank those same people for their support and advice. My mother and father, who showed excitement for my passion to write -

even those awkward stories written from the singularly innocent perspective of a child.

To my brother Jimmy, who asked the obvious question no one else would ask: Why hadn't I done this all my life?

Thank you, Charlie, who took time from his political non-fiction to placate a brother's ego.

Thank you to my sister Tracey who has always been strong in her beliefs and from whom I re-earned a treasured trust.

Thank you, Clan Valhalla, for your support and interest in all things Craig Rainey.

To Karen, my first fan who never let me quit, thank you for your faith and devotion.

My deepest thanks go to my love Alexandra. If it hadn't been for you, I would never have finished *Massacre at Agua Caliente*. If it hadn't been for you, I would not have found the ability to follow the writer's path.

Thank you, dear reader, for allowing me to tell you my story. Your time is of value and I am grateful you are investing it in me.

I thank God, above all, for the gifts he bestowed upon me at birth, among which writing seems to be a part.

CRAIG RAINEY

# Prologue

Juarez was known as the kidnapping/murder capital of Mexico for many years before the Cartel took over the country's politics, commerce and economy. The years that followed advanced the violence to a frantic pace.

The citizens of the large city were poor, offering little to obtain from which the Cartel could profit. Drugs, stolen goods, and cash were far from the only source of profit for the Cartel.

Pablo Rojas had ascended to his position as head of the Cartel through a powerful combination of cunning and ruthlessness. Both traits were respected and feared within his organization.

The newspapers and TV anchors referred to him as *Cabeza de la Serpiento,* Head of the Snake. He disliked the term from the first. The name was never uttered by anyone within his organization after the hangings in Nueva Laredo. The hangings represented the ruthlessness in his formula for success.

He considered Juarez, like all cities on the Mexican/American border, a working farm from which he harvested, but never had to plant or maintain. The crops he sowed grew naturally and readily like a weed or invasive grass. In decades past, the harvest was only a supplement to the considerable profits the organization realized from a thriving drug trade.

The dominance of Human Trafficking and White Slavery within the Cartel wasn't prevalent because of the pressures of an escalating War on Drugs. The seizures of product and personnel represented a quantifiable cost of doing business. He ran the operation as any large corporation might, accounting for adverse environmental and process conditions. Human Trafficking moved to prominence in his business model due to the growing number of states moving towards the legalization of Marijuana. Profits shrank with the lessening demand.

Beautiful girls would never be regulated nor legalized in any state or country. The demand, particularly in the United States, was immense.  His farms were closer to the marketplace than his drug suppliers. His was a perfect world of supply and demand.

Selection and distribution of young girls was handled on a case by case basis. The harvest was targeted and specific to a very exacting definition of the type of girl the market demanded.

The large number of kidnappings and murders in Juarez consisted of a diverse demographic within which the organization easily hid a comparatively small number of abductions of young girls. The disappearances were included in the general tally by law enforcement and news organizations. A small number of special interest groups and involved citizens railed against the kidnappings. Their warnings of the prevalence of enslaving young girls was a weak message largely ignored by the news editors and the news station managers. The newspapers rarely gave his Trafficking activities more than an upper right-hand column in the Editorials.

Three dark trucks choked the few people who were outside their houses with a thick cloud of dust. Inside the lead vehicle, Elias Uriegas relaxed against the passenger seat. He was a thin man with a thick mustache. His bucked teeth were yellow stained with stripes of brown from snuff and chewing tobacco. He rarely spit, preferring to swallow the juices.

Tonight was another pick-up and delivery. He was paid handsomely for his work. Years of providing the finest product had raised his pricing to the highest amongst his contemporaries. His success was chiefly due to his preparation. He had a nine-man team. All of them were in the trucks behind his. They were scouts, acquisition fronts and harvesters. Elias grinned, baring his dull striped teeth. The boss liked to call the worst jobs in the organization by neat, harmless titles.

His "Scouts" were those who wandered the streets looking for suitable girls. The scouting process could take up to three years depending upon the age of the prospect (another Rojas term). Elias kept the names and locations of the girls on a note pad. Computers and the internet were too vulnerable to be trusted with the damning information.

The men who Rojas called "Acquisition Fronts" were the most attractive and appeared the most innocent amongst his crew. They got close to the girls, learning about the girls' habits and home life. The information was critical in the success of the harvest.

The "Harvest" was a quick and violent snatch and go.

The three trucks and the nine men sped towards the city where they would harvest the next crop.

Nina, Maria and Christina leaned against the chain link fence outside of Christina's small home in Juarez. She drew circles with her toe in the dirt along the inside of the fence. Nina and Maria stood outside the fence. The sun had only just dropped below the dusty horizon, but Christina felt prickles of alarm, causing her a growing anxiety. Everyone knew that it was unwise for teenage girls to remain outside their homes after dark. It had been several weeks since the last kidnapping, but the danger was no less real.

"Come inside, *meja*", her father called from within the small house. The front door was open, the screen door guarded against the clouds of flies. The soft glow of the living room lamp and the flicker of the TV comforted her.

"*Si, papa*", she called back to him.

"You are such a good girl", Maria chided her.

They giggled at the dig.

Nina lifted her head to listen. The sounds of the night seemed to have changed. The others paused, watching her with puzzled expressions.

"You too?" Maria asked Nina.

"Listen", Nina said, lifting a hand.

The two girls canted their heads to listen for what Nina claimed she heard. Gradually the other two heard a growing din of noise as yet unidentifiable.

"What is that?" Maria asked of no one in particular.

The intersection nearby glowed with the light of approaching automobiles. The sound became the clearly defined noise of gravel under tires and the roar of engines. Three trucks heaved into view, sliding as they turned onto the street.

The girls were frozen in place, fear rooting them to the ground.

The stories were familiar. The three trucks were the specters of every girl's nightmare. Their nightmare was approaching terrifyingly quickly.

Maria and Nina turned to run as the trucks slid to a stop before Christina's house. The doors flung open and men spilled from the trucks, giving chase after the two girls.

Christina ran across the yard and up the stairs. She yanked the screen door open violently. She ran into the house where her father sat.

"*Papa, Papa! Ayudame, Papa!*"

Papa stood from his chair before the TV.

The screen door burst open and a short but powerfully built youth entered the room. He carried a black revolver in his right hand. Papa moved forward, pulling Christina behind him. The young man strode directly before Papa and bashed him across the face with the big pistol. Papa went down with a groan. The thug kicked Papa and grabbed Christina.

Christina screamed and clawed at the iron grip. The man pocketed the pistol and covered her mouth with a strong sweaty hand. He dragged her out past the broken screen door and to the trucks where several men waited with Nina. As he brought Christina through the gate, three men returned to the trucks, Maria struggling with her captors. The girls were bound with large plastic slip ties, their mouths sealed with duct tape, and dropped into the bed of the first truck.

Elias grinned his filthy smile as he looked over the girls. He nodded at Christina. She was singularly beautiful. Elias grabbed her ass as he leaned towards her over the side of the truck.

"Time to ride the *Vaca* Train, *Meja*."

The men hurried to the trucks. Soon the little house on the dusty street in Juarez was quiet once more.

# Chapter 1

A thick blue smoke cloud fogged the dark bar. A popular country tune twanged an empathetic broken-hearted message from the corner jukebox. Carson Brand sipped bourbon rocks from a heavy high ball glass. His thoughts rankled him. He was troubled by his strong doubts of Natalie, his girlfriend of eight months. His brow furrowed in anger as he studied the drink before him. He was convinced that Natalie was cheating on him.

Like a strong wind driving dry leaves before it, a looming danger scattered his troubled thoughts. A sense of impending violence provided him a strange relief from the painful images in his mind - Natalie lying in ecstasy beneath another man. He looked up in alarm.

Normally, any diversion from his dark suspicions would have been a welcome interruption. The danger of the moment, however, was a diversion as dire as his jealous doubts.

His gaze moved left towards the ominous presence which had roused him from his quiet thoughts. He didn't want trouble, but here it was.

He felt a grim surprise that he registered no internal alarm at the impending threat before him. He realized, with habitual practicality, that his reluctance to fight was more related to the five dollars he had recently sacrificed to the merry glow of the digital juke box, than the threat of imminent danger descending upon him.

He was well into his favorite part of his daily ritual: getting to the bottom of the first of three bourbons: a hard and fast after-work therapy. The haze of an infant buzz had just begun to weave a dull screen through which life would soon appear pleasant and full of possibility.

"Fourth of the one-thirty-third, huh?"

A bearded man stood just outside of foot range. His tattooed, logger-size arms were crossed over an airborne T-shirt which struggled to hide a barrel chest and lean washboard stomach.

He referred to the Texas Army National Guard unit with which Brand had served years before.

Brand did not immediately react. Sometimes one paid for friendly intentions. In bar life, one thing led to another thing, and the last thing was Brand making a friendly connection with a military brother at the bar.

"Last time I checked, that was a weekend warrior F.A. battalion."

Airborne pointed a thick accusing finger at Brand.

"You were never in Falusia, because they were never in Falusia."

The oaf was right. His former National Guard field artillery battalion had never seen any service in the desert. The forbidding heat of Fort Hood for two weeks every summer was no picnic, but it wasn't life threatening if you observed proper heat discipline.

Resigned to the inevitable looming conflict, Brand drained his drink. Ice fell rebelliously onto his upper lip. A small cold stream escaped his chin and darkened his shirt.

Karen, the dark-haired bartender, watched the developing situation dubiously. Brand glanced at her to gauge how far he could go without the police intervening.

Karen was a veteran of countless bar conflicts and seemed nonplussed thus far. He smiled weakly at her. She was more than his bartender. She was his friend and a former lover. She had placed him firmly into the friend zone once she had learned he was married at the time they dated. He was no longer married, but he remained in the friend zone, nonetheless.

Karen was one of the few blondes who colored their hair brunette. He had only known her with dark hair. Blonde was the hair color of her old life. This new chapter was likely as dark as the hair change.

Mr. Muscles was growing impatient with Brand's wool-gathering.

"You'd best come out of it, Mr. Nasty Guard."

Brand returned his glass to the moist coaster, embossed with a colorful beer logo. He wiped the ice trail from his chin with a disapproving frown. He considered the indignant big man impassively.

The unavoidable conflict to come had little to do with the insult of the exaggerated claims of his military service. The underlying cause of this confrontation was the large breasts and gym-honed curves of the dusky brunette at the end of the bar.

Her name was Gwen. She was a real estate broker with a big national firm. She drove a Saab and lived in a million-dollar house in the hill country. She had arrived early for her date by more than two hours. She had spent most of that time downing dirty Martinis and putting Brand in his place.

The latter was recompense for his loitering gaze and friendly small talk. In his experience, beautiful women displayed their interest through deprecating comments, delivered in the context of helpful advice regarding the hopelessness of winning their favor.

His philanderer buddy, Bert, had an opening line that never failed. Women like Gwen were his favorite quarry. He began with an hypothesis:

'Is it fair that when a woman has many sexual partners, she is considered a slut, but when a man has many partners, he is considered a stud?'

No matter the answer, he invariably followed the first question with an unlikely challenge. He would say in a low conspiratorial tone, 'When I tell you why, you will agree that it is not only true, but completely fair.'

Invariably, his challenge was accepted, and his prediction of their agreement summarily rejected.

In Brand's opinion, Bert was halfway there merely being given the time to work the angle. He had successfully made it to the "chair."

Bert would explain to the skeptical woman that a man's nature is to meet women. If he is not good at it, he has a faulty *Approach Mechanism*. A woman's nature is to reject the man. How the man handles the rejection determines whether he is an appropriate mate or not. If a large number of men get through the screening process, she is said to have a faulty *Filtering Mechanism.*

Mr. Muscles shifted his weight, frustrated with Brand's delayed reaction to the danger he represented.

Brand understood the reasoning behind the theory, but he suspected that the line only worked if delivered with proper skill. Brand had never been much of a lady's man. Drunken Gwen was just hot enough that he had given the method a try. The line got her attention but failed to impress her in the payoff. Luckily – maybe that was not the right word – she found Brand attractive enough to flirt with him in return.

Brand's eyes brightened as his thoughts returned to the angry bigger man.

"Let's get down to what is really bothering you, big boy. Your girl chatted me up before you got here. From what I gather, she is the brains of the operation. She is also, apparently, pretty proud of how much of a woman she is."

Brand raised his voice a fraction to include Karen.

"I'm gonna need another in just a minute, sugar."

Karen moved forward cautiously and collected his glass. He nodded his thanks and continued his thought.

"You are backing a losing cause. I was minutes away from hitting that in the parking lot when you arrived. I'm having girlfriend problems of my own, so she caught me in a weakened state."

Mr. Muscles lowered his huge arms. He flexed his hands as his rage grew. He was big, at least six-five. He likely lived in the gym. He was former military, confirmed by their earlier conversation, his taking offense at Brand's boast of military combat service, and the Airborne T-shirt.

Although Mr. Muscles was a formidable adversary, Brand felt pity for him. The poor guy had arrived to his date a doomed man. Drunk Gwen was past her Filtering stage and was well into the next. Brand wasn't sure how Bert would characterize the metamorphosis, but he saw it as the phase where rejected hot girl sic's intimidating boyfriend on guy with faulty Approach Mechanism.

The inevitability of the battle to come galvanized Brand in his reaction to the threat. There was no point taking this thing sitting down.

Brand stood to his full six feet and faced the behemoth. He was in good shape for a regular guy who ate what he wanted and drank frequently. He was thick in the right places and his arms and legs were sturdy from a lifetime of outdoor labor. His dark blue eyes reflected a menace the bigger man innately recognized.

"This is about to go bad for you", Brand said calmly. His tone belied the rage growing within him in reaction to the confident aggression of the bigger man.

He glanced at Karen with a look meant to assuage her rising sense of alarm. Her expression assured him she was not assuaged. He looked at the big man once more.

"Being a big guy has kept you out of fights. Most guys don't like to tangle with six-foot-five assholes."

Brand felt a familiar heat rising deep within him. His anger at Natalie's likely indiscretions, coupled with the threat of violence, narrowed his eyes and stiffened his back. He awaited the hum of adrenalin which always led to the next stage, a release deep within him which blossomed into the freedom of full, unbridled fury.

Although his passions mounted, his voice remained even.

"I've got bigger problems than you right now. Why don't you go back to your girl and your drink while you can."

He pointed mildly towards Gwen and the nearby empty seat.

The giant made no move to retreat.

Brand was near the point where he would no longer be able to resist the growing desire for conflict. With his remaining calm near its end, he tried to reason with the big man.

"As I said, you are a big guy and that has gotten you out of a lot of trouble. If you were a smaller man, I would feel guilty about stomping a mud hole in your ass. If you keep annoying me, I am going to whip your ass right in front of that slutty girlfriend of yours."

Brand watched the giant's eyes. He saw the dullness of fear and doubt cloud them. Mr. Muscles had never been faced down before. This was unfamiliar ground for him.

Brand's lips tightened into a disapproving tight line. He watched fear grip the bigger man. He clearly saw the man's mind working to understand this new approach to backing down from a fight. Unexplainably, the brute's growing doubt drew a deeper anger from Brand.

Mr. Muscles experienced a troubling quandary at this uncharacteristic reaction to his aggression. He had been in this position many times. The expected flurry of retractions, apologies and calls to reason were not being used here. This smaller man was, in fact, skipping the part where he hurled impotent threats and promises of violence intended to bluff his way out of the fight. He was moving with unflinching purpose towards the physical conflict phase at a tempo the big man had never before experienced.

Brand recognized a growing reluctance in the bigger man. He worked to master the rising wave building within him. He felt genuine pity for the man. Gwen was getting what she wanted, but at the cost of a good man's pride. The pity, however, was not enough to halt his headlong descent into violent rage.

With a visible effort, Brand relaxed his body language, though not enough for his stand-down to be perceived as fear.

"Go back to your girlfriend", he muttered dismissively. "I'll buy you a drink for the exaggeration about my military record."

Brand sat again, dismissing the giant. Karen placed a fresh drink before him, watching Mr. Muscles suspiciously.

The big man stayed in place for a long moment, unsure how to proceed. Finally, he moved slowly behind Brand and back to the end of the horseshoe-shaped bar where Gwen glowered at him silently, eyes blazing.

"This isn't over", Karen confided in a low voice.

"Maybe", Brand replied, sipping his drink. He struggled to master the surplus energy of his untapped rage.

The couple at the end of the bar argued in hushed but urgent tones. Brand knew she was excoriating him for his cowardice. Mr. Muscles was likely trying to explain away his retreat with a combination of reasonable assertions for avoiding trouble, and swaggering boasts of how the smaller guy wasn't worth his time and effort.

Gwen wasn't buying it – not one bit.

Karen served Mr. Muscles the drink and gestured across the bar towards Brand, crediting him with the purchase.

Mr. Muscles looked at the drink. All the while his girlfriend poured poison into his ear. Finally, her goading took hold.

He slammed both fists on the bar and threw the drink onto the stained floor. Glass exploded, and amber liquor splashed his boots. He left his chair at a sprint. He lowered his shoulders in a wild and woolly move to tackle Brand.

Brand saw this immediately. He rose, grabbing his sturdy wooden and steel bar chair. He threw it at the attacker's feet.

Mr. Muscles' boots tangled in the heavy falling chair. He grabbed the stout wooden trim at the edge of the bar, trying to catch himself. His head rose as he struggled to right himself.

Brand hammered a right into the middle of his straining visage. The crack of his breaking nose sounded like a pool cue broken over a knee. Brand followed the blow with a left to the side of his head, just behind the ear.

The giant landed on his battered face, out cold.

Brand waited in surprise. The behind-the-ear shot had been luck. He fought by the credo 'hit hard and hit often.' His military training, albeit on weekends and two weeks each summer, had included handgun training. In shooting, it was called a double tap. Never trust in a single shot – or blow. The lucky finishing punch was a last resort as his target fell out of range.

Karen looked directly at Brand with a helpless expression.

"I'm calling the police...guy who I have never seen before."

She went to the phone and dialed 911 as Brand dashed out the front doors.

# Chapter 2

His name was Christopher, and he was not enjoying the heat. His journey home from school was a daily pilgrimage which ended in the dark cool sanctuary of his small bedroom. Within those hallowed walls lay a wonderful portal to a world in which he was the lone master.

His rule was law and his digital subjects saw clearly the flawless hero which he knew slept deep within him in the real world. This, yet unseen personal attribute was, to him, a character trait he concealed from those unworthy critics at school and on the playground.

His castle was a thin computer screen, aglow in his dark bedroom. His kingdom was a digital video game world in which anyone could be anything. He viewed the long walk from the school to his home as a daily penance, for which he suffered the heat and the humiliation of passivity.

His slow shambling steps lifted in an increasing but reluctant tempo. The thought of his awaiting fantasy world beckoned. He wiped his moist brow with the back of his hand. He dried the hand on his baggy jeans. The heat was thick and clinging like a barber's towel. His white button-down was dark with broad stains, and moist with sweat beneath the shoulder slings of his heavy backpack.

Despite his discomfort, Chris smiled at the boyhood memory of his parents' favorite method for escaping the relentless summer heat. He and his sister Lea would walk with Mama and Papa, enduring the baking Sun. Slowly they would make their way to Garcia's Grocery.

The small family would enter as any legitimate customer might. Mama and Papa would feign interest in the specials and weekly advertised sales. Pulling a basket from the racked carts, they would stroll the cool aisles, occasionally selecting an item from the shelves, dropping it in the basket. The cool air was soothing, and their visits were long.

He and his sister always stayed close and quiet. Running and playing upon the cool vinyl floor tiles was not tolerated. Christopher learned early to be inconspicuous in order to maintain the comfort of anonymity.

His long walk to and from school had included no nearby grocery store to offer him respite from the early summer heat. Instead, he trudged wearily upon the graduated segments of scorching sidewalk. Bordering the dusty street were rows of white clapboard houses behind dull chain link fencing.

He was lost in his thoughts when a small but voracious dog slammed against the fence, howling and barking as if Chris were a hapless cur trespassing within the dog's claimed territory.

The boy stumbled away from the attacking dog with a gasp and quickened heartbeat. He muttered under his breath, cursing the little beast and his own easily thwarted courage.

The dog represented the most recent insult Christopher had weathered that day. He was only an hour separated from the latest ridicule of many perpetrated upon him by the class bully, Joel. The humiliation was fresh, and the dog added a painful reminder that Christopher's was the tragic plight of the weak.

At the beginning of the school year, early in the tirade of Joel's pranks, Christopher had confided in his father about the evil bully. His father had assured him on that, and several subsequent occasions, that Joel would desist if ignored. Chris did his best to follow his father's advice, but it was difficult to ignore a kick in the pants, or a spit ball to the face, or being tripped from behind in a crowded hallway. This last was the most recent prank Joel had visited upon Chris. From his prone position on the hallway floor, Chris had looked up at the bigger Joel. The sadistic boy was surrounded by students who joined him in laughing and pointing at his fallen victim.

Chris suspected that many of the onlookers probably felt relief that they were not the fallen in that moment. He was certain that many within the laughing crowd had taken their turn as the victim to Joel's pranks.

Sufficiently dispirited, Christopher moved away from the annoying din of the little mongrel. He felt frustration tighten within him to the point of pain. His thoughts darkened as he reflected upon the prospect of a school year filled with pain and suffering at the hands of the bully. To his troubled mind, the occurrences combined as one huge offense whose scope was enormous and unforgiveable.

Christopher lapsed into a fantasy version of that afternoon's event. But in this version, he rises angrily from the cold floor tiles and rushes Joel, fists flailing. His pale lips open with a torrent of curses and epithets rained upon his surprised and cowering victim.

In his imagined victory, Joel reacts with an impotent, off-balance retreat. Although his victim falls away from him, Christopher continues to pummel the bully until Joel lands heavily on the floor, his cries for mercy unheeded.

Christopher's imagined triumph faded as he again focused on his pitiful reality. He walked slowly along the hot sidewalk, thankful when the next dog did nothing more than watch him pass with lolling tongue and curious eyes.

Christopher watched with a casual regard as an aged white car slowed visibly as it drew closer, approaching from the opposite direction. He could see the dim silhouettes of two people in the front seats.

A small tickle of prescience grew like a faraway voice, calling out a warning. He was unaccustomed to hearing, much less heeding, the curious sensations of his innate survival instincts. He didn't know that this unfamiliar danger signal was something bestowed upon all living creatures since the first single cell organism evolved into a creature which drew fearful breath. Animals in the wild depended upon this instinct as much as they depended upon their hunger to signal their need to feed.

His mind had just begun to register the warning when the car stopped alongside him, and a grim-faced Latino male pushed a large pistol out the window upon a stiffened arm. Flame leapt from the dark muzzle and Christopher felt a sharp hot pain pierce his chest. The impact of the slug struck a bone deep inside him, knocking him flat upon the hot sidewalk.

He tried to draw a breath to relieve the pressure building within his chest. He felt a strange rattling in his throat. He heard the car's tires squeal as the shooter fled. He couldn't move, his vision clouding with a red hue.

Tears darkened the fresh dust at the corner of his eyes as he died. His last thoughts were of Joel lying on the hot sidewalk. Joel should have been there to pay for his sins.

It was hot. Momma and Papa should take Lea to the store today.

# Chapter 3

Miguel wiped the tears from his eyes. He could hardly see to drive. He was *Mu-Ha* now - his final test passed with flying colors. He felt real pride for a fleeting moment. For scant seconds the dying eyes of the frightened teen fell from his thoughts. The reprieve was brief. His swelling pride fell violently to guilt and despair, as the kid had fallen to his colt revolver.

Next to him Javier watched the driver with keen interest from his place in the passenger seat. He was only a few months removed from his own *Probar*. Everyone did it. Everyone wept. That was the process. He felt an urge to console the *Driver* with this information. Instinctively he knew it wouldn't help. His *Shotgun* hadn't said a word to him when he was the *Driver*. He said nothing to this *Driver*.

Miguel managed to merge the road worn white Toyota Corolla into the speeding traffic of the freeway. Hot wind buffeted them as the exits moved slowly past. The sun wouldn't set for hours. Without the benefit of darkness, they had to move carefully, exposed and vulnerable in broad daylight. With anxious glances, they searched the mirrors and the rear window.

Their nervous vigilance relaxed only after they reached the safety of the South Side. They left the freeway and followed the access road for a few miles before turning onto a narrow residential street lined with 1940's style houses. White clapboard and chain-link fencing defined the style within the neighborhood.

Miguel turned the Toyota into a caliche alley and soon parked before the closed doors of a dilapidated detached garage. One of the rickety garage doors rose on rusty tracks, and a thin older man watched them exit the car. Miguel felt as if he was wading through the tepid waters of a dream.

"Bring the car inside", the older man urged sharply.

Clumsily, Miguel rushed to obey. He started the car and hurriedly pulled it into the cover of the structure.

Javier ducked into the wide doorway as the man lowered the garage door with a worn nylon cord. Miguel stepped from the car and moved next to Javier. The man of some fifty years of age turned from the closed door and faced the two. He was the leader of *Muchachos Hablidad*.

"It is done?"

Miguel remained mute as if the question held some hidden puzzle he must solve before answering.

Javier turned from his observation of Miguel and spoke for them both.

"*Si, Señor* Fuentes. It is done."

Fuentes watched Miguel for a long moment. Finally, he moved towards a side door and left the garage. Javier pushed Miguel gently ahead of him and they followed the older man. The sidewalk hugged the vine covered chain link fence which enclosed a small backyard with an old swing set, abandoned and slightly akilter.

The house was of the same aged architecture as the detached garage. Fuentes climbed three concrete steps and opened the side door. He entered the house and the two followed him into the cool darkness within. Dripping window units forced chilled air into the house, creating a din like a small sheet metal plant built upon a floating barge. The old air-conditioning units bubbled and groaned at their tasks.

Fuentes led them through a narrow kitchen and into what had been a living room when the building was used as a residence. It now looked like a communications bunker for a special operation's military unit.

Mounted in a rough wooden shelving unit, a bank of eight 12" black and white monitors displayed scenes of gates and security doors for industrial buildings and warehouses. Others offered rounded views of the house's entrances.

A long squat table supported two of every kind of radio known to man. Every level of wireless technology from hand held walkies to CB radios and even HAM units shone with green and red LCD gauges and displays. The volume controls were adjusted to the lowest setting. The radio noise added to the air conditioners' roar a staccato buzz like the rise and fall of scores of cicadas crowding mesquite trees on a hot Summer day.

Fuentes moved a roller chair from behind a large green metal desk. He opened the narrow under-table drawer and withdrew two stacks of bills. He tossed the larger of the two to Miguel and the thinner to Javier. He watched the two as they looked at the money with a mixture of surprise and confusion.

Fuentes ran his operation based upon the simplest of credos. He paid cash on delivery and tolerated no mistakes or excuses.

"Sit" he instructed the two youths.

He lowered himself into the heavy metal office chair and pulled himself up behind the large desk. He rocked against the creaky steel springs under the chair, as he waited for the young men to pull over two chairs and settle upon them. Once the scraping of chairs across the scarred hardwood flooring ceased, he leaned forward, crossing his arms in preparation for the important information he would share with these young men. His rough wards finally settled, and the room was silent other than the dull hum of the air conditioners and radios.

"It is time you both became one with *Muchachos Hablidad*. My concern is not just for what you can do for me, but also what I can do for you in return.

Fuentes leaned back meaningfully.

"We make sharp edged tools here. These tools must be formed from the hard steel of strong-willed men. Taking a life is a thing. This thing is done by accident every day. This thing is done out of anger or jealousy every day. Everyday this thing is done carelessly and with little meaning."

The two young men looked at each other with confusion. They had both taken lives recently with no thought or care to the meaning of the act other than to enter the *MuHa* organization. Where was the meaning otherwise?

Fuentes nodded as if he read their very thoughts.

"Tools must be forged in fire to create hardness and temper. The tempering process also involves hammering away the impurities in order to leave only true steel. You have been forged, now comes the tempering."

Fuentes looked at each man earnestly. He gave them a look of critical scrutiny before continuing with his instructions.

"You both will report to my associate, *Señor* Salazar. He is building a large concrete foundation near downtown. You will work for him every day until I call for you."

Both young men stiffened in their chairs. It was obvious that they had imagined their new lives differently.

"Is there a problem?" Fuentes asked with a mild innocence to his tone.

Javier cleared his throat nervously.

"*Señor* Fuentes, my father toils in the hot sun. I will not be my father."

Fuentes considered Javier through narrowed eyes. After a moment he nodded to Miguel.

"And you?"

Miguel looked down, uncertain of the proper response. He marveled at the workings of his mind. There was a logic to Fuentes' methods. Maybe his was a unique case compared with others who had completed the *Probar*.

For an unknown reason, his memory locked in upon a day some ten years past. In the memory, his uncle Raymond grinned at him. He sat in a scarred wooden chair. A man with burly arms, tattooed from knuckles to rotators leaned in close as he scratched ink into his uncle's bicep. The tattoo pen buzzed like an over-revved electric razor.

Eight-year-old Miguel watched his uncle's face with open awe. Uncle Ray's eyes sparkled at the boy. His teeth clenched in a set grin at the pain he was enduring.

"Does it hurt, Uncle?" Miguel had asked.

"Of course, *Mejo*", was the tight answer. "Today's pain is the price for tomorrow's gain."

Miguel leaned back in the hard chair as he recalled the days following that one. His uncle had occupied the sofa in Miguel's father's living room for months. Miguel relished the time he spent with his Uncle Raymond.

Raymond was nearly the same age as his brother, Miguel's father, but he had none of the harsh criticisms nor the ready corrective judgement of Miguel's father. Uncle Raymond was a man who had never progressed past the mischievous openness of boyhood. He treated Miguel with an equanimity which elevated the youngster to the coveted level of a peer rather than an adolescent subordinate.

Several days had passed after which Raymond had shown Miguel the new tattoo. It had changed magically from a colorful scabbed mass to a vivid image with as much allure in its detail as the man who wore it.

Raymond told Miguel that the pain no longer defined the moment. But because of the pain, the tattoo was now a testament to the man who bore its mark.

He lived with his uncle Raymond now. His father had been deported years before, and his mother had remarried and invested no effort to staying in touch with him. Raymond's tattoo had faded over time, but its message was one Miguel still treasured.

Miguel raised his eyes to Fuentes. The *Probar* was his tattoo. His instincts told him that the pain would pass, and the experience would live within him as a badge of honor like Raymond's tattoo.

"I am what you would have me to be, patron."

"Good. You will be texted the address and date to start your journey to *MuHa*.

"You", he continued, speaking to Miguel but looking at Javier, "Are free to leave as you arrived."

Miguel stood. Fuentes nodded and Miguel left the room. Javier remained in his seat. Fuentes withdrew his cell phone from his pocket and manipulated the screen. He seemed not to notice that Javier continued to occupy his seat. He tapped the screen, typing out a text message.

"*Señor*?"

Javier's voice quavered nervously.

Fuentes answered but did not look up from his manipulation of the phone.

"You are excused."

"*Señor* Fuentes, I joined you to be more than some common *Mojar*."

His voice strengthened with the resolve of his statement.

Fuentes looked from his phone finally. He sat the phone on the heavy desk, resting his hands lightly on the green top.

"You agreed to obey me when you joined me…"

"But I didn't know you would want me to dig ditches and sweat like *el Trabajador*."

Fuentes frowned at the interruption.

"Your words are more important than mine, I see."

"I didn't say that. I said, I didn't sign up to be a *peon*."

"So, my words are not only unimportant, but wrong as well."

"Again, you are putting words in my mouth. This is bullshit!"

Fuentes seemed unmoved by Javier's outburst.

"I will give you one last bit of wisdom. That which got you here is no longer sufficient to keep you here. That which keeps you here is no longer available to you. Get out."

Javier opened his mouth to speak.

"Do not talk. Get out while you still can."

Javier paled. He had not seen the danger until he had descended within its deadly depths. He rose slowly and backed from the room.

Fuentes lifted his phone and returned his attention to his texting. He exhaled audibly as he composed the message. He touched the send button, returned the phone to the desk top, and leaned back. He looked around him blankly, distracted by his thoughts. He rose and moved around the desk. He lifted the two chairs, returning them to their original places.

Outside, Javier returned to the little garage. The white Toyota was gone, and the empty garage once again was dark behind the pull-down doors. His driver had left him. He pulled his cell from his jeans pocket. He pressed a quick dial button from his contacts and awaited the ring tone. He heard squeaking brakes as a car stopped beyond the garage doors. He terminated the call and pocketed his phone. He returned to the side door and left, headed to the alley.

He pushed open the gate. Clinging vines broke as he pushed through. Apparently, the gate was never used. In the alley he halted in surprise. The car was not the white Toyota in which he had arrived. It was a shiny black SUV. Its clean paint seemed absurdly out of place in the hot dusty alley. A well-dressed, swarthy-skinned man in his early 30's opened the passenger door and placed a shiny expensive shoe upon the dust of the caliche alley. He stepped backwards and opened the back door of the SUV. He waited beside the open door.

Javier paused, uncertain of his next move. Finally, he walked over and entered the SUV. The well-dressed man closed the door and re-entered the truck. The driver backed the SUV, then drove away from the little garage.

# Chapter 4

B rand parked his truck in the only available slot in the packed parking lot. He pressed the lock button on the key fob, and the truck honked its confirmation. With one last glance at his truck, he walked towards the tight grouping of two-story buildings comprising his apartment complex.

He entered a shady canopy of dense trees under which a smooth sidewalk wound. The walkway soon skirted a sturdy wrought iron gate enclosing the beckoning blue waters of a large swimming pool.

He surveyed the occupants within the pool area. A squat Mexican woman leaned precariously over the water as she scolded one of her five swimming children in terse Spanish. In two chaise loungers were a pair of darkly tanned, thin men Brand knew to be gay. Two chairs down, he spotted her.

She lay flat, her skin shiny with tanning lotion. Her arms were stretched above her dark hair. Her bikini reluctantly concealed her most intimate regions. Large sunglasses shaded her eyes, making it impossible to determine if she saw him. As always, he experienced a mixture of pleasure and doubt as he admired her.

He released the gate latch. The iron hinges complained as he opened the gate. He circled the pool, approaching the dark-haired beauty with measured steps. His dusty jeans and heavy work boots felt shoddy and inappropriate. He was conspicuously out of place, as if he had suddenly been transported to a tropical island and had forgotten to pack for the trip.

As he drew near her, his eyes loitered in their survey of her taut body. His desire for her scattered much of his discomfort at his doubts of her, a temporary salve for his jealousy. He halted a short distance from her. He remained far enough away so as not to cast a shadow. He suspected by the irregular rise and fall of her dark abdomen that she knew he was there. Still she acted as if she hadn't noticed him. He smiled slightly at the ruse.

"Natalie" he said softly.

She stretched with a sigh, feigning surprise behind her sunglasses.

"Hello, baby. How was your day?"

His grin grew to a smile despite his insecurities.

"Busy. Are you ready to come in?"

She rose up on her elbows and looked him over from behind the glasses.

"Do I look ready?"

Her words were playful and welcoming.

He grinned.

"You look like you were born ready."

She smiled at his trite compliment. She rose, gathering her towel and tanning products. His eyes completed their inspection of her.

With a woman like her, he thought with a weak acquiescence, your days were always numbered. In that moment he committed himself to follow a nihilistic path. Enjoy what you have today.

The gay couple, and even the mother of five, paused to watch Brand and Natalie make their way to the gate. Brand knew he was an impediment to their view, rather than the subject of their scrutiny.

He pulled the gate closed behind him and a short walk brought them to a steel paneled door and the entrance to their shared apartment. He turned the key and they entered their modestly furnished one-bedroom flat.

Natalie disappeared into the bedroom and Brand dropped onto the microfiber sofa. He checked his phone for calls he knew he had not received. Money was always elusive in the construction business.

He smiled faintly at the memory of Mr. Muscles. Was he back home with his girl? How would that conversation go tonight?

His cell rang. He answered immediately.

"What's up, Bert", he said brightly.

"I'm here at the Dog. The cops just left. It seems some guy whipped some ex-badass's ass."

"You don't say", Brand said innocently, amused at the timing of the call coming just as he wondered about the outcome of the afternoon's conflict.

"He told the cops the guy hit him with a chair."

"That doesn't sound fair. "

"Nope. He said it wouldn't have gone that way if the other guy hadn't jumped him from behind."

"Very unsporting of him."

"You home?"

"Just got here. Are you out for the night?"

"Donna thinks we are working late."

"Damn, Bert. Do you walk around with a perpetual hard-on? You better hope she doesn't call me. I am done lying for you."

"Don't lie. Just don't pick up the phone."

"What if she calls Natalie?"

"She wouldn't do that. She doesn't like her. She's too hot."

"Tell me about it", Brand agreed grimly.

Natalie returned from the bedroom, tucking her tee shirt into her skinny jeans.

"What if who calls me?" She asked.

"Donna", Brand said casually.

"Dammit, Brand", Bert spat. "Can't you keep anything between us?"

"I can't, Bert. She's too hot. Gotta go."

He ended the call and followed Natalie into the kitchen.

# Chapter 5

It was early morning when Brand parked his truck a few yards from the knotty skeleton of rough framing which would one day be a luxury apartment building. Its walls were ribbed like a giant stick house, revealing a confusing network of lumber.

Two men sat upon a lumber pile, watching expectantly as Brand approached. Brand looked around the expansive job site. Numerous service trucks and vans were parked around the buildings in the complex. He saw no shiny black sports car.

"Is Bert here yet", Brand asked knowing the answer.

The older of the two men was Lance. He was weathered and dark from years of working in the Sun. His lips parted in a white toothy grin. He had been Brand's top hand for several years and knew much about the odd relationship between Bert and Brand.

"It's a work day, ain't it?", Lance said through squinting eyes.

"So that would be a no."

"Yep."

Brand moved to the rear of his truck and dropped the tail gate.

"Let's get rolled out, Lance. Bert will be here directly."

Lance rose with a doubtful shake of his head.

"Off your ass, Brett."

The second man was younger and appeared to be suffering from the effects of a long night of drinking. He rose wearily and followed Lance to Brand's truck.

In turn, each man pulled tools and hoses from the truck and arranged them around the work site as was needed. Brand produced his phone and pushed Bert's contact icon. He looked around as he waited for the ring tone. As expected, the call went to voicemail.

"Get your hung-over ass to work."

Brand ended the call and pocketed the phone. He grabbed his tool bags from the truck and buckled them tightly around his waist.

An hour later, Brand, Lance and Brett grunted, lifting a heavy engineered beam into position. Bert's black sports car approached smoothly and pulled into position next to Brand's truck. The dull thump of a hip-hop bass line rattled the car's license plates with a loose buzz.

With a strained push and a groan, Brand placed the end of the large beam into its pocket. He shot nails into the beam with a heavy nail gun.

He exhaled audibly as he watched the newly arrived sports car. The driver remained within the air-conditioned car for an annoyingly long time before he finally turned off the engine and opened the door.

Bert was a tall heavy man with a full beard and expensive sunglasses. He wore slacks, a silk shirt and leather mesh sandals. He smiled at Brand as he surveyed the morning's work.

"Get to work. We're burning daylight", Bert called brightly.

Brand registered only annoyance.

"We start at seven, Bert."

"Thank god someone does. You wouldn't believe the night I had."

"Are you going to work today?" Brand complained from his position atop the ladder.

"I just need to change my clothes", Bert assured him.

Brand's frustration was obvious.

Bert spoke to him with his typical manner of a man who patiently and cheerfully explained the obvious to a dullard.

Brand lowered the nail gun to the slab by its thin blue hose.

"I'll be back", he informed the two carpenters. "Lay out this beam and line it. Numb nuts should be dressed by then."

Brand descended the ladder and moved to join Bert at the open trunk of his car. The trunk looked like a hamper. Clothing of all kinds was mixed together with no thought to organization or care.

Bert adroitly conjured a toothbrush and toothpaste from the confused mess. The toothbrush had apparently spent some time under the pile. The bristles looked as disheveled as an Irishman's beard after a weekend drunk.

Bert squeezed toothpaste onto the bent bristles. The dentifrice disappeared into his mouth and he sawed at his molars enthusiastically.

Brand waited patiently as Bert smiled at him through a mouth full of roiling foam. Finally, he spit a white stream and rinsed with a large pull from a mouthwash bottle. He spit once again then wiped his face on a tube sock.

"You truly are a child of the eighties. Tube socks?"

Bert rooted around the pile and produced what appeared to be a leopard-skin strap.

"Man thong", he announced proudly.

"You actually wear a thong?"

"I'm wearing a red one now."

Brand laughed despite his frustration with his friend. Bert was unique, if nothing else.

"Have you slept?"

"Not since night before last, but I don't need much sleep."

Brand knew of his friend's sleeping habits: rather his lack of sleeping habits. They had been friends since they were seventeen years old. Bert had been his first acquaintance when he joined the National Guard. They had been inseparable since that day.

"Get dressed", Brand ordered, "We need to get this porch built by close of business or we don't draw a check this week."

Brand walked back towards the awaiting carpenters.

Later that afternoon, Brand sat in the cool darkness of Rod Dog's Saloon. He occupied the same bar stool with which he had tripped Mr. Muscles the previous day. Bert sat beside him, trying to catch the eye of a drab, middle-aged woman across the bar.

Karen watched Bert with disapproving interest. This was a show she had seen often over the years.

Brand sipped his bourbon then looked at Bert.

"We have to drop the frame package on the new slab next week. Concrete is being poured on Monday."

Bert lifted his glass and sipped his *Copper Penny* through a thin bar straw. He replied distantly, his gaze locked upon the woman who was desperately avoiding eye contact.

"I ordered it yesterday."

Brand eyed him skeptically. Bert was inefficient by nature. This claim of proactivity roused his suspicions.

The usually unflappable Bert sensed Brand's reaction and turned towards him. He noticed the doubtful look on Brand's face and frowned in an uncharacteristic display of annoyance.

"You can call the superintendent if you don't believe me", he said testily.

"I hope you understand that we are an endangered species in the south Texas construction business. We are white, English speaking and we charge too much money for what we do. We have to do it better and cleaner than the wetbacks taking over the trades."

Supes isn't that tough", Bert disagreed. "He likes our work and he still believes there is honor in being a tradesman. The illegals are fast, but their work is shit and you never know when I.N.S. will show up and empty the site."

Brand sipped his drink. His eyes searched Bert's face for any sign of subterfuge. He looked for minutiae which would betray the joke to come. Instead, he detected only pain at Brand's doubtful attitude.

"Alright", Brand finally conceded. "When is the lumber drop scheduled?"

"Monday."

They were silent for a moment, each processing his own thoughts. Brand let the subject drop. He sipped his drink and glanced mischievously at his friend.

"Any plans this weekend?"

Bert lifted his head abruptly.

"We are supposed to go to Mexico this weekend!"

Now it was Bert's turn to evaluate Brand's intentions. Brand never forgot anything, particularly if it was a scheduled event.

"Stop messing with me, *swine bait*."

Brand grinned at the pet name. They had come up with their own unique language in their teens and occasionally they reverted to the rare reference from those days so long ago.

"I remember, Bert."

"You better. We planned this trip weeks ago."

Bert's attention moved from Brand to a point across the bar.

Brand followed the look until his eyes fell upon a shapely blonde taking a seat at the opposite side of the horseshoe shaped bar. Bert forgot the middle-aged woman as if she was the last bite of a meal and desert had just been served. The new blonde was not a regular. Among the blue-collar patrons, she stood out like a Lamborghini at a Yugo dealership.

"She is hot", Bert said unnecessarily in a voice pitched for Brand alone.

"Must be lost", Brand surmised.

"Definitely", Bert agreed. His voice held a far away, dreamy quality.

Brand looked at his friend. Bert had forgotten him in his preoccupation with this new focus of his insatiable desires.

Brand dug in his pocket and produced a twenty. He tossed it on the bar and waved to Karen. He slapped Bert on the shoulder. The big man made no move in reaction to the blow. He was already far gone on this new quest.

"Get some sleep tonight, Bert. We need you strong tomorrow."

"No problem", Bert replied with the voice of a psyche patient under hypnosis.

Brand headed for the front door. Outside, the day was still bright and hot. He found his truck and headed home.

After only a few minutes on the road, his phone rang. Natalie's name was displayed on the dash screen. He pressed the blue tooth answer button on the touch screen.

"Hey baby. Headed home now. I just left the Dog."

"I was thinking of going out with the girls tonight."

Brand made no reply immediately.

"Are you there?", she prompted.

"Yeah, I'm still here. You going out with Victoria again?"

"She is going through a hard time with the break-up and she needs someone to talk to."

"Natalie, it is a bad mix when the focus of the "girls' night" is a man-hating, tore up divorcee, trying to kill her pain by luring equally lonely men into short term physical relationships. The remainder of the 'girls' find themselves hit on by the same type guys, particularly the hot friend in a committed relationship."

"Since when are you jealous, tough guy?"

Her tone was light and playful. Brand felt the pain of jealous doubt take its place once more. His voice registered weary acquiescence.

"Get home at a decent hour. I have to work tomorrow."

"Well don't wait up for me", she advised firmly.

"I don't wait up for you. I wake up when you get in and I have trouble getting back to sleep."

"Poor baby", she chided him in the same playful tone.

The phone went dead. He hated it when she did that. She believed saying hello or goodbye to someone you see every day was silly and insecure. Brand considered it common courtesy.

He turned the truck onto the next intersecting street and headed back to Rod Dog's. The prospect of an evening alone with the TV and pizza delivery depressed him. Bert was always good for an entertaining show when he was on the hunt.

His former space in the parking lot was still available. He locked his truck and entered the bar. The double glass doors, emblazoned with the Rod Dog logo, featuring a cartoon dog with a tall cocktail, fed into a makeshift entry vestibule. A poster-littered dividing wall blocked the entrant's view and unwelcome sunlight from the dark interior of the bar.

Brand turned to the right towards the side of the horseshoe bar where he and Bert had sat earlier.

New customers occupied both seats. Brand shifted his search to the seat across the bar where the attractive blonde had drawn Bert's attention. Predictably, Bert occupied a seat beside her, chatting her up.

Brand nodded to Karen and she fetched a clean high ball glass from the drying rack and moved to make him a drink. He circled the bar, taking a chair on the other side of the blonde from Bert.

"Look whose here", Bert announced happily. "Natalie's out with the girls again?"

"Nice call, Mr. Psychic."

The blonde looked Brand over thoroughly.

"This", Bert said with a flourish, "is Carson Brand. Brand this is Debbie."

"Hello Carson", she said and stuck out a hand.

"His friends call him Brand", Bert corrected her before Brand could respond.

"Hello...Brand", she said carefully.

Brand took her hand.

"Glad to meet you."

"Debbie is a V.P. at Progeny Bank downtown", Bert said proudly. "She got stood up for dinner at the restaurant next door. She decided to drown her sorrows."

"It's not like that, Robert", she said firmly. "The night is young, and I am off tomorrow."

"His friends call him Bert", Brand said with a wink.

Bert frowned at Brand. Brand had started the Bert thing many years ago and he was powerless to stop it, or he would have long before it stuck.

"Bert?" she asked with a wrinkle of her nose. "Where's Ernie?"

"Never heard that one before", Bert mumbled in annoyance.

"So, who is Natalie, Brand?"

"My girlfriend."

"So, your girlfriend is out with the girls on a Monday night?"

"So, it seems", Brand said testily and nodded his thanks to Karen as she sat his drink before him.

Karen glanced at Debbie, then Bert. She shook her head with a deprecating smile and returned to her duties. Her expression conveyed, 'Bert is up to his old tricks again.'

Debbie missed the reaction from Karen as she favored Brand with a dirty look at his mocking comment.

Brand looked forward at the stair step display, where a multi-colored glass menagerie of liquor bottles rose towards the ceiling, his glass held between open palms. The cold glass comforted him as he grappled with his feelings about Natalie's frequent "girl's nights."

# Chapter 6

Brand left the bar just before midnight. It was his private policy to leave the bar before a buzz took hold. The last thing he needed was a DWI. His experience had taught him that it took an average of twenty minutes for alcohol to take full effect. His apartment was within ten minutes of the Dog, allowing him to take advantage of this self-imposed rule.

As expected, the apartment was empty. Brand went into the bedroom and stripped to his boxers. He flopped onto the bed and grabbed an old western novel from the nightstand. He hoped a little reading would coax his troubled mind into a state of slumber.

It seemed nearly an hour before he turned off the light, sleep beckoning him. He was sleeping soundly when he was awakened by the front door opening and slamming closed. He heard Natalie and Victoria giggle in their unsuccessful attempt to be quiet. They were drunk.

Brand turned on the light and pulled on his jeans. He left the bedroom. In the kitchen he saw the girls rummaging through the fridge. Natalie wore a short red dress with a plunging neckline. Her spiked heeled pumps made her legs look great. Victoria was slightly older than Natalie, and more thickly built. She had curly hair the color of copper. She wore a frumpy skirt and a sleeveless blouse.

Natalie turned from her search of the fridge and saw Brand shirtless, standing in the living room

"Hey babe", she said thickly. "You showing off for Victoria?"

"Hey Brand", Victoria greeted him. She eyed him hungrily. "Why don't you join us for a bite?"

Natalie gave her a warning glance which she softened with a good-natured laugh.

"Leave the biting to me, girlfriend."

"Such a spoil sport", Victoria said with a tone of mock disappointment.

Brand watched Victoria pick at a bowl of cheerios, obviously tipsy from the effects of alcohol. She had never flirted with him before. Conversely, she typically spoke to him with disdain. He was not enamored with her, considering Natalie's recounting of her many criticisms of him. His impression of the woman was that of an angry and lonely spinster who harbored a poor opinion of any man who was in a committed relationship with any of her friends.

According to Natalie, Victoria's husband left her for a younger woman less than a year before. Natalie guessed that Victoria assigned to Brand the same weakness of character which she believed motivated her husband to leave her. It didn't help that Brand was known to have cheated on his last wife prior to his relationship with Natalie. Warranted or not, Victoria hated him. For Brand, this flirting was strange and unwelcome.

"Did you get that guy's number?" Natalie asked Victoria as she took a seat at the bar top.

"Oh yeah", Victoria replied, pointing significantly with a dripping spoon. "He is CEO of a start-up tech company. He is loaded."

Natalie nodded her appreciation.

"He's hot. You like bald guys anyway."

Brand laughed.

"Is there no credit given to guys who have hair?"

Both women leveled him with looks of ridicule at his ignorance. He obviously had no idea what women liked in men.

"That is a shallow point of view", Natalie chided him.

"I see what you mean", Brand agreed with an enthusiastic nod. "It is way more sensitive to judge him by his job and income."

"It is as easy to love a rich one as it is to love a poor one", Victoria preached.

Brand favored Victoria with a deprecating look.

"That is no different than the misogyny of a man judging a woman based solely upon her bust size or how tight her ass is."

Natalie frowned at him and Victoria compressed her lips into a disapproving line. Brand saw the signs of a growing storm and decided to avoid a drunken argument.

"I'm going to bed before you two progressive feminists murder me here in my own kitchen."

Brand returned to his bed. His ears rang with the hushed conversation, excoriating him for his lack of reason and understanding.

# Chapter 7

Piedras Negras was an expansive, dingy, border town. The small city seemed perpetually cloaked in a haze of pollution and airborne dust. Upon crossing the newer of two international border crossing bridges and customs stations, the street narrowed into a roughly paved lane lined with clinics, pharmacies, and curio shops.

Old buildings were filled with festively decorated businesses catering to American tourists. The entry road terminated at the edge of a small dusty square. The square was an aged cluster of 'dobe buildings amidst ancient pin oaks.

The two Americans entered the square on foot. Brand had lobbied to drive into Mexico. Bert had cautioned against it. American cars, particularly four-wheel drive trucks, were in high demand among the local thieves. It was rumored that the police aided in the thefts and extorted large amounts of cash in the process.

Brand's truck was relatively new, and the aggressive tires and highly polished chrome rims would draw attention they didn't want. Bert vouchsafed that his last trip had cost him more than a grand. No need to raise the stakes.

Bert made frequent trips to Mexico and was a veteran of Border town procedures. His block of instruction to Brand was simple and inviolate: Leave your truck in a parking lot on the U.S. side. Cabs were cheap and easily available. Cell phones were worthless across the border unless you ponied up sixty bucks for a month of international calling. The vegetables came from the U.S. and were usually *e-coli* free. It was best to exchange dollars for *pesos* at the bank on the square, or the locals would take liberties in their calculations of the exchange rates. Finally, and the most important, don't buy a whore in *Boy's Town* until the night shift arrives after 8 PM.

"Are we going to Boy's Town?" Brand had asked doubtfully.

"Probably not", Bert had admitted, "But your orientation would not be complete if I didn't bring it up."

They moved towards a line of small cabs parked along one of the peripheral streets of the square. The first cab in line was a tiny, dented, white, nondescript, four-door. A smallish, swarthy-skinned man, with a sweaty beard-darkened jaw, pushed away from his relaxed posture against the car. He smiled a stained welcome to the Americans.

"Take us to a good bar where we can meet women", Bert said in a loud voice.

"I know just the bar for women", the driver said. His heavily accented voice was hardly audible over the creaking door hinges as he pulled open the back door to the ancient cab.

Brand entered the back seat, pulling the door closed with a solid bang.

Bert moved around the car and took a seat in the front.

Brand leaned forward in the back seat.

"Bert, let's get some authentic Mexican food before we go on our drinking binge."

Bert looked at the driver.

"No tourist traps", he warned the driver.

The cabbie gave him a hurt look.

"Of course not, *Señor*."

The driver turned the key, and the little motor shook the occupants and car mercilessly. Finally, the little vehicle found its rhythm and the cabbie engaged the forward gear. They lurched into traffic.

The cab was not air conditioned, leaving the passengers at the mercy of the billowing dusty air, buffeting them as the little car gained speed.

Brand was occupied with his impression of the city. They passed a shopping center. There was little glitz or glamour to the retail shops. The brightly colored signs, touting bargains and sales, seemed like gaudy paint splotches on a faded canvas. Other than the rare glimpse of a shiny sedan or massive S.U.V., the bulk of the traffic consisted of small dusty cars in various states of disrepair.

Their cab driver ran a red light, narrowly avoiding a collision with a fast-moving pickup truck. He weaved through traffic, selecting lanes as if he were controlling a vehicle in a video game.

The little cab flew past a parked police car and whipped around a corner. The dangerous maneuver drew no attention whatsoever from the officer inside. It was apparent to Brand that traffic laws were more suggestions than rules here.

Horns continually sounded from all directions: some were a direct result of the cabbie's recklessness at the wheel. Otherwise, it seemed that most of the horn blasts were sounded as a procedural component of driving in Mexico. As with most things in Mexico, driving appeared to involve a large measure of verbose display.

Brand was glad he hadn't brought his truck. The danger of theft seemed trivial compared to the risk of a collision.

Bert leaned in towards the little driver so he could be heard.

"What's your name?" he asked, his voice raised to a volume which was audible over the loud engine and wind noise.

"I am Carlos."

"My name is Bert."

He jerked a thumb towards the back seat.

"He's Brand."

They drove a few minutes more before Carlos pulled his cab roughly into a dirt parking lot. He parked the car in a narrow space next to a squat building with a full glass front. Brand eagerly escaped the confines of the small back seat. He stretched and looked around him.

Bert extended to Carlos a crisp twenty-dollar bill.

"Come in and have a bite with us, Carlos."

Carlos hesitated, his gaze coveting the money. He snatched the bill and opened his door.

They entered the double glass doors and found a seat at a Formica topped steel table. Behind a counter, within a glass enclosure, hung a slab of roasted pork. Heating lamps illuminated the meat with a red glow.

"*Puerca*", Carlos explained needlessly.

A waiter appeared before them. He wore black slacks and a long-sleeved white button down, secured at the neck by a black clip-on bow tie.

"*Buenos Tardes*", the waiter greeted them with a nod.

Bert interlaced his fingers.

"*Cerveza por favor.*"

Brand put up three fingers.

Carlos made a feeble protest as the waiter left to place the order.

"Just one beer, Carlos", Bert assured him.

Within the hour they were back on the road.

Carlos mashed the gas pedal and they turned onto the pavement. The beer and the tacos did nothing to alter his driving style. The little cab again was pressed to its limits as Carlos ran the race towards their next destination.

Bert leaned towards Carlos to be heard once more over the noise.

"How far to the cantina with the women?"

"Not far", Carlos said with a sly grin. "Fifteen minutes."

"Is it outside of town?" Brand asked sarcastically.

He doubted they would still be in Piedras Negras in fifteen minutes at their current rate of speed.

"Very funny, *Señor*", Carlos laughed good-naturedly.

They soon exchanged the shoddy business district for what appeared to be a residential neighborhood. Squat adobe houses with dirt yards, littered with all manner of junk, lined both sides of the cracked, filthy, paved street.

Carlos adroitly careened the cab around a corner. He whipped into an available parking space before a two-story brick building. A flat painted sign proclaimed the establishment's identity: *El Capitan Cantina y Hotel*.

"Welcome to *El Capitan, Amigos*" Carlos sang out.

"How much do we owe you, Carlos?" Bert asked as he reached for his wallet.

"Thirty pesos, *Señor*."

Bert glanced back at Brand. That's about ten bucks, Bro", Bert said in a low voice to Brand. Bert brightened and returned his attention to the cabbie.

"How much longer are you working Carlos?"

"I just started my shift."

"How much do you typically make in a day?"

Carlos squinted as he tried to divine the meaning of Bert's questioning.

"Mostly a hundred pesos a day."

"Tell you what", Bert said. "We'll pay you $100.00 American for you to drive us the rest of your shift."

Carlos gave Bert a confused look, almost as if he had lost his ability to understand English. Once he completed the arithmetic in his head his face blossomed into an accepting smile.

"Agreed", Carlos said simply.

He shoved the gear shift into park and turned the key. The little cab shuddered into silence. Carlos led the way to the dark front door of 'El Capitan.'

He spoke briefly in Spanish with the large bouncer at the front door, after which they ascended a narrow-paneled staircase up to a large room decorated with the colors and lighting of a 70's discotheque. They took seats at the bar beside two busty Latinas.

Sometime later, Brand beamed at the two young women through a warm bourbon glow. His gaze fell upon Carlos and his face cracked into a full grin.

The cabbie was slack jawed with desire for the young beauties. Cheap Tequila had darkened his eyes with a romantic melancholy.

Bert seemed no less sober than he had been upon their arrival. Brand had grown accustomed to his friend's resistance to the effects of much alcohol. He had never seen the larger man drunk beyond a mild buzz. On the other hand, Bert had helped Brand home many a night, sodden with the effects of strong drink.

Bert placed his full attention upon Carlos. He seemed curious and even intrigued by the Mexican's desultory manner.

"Carlos", he said. "Drink up. You seem to have a heavy heart. No party poopers tonight."

Carlos pulled his dull eyes from the lusty beauty of dark cleavage.

"What is the 'Party Poopers'?"

Bert's laugh rose hearty and deep from within his big frame. He stood dramatically. Brand laughed to himself. He knew his friend. He knew what was to come.

"Carlos", he said warmly, placing a reassuring hand on his shoulder. "I will save you from becoming one."

Bert lifted the nearest buxom beauty's chin gently with his curled index finger. He looked at the lovely girl but spoke to Carlos with a thoughtful warmth to his voice.

"Do you know how men learned the ways of drink and spirits, lad?"

Bert's American manner changed by degrees until he soon affected a full Irish brogue.

"It was handed down by the god of humor and twisted by the fickle whim of the human heart."

Carlos looked at Bert for a long silent moment. Even the consorts, who understood almost no English, seemed to contemplate his claim.

Brand shook his head. Bert was a regular at the Renaissance Faire held near Houston each year in the fall. His soliloquy was well-known among the *Rennies*. Brand always enjoyed Bert's sense of theatre which he invested in the telling of the 'Tale of Booze.' His favorite aspect, however, was the reaction of the audience to the story. Whether it was the story itself, or the transformation of the large bearded American into a sage spinner of yarns.

A look around the bar assured Brand that he would be the only audience member to gain any insight from the tale, and he had heard the story enough times to tell it himself.

"Bert", Brand said with a raised hand, "spare us this once. The story is too long and involved for an audience with so little English."

Bert held his breath as he thought over the entreaty. Once released, his oratory urge was difficult to recapture. Finally, Bert settled onto his barstool and sipped his drink.

Soon after, Carlos announced that his shift was nearly over and that he must return the cab and fare before long. To the protests of the buxom Latinas, they paid the tab. Bert tipped the girls and accepted their hugs and kisses of gratitude.

The Sun was low on the horizon when Carlos dropped them at the dusty square where they had met.

Bert tipped Carlos an additional twenty dollars and bid him farewell. The Americans watched the little cab as it lurched into the light traffic moving about the square, disappearing down an adjoining street.

Bert clapped a hand on Brand's shoulder.

"It is time to meet Arturo, Brand."

Brand gave Bert a withering look. His senses swam with the effect of their last round of drinks. The idea of a cool motel room, and the stiff sheets of a firm double bed beckoned. Instinctively he knew his needs would have to wait. There was no winning this debate. Bert was persuasive, and besides, he had Mexico on his side.

They travelled east, moving along a narrow, rough street, lined with dilapidated buildings. They passed a three-story brick building with open windows and Juliet balconies across the front. A faded sign reading *Hotel Rojas* hung from one corner.

Another corner building was unusually modern in contrast to the surrounding buildings. The windows were boarded up and graffiti colored its larger walls like tattoos on a convict's back.

The small Mexican village bore all the features of a formerly robust tourist town. The prevalence of drug cartels and greedy politicians had done more to kill progress and commerce than American border laws ever could have.

Bert pointed towards a dark doorway.

"That's it."

They entered a small dark cantina. The bar was dank and mysterious. Brand got the impression of a beer-scented cave. Two bare light bulbs hung by long gray wires from a tall ceiling hidden somewhere in the darkness above. The bare bulbs illuminated the small room with a limited glow, unable to plumb the darkness shrouding the farthest corners. Three folding tables, hosting metal folding chairs, claimed their rightful territories within the remainder of the barroom.

Brand looked around with an expression of unrealized expectations.

"Why do you like this place, Bert?"

"It is authentic. Who wants to go to some tourist trap? Besides, I like Arturo."

They settled atop the only two stools at the bar. Behind the short dark bar stood the tallest Mexican Brand had ever seen. He must have been six foot six. He was whipcord lean and sported a huge mustache. To Brand, he appeared a caricature.

"*Señor Roberto*! Good to see you again", the bartender said in a deep but pleasant voice. "You bring a friend. I am Arturo."

He bowed slightly to Brand.

"Brand", he replied with a polite smile.

"*Micheladas*?"

"*Si, por favor*", Bert answered before Brand could protest.

"Beer and clamato?" Brand protested.

"You have to taste Arturo's *Michelada*."

"I hope my years working Schumann's ranch and eating with those wetbacks is still affecting my gut. Tomatoes are a bad thing to swallow in Mexico."

"As I explained, they import everything from the U.S. now. Besides, the Clamato is out of a bottle."

"I'm sure Arturo orders weekly from his American supplier. If the garnish is vegetable-based, we are gonna spend some quality time in the shitter tonight."

"Every party needs a pooper, that's why we invited you", Bert chided him in a sing song voice.

Tall glasses filled with a red tomato-looking beverage appeared before them. Ice and celery floated within the tall beverages. Brand gave Bert a sidelong glance then lifted the cold glass and took a deep swig.

"Tasty but deadly", he predicted.

Bert lifted his *Michelada*.

"To Mexico", he said looking in Arturo's direction.

Brand lifted his drink.

"To Mexico", he repeated.

Arturo beamed as he watched the Americans drink.

# Chapter 8

Nighttime had transformed the narrow street when Bert pulled Brand through the door of the bar. Passersby were fewer and consisted primarily of staggering drunken Americans. Few locals stalked the dark street. Those who did, appeared suspiciously attentive to the unsure movements of the tourists.

They turned to their right onto the narrow sidewalk.

"I think we are going the wrong direction, Bert", Brand said thickly. He leaned against the wall and breathed deeply, trying to clear his head.

Bert looked around him.

"You're right", Bert agreed, looking around him to gain his bearings. "The hotel is there. Come on *Whetto*."

Bert reversed their course, leading the way. Brand noticed two locals eyeing them covertly. There were no groups of college kids as he had seen in years past. He and Bert were the only foreigners in sight.

"The cartels have really ruined the tourist trade here", he observed.

"Indeed", Bert agreed. "This is the real Mexico my friend."

"Yeah", Brand agreed. "A bona fide third world country at our southern border. Just keep up the pace, brother. It's after midnight and I don't think we are very popular here."

Before long, they began the climb along the smooth pavement of the road leading to the international bridge. They didn't go far before their progress was blocked by large pipe gates closed over the road. The walk path entrance too was closed and padlocked. A large sign read in both Spanish and English that the bridge closed at 11 PM. In smaller letters, a notice explained that the secondary bridge was open twenty-four hours per day. A strip map with basic landmarks and street names illustrated the route to the second bridge.

Brand spoke for them both.

"I hate walking when I'm drunk."

Bert shrugged and turned on his heel. They retraced their steps to, and beyond Arturo's little bar.

The street was dark. Their imaginations inserted shadowy characters crouched in the darkness. Brand imagined their trek marked by mysterious menacing eyes like villains in a *Henry Selick* film.

The road upon which Arturo's bar sat stretched somewhat parallel with the river. Neither man was sure of the distance to the second bridge. They walked for easily a mile before they saw a sign indicating the bridge was 500 meters further.

In minutes they were upon the bridge walkway. The broad steel girders and rusted railing gave an accurate indication that the bridge was very old. Mercury vapor lighting cast an alien orange glow to the night as they gained the bridge's center.

They approached the Mexican border shack, their passports ready for presentation. Brand handed his passport to the guard who eyed him suspiciously.

"Are you bringing any items back with you?"

Brand looked down at himself with an incredulous grin. His jeans and tee shirt would not have hidden anything of size.

"No, sir", he replied with a forced grin conveying his sarcasm.

The guard held Brand's passport and eyeballed him for a long moment. He made it apparent to Brand that he served attitude at his own peril.

Bert handed the guard his passport in turn, sharing a disappointed look at Brand. He silently conveyed his agreement and mutual disappointment at Brand's condescending manner.

The guard favored Bert with a frown for his poorly conceived ploy to curry favor in order to pass the guard shack unmolested. He returned the passport and indicated they move along.

The Border guard at the American side was equally unfriendly.

"Where are you headed?" the American guard asked.

"America", Brand informed him.

Brand was getting tired of the international border game. Bert nudged him.

"We are from San Antonio", Bert said with a smile.

"What was the purpose of your visit to Mexico?"

"Pleasure, wine and food", Bert replied brightly.

"Do you have anything to declare?"

Brand bit his tongue. He felt it wise to keep his mouth shut and get back to their motel.

"No, sir", Bert said.

"And you?"

The border guard's eyes narrowed in readiness to handle this potentially unpleasant entrant with any necessary means.

"Nothing to declare", Brand replied obediently.

The guard returned the passports and released them onto American soil.

# Chapter 9

B rand heard yelling over the staccato reports of nail guns and the roar of growling *cherry pickers* conveying heavy bundles of building materials around the large job site.

He climbed higher upon the skeleton of framing they were building. He looked down and saw a group of roughly dressed Mexican workers yelling and gesturing at Bert. The large, bearded Bert stood at a distance with his hands raised as if to deflect the growing ire of the workmen.

Between the two factions and at a slight distance, stood a stunningly beautiful Latina woman. She wore high heels and a form fitting cocktail dress. The neck line was as plunging as the hem line was high. Brand couldn't help but admire her despite his friend's compromised position in the growing fray.

Brand shook his head wearily. Bert's all-consuming desire for the fairer sex seemed to keep him continually poised at the brink of catastrophe.

With the agility of years on job sites, Brand descended the wooden framing smoothly and rapidly. He dropped his tool bags on the hot concrete.

He arrived at Bert's side as an angry older man approached with his head down and his steps deliberate. Brand recognized the Mexican as the lead concrete man and, as Brand knew him, the owner of the concrete company. Brand recalled his last name only.

"Salazar", he called in a friendly but authoritative tone. "What is the problem here?"

Salazar was a squat but powerfully built Mexican with light blue eyes. Brand guessed there was more Castilian in his lineage than Indian. The angry Salazar considered Brand for a long moment. His jaw worked as he attempted to compose himself. He recognized Brand as one of the regular subcontractors for many of the prominent general contractors for which they both worked.

"Your man had his hands on my girlfriend."

Bert shook his head slowly and drew a breath as he readied his disclaimer.

"Bert", Brand said in a low but firm voice, "Let me handle this for now."

Bert looked away from the menacing group of workmen and at Brand. His expression reflected amused interest. Brand had seen that look before. Bert seemed to revel in Brand's travails at extricating him from these types of situations.

"This is your girlfriend?" Brand asked incredulously, looking once more at the attractive woman. She looked askance as if the conflict had nothing to do with her.

He recovered quickly as a frown stretched the man's angry face at Brand's disbelieving look and doubtful remark.

"Well done", Brand said quickly, attempting to cover his surprise. "I'm sure Bert meant no disrespect. Did you, Bert?"

Bert shook his head innocently.

"She said her neck was sore and I offered to massage it to take out the kinks."

Brand shot a panicked look at his friend.

Salazar caught the look and his anger flared once again.

"You admit it, *gringo*?"

Brand bristled.

"Go easy with the *gringo* talk, Salazar."

"Fuck you too, *pinche guero*!"

The Mexican was angry, and he felt he must not allow his men to see him cowed by these white men. Too late, he saw that he had pushed Brand too far.

"You got a big mouth on you", Brand said menacingly.

Salazar sized up the white man with a critical eye. There was something about him that gave Salazar pause. This was not someone to bluff out of a fight. His voice lost some of its force,

"You better take care of your man, or I will."

Brand's jaw worked under his thin razor stubble. He saw the fear in the smaller man and this last warning was a weak ploy to save face and perhaps to find a way out of impending violence.

Bert watched Brand expectantly. He knew his friend, and he recognized a tipping point at which this encounter would either dissipate or escalate to violence.

Brand counted six men in Salazar's crew. They looked, to a man, like dogs held back from the fox. In their camp was only Bert and himself. Lance and Brett were not to be counted upon in a fight.

Although Bert was a large man, he was not experienced in a fight. His size had kept him out of conflicts. The odds were not ideal. Brand knew he could not run away from a fight – even when the outcome was so surely against him.

He stood stock still, his eyes never leaving Salazar. No matter what happened, he planned to bestow upon the concrete man injuries he would never outlive. Salvation arrived from an unexpected quarter. A new shiny truck pulled up to the group. A tall man with a hard hat and a large gut stepped out of the cab.

Salazar's helpers dispersed nervously. Bert looked down and examined his nails. Brand and Salazar waited where they were.

"What is going on here, Brand?" the newcomer asked with an unmistakable tone of authority.

"Nothing, Supes."

"That's not how it looks from where I am standing."

Brand relaxed his posture.

"We were just talking about how lovely Salazar's girlfriend is."

The superintendent glanced at the shapely Latina. He was not pleased.

"Get back to work before I find someone who will."

Without a word, the two combatants turned and returned to their separate work areas.

Salazar returned to the open forms and the tied steel within which his foundation would be poured. A young man came near.

"The *whetto* has no respect. He should be taught manners."

"Which one?" Salazar asked impatiently.

"Choose", replied the self-possessed young man.

Salazar gave the youth his full attention. He detected a serious intent behind the casual conversation. He recognized him as one of Fuentes' men. The old man was a good source for unskilled labor when the job required nothing more than a strong back.

"What is your name?"

"Miguel Luna, *Señor* Salazar."

"Ah yes. I remember now. What is in your mind, Miguel?"

"Do you know much about what we do for *Señor* Fuentes?"

"It is best to keep one's eyes on his work."

"You are wise, *Señor*."

Miguel looked over to the lovely Latina. She remained within the shade of the lone tree in the center of the road base which would one day be a parking lot. As she had during the entire dispute, she watched mildly. Her eyes met Miguel's and she smiled at him as though she knew him, and they shared a secret knowledge.

Miguel returned his gaze to Salazar.

"You were kind enough to provide me a job. I will take care of the white men for you."

"That is not necessary, Miguel."

Miguel lifted a hand and quieted Salazar's protests.

"It is just a thing. It is nothing at all."

# Chapter 10

Workmen loaded tools on trucks in preparation to leave for the day. Brand rolled a blue air hose. Bert gathered the nail guns strewn throughout the job. Lance and Brett carried a big green air compressor to Brand's truck. The men were tired, and the day was hot.

Brand tossed the hose in the bed and slammed the tailgate on his truck. Bert stood close by. He watched Brand. Thoughts milled busily in his head.

Wearily, Brand leaned against the truck bed.

"The Dog?" He asked perfunctorily.

"Indeed", was the simple reply.

"I'll meet you there."

Karen was busy mixing cocktails and delivering them at high speed. The hour was early, just after 5 o'clock. Rod Dog's was a happy hour bar. The after-work crowds were primarily regulars and she knew most of their drink selections by heart.

Brand and Bert arrived to find the place packed to capacity. The horseshoe shaped bar was completely seated, and several patrons stood at the packed bar top chatting loudly with seated patrons.

The tightly packed low tables hosted men and women in every manner of dress. Here, a tightly packed group of men and women in suits and business formal attire laughed and joked, sipping at their martinis and scotch and sodas. There, round tables were circled by tanned men in tee shirts and heavy jeans. Cold beer washed away the hot labor of a long day outside. Against the far wall, near the big flat screen TV, the digital dart board suffered the competitive attack of a national retailer's sales staff dressed in blue golf shirts and khaki slacks.

Fortune was with them, and two men wearing button downs with sewn on tabs featuring their names and company logos, stood. They paid their tabs and left.

Bert and Brand managed to slide into their seats near the waitress station at the bar. Karen sat two high ball glasses before them.

"Hello, you", she welcomed Brand. "How are you, Bert?"

Bert smiled and nodded as he lifted his cocktail to his lips.

Karen considered Bert for a moment before she moved across the bar to serve another patron.

"She sure is icy today", Bert complained.

"She knows you, Bert."

"What is that supposed to mean?"

"How many of her girlfriends have you banged?"

"How does she know about that?"

Brand regarded Bert with an incredulous look.

"Everyone knows."

Bert again sipped his drink, weighing his friend's words.

"That thing today with the concrete guy's girlfriend: what were you thinking?"

Bert chuckled.

"That was an innocent mistake."

"After a while, the mistakes are no longer innocent, Bert."

"We could have taken them, Bro", Bert assured Brand with a good-natured slap on the shoulder.

Brand grimaced, looking at his drink. Bert was joking about something that could have been disastrous. To Brand's knowledge, Bert had never been in a fight. As with most things between them, Bert was pretty free and easy in heaping his troubles onto Brand's shoulders with a willingness which shouted, 'I don't care about anyone but myself.'

The young Latina was forbidden fruit. Bert demonstrated time and again that his dick ruled his actions. From the time they were privates, just sworn in, Bert showed a preoccupation with females at a level which, to Brand, indicated a psychosis. Was it his insecurities that compelled Bert to treat every woman he encountered as a test of his manhood and virility?

"Your dick is going to get you in deeper shit than you or I can get you out of", Brand warned his friend.

Bert looked at Brand for a long moment. It was doubtful that Bert was thinking of anything more than a quippy retort intended to lighten Brand's dour mood.

"My dick naturally avoids deep shit. I don't like back door action."

Brand shook his head: so predictable. He sipped his drink as he organized his thoughts. He knew the effort was futile, but he had to try.

"Let's analyze the roll sex plays in your life, Bert. You are packing around a huge dick. You prefer to go down on a woman rather than use it. Your definition of a successful sex act is, A: It must last at least eight hours; B: The woman must either collapse from orgasmic exhaustion, or she should be in a state of dehydration from fluid loss; and C: She must be properly chafed inside, and her body must ache from being contorted into impossible angles.

"Sometimes you don't cum and that is okay with you. In fact, you consider it an act of valor in that you sacrificed your satisfaction for that of your lover. By the way, the not cumming thing is not normal and indicates a deeper problem."

Brand glanced up, surprised to see Karen committed to a rare still moment. She stood at a distance, monitoring his analysis of Bert with a curious look on her face. She had talked with Brand on many occasions about Bert. She agreed he was an oddity and very much unattractive due to his strange treatment of women. She turned from her scrutiny and moved to make another drink.

"I'm not sure how big I am compared to other men", Bert said with feigned modesty, "But the rest is absolutely true. I sense a little envy in your criticism."

"Bert, you have heard it before, but I need to remind you that sex is not the goal of a relationship. It is a very pleasant side effect of a healthy relationship."

"We disagree on the smaller points, but I think you see where I get my motivation. That first moment when a man and a woman join physically is the greatest pleasure in the world."

"You have been married for more than twenty years…"

"Twenty-three."

"You have two daughters and about four cats."

"The cats are a result of my not being able to say no to my girls."

"Isn't it time you reset your priorities to include a long and happy family life, and an end to philandry?"

"That's not a word."

"Fucking a woman into oblivion is not love."

"Never said it was."

"That's my point. Work on the love part and don't play around."

Bert stared at Brand for a long moment. His gaze searched his friend desperately.

"What have you done with Brand, you bastard?"

"Fuck you."

"Nice come back."

Brand finished his drink. Karen moved his way to refill his glass.

"Cash me out, Karen. I've gotta get home."

"And that's another thing", Bert complained. "It's pretty easy to advise me to turn off the pussy tap when you have a smoking hottie at the house."

Karen brought his tab and Brand passed her a credit card. She moved to the cash register. Both men watched her absently as they processed their individual thoughts.

Brand again experienced his own share of mental anguish at the thought of Natalie's potential infidelities.

"Mexico this weekend?" Bert asked brightly.

"We just got back", Brand complained.

"It's still early in the week. We'll revisit this in a couple of days."

Brand signed his tab and stood, pocketing his wallet.

"Later."

"Tell Natalie I said hey", Bert said by way of adieu.

"Get home and get some sleep. We need you at full power tomorrow."

"I will."

Brand rewarded the promise with a doubtful look.

# Chapter 11

Friday night they crossed the main international bridge into Piedras Negras. The sun dropped reluctantly below the horizon. The velvety dark blue of the evening sky wrapped the dusty town in a lovely cloak. Her gaudy lights offered the seductive promise of raucous tourists and lively revelry. Brand had no idea this evening would be his last with Bert.

They searched for Carlos and his rattle trap cab among the line of taxis at the northern edge of the square. Instead, they found only the eager yellowed smiles of other drivers. A short conversation brought them to the decision of a drink or two with Arturo, then an early evening back at their motel. They were both tired after a long week on the job site under the pounding of the early summer heat. It was agreed that Saturday would be their big night in old Mexico.

The street before the ancient Hotel Rojas teemed with American tourists. Eager white faces cast fascinated looks in every direction, savoring the timeless authenticity of the dingy border town.

They entered Arturo's bar. It hosted a markedly different atmosphere than it had previously. The place was packed with locals and tourists alike. Arturo towered over the rough bar. He moved at a pace appropriate of any veteran bartender. Lost was his languorous manner of their previous visit. He spotted the two Americans with a welcoming smile. He gestured for them to stand at the end of the bar.

"*Micheladas*?" he asked eagerly.

Bert quickly responded in the affirmative as Brand responded with a resounding 'no.'

"*Cerveza por favor*", Brand said quickly.

They took their places at the bar.

"Now this is what I'm talking about", Bert announced heartily.

"Not bad, Bert", Brand agreed.

Brand looked around him with mild interest. He noticed two dusky beauties at the opposite end of the bar. They appraised the American newcomers with open interest.

"Working girls", Bert pointed out unnecessarily.

The drinks arrived with a truncated welcome from the pleasant, but harried, Arturo. They drank deeply of their first cocktail, the typical manner in which they initiated a night of drinking.

"I love these things", Bert reported, holding the tall red-filled glass high for his friend to admire.

"Too much veggie action for a decent cocktail", Brand said.

Bert shrugged and drank deeply once more.

Brand sipped his beer as he committed himself to the business of people watching. The room was filled with a bountiful variety of clientele for the endeavor. Other than the two prostitutes, the bar was lined with tourists. The largest group was comprised of six rowdy college guys. Brand guessed them part of a fraternity. They spoke loudly, and each drink was a celebrated accomplishment. The frat boys acted demonstratively, showing off for the pretty Mexican girls at the end of the bar.

Brand swallowed a knowing grin. The prospect of the frat boys making it home tonight with their money was doubtful if these professionals got hold of them.

Nearer Brand, seated at the bar, were three older American men. Brand heard them speaking English. He guessed them to be hunters or fisherman. Likely they crossed the border for a night of drinks and Mexican culture.

The three folding tables hosted large groups, seated in the folding chairs and standing. Most of these seemed to be locals. Brand suspected a few of the patrons among the large assortment of locals were from America. Their clothing was of a Walmart style. The biggest difference were the shoes. Mexican natives typically wore rough work shoes or, if they had higher social position, black dress shoes of the winged tip style. The occasional American sports shoe was worn by few locals with the cash to afford them. Those were usually outlandish and gaudy. The unlaced, garish style was common to those worn by American inner-city blacks. The Americans among the locals wore casual sneakers or gym shoes, laced and tied.

Brand and Bert finished their drinks at the same time.

"How did you drink that *Michelada* so fast?"

"What is taking you so long?"

They ordered another round.

Time passed as they chatted casually, enjoying the atmosphere of the small bar. Bert's interest in the women at the end of the bar grew as the drinks continued to appear before him. At one point he ordered tequila shots for he and Brand, and the two prostitutes.

The women lifted their shot glasses in tribute to the Americans and tossed back the bitter liquid with the equanimity of seasoned pros.

Brand saw the front door open. A young thin man entered the bar. Brand wouldn't have noticed him if he hadn't been looking towards the entrance at that moment. He noticed the newcomer before he was seen.

The man stopped just inside the door and scanned the bar. His eyes settled upon Brand as if he were searching for him particularly. When he located Brand at the bar, their eyes locked. The kid didn't look away as Brand might have expected. He gazed intently at him as if to challenge him.

Brand searched his face with a passive scrutiny. Why was this guy familiar? Brand looked away casually as if he had only noticed the new man in passing. He allowed his gaze to come to rest on a few other patrons to assuage any suspicions the newcomer might have gained at being seen. Brand was unsure why he continued the ruse. Something about the young man set him ill-at-ease. Brand was sure the new man was familiar. He couldn't place him immediately. He was certain, however, that the curious stranger was someone he had seen recently.

He turned to Bert to ask if he recognized the Mexican. Before he could pose the query to his friend, recognition hit him with a subtle shock. He had seen the newcomer with Salazar's crew earlier in the week. In fact, he remembered that the man had spoken with Salazar immediately after the Latina confrontation.

What were the odds that one of Salazar's men would patronize this particular bar, in this particular border town, while they were there? Brand felt a sudden surge of dread issuing from deep within him. His instincts screamed trouble with an irresistible call to action. He looked towards the door. The skinny kid was no longer there. He had moved to one of the folding tables. He spoke with an older man in mustaches and rough clothing. They invested much theatre in acting as if they weren't talking about the Americans. Two other men leaned in closer as the older man spoke to the newcomer. One of the two glanced in Brand's direction.

"Bert", Brand said, turning his back to the bar room. He sipped his drink and leaned back casually. He was unsure if the kid was sharp enough to discern whether Brand had recognized him or not.

Bert looked at his friend expectantly. A happy grin pulled at the corners of his mouth.

"Brand", he returned lightly.

"We are in trouble. Do not look around you no matter what I tell you. The next few minutes may be critical to our getting out of Mexico in one piece."

From the corner of his eye, he saw Bert stiffen. To Brand's surprise, Bert kept his gaze forward as he followed instructions.

"One of Salazar's crewmen just walked into the bar."

Bert looked at Brand in alarm.

"Are you serious?"

"That's not the worst part. He is talking with three other guys. They look like locals and they look a little rough. This has to be about that Mexican chick from the job site."

"Shit, Brand. We need to get the hell out of here."

"Agreed."

Brand glanced toward the prostitutes at an angle where he could just see the group of men with his peripheral vision. He smiled and nodded as if he was acknowledging the women.

"I'm going to go talk to those women. The guys at the table will watch me. You head towards the restroom like you have to pee. It is important that you act naturally. They will see you, but I don't think they know we are onto them. At the wall, head towards the front door. Hit the door and turn left. Get your ass to the bridge as fast as you can run."

"I'm not much good on foot, bud."

Brand nodded.

"I know partner. I'll do what I can to slow them down."

Bert looked at him with concern.

"Don't worry about me. They will focus on you when you leave. I'll catch up with you before you hit the square."

Brand saw Bert pale under his tan. His eyes bulged with fear.

"Keep your shit together, Bert. When you turn towards the front door, the act is no longer necessary. They will react to the situation. I'm counting on that."

Brand put a hand on Bert's forearm.

"Wait until I talk to the girls."

Bert swallowed visibly. Brand felt a pang. His friend was genuinely afraid. In a brief self-analysis, Brand wondered at the truth that he felt no fear. He felt only a galvanizing sense of purpose.

There was real danger in his plan. It was predicated purely on instinct and a response from an adversary he did not know, based upon a guess at how they would react to a weak subterfuge. He forced himself to smile at Bert, partially for the theatre of their ruse, and partially to bolster Bert's flagging courage.

Brand moved towards the girls, feigning a timidity he thought one might affect when approaching strange women in a bar. He rarely approached women in bars, but he was never uneasy or awkward. He did, however, want to appear innocuous to the watchers.

He saw, via peripheral vision, that the four men watched him carefully. Brand figured they were confident in their numbers and their presumed anonymity.

The nearest of the two women turned in her seat to face Brand. Her demeanor was welcoming, and her eyes showed interest.

"Hi", Brand said with a half-hearted smile.

"*Ola*", she replied with a seductive smile in return.

"I have been watching you all night and I wanted to come over and introduce myself."

Brand glanced at Bert. He had not moved from his stiff posture over his forgotten drink. He did not look at Brand. He seemed to see only inward. Perhaps, Brand thought, he was examining the events which had brought him to this dire predicament.

"Have you?" she replied with a thick accent. She leaned forward to present her ample bosoms. "I noticed you too. You are very handsome and very strong."

Bert rose slowly and turned towards the sign reading 'Banos.' He looked straight ahead, making his way slowly towards the bathroom. Brand saw the group of men break with their scrutiny of him to keep an eye on Bert's whereabouts.

"Let's fuck right here", Brand announced loudly.

He grabbed her and pulled her into him roughly. He locked her lips against his. Her reaction was immediate and violent. She pushed against him and cried out in alarm.

The college guys turned towards the commotion. The four adversaries did likewise.

Bert reacted to the commotion as if a starter's gun was fired at a track meet. He bolted for the door. The Mexican Brand recognized from the job site stood when he saw Bert attempting to escape. The other three noticed Bert's flight a split second later. They rose from their chairs and turned towards the closing door.

Brand grabbed the woman's half-full beer bottle in his left hand and ran headlong into the group. The mustached man turned towards the movement and Brand broke the bottle against his face. He brought a powerful right fist under the next man's jaw. His teeth crunched together, and he collapsed beside the beer bottle recipient.

Salazar's man turned in time to receive Brand's shoulder in his chest. He went down, grasping at the air with flailing arms. The fourth man retreated in alarm, falling into a nearby table, toppling the occupants with him.

Brand hit the door at full speed. He turned left and ran, dodging pedestrians. He did not immediately spot Bert. He zig-zagged through the crowd, unhappy with his slowed progress. Finally, he came to the first intersection. Traffic was heavy as he crossed the street. He weaved through the cars to the vigorous honks of testy drivers. He heard the crash of the bar door slammed open behind him. The four men spilled out of Arturo's bar and looked about wildly. They spotted Brand and yelled in alarm, encouraging one another in the pursuit.

Not far ahead, past the intersection, Brand saw Bert. He was moving heavily through the crowd. Those revelers he didn't crush with his large frame, were roughly shoved out of the way. Many staggered or fell aside before the panicked big man like waves before the prow of a ship.

Brand caught him easily, following the swath he cut through the crowd. He turned quickly to check the progress of the pursuers. He saw them clearly, no more than half a block behind. They were near enough he could see the blood and anger on their faces

Brand moved past Bert. Sweat shone in large beads on his friend's face.

"Come on, Bert. Get that big ass moving. They're gaining."

Bert conserved his breath and said nothing. His mouth was set grimly. His face was lined with concern and the effort he was applying to his escape.

They broke out of the street throng and entered the less compacted crowds strolling the square. A band played wildly with the cries of brass horns and voices raised in Spanish harmonies. Brand led the way. He reluctantly slowed his pace so as not to lose Bert.

They finally reached the road which led to the international bridge. Brand slowed to a walk. His fists clenched in frustration. Mexican policemen were closing the chain-link gate, blocking the bridge to crossers.

It must have been after eleven. Brand hadn't considered the time in his plans. Bert stopped beside him, drawing heavy, labored breaths.

"Shit", he said through rasping pulls of air.

Brand looked around them. He saw a narrow dark alley between two buildings whose windows were crowded with cheap curios and brightly colored tourist items.

"Follow me, Bert."

He scanned their surroundings with a quick turn of his head as he led Bert into the dark alley. He didn't see the pursuers. He was troubled by their absence. They should have caught up with them by now. The obvious answer was that they knew there was no escape over the main bridge. Of course they would know. This was their home. They would expect the Americans to make for the second bridge.

Brand guessed the Mexicans would head for the second bridge road and await them there. He remembered from their previous visit that the second bridge was some two miles away. Once they reached the road leading to the bridge, it was a gauntlet of tall chain link fencing and heavy railing. The bridge road was approximately a half mile long, mainly uphill, and without cover.

They picked their way amongst the junk and trash cans littering the alley. They made every effort to remain silent and unnoticed. On both sides, crappy little houses bordered the dirt alleyway. Most of the houses were dark. Many of them seemed empty. Only here and there dim lights shone through dingy windows.

Their progress was slowed by the caution required to avoid disturbing the junk that filled the lane. Bert's breathing was no longer loud pulls of air. He was catching his breath as a result of their slower pace. Brand searched for a place where they could rest and formulate a plan.

The alleyway met no cross streets. To their left, unseen beyond the trashy houses, and a few rods distance, was the river. To their right were the tourist areas of the border town, then the city proper beyond that. Access to the river was limited. Brand presumed there was much danger in approaching the Rio Grande so close to an international border crossing. Earlier, he had seen the border fence some distance from the river bank. Beyond that was thick underbrush all the way to the river's edge. They would have a difficult time getting to the river at all, much less the unlikely opportunity to swim across.

Ironically, if caught on this side, the Mexican authorities would likely apprehend them and toss them into the deepest darkest Mexican prison they could find. Mexican immigration laws were far stricter than those of the U.S.

Even for Mexicans, crossing the river illegally was not a casual matter. The process was carefully planned and implemented in specific areas scouted and protected by the cartels and led by organized runners called *Coyotes*.

If they attempted to cross the second bridge, they would be walking into an ambush set by foes far more familiar with the lay of the land than they. If they happened to escape the ambush and mount the bridge access road, they would have to outrun their pursuers over a huge distance on foot, and in the open, before they came to the first guard post.

Bert had faltered after only three blocks of running. Brand was in good shape for a guy who didn't run much and hit the gym even less. He wasn't a long-distance runner, and their adversaries might be excellent on foot.

Bert tugged on Brand's shirt from behind. He turned as Bert slumped down wearily onto an old fiber barrel. He rested his elbows on his legs, his head drooped wearily between his broad shoulders.

Brand sat across from him on a long rickety wooden box. He listened to Bert's breathing, his thoughts on their predicament.

"I can't believe they are this upset about a girl", Bert said in a husky voice.

Brand couldn't see Bert's face in the gloom. Conversely, his friend couldn't see the wry look Brand made at the statement.

"I think those assholes will stake out the second bridge, Bert. There are no other crossing points within a hundred miles."

"We could swim for it."

Brand shook his head. He suspected Bert was being glib.

"This alley is a trap. Based on our last walk to the bridge, there are no cross streets that intersect with this alley. There is only one way in and one way out. I figure it goes all the way to the second bridge access road, if it goes that far, then stops at the fence that isolates the road. They will figure out where we hid at the main crossing if they haven't already. We may already be in their trap."

Dimly, he saw Bert's head lift as he looked for unseen foes.

Bert looked back towards Brand. He chuckled.

"Do you remember that time we were in the Guard and we stayed out all Friday night? We nearly missed formation. All day we were committed to going home and sleeping for twelve hours. It's like we got our second wind around three o'clock Saturday afternoon."

Brand nodded, grinning at the memory despite their situation.

"We changed into our civvies and jumped in the truck headed for 'The Corral Dance Hall.' You fell asleep at the wheel at least three times in the first ten miles. I took over and kept falling asleep too. We finally pulled over after getting maybe halfway there and slept in the car. We were committed to partying, brother,"

Both chuckled at the story. It was a tale they had rehashed many times since that day. Brand's smile faded as he considered Bert critically. His friend was referencing a distant memory while danger closed in upon them. Brand suspected his retreat into nostalgia was a coping method.

Again, he felt a warm sympathy for his long-time friend. He had never seen him under duress before. Bert's relief seemed to come from diverting his thoughts elsewhere.

"You could use some road work", Brand commented light-heartedly.

Bert made an emphatic grunt.

"That's true. These damn biker boots don't help much."

"Those things gotta weigh ten pounds each, Bert."

"At least. They are also half height and laced all the way up. My ankles are trussed up like a traction patient."

Brand stood resolutely.

"We don't have time to wait around, bro. When we don't show up at the bridge, they will come looking for us. We may have done what they expected us to do already. We've gotta get out of this alley."

Bert stood stiffly.

"Which way?"

"Let's keep going. Maybe we can find a break between the houses."

They picked their way along the alley for another hundred yards until thick foliage covered the alleyway in an impassable bramble. They looked at the thorny blockade dejectedly.

"This is bad." Bert, as was his manner, stated the obvious.

"We have to go back."

Brand glanced towards their back trail. He was certain there was no way their assailants didn't know where they were. He and Bert were trapped in this alley. He looked around him for something he could use as a weapon in the inevitable fight before them.

He heard chain link rattling nearby. He turned in time to see Bert clambering over the fence and into a narrow back yard of one of the houses.

Once across, Bert paused, looking at Brand.

"As I see it", he observed, "We have one option – other than going back and being killed at the road."

Brand considered Bert's intentions.

"If we break into that house and people are in there asleep", Brand warned, "We will have the cops to deal with too."

"Tomato – *tomatillo, Vato*. We are cooked either way."

Bert's tone betrayed the casual content of his comment. His voice was tight with stress.

Brand shrugged then climbed the fence. They approached the rear of the darkened house cautiously. Brand strained his ears to detect any sound within the house. His search for external signs that the house was occupied were fruitless. It seemed that all the structures in that district were in dire need of repair and displayed a forlorn impression of abandonment whether occupied or not. Interestingly, the buildings were built one jammed against the other. Their only egress would have to be through the building.

At the center of the dark back wall, a ramshackle plank door hung to its frame. It clung precariously, as if it treasured its final moments before it surrendered to the inevitable forces which ultimately ruined every door in the neighborhood.

Brand tested the inadequate latching mechanism, more for noise than the degree of effort necessary to force the door. Surprisingly, the door surrendered easily and noiselessly save for the muted complaint of rusty hinges.

Stealthily, Brand led Bert into the darkness within the small house. The structure had no interior walls and the two dingy windows at the front of the house allowed but scant light to show the way. Brand saw dark shapes on the floor which he reasoned were piles of debris and trash. The floor was compacted dirt. The air inside the hovel smelled dank, like a crawl space or primitive basement. His imagination provided him the unwelcome comparison of the smell to that of a freshly dug grave. Brand tightened his jaw at the grim thought. He would allow no foreboding fantasy, or whim of fancy to cloud his judgement.

They were, by no means, clear of danger once they emerged; but he determined to grade their progress incrementally. This was a victory in his book. There were many unanswered questions related to their dire predicament. He felt a small satisfaction that they provided themselves a measure of hope with this minor maneuver.

Brand led Bert to the window at the right of the door centered in the front wall. He searched the area immediately outside. The house faced the rear of a large brick building. There were no windows in the tall structure, but Brand thought it was probably the back wall of the Hotel Rojas.

A crashing sound from the alley behind the house startled them. Bert pressed a large hand on Brand's shoulder.

The hunters were in the alley, Brand thought. The bramble barrier was near, and it wouldn't take long for the pursuers to determine their escape route.

With renewed urgency Brand moved to the door and tried the dusty knob. It turned easily, but the door moved only a fraction before it jammed solidly with a metallic sound and a strong resistance.

Brand deduced that the door was locked from the outside with a clasp and padlock. That was the only explanation. They had the benefit of one remaining unknown. Their pursuers had not determined by which house they had escaped.

Brand believed they would have to exit the shack through one of the windows. If it wouldn't open, he would have to break the glass. The noise would give away their position as surely as if a spotlight had shone upon them in the dark.

Brand tested the sash from all directions. The window was sealed either by design or with age.

"Bert", he whispered to his companion. "We are going to have to run again."

"I know", Bert replied in a strained voice. "Hurry up and break it."

Brand moved away from the window and felt around the floor until he found something that would protect his skin from broken glass. One of the dark shapes on the floor was a small metal pail. Brand lifted it and shook out any contents, dust, or spiders awaiting within. He returned to the window and punched through the glass, his hand inside the pail.

The noise of the breaking glass was deafening to their desperate ears. In reaction to the window shattering, a sound of clatter and movement announced that those in the alley had located their quarry's escape route.

The need for stealth was behind him, so Brand noisily knocked the remaining sharp edges of glass from the window frame. He dropped the pail and climbed through the window. The wooden frame felt rough in his palms, but he had successfully removed all the glass. He dropped to the dirt below the window and turned to help Bert. The big man emerged from the dark house with surprising agility

They sprinted into the narrow road behind the hotel and turned left in the general direction of the bridge. Behind them, the small house was alive with the sound of scrambling feet and the grunts of laboring men.

It sounded to Brand like the noises were those of three men. Their pursuers had been four at the beginning. Either others had joined their number, or only one man held watch while the other three flushed the Americans from cover.

As Brand expected, they were able to reach the street before the hotel via a small gap between the hotel and an adjoining building. He paused, then peered around the corner into the lane fronting the hotel. The street was empty except for a few drunken party goers headed home.

Bert pushed Brand impatiently, and they entered the open sidewalk. They moved cautiously, casting nervous looks in all directions. Their instinct was to run, but Brand forced himself and Bert to maintain a slower and less obtrusive pace.

They moved quickly but cautiously, passing Arturo's bar across the street. It was dark, the door locked. They crossed the street and rounded the first intersection to their right. Brand picked up the pace by half. He listened intently for the sounds of their pursuers. Soon he heard a disturbance behind them. The sounds were muffled by distance and the corner buildings they had just passed. The footfalls were unmistakable. The enemy was closing in upon them.

Brand crossed the street and ran as far as the corner of the next block. This area seemed to be more of an industrial district rather than the festive tourist-friendly businesses comprising the previous lanes. Warehouses sat far back from the road across from where they walked. On their side of the street, the lane seemed to be lined with office spaces. Rather than gaudy bars and tourist dens, these buildings were filled with offices sporting desks and fake trees.

They had nearly traversed the full block when Brand led Bert into a space between two office buildings. The evasive move was not a second too early. The sound of multiple heavy footfalls filled the night behind them as the pursuing adversaries moved onto the street they had just left.

They heard rough voices speaking but could not make out distinct words. Neither Bert nor Brand spoke enough Spanish to have benefited from hearing their conversation clearly. They backed into the darkness of a narrow alcove which housed a roof access ladder and a drain pipe. They were belt buckle to belt buckle in the narrow niche.

The pursuit passed the alley with only a short pause to peer into the space. The shallow, narrow alley was quickly determined an unlikely hiding place for their quarry. Brand clearly discerned three individual voices. He was correct in the number of their enemies. Where was the fourth man? The three voices faded into the distance.

They did not move from their intimate hiding place. Bert took a deep breath and Brand felt his stomach pressed against Bert's.

"I think they have invited a few more friends to the chase", Bert observed.

"I think you are right. Who the hell are these guys?"

"I would guess they are part of some goddam drug cartel or something."

Brand leaned out of the alcove and into the less compromising space of the small alleyway.

"Or something", Brand echoed absently, his mind working on their next move.

"How far do you think we are from the bridge?" Bert asked softly.

"Maybe a mile. We need to approach the bridge road straight on. We have dodged around enough that I don't believe they will expect us to be bold in our approach."

"What makes you think that?"

"It's just a hunch."

"A hunch", Bert repeated thoughtfully. "That's a pretty big gamble."

"That's what those Mexicans will be thinking too."

Brand moved back to the edge of the street. He saw no movement. He strained his ears to hear any telltale sounds of the hunters. Nothing he heard helped him. The city was strangely quiet. He guessed the time to be after midnight.

"Let's move, Bert."

They struck out at a brisk walking pace. They paused cautiously at the next intersection and surveyed the area in all directions before they crossed. They made good progress and within a few minutes they were at the intersection of the road leading to the second international bridge.

Brand peered around the corner, exposing only enough of his face to get a good look in the direction of the bridge. Because of their diversion, they were two blocks over and some half a mile from the bridge. He could see the orange glow of the bridge lights and further away, the glare of bright security lights, like an aura over the tops of the buildings and trees. He saw no one on the streets ahead. He was encouraged that it appeared he was correct in his prediction regarding the actions of their adversaries.

Brand turned to Bert and spoke in a tone just loud enough to be heard.

"We need to cross here and go one more block. We will double back around the next block."

"I thought you wanted to take the bold approach."

Bert's voice registered annoyance, likely spurred by growing fatigue and the desperation of their situation. Nevertheless, Brand was also tired, and his patience was not adequate to conceal his intolerance of Bert's doubtful manner.

"Do you want to run for it from here? It's only about a mile to the U.S. You can make it easy."

"I got it! You lead."

Brand checked once again, then moved briskly across the intersection. Bert followed as though they were still pinned together in the building alcove. They paused under a metal awning covering the front door of a corner building. Brand checked for pursuers once again. As before, the street was empty as far distant as he could see. He was uncertain how accurately he could detect awaiting adversaries in the dim street lights spaced at lengthy intervals along the street.

They moved silently, ears hyper-sensitive for any hint of human activity. The entire district was shrouded in an eerie silence. There was an absence of the normal city noises typical of any urban area – even late in the night. It was almost as if the very city watched and waited to see how their drama would play out.

They reached the end of the block. Brand again repeated his surveillance ritual, scanning their surroundings.

He was growing suspicious. Where were the three men who had followed them so relentlessly? Had they changed their tactics? Were they lying in wait? He dared not hope they had moved farther into the city, thinking the Americans might hole up and wait for the morning to catch a cab to the border crossing.

Brand grunted softly. That seemed like a good idea to him at that moment. He shook his head, clearing all but his current plan from his mind. This was no time to doubt himself or change course midstream.

He turned to Bert. The bigger man was watching him with keen interest. Brand patted him on the shoulder. The last thing he needed was to do anything which might cause Bert to doubt him. They needed to remain sharp if they were going to survive this thing.

Brand turned the corner, staying under the darkness of the flat metal cover over the narrow sidewalk. They moved along the building until it ended at a vacant lot at the next corner of the block. The crossing street ran from their position west to the square. Brand bent low as he moved across the lot, abandoning the sidewalk in favor of the diagonal shortcut. Bert followed.

They paused at the side of a 'dobe building bordering the empty lot. They stepped carefully over trash, broken lumber, and rusted pipes piled haphazardly beside the building. Brand inched close to the corner of the house and once again peeked around the building. He quickly withdrew.

Three men stood on the porch before the building. They were silent. He had seen them only because of the cherry glow from the ends of their cigarettes. He suspected these were the same men who had pursued them from the alley.

Bert pressed forward, and Brand gripped his arm tightly. He placed his index finger to his lips. He raised three fingers close to Bert's face. He pointed towards the front of the building.

Bert nodded his understanding.

Brand bent low and inspected the pile at their feet as best he could in the darkness.

Amongst the old wood were a few heavy galvanized pipes, some two or three feet long. He carefully extracted them from the mess. He moved slowly and deliberately, supporting surrounding materials with his other hand. In this way he was able to retrieve two of the pipes without making any noise. He handed one to Bert.

Brand hefted the pipe meaningfully, testing the weight. Bert gripped his pipe until his hand ached. He knew his friend well. Brand was fed up with running. Bert had seen this side of him many times. In his rare appearances in crowded social settings, Brand displayed this side of his personality when he experienced passive aggressive behavior disguised as humor or ill manners from someone. Once he reached the limit of his tolerance, he acted quickly and decisively.

In this instance there was no disapproving girlfriend nor were there social protocols to hinder him. There was no significant fear of police action. He was free to run amuck. Bert could almost feel his friend's internal mechanism spinning up to a fury he would tap to engage the three unseen enemies around the corner.

Without a word, Brand turned the corner. He moved quickly, but with the control and deliberation of one measured in his commitment and sure of his intentions. Bert followed automatically. He wasn't certain how he could help, but he determined that he would do what he could.

Brand's first blow crushed the side of the nearest man's head. He went down with a wet cry. The other two men lost critical seconds processing the attack. Brand brought the pipe up the next man's body under his chin. The blow did no more than stun him. Brand, however, used that instance to crush his larynx under a broad fist. The third man, by this time, was fully engaged in his reaction. He reached into his pants and produced an evil looking thin knife.

Brand hissed a low snarl at the sight of the weapon and tackled the man. His weight landed on the man's chest. The knife wielding Mexican's breath was crushed from his lungs. He forgot the knife as he struggled to breathe. Brand brought the pipe up and down fast as a cat's paw. The heavy pipe crushed his face with a meaty crunch. The knife clattered away onto the street where the blade glimmered in the dim ambient light.

Brand kept his hold on the pipe as he rose. He resumed his journey towards the bridge road.

Bert caught up with him.

"Those aren't the guys from the bar."

"I saw that", Brand agreed. His voice was no longer contemplative. He spoke with the firm resolve of the warrior. He was prey no more.

"Don't get careless, Brand. We have gotten this far. Let's keep cool."

Brand made no reply. He merely crossed the street in preparation for the right turn that would put them onto the bridge road.

They arrived at the bridge road and turned right towards the border crossing. The roadway rose gradually, ascending to the highest level of the international bridge. Dense trees and thick underbrush grew closely against the tall chain link fence on each side of the wide road.

This had been the main crossing for years prior to the construction of the new bridge.

Soon the road surface changed from tarmac to concrete. They were on the bridge structure. The Rio Grande was a considerable distance farther along the bridge. They approached the first mercury vapor street light.

Brand looked at the pipe clutched in his right hand. It would not do for the Mexican guards to see them armed. He tossed the pipe over the high fence. The heavy pipe cracked limbs and crushed foliage as it fell from thin branch to thin branch finally coming to rest on the ground far below them. Bert disposed of his weapon in the same manner. They walked briskly, the warm night air close around them.

As if the day were dawning prematurely, the night grew brighter around them. At first the growing illumination seemed a trick of their imaginations. Soon. the sound of a car's revving motor caused them to look behind them. Two sets of headlights brightened the night around them as two vehicles sped towards them up the bridge road. A third turned onto the bridge and followed at a distance behind the first two.

As one, they increased their pace to a full sprint. They made desperately for the gathered bright lights of the border crossing with the urgency of panic and fear. The cars gained with dreadful speed. The Mexican guard shack was a disheartening distance ahead.

"Run, Bert", Brand yelled as he raised the pace to a full sprint.

Bert accelerated impressively. Adrenalin fueled his muscles, overcoming the fatigue that weakened them. The effect, however, was temporary. Bert began to lose ground. He clenched his teeth as he willed himself to stay in contact with the quicker Brand.

Brand glanced over his shoulder. Bert had fallen dangerously far behind. Their only hope was to reach the Mexican guard shack before the three cars caught them and cut off their escape. Desperately Brand decided the best chance for the faltering Bert, was for him to move ahead at speed. Brand thought he would convince the guards to help. If not help, perhaps the presence of government officials would discourage the pursuers.

Purposefully, Brand pushed himself. A rearward glance showed a look of despair and abandonment on Bert's weary, frightened visage. Brand gave his full attention to his efforts to quickly reach the guard shack. He hoped these villains would be reluctant to commit violence in plain view of the authorities.

Brand arrived at the Mexican guard shack. He looked behind him. Bert was still some fifty yards distant. His pace had faltered to no more than a shambling walk. The headlights were now distinctly recognizable as automobiles. The security street lights shone off the shiny paint of three large black SUV's.

Brand beat on the steel and glass door of the guard shack. A uniformed sentry frowned at him. He stood slowly and donned his khaki policeman's cap. Brand glanced behind him. Bert was only about thirty yards away. The SUV's were almost upon him. Brand again gave his attention to the slow-moving guard. The apathetic sentry opened the door and eyed Brand suspiciously.

"Passport?"

"*Señor*", Brand said breathlessly. "My friend is in danger."

He pointed at the laboring Bert, head down, walking with an exhausted gait.

Tires squealed as the SUV's slid to a halt between Bert and the guard shack.

"Help us", Brand yelled impatiently.

Men stepped out of the trucks. They looked directly at Brand and the border official. Salazar's man was the last to step onto the street. He eyed Bert hungrily. His gaze moved to Brand and he favored him with a cruel grin. He pointed at Bert and the men moved to surround him. The guard surveyed the men impassively. He returned his attention to Brand.

"Passport please, *Señor*."

"Motherfucker!", Brand yelled and looked once more towards Bert.

The men moved in. Two of them grasped Bert's arms and dragged him to the nearest SUV.

Brand took two steps towards the group. The guard pulled the snap on his leather holster. He grasped the butt of his service weapon.

"On the ground, *gringo*", he commanded as he drew his pistol.

Brand spun on his left foot and dropped the guard with a hard right to the face. He moved with him as the guard fell. He punched him twice more in the face.

The stunned guard lay on the warm tarmac bleeding from his nose and mouth. Brand grabbed his pistol and chambered a round. He ran towards the two SUV's.

Bert struggled against his captors. Brand pushed the gun ahead of him and fired two shots. The first broke the window out of one of the open doors of the first SUV. The second punched a hole in the door below the broken window. The men drew weapons and sent a volley of bullets at Brand. Luckily, the bullets flew wide as they jumped for cover. The distance was great for hand guns. Brand leapt to the side and fired rapidly, perforating the lead SUV with multiple hits.

A total of four men forced Bert into the second SUV. He resisted mightily until one of them struck him in the face with a pistol. They finally wrestled him into the back seat.

The last Brand saw of his friend before they closed the door was his face contorted with a terrified look of despair. Brand stood with the pistol hanging at his side as the men entered the vehicles with slammed doors. They put the trucks in gear and sped away from the border crossing. Soon the taillights faded into the dull night.

Brand heard the guard moan as he slowly regained his faculties. Brand returned to him quickly.

"I should kill you", Brand threatened through clenched teeth. "Where did they take him?"

The guard glared at him. His cut and bloodied face showed no intention of cooperating.

"You are next, Carson Brand", he said spitting blood.

Brand straightened and drew a surprised breath before he brought the gun down hard into the man's hate-filled face. He pulled the clip and cleared the breech. He moved to drop the pieces on the pavement. After a quick reconsideration, he threw the weapon's components off the bridge. He turned north and crossed the bridge, the Rio Grande unseen in the darkness far below.

## Chapter 12

When he reached the American side, Brand was met by a large contingent of border patrol officers. They watched him with grim expressions. The lone American, approaching slowly, made for a curious image after the sound of so much gunfire only moments before.

Once Brand crossed the thick white line painted on the roadway, indicating the American side of the border, he was ordered on his face. He was handcuffed and searched. The officers took his passport and his wallet. They lifted him onto his feet then led/carried him into a tan metal building. Inside, he was pushed into a hard metal chair before a small steel table in a narrow room illuminated by a long fluorescent light fixture.

Without a word, the officers left him alone in the small room. Brand heard the lock engaged from the outside of the door. A half window reinforced with steel mesh showed him an empty hallway. The walls were covered with various notices and warnings in both English and Spanish.

Anguish gripped him as his mind went back to the abduction of his friend. The look on Bert's face as they pushed him into the SUV haunted Brand. His instinct was to tell the American officials everything about that evening. The sooner they acted, the more likely Bert could be saved.

The minutes passed as he sat alone with his thoughts. As the events of the last few hours played in his mind, Brand considered a dawning reality which overrode his desire to tell all. Many crimes had been committed in Mexico. He had assailed at least six men and a Mexican official. He had also taken an official's service weapon and opened fire upon citizens of Mexico.

Obviously, the guard knew exactly what was going on and was complicit with the men in the S.U.V.'s. What were the rules in dealing with an international incident involving actions which were felonies in the U.S.? How did the guard know his name on sight? He suspected that the relationship between Mexico and the U.S. in instances like this one was more cooperative than it might be with other more distant countries. The ongoing issues with illegal immigration, and the political climate surrounding it, may compel American authorities to work with the Mexican government as a sign of good faith.

None of this was clear to Brand. He was in strange waters here. He felt, under the circumstances, that it might not be in his best interest to clear up a confusing matter. Perhaps the unknowns might keep him out of Mexican hands.

Two uniformed officials appeared at the half window of the locked door. They unlocked the door with an abrupt noise of heavy tumblers and stiff hinges. They entered and closed the door. One of the officers took the seat across the table from Brand. He held Brand's passport and wallet. The second man stood to the left and behind Brand.

The seated officer placed Brand's possessions on the table between them.

"My name is Officer Worth."

He nodded towards the standing officer.

"This is Officer Collins."

"Carson Brand, it seems you have had an interesting evening."

Brand looked at him suspiciously. Had they already heard from the other side? What did he know? Brand decided to play things close to the vest.

"The end of it was pretty interesting."

"How do you mean?"

"There was some kind of shootout near the Mexican border. It was a ways from me, but it looked like it might be a cartel thing."

"What makes you think it was the cartel?"

"Isn't everything down here about the cartels?"

Worth glanced at Collins. They were not satisfied with his responses.

"You are acting pretty calm for a guy who was just in a shootout."

"I wasn't in a shootout. I heard shots from a ways down the bridge from the Mexican border. I'm prior service. I have heard and seen guns fired before."

"Prior service? What branch?"

"Army."

Brand thought a moment. He pictured the bearded airborne prior service guy from Rod Dog's in his mind.

"Army National Guard", he added.

"What was the purpose of your visit to Mexico?"

"I just wanted to see the sights."

"Alone?"

"Yessir."

"No one crossed with you when you entered Mexico yesterday evening?"

"There were quite a few people in line when I went through the check point, but they weren't with me."

"Your address is still 12346 Bentwood, apartment 114 in San Antonio?"

"It is. What is this about, Officer Worth? I have told you what I know. I am an American and I had nothing to do with some shootout in Mexico. I guess if I am guilty of anything, it is coming back home too late."

"You feel like you are guilty?"

Brand leaned back and considered Worth with a look of incredulity.

"I'm tired and would like to get back to my truck."

Brand carefully avoided revealing he had checked into a motel. He was unsure how many people might have seen him with Bert there.

"Are you driving back to San Antonio this morning?"

Yessir."

"Have you been drinking?"

Brand stopped himself before he answered. He covered the pause with another impatient look. If he said he had not drunk in several hours, it would bring up the question of what he had been doing in the intervening hours.

"I am not drunk, but I will not drive if I feel like I am unable."

"Answer the question."

"I had a few drinks at a bar near the main bridge."

"Which bar?"

"It didn't have a sign out front. I didn't catch a name."

"You just happened into a bar with no name?"

"I saw a group of tourists go in, so I followed."

Worth watched Brand intently, searching his face for tell-tale signs of fabrication or subterfuge. Finally, he leaned back.

"We are going to detain you here for a few hours until we can confirm your story with the Mexican officials."

Brand looked down at his feet. He dared not trust his reactions. He composed himself, hoping his inner conflict appeared to be the frustration of an innocent tourist wrongly ensnared in a bureaucratic mess. Once he settled upon the thoughts of his desired appearance, he looked up at Worth.

"I'm sorry, officer. I don't understand how I am involved in a situation that is obviously a matter for the Mexicans. I read about this kind of thing all the time in the paper and on-line. I am tired and would like to go home."

"It's just for a few hours, Mr. Brand, then we will have you on your way."

Worth stood, leaving Brands things on the table. He moved around the desk.

"Are the cuffs necessary, officer?"

Worth paused and gave Brand a strange look. Obviously, the officer was not buying Brand's story. He and Collins left the room.

Once more alone in the tiny room, grief and worry were again his companions. Bert's face haunted him. Committed to the hands of those ruthless men in the ominous black SUV's, was akin to being handed over to the very devil himself.

Brand had learned when he was a kid that "The wages of sin are death." Bert's sin seemed a trifle compared with the punishment. Bert had flirted with a girl. The result was an all-night pursuit and a gunfight resulting in his friend's abduction.

Brand shook his head sadly. Didn't he predict only a few days ago that Bert's dick would be the death of him? He was no sage and there hadn't been serious foreboding in the prediction, but he somehow felt he was partially responsible for the result. No matter how his reasonable mind vied for clarity, his imagination would not give up the idea he was somehow at fault.

Several hours passed in this way until Officers Worth and Collins again took their places in the informal prison cell. Brand was weary from a lack of sleep and worry. He was also suffering thirst and hunger pangs. Additionally, he really had to pee.

"Mr. Brand", Worth began, as he made himself comfortable across the table as before, "Do you have anything else you would like to add to your story while you still can?"

"My story?" Brand protested weakly. "Am I free to go or not? You have kept me locked up in this room all night for no cause other than you are waiting for a phone call or something."

"Mr. Brand, your attitude would better serve you back in your pocket. It is in your best interest to cooperate with us."

Brand sensed that Worth was on a fishing expedition. He guessed, based upon their previous Q and A session, that the Border official was very direct in his manner. Opening this new interrogation with so vague and general a question indicated they had nothing with which to hold him.

"Have I done otherwise since you locked me up?"

"I believe you are not telling me everything."

"Officer, Worth, I believe you are stretching our time together in a vain effort to gain intel I don't have. I'm tired, and certainly not too drunk to drive. I told you everything I know about last night. Our time is finished here, unless you want to buy me breakfast, sir."

Worth seemed to have no sense of humor. Brand was now certain he also had no probable cause to hold him. He had seen on TV that he could be held no more than twenty-four hours without being charged with a crime. He hoped Worth would not exercise that right.

His relief in his suspicions that he was free to go also nagged at him. Why wasn't he weathering a serious grilling about the assaults on six men and a border guard, the subsequent discharging of an officer's service weapon, and participating in a gunfight with what appeared to be members of organized crime.

"Stand up, Mr. Brand."

He obeyed, rising stiffly. His bladder ached dangerously. Collins moved in behind him and removed the handcuffs. Brand rubbed his wrists as everyone did. He collected his belongings from the table and pocketed them.

"You are free to go", Collins said unnecessarily.

"Is there a bathroom nearby?"

# Chapter 13

Brand walked away from the metal buildings and the dingy glow of quartz vapor lights. Leaving the border crossing behind did little to relax his knotted gut. What relief he felt at being released without penalty for his numerous crimes provided scant aid in assuaging his fears for Bert. The urge to cross back into Mexico and attempt a rescue was powerful. The reality of the logistical constraints, in large part, stayed his hand. He had no idea how he would cross, and once there, he was unsure how he could find his friend.

The words of the Mexican border agent troubled him greatly. He had known his name and seemed nonplussed by the violent abduction occurring nearby. Why had the attack and the disarming of the guard not been reported to the American authorities? Worth had indicated they would confirm his story with the Mexican authorities. The guard's silence was troubling. By all indications, Brand was involved with a well-organized group comprised of both criminal and law enforcement elements.

He finally arrived at the parking lot where he had left his pick-up. The shining blue truck seemed undamaged. He retrieved his hide-a-key from under the rear fender well. The truck cranked on the first try and he put it in gear. He drove through the early morning darkness.

Eagle Pass slept at that hour. He travelled empty streets, signal lights blinking their weary caution at the only vehicle on the road.

He parked the truck in a space across the parking lot from his motel room. The lot was packed to capacity. Many of the vehicles were heavy service trucks emblazoned with logos of national companies. It was apparent that many service industry employees were billeted there while employed in varying aspects of a busy international crossing point.

He inserted the key card and entered the cold dark room. He and Bert always dropped the temperature to arctic levels when they arrived. He found a light switch next to the door and clicked it on.

His was a typical cheap motel room with two double beds. Bert's blue tote bag lay on the nearest one. A pair of pants, a shirt, his cell phone and a wad of receipts lay next to the bag.

Brand rushed to the bathroom and satisfied his long-denied need to pee. After washing his hands, he returned to the bed nearest the door. Brand looked at Bert's belongings with a heavy heart. He remembered their happy chatter as they readied themselves for the evening out.

Brand pursed his lips helplessly, his eyes on Bert's phone. Sixty bucks for a month of international calls might have saved them both last night.

Their bags and their clothes had been discarded with little attention paid to tidiness. Brand regarded the items with the reverence of a monument. His heart ached. With a mighty effort he thrust from him the fears and misgivings fighting to take their places in his mind. He would not give up hope that Bert would return. He might be the worst for the experience, but he would return with a valuable lesson learned.

He made his way around to the second bed. He unzipped his black gym bag embroidered with the name and logo for Olympic Gym, a muscle head workout facility in San Antonio. He retrieved his cell phone and checked it for calls. There were none.

He thought about calling Natalie but decided against it until he knew more. Upsetting her would serve no purpose. He wasn't sure how he would handle talking about what he had just been through.

The red LCD numbers on the alarm clock read 6:34AM. Brand found the remote control for the small wall mounted flat screen. He clicked the power button and waited as the TV lit with a grainy display. He turned the channels, searching for a local station. The hour was early, but he hoped he could learn something that might help.

He watched every news show he could tune in until programming reverted to either sports programs or, for the smaller market stations, infomercials. The two stations he found originating from Mexico offered no help either. He saw nothing related to any incident in Mexico.

With one last look at Bert's things, he moved wearily to the bathroom where he turned the shower valve and adjusted the temperature. He undressed and stepped into the tub/shower combo. The hot water soothed his weary muscles. The efforts of the last twelve hours dragged upon him.

After a quick soap and rinse, he stepped out of the shower and dried himself with a stiff rough towel hanging on one of the two racks. He returned to the room and dressed in fresh clothes. He was ravenously hungry.

He left the room and crossed the parking lot. Many of the cars and service trucks were gone. His truck waited alone in its spot next to a tall fence. He walked to the busy café which shared the lot and found an empty booth at the rear of the restaurant.

A cheerful waitress brought him coffee and placed his order for the "Cowboy Breakfast". He blew steam off the surface of his coffee then gingerly brought the cup to his lips.

When the plate arrived, he shoveled his way through eggs, bacon, grits and biscuits in quick fashion. The waitress returned to refill his coffee. Her buxom figure quaked merrily as she laughed and shook her head at his empty plate.

"Check?" She asked with a chuckle.

"Yes, please", he replied, reaching for his wallet.

He returned to the room and lay down atop the blankets. He thought he might try to rest for an hour or so. He doubted he would be able to sleep with all that troubled him.

He was surprised when he awoke. He felt that several hours had passed since he had fallen asleep. He experienced a keen sense of the surreal as his mind struggled with the memory of the previous night's drama. Only the sight of Bert's things on the bed confirmed the worries which gnawed at him. The alarm clock read 5:15PM. The late hour caused him a surge of panic as if he had missed out on important events.

He grabbed the remote and again turned on the TV. He endured several minutes of commercials before the nightly news came on. The anchors talked about local traffic and weather for a few moments. A red banner spread across the bottom of the screen. The words "Breaking News" appeared in the strip of red.

"Just in", the overly coifed news anchor began. "Federal authorities made a grim discovery this afternoon. Fernando Lopez is on the scene. Fernando."

Brand turned up the sound on the TV. The hushed but obtrusive din of the air conditioner added a white noise aspect to the motel room which made Brand feel he had to strain to hear details. The news story drew his full attention, and the air conditioning unit distracted him annoyingly. He sat erect on the edge of the double bed. The stiff bedspread gave reluctantly to his weight.

The reporter spoke in a toneless voice with practiced, syncopated mid-sentence pauses throughout his soliloquy.

"We are on the scene of a (pause) grisly crime scene. Early reports indicate the body of (pause) a man in his late thirties was discovered by a passerby this morning (pause) before dawn."

The shot cut to video of policemen gathered around a body covered with a dark blanket.

"The body was recovered in shallow water (pause) in the Rio Grande. Due to the injuries to the body (pause) the police suspect foul play here."

The shot returned to the reporter.

"Officials say they have (pause) identified the victim, but they are withholding his name (pause) pending notification of next of kin."

The shot returned to the scene footage.

Brand kneeled before the TV, getting as close as he could. He felt the blood drain from his ears. Obstructed by the circle of working police and medical examiners, Brand caught only a glimpse of the covered body, but it was apparent it was that of a large man. The body could have been anyone. Unmistakable to Brand, however, were the large black boots protruding from beyond the reach of the blanket. The dead man wore half height biker boots, laced to the top.

Brand leaned back against the bed. He sat heavily on the thin carpet.

Bert was dead. Again, in his mind's eye he saw Bert's face at that moment when they pulled him into the SUV. His expression was clearly that of despair and loss. Brand felt tears burn behind his eyes. Disbelief fought impotently to soften the blow. There was no doubt here. The events of the previous night replayed in detail from the bar to his interrogation at the hands of the U.S. officials. It was all so unreal to Brand. All of this for a slight affront? Who was Salazar that he could conjure this level of response from across the border? He was a concrete guy.

The Mexican border guard had known Brand's name and warned him he was next. Brand rose suddenly, his senses strung tightly. If they knew his name, maybe they knew more. Brand moved to the night stand and picked up his phone. He pressed the name 'Natalie' and waited for the ring tone. The connection went directly to voice mail.

"Shit", he muttered.

Brand terminated the call and slid the phone into his pocket.

Quickly he gathered his and Bert's belongings and vacated the room. He threw the gym bags into the back seat of his truck and settled behind the wheel. He had a two-hour drive back to San Antonio.

Traffic was light as he left Eagle Pass. He drove through the desolate brush and red sand of the desert, his thoughts crowded with snippets of scenes from his years with Bert. His memories paraded through his mind in no particular order. Each grim thought of the previous night summoned a different and unique image of Bert in their past. His mind whirled with a lifetime of memories throughout the nearly twenty years they had been friends. A deep sadness, hardened with the disbelief that his best friend was gone, occupied his attention, leaving the long miles unnoticed.

Again, he questioned the sense of it all. Why had so much effort been committed to the pursuit and kidnapping of Bert? Brand frowned at the thought that he too was a target of the efforts last night. The guard's fierce warning confirmed this without question.

His mind churned with a mixture of disparate thoughts and images. He knew that if left to do so, his mind would find a clear path in this matter. He focused his priorities on getting in touch with Natalie as soon as possible. The next step would include his reaction and subsequent actions in reprisal for the murder of his friend.

Since youth, Carson Brand had never felt confusion in his sense of purpose. He had never analyzed his process when faced with conflict or fearful situations.

During his two semesters in college, he roomed with an ROTC cadet, Patrick Gentry, who had trained with several special ops teams while serving in the 82nd Airborne Division. Patrick often spoke of his training. He pared down the philosophy behind all training to the fact that there were two instincts to which people resorted when faced with danger. They were either fight people or they were flight people. Patrick said that ninety percent of all people defaulted to flight. Only ten percent were fighters. Law enforcement and special ops alike trained for the difficult task of dealing with the ten percent.

Brand had given Patrick's theory a lot of thought over the years. He wasn't sure if he were truly a fight person, or if he just flattered himself as such. Natalie assured him, during one of their few intimate conversations, that he was definitely a fight person.

She had postulated that everyone believed they were good drivers, had a great sense of humor, were smart, and courageous. She informed him that those things could only be confirmed by an impartial third party.

Brand had grinned and shrugged at the time. He liked her best when she paid him genuine friendly attention. He cherished any sort of compliment from her. Nowadays those moments were rare.

With a twinge of guilt at the long interval since his last attempt to call her, he again tried her number. As before, it went directly to voice mail. It wasn't unusual for her to miss his calls. Sometimes she was at the pool where she was known to silence her phone. She might have gone home to visit her mother for the weekend.

Brand didn't permit himself to speculate on the possibility that she might be involved with entertaining some other man, not expecting him until the following day.

His was not naivety. Rather, he needed no additional gloom in his life. Natalie was unpredictable and decidedly willful. She enjoyed attention and she was a natural magnet for men and women alike.

Their collection of friends was vast, and this was largely due to her connector personality. Brand was likeable and engaging, but in the event they split the sheets, Brand doubted that even a half of their mutual acquaintances would remain in contact with him.

Bert had been his only real friend based upon Brand's definition of true friendship. Even Natalie, after almost a year, knew less about Brand than Bert did. Their relationship had started hot and impassioned. It seemed to Brand that their regard for one another had cooled noticeably over the past few weeks.

Where before she would have jealously coveted any spare time he allowed himself, she now agreed to his sojourns with Bert with a shrug and a ready dismissal.

He had to admit that his remaining fascination with her was more about her physical appeal than any attraction of the heart. His concern presently was spurred to a greater degree by the attachment of familiarity than by the concern for the safety of a loved one.

He entered the western city limits of San Antonio. Sprawling subdivisions filled with boxy two-story beige tract homes appeared more frequently as he neared the city's greater populated central districts. The blue Ford ascended the long sweeping ramp of a towering fly-over and he was soon in heavy freeway traffic.

Brand tried Natalie's number once more. To his surprise she picked up.

"Why are you blowing up my phone, Brand?"

He paused to take a breath and cleanse his pallet of a hot retort. He knew he was filled with grief and it would not help to vent at Natalie.

"Are you at home?" He asked evenly.

"I'm at Mom's", she replied. Her voice dragged with a careful pace indicating that she was weighing his words suspiciously.

"Are you sleeping there tonight, or did you plan on going home?"

"What's wrong?"

Her intuition was always keen.

"I'd rather not talk about it on the phone."

"Brand, are you in some kind of trouble?"

"It's Bert."

"That figures. What did he do this time?"

Brand detected a lightening of her manner at the suggestion of what had become a usual occurrence on Bert's account.

"Mom is making dinner for us. I planned on going home later. Are you still in Eagle Pass?"

"No", Brand replied a little too quickly. "I'm headed home. I'm back in town."

"What has happened?"

Concern dropped her tone to a lower register.

"Bert", he replied. He didn't trust his voice on the subject.

"Is he alright?"

"I'll tell you all about it when I see you", he said with a finality that indicated he wanted to close the matter for now. "Stay at your Mom's this weekend."

"I didn't bring a change of clothes."

"You're bound to still have some things at your mom's house."

"Kid's clothes", she protested.

"Don't worry. The Miss America pageant is next week. You can take the weekend off."

"Funny, Brand. Why can't I come home?"

"Bert and I got crossways with some people and I think they may drop by."

"In Mexico?"

Her voice was suddenly shrill with alarm.

"Yes."

"So, Bert got crossways, and you are having to bail him out again?"

"Nat, I have to let you go."

"Don't call me that. You need to tell me what's going on, Brand."

"I can't right now."

Natalie said nothing and they listened to dead air for a long time. He sensed she was processing the conversation. Brand was certain she was waging an internal conflict on whether to heed his warning or not.

"I can tell you", he said gravely, "that this is serious enough that you may not be able to ever come back."

"What did you do, Brand?" She cried desperately.

"Give me a couple of hours and I will drop by with some of your clothes. Text me a list of what you want me to gather for you."

"Are you breaking up with me?" she asked hotly. She was having real trouble getting her head around this thing.

"No, baby", he assured her tenderly.

Her tone softened with emotion.

"I just don't understand."

"I'm almost home. Like I said, text me a list. I'll see you in a couple of hours. Eat with your Mom. It's okay."

"Be careful."

"I will."

She ended the call without ceremony, and he dropped his phone on the seat next to him.

## Chapter 14

Brand was close to their apartment complex. He searched the streets for any suspicious-looking cars. He was unsure what would qualify as suspicious, although big black SUV's were at the top of the list.

He turned into a side entrance to the property, driving slowly. He approached his apartment building carefully. He thought it likely that if they knew where he lived, they would also know what he drove. There was no evidence they knew either, but he was taking no chances.

He pulled the truck into an empty space three buildings away from his apartment building. He shifted the truck into park and looked around him. His gaze fell upon Bert's gym bag in the back seat. He felt a twinge of sorrow at the prospect of carrying the bag inside with him. He worried, however, that if he left the bag in his truck, it might draw the interest of a thief who might break in and steal the bag.

He groaned at the realization of his only course. He shifted into reverse and left the parking spot. His jaw worked as he screwed up his courage for the task ahead. He would have to face Donna with the news of Bert's death when he returned his belongings to his house.

His attention to the region around him did not falter with his reluctance. He searched for black SUV's, but also any vehicle that might appear out of place. He arrived at Bert's house in less than a half hour. Bert and his wife, Donna, lived in a beige tract home in a subdivision of beige houses. As a construction industry professional, Brand detested the broad, square, boxes with shallow pitched roofs. To him they represented a closing of a chapter in America.

The mantle of 'Skilled Artisan' used to carry with it a deep sense of honor and tradition. Today those careers were considered "jobs no American would do." Politics and a politically motivated media awarded his life's pursuit to illegal labor. The result was bland tract homes built by the hundreds.

He parked at the curb before Bert's house. He felt relief at the empty driveway. There was no car in the garage because Bert and his wife, Donna, stored what would not fit in the house, in the two-car garage. The large space was completely filled with unwanted junk neither had the will to throw away.

Brand stepped out of the truck and circled to the rear passenger side door. He pulled open the door and collected Bert's gym bag. He felt raw emotion fighting for release as he walked up the concrete walkway towards the front door.

He rang the doorbell and waited an appropriate amount of time before he hid the bag behind a line of flowerpots. He turned and returned to his truck.

As before, a half hour's driving brought him back to his apartment complex. He found the same parking space empty and he pulled in. He retrieved his overnight bag and locked the truck.

On foot he took a circuitous route to his apartment, crossing manicured lawns and intricate landscape features. In this way he finally arrived at his front door. It was locked and undamaged.

Brand looked around one last time before inserting his key into the deadbolt. The tumblers turned easily, and he entered. Nothing seemed abnormal or out of place.

After a quick survey, he found the apartment empty. Natalie had left the place in a condition which indicated she was planning to be gone only a short while. Two small piles of folded clothes rested on the sofa where she had likely watched TV as she did the laundry.

He moved to the bedroom. The bed was made, and two outfits lay on it where he imagined she had tossed them as she decided what to wear to her Mom's.

He entered his small walk-in closet and dug around in the stacks of boxes and seldom used bric-a-brac on the upper shelf. He felt around until he gripped the heavy cold weight of his pistol. He pulled the gun clear, careful not to dump any of the piles.

He held his Model 21 Glock. He opened the slide slightly. A .45 caliber round was in the chamber. He pulled the clip. It was full.

He sometimes joked with Natalie about the weapon, calling it his 'throw down piece.' The pistol was unregistered to him or to anyone else. He had purchased the Glock for $300.00 from a friend who had found it in a rental car.

He came in possession of the weapon when his friend Jack had flown into San Antonio on business from Dallas, where he lived with his son. He had rented a car from a locally owned car rental service, rather than a national chain.

Jack told of his having to slam on the breaks at a signal light, where the gun had slid forward into the passenger side floorboard. Apparently, the small rental agency was lax in its cleaning of returns.

That same week, Brand had met Jack and other mutual friends at Rod Dog's for a cocktail. The conversation led to Jack telling his story of how he had acquired the weapon.

Brand had offered to buy the pistol if Jack was interested. Jack sold it to him rather than deal with the issues of bringing back an unregistered pistol on a flight to Dallas.

Brand knew an old schoolmate who worked for SAPD. After a brief catch-up conversation, he asked if he might run the serial number. Although reluctant, his friendship with Brand won out and the officer ran the check. Nothing came back locally, federally or even on Interpol.

Brand had never fired the weapon since the day he purchased it. He kept it around for home protection only. Few of his friends and acquaintances even knew he owned a gun.

He moved to his chest of drawers. He laid the gun on top and opened the top drawer. He quickly changed into shorts and a tee shirt. He intended to get a couple hours of sleep, but he refused to allow himself the vulnerability of a shower. He collected the pistol and returned to the living room.

Retrieving a dining room chair from the small table, he jammed the back of the chair against the door knob. He approached the sofa and moved Natalie's laundry piles to the coffee table and dropped wearily onto the sofa. He secreted the pistol between him and the sofa back, behind the bottom cushion.

He waited for fatigue to pull his troubled mind into the welcome oblivion of sleep. In his pocket, his phone signaled a new text had been received. He rolled on his side and extracted the phone. Natalie had texted her list. He darkened the phone and set it on the coffee table near at hand.

No longer kept at bay by his preoccupations and activity, grief moved into the vacancies usually left for sleep and rest. Brand lay on his back, eyes wide. He did not see the popcorn ceiling. Rather, the white ceiling was a canvas upon which was painted scenes of the previous night. He struggled to maintain the sobriety of reason by avoiding a detailed reflection of the details regarding Bert's death. Despite his intentions, focus he did, with uncontrollable regularity.

Brand mourned Bert and the sleep he was convinced would never come. Exhaustion was his sadistic companion. Grief and weariness took their cruel turns on him. Brand forced himself to remain prone and motionless in the face of the mental beating he was receiving.

Eventually, fatigue triumphed over his frazzled emotions and he drifted into a deep sleep.

# Chapter 15

Fuentes sat behind the metal desk, his cell phone to his ear.

"*Si, Señor*", he said in a tone of obedience and deference to the man on the other end.

He held his comments as the man on the other end of the line spoke. Fuentes paused a full five seconds before he replied. It would not do to interrupt or to seem lacking in self-control. He replied in Spanish and with a measured control of his comments:

"(He is one of ours.)"

He listened intently as the man on the other end spoke.

"(It is not safe for him to return until the trouble has died down there.)"

Pause.

"(He was not following my orders, sir. I knew nothing of this.)"

The other speaker continued his tirade and Fuentes searched the room as if he sought answers from the wall of black and white TV monitors, the table of radio equipment, and the whirring air conditioners. The green and red LCD's merely blinked at him bright and uncaring.

"(I am responsible for all that my men do. Had I been notified that he gathered your assets in this matter, I could have intervened. That is all I am saying.)"

Fuentes listened with heightened interest.

"(Who is this dead American?)"

Fuentes pulled the phone a small distance from his ear. The man on the other end of the phone spoke with unleashed passion. The little phone speaker distorted with the increased volume of the speaker on the other end.

"(As I mentioned, *Señor*, I knew nothing of this matter. Tell me what you have learned from Miguel and I can facilitate on my side of the border.)"

Fuentes drew a yellow legal pad from the narrow drawer below the desk top. He clicked a blue gel tipped pen and jotted down notes as he was given the details he requested. As he wrote, his expression grew stony with anger.

"(I will collect Miguel at the crossing myself.)"

Fuentes waited as he listened, the pen poised just above the yellow paper, forgotten in his rising anger.

"(It is not necessary, *Señor*. I can handle Miguel within my organization.)"

Fuentes lowered the pen and laid it atop the pad. He leaned back in the heavy chair.

"(As you wish, *Señor*. I will be here when your men arrive with him.)"

Fuentes ended the call and laid the phone beside the pen.

The second American, Carson Brand, was a problem. His contact was clear on that point. Fuentes moved the phone and read the name written in blue ink once again. Next to the name was the address, 12346 Brentwood, apartment number 114. Next to this Fuentes wrote Rockledge Apartments.

# Chapter 16

Brand couldn't get any closer for some reason. Natalie was there with the skinny young Mexican he had seen at Arturo's bar. They kissed passionately, and she appeared to be the catalyst. Her passion seemed to intimidate the young guy but there was no quit in him.

She had long dark hair, a perfectly fit tanned body with no tan lines, large breasts, and she wore nothing but earrings. Brand struggled to move closer – to intervene. His anger was high with the jealousy he felt. He struggled to no avail. He managed to move a scant few inches forward. The lovers collapsed onto the bed, kissing passionately. She held the Mexican's head in her hands and seemed to be sucking his heart out through his yearning mouth.

He tweaked her nipple and she smiled within the kiss. She rolled over and steadied herself on all fours. The kid moved around behind her, his eager hands all over her. Desperation gripped Brand's heart as he watched, helpless and frozen in place.

Three loud booms, which sounded like nearby explosions, shook the dark room around the lovers.

Brand sat bolt upright. He was on the sofa in his apartment. Three more booms sounded nearby. At first, he thought someone was trying to break the door down.

Through bleary eyes and a sleep-fogged consciousness he saw that the dining chair still leaned securely against the knob. Again, a heavy knock shook the door.

A voice from outside boomed with authority.

"Mr. Brand, open the door, San Antonio Police."

Brand stood. He ensured that the Glock was securely hidden behind the sofa cushions. He went to the door and removed the chair. He carried it to the table and replaced it in its proper position. He returned to the door as another blow shook the door. He opened the door to two burly officers in navy blue police uniforms.

"Sorry", he explained, "I was sleeping."

"Do you own a blue F150, Mr. Brand?"

Sleep fled from Brand's tired mind at the mention of his truck.

"I do. What...?"

"It has been vandalized, sir. Please come with us."

Brand followed the officers in his bare feet, closing the door behind him. He padded along the sidewalk. He watched the broad Kevlar armored backs of the officers stretch the stiff uniforms they wore. The hour was early. He saw a pink hue coloring the eastern horizon. He guessed it was before six in the morning.

They rounded the corner of the last building, bringing them to the lined parking lot. More police officers, a fire truck and several spectators watched his truck burning in the early morning darkness.

Brand rushed past the officers. They protested and reached for Brand. He avoided their grasp but advanced only a short distance before he halted of his own accord. The heat from the blaze prevented his approach. Firemen worked to extinguish the flames as Brand watched helplessly.

The officers took positions on each side of Brand in case he tried to bolt once more. They watched together as the firemen doused the fire raging within the cab of the truck.

"It looks like someone broke the driver's side window and tossed in a make-shift Molotov cocktail", one of the cops explained.

The other turned slightly to face Brand.

"Do you know of anyone who might dislike you enough to torch your truck?"

Brand considered the officer as thoughts of cartel thugs in black SUV's occupied his mind.

"No. Not off the top of my head. Are there any witnesses?"

"We are questioning neighbors, but so far no one has claimed to have seen anything."

The second officer opened a small steno pad and clicked a ball-point pen.

"We need to collect some information from you, Mr. Brand, before you go anywhere."

"How did you know how to find me?" Brand asked before it occurred to him that they likely ran the plates on his burning truck.

"We ran the plates."

The officers proceeded to ask a battery of background questions of Brand. A flat bed tow truck arrived as the officer folded his notebook and released him to return to his apartment. Inside the apartment, he called the insurance company to begin the claim. His next call was to Natalie: surprisingly, she immediately picked up.

"Did someone light your truck on fire?"

"How did you know?"

"I got a call from Sydney in 318. It's all happening in front of her place. She saw you talking with the police."

"Yes. It's my truck. No. I don't know who did it."

"Do I need to come get you?"

"Please. I'll meet you at the parking lot near the pool."

"On my way."

Brand changed into jeans and a golf shirt. He left the shirt untucked to cover the Glock which he placed in the waist band. The big pistol was uncomfortable at the small of his back. The movies always portrayed hiding a gun in one's trousers as clever and practical. The Glock tended to dive into his pants, requiring regular adjustment and correction to keep the weapon in a position where it was accessible, comfortable, and at the ready.

Brand waited near the parking lot for some ten minutes before he saw Natalie's car turn into the lot. She drove slowly as though she was a cop searching for known hidden perpetrators.

She stopped the car close to Brand. He entered quickly, and she pulled away from the curb. Soon they were traveling along the neighboring streets. He struggled to decide how to begin his tale. Her presence soothed him. He had not counted upon the comfort of her company. Lately he found himself focused solely upon his doubts of her loyalty. In that moment she was familiar and available as he had not felt of her for some time.

"Pull over here", he directed.

She entered an expansive parking lot before a large store, nearly empty at that early hour. She parked the car in a space near the street. She pushed the shifter into park, then settled herself into a comfortable position and waited expectantly for Brand to speak.

Brand collected his thoughts. He wanted to deliver his story in a manner to which she would react gradually. An explosion of emotion, or worse, a rush to judgement, would derail his intention to keep her on his side. He could never be certain how she would judge his role in any situation. His best bet was to stay on task and keep the facts straight in the telling of his story.

"Natalie", he began. "Bert is dead."

She endured his pause in the story as expected. She was disbelieving and even more doubtful of his intentions.

"Seriously", he affirmed. "He is dead."

Natalie searched his face for a secret code or some unfathomable meaning to his revelation.

"We checked into a motel in Eagle Pass. We crossed the border and had a few drinks at a bar, the same one where we drank on the last trip. A guy on Salazar's concrete crew, who I recognized from the job, showed up. You may not have heard, but Bert flirted with the concrete guy's girlfriend and there was an incident."

She shook her head, her eyes searching his face as she tried to make sense of the story.

"Anyway, I had a feeling that the coincidence was too convenient. It turned out that my instincts were right. We spent the rest of the night running from what I figure are members of a Mexican cartel. I made it back. Bert was kidnapped at the border. I saw his body on the news this morning. He was found in the Rio Grande dead."

Natalie stared at him. He could not detect any distinct emotion in her wide-eyed mute reaction to his words. Patiently, he waited for her to speak.

"How did you and Bert get involved with a Mexican cartel?" She asked in a reasonable tone. Brand thought her manner remarkable considering the gravity of his revelation.

"As I said, we had an altercation on the job where Bert, evidently, flirted with the concrete guy's girlfriend. Things were getting heated, so I intervened."

"So, the *concrete guy*", she emphasized his term as though he were using bad grammar, "killed Bert for flirting?"

Brand considered her summary with interest. Her observation was short but succinct. Bert had been killed for flirting. The irony was arresting in its gravity.

"So, you saw the 'concrete guy' in the bar last night?" she asked with a look which betrayed disbelief at his explanation for the events leading up to Bert's kidnapping.

"No. I saw one of his guys there. I don't think the concrete guy was directly involved in the pursuit or the kidnapping."

"Pursuit? Kidnapping? And now they have car bombed your truck. Brand, are we in trouble here?"

"I'm sure of it", he answered simply. "I wasn't sure what they would do, but I know they are after me now."

"There has to be more to the story, Brand. No one kills someone for flirting. Did you threaten or kick somebody's ass? Did you escalate this somehow and you are not telling me?"

Brand leaned back in his seat. Predictably, she had arrived at the point where she assumed all of this was his fault. Maybe she was right. What was he missing in this thing?

She looked out the window at the light early morning traffic.

"What am I going to do, Brand? Am I in danger too? They know where you live and what you drive. They must know about me."

"I figure they do. That's why I asked you to stay at your mom's tonight."

"Then why did you want me to come get you?"

"Someone doesn't torch your truck if they are lying in wait for you. Someone sent me a warning. Bad guys are not going to sit around while a dozen cops and a score of witnesses are milling around a crime scene."

"Okay, so what do we do now?"

"We need to stick together. Tomorrow is Sunday, so I may not be able to get a rental until Monday."

Natalie turned the key. The car started smoothly.

"Today is Sunday", she corrected him.

She pulled the shifter into reverse and backed out of the parking space.

# Chapter 17

Miguel sat in the back seat of an old sedan. All four windows were open, flooding the car with cool evening air as it rocked at a dangerous speed along the rough road. He wrinkled his nose at the sour odor of sweat and years of dirt and rust which permeated the darkest regions of the car.

Beside him, an unshaven Mexican man looked out the window at the dark countryside. In the front seat, two men kept their attention on the road ahead.

The last few days had been enlightening. Miguel had experienced a spiritual and personal renaissance. Since the day of his *Probar*, he had felt a power growing within him. Following the jarring shock of the initiation ritual - the killing - a defining feeling of power had taken its place. He had the freedom to mold himself and those around him with violence. The innocent boy was gone. Within the youthful appearance of a youngster dwelt a man of stolid purpose and decisive actions.

Following the killing of the bearded American, his self-worth had grown as had his value to the organization. His elevated status was apparent in the regard paid him by the ground troops within the cartel.

His old life had been mundane at best. Now that he was a part of *MuHa*, he was powerful in his own right. Add to that the ability to summon his cartel brothers with a whisper, he felt a strength of will and a galvanizing purposefulness which gave him a clarity of direction in his life.

After the killing of the big American, he had weathered the doubts of the Mexican Don. The leader did not know him at the time. The phone call between Don Rojas and Fuentes had been concerning. The conversation demonstrated a polarizing contrast between the Mexican operation and its American representation. Despite the Don's position of authority, Fuentes possessed a position empowered by his access to America and his ability to control personnel and activities capable of working on both sides of the border. Miguel sensed that Don Rojas suspected that Fuentes would use the advantage to exert his will upon the situation. The suspicion seemed to nettle the leader.

Because of Fuentes' displeasure at Miguel's ambitious mission, he had been uncertain of the cartel's recourse for his independent actions against the two Americans. Killing the bigger man was a risk, but likely the preferred outcome. The second man's escape was a mistake he suspected might yield graver consequences.

Fortunately, Don Rojas had settled upon a reaction of cautious approval. The one-sided telephone conversation between Rojas and Fuentes ended in support for Miguel's actions despite the obvious displeasure of the security man.

Although he was being spirited away in the night, he felt an innate sense of safety and belonging. His value to the collective had been somehow elevated with his killing of the American. He sensed that he was regarded as a celebrity among his peers.

It was clear that the murder was likely to cause problems, but the deed also exposed a quality in Miguel that increased his value to the organization. He was not a bona fide *Sicario* in this new context, nor did he consider himself an enforcer. But his efficiency in dispatching the American had elicited an unmistakable respect among those who mattered. Miguel might be mistaken, but he had seen what he thought to be fear in the eyes of his brothers after the brutal killing. Rojas' sparing his life further confirmed his value.

Fuentes did not know of the desire within the Mexican branch of the cartel to eliminate the American. The beautiful, Christina had made him aware of the sanction.

Miguel suspected that he was accompanied on the return trip to the U.S. to support his unauthorized actions in Mexico, in case Fuentes harbored a desire to punish Miguel.

The driver turned to the right off the primitive black-topped highway and onto a narrow caliche road. The headlights were extinguished and the men in the front donned night vision goggles. The darkened car maintained an uncomfortably brisk pace. Miguel could see nothing ahead or out the windows in the darkness. The driver was able to see clearly with the NVG's. The acrid dust flung in the air by the speeding car wafted into the back seat. Miguel wrinkled his nose and limited his breathing as best he could in order to avoid inhaling dust. They travelled the rough road for some half an hour. The driver pulled over, settling the car into a gulch only he and his co-driver could see with their NVG's.

The driver turned the key and the car died with a reluctant sputter. The four men exited the auto. Driver and co-driver moved to the rear of the car where they opened the trunk which yielded with a rusty groan.

Four heavy back packs were distributed among the men and slung upon their backs. The driver slammed the trunk and turned away from the car. The two men in NVG's led, and they made their dim way along a shallow ditch for roughly a quarter of a mile.

The driver finally halted. He bent low and Miguel could just make out that he dug his fingers around in the dust until he grasped something. He stood, lifting a rope which crossed their trail. The others followed as he traced the length of the rope to their right.

Fewer than a dozen yards farther, the end was tied to a broken stump where a thick bush had been cut. Near the stump protruded the partially buried, round top of a barrel drum laid on its side.

The driver dropped the rope and raised the drum lid like a trap door set in the side of the gulch. The partially buried drum served as a tubed passageway leading into the side of the small hill.

In turn each man bent low, shoved his heavy duffel bag inside and crawled into the barrel like clowns entering a tiny circus car, Miguel watched the others vanish into the narrow mouth of the 55-gallon drum. In turn, he pushed his backpack inside ahead of him then entered the make-shift tunnel. He carefully pulled the lid closed behind him. The entry container was only the first of nearly a dozen barrels which formed a narrow tube. The metal chute fed downward at a shallow angle. The last barrel opened into a larger cavern. Miguel stepped down and was once more among the other three men.

The cave was dark as pitch. He could see nothing at all. He sensed that the two men with the NVG's looked at him. Miguel imagined they were enjoying their advantage over the two blinded men.

Miguel felt a hand grasp his shoulder and turn him to the left. Another unseen hand guided his right hand until he gripped a hanging strap at the bottom of the backpack of one of the men ahead of him. He clung to the strap and was pulled along the black tunnel. To Miguel, the close air smelled like a freshly dug grave. He battled his imagination for control of his rising sense of panic. He drew a tenuous comfort from the company of the other men. He forced himself to trust in the experience of the others whom he assumed had travelled this unsettling route before.

Miguel shuffled uncertainly for another fifty yards or so when, like a lightning strike, the tunnel suddenly blazed with a bright white glow. Miguel's aching eyes struggled to adjust to the brightness. Through squinting, straining eyes, he saw that the driver no longer wore his

NVG's. He wore a miner's hard hat with a powerful lamp sending a brilliant light down the long narrow tunnel.

As his eyes strained to adjust to the lighted environment, Miguel could see heavy timbers, presumably placed to prevent the tunnel from collapsing. The sides of the tunnel were comprised of loose dirt rather than a firm sediment which would seem a better and more stable material for a tunnel.

They moved for some time on a level plane. After what seemed to Miguel more than five minutes, the ground below their feet began to drop away, taking them deeper underground. In this way, they descended for many minutes.

The cave became cooler and their feet sloshed along the moist bottom of the tunnel as they moved forward. In the dim light of the miner's lamp the soft sediment of the tunnel's sides appeared more solid and shone with dampness.

Miguel touched the right-side wall. His hand came away muddy. He guessed they were beneath the river. The construction of the tunnel changed as they reached the deepest point. The wooden supports were built more closely together in this region and between the more closely placed beams were stones along the sides. The additional structure and support presumably carried the increased weight and the heavier wet soil beneath the river bed. They reached a short flat region where moisture dripped from the ceiling. This level section of the tunnel covered only a short distance before it pitched upwards.

Miguel felt relief as the ground rose again beneath his feet. Long minutes later they reached the northern terminus of the tunnel. They climbed into another steel barrel tube. This one was slightly longer than the barrel access on the Mexican side. The driver extinguished his helmet light and they were once more left in utter darkness, red and violet spots danced before Miguel's eyes. He followed the three men out and once again savored the fresh air of the open night.

The driver and co-driver once again donned the NVG's. They guided the other two men along the bottom of a winding draw. Small animals could be heard here and there scurrying within the spare underbrush on the level above them. They followed the dry bed for just over a mile. The moon peaked over a dark horizon, providing scant light. The dim glow was enough, however, for Miguel to recognize that the leaders halted in a small depression just off the level grade of a single lane dirt road.

They didn't wait more than five minutes before headlights brightened the northern horizon in a half circle glow. Within minutes the glow evolved into distinct headlights. The roar of a car motor grew in volume until the car stopped on the road just beyond their hiding place. Quickly, the four men hurried onto the roadbed, dragging their packs. They entered the car, setting the heavy packs on their laps. Once the doors closed, the car U-turned and made its way back to the north.

# Chapter 18

Fuentes swallowed his anger. Miguel sat in a chair at the edge of the room with a smug look on his face. The three cartel escorts stood nearby with arms crossed. The phone rang precisely at 9:30 as agreed. Fuentes answered on the first ring. The conversation was in Spanish:

("*Si*. They are here. The payload is here as well.")

Fuentes looked at the men vacantly as he listened to the voice on the other end of the phone.

("Of course, Patron. The packs will be full for the return trip as always.")

Another pause as he listened.

("A warning has been sent to the American.")

He looked menacingly at Miguel.

("Our new enforcer will take care of that, *Señor*.")

Miguel shifted uneasily. No matter his comfort level with his newfound notoriety and perceived value, Fuentes caused him distress for some reason unknown to him. His sarcastic reference to him as an enforcer rankled his newly acquired pride.

("I will see to it. This matter is as nothing to you, I swear it.")

Fuentes returned the phone to the table. He looked to the three standing men.

"Come."

He moved from behind the desk and made his way towards the kitchen entrance through which Miguel had passed after his *Probar*. Fuentes held a finger in the air, indicating Miguel should wait. He pointed at the four black backpacks on the floor, motioning that the others should bring them along.

Miguel waited, listening to the receding footfalls. He understood from Fuentes' side of the conversation that he would take care of the remaining American. His heart leaped in his chest with anticipation. His calling was clear.

Fuentes said it with derision, but Miguel knew the truth. Like a potter, whose craft requires the work of deft fingers at the wheel, his skillful art would be the taking of life.

Fuentes returned unexpectedly with no sound of footfalls. Miguel covered his start as best he could. Fuentes, however, noticed Miguel's startled reaction to his return with a satisfied expression. This upstart was no more than any of a score who had come before. Mexico overestimated his value. An accounting would come soon enough.

"*Señor*, Fuentes", Miguel said in as self-assured a tone as he could muster. "Thank you for entrusting this task to me. I will not fail to complete it."

"Perhaps."

Fuentes again took his place behind the steel desk.

Miguel heard footfalls as the men returned. The packs were full as before, though they may have been a bit heavier than when they were taken from the room. The men carried them hanging at arm's length, finally laying them in a pile on the floor.

They approached the desk expectantly. Miguel remained in his chair.

"You know the protocol", Fuentes recited. "A driver waits for you outside. Go with God."

They nodded ceremoniously. Miguel thought the reverence ridiculous. He also knew that they reacted involuntarily to the spiritual context of the dismissal as all good Catholics would. Their upbringing demanded it.

They gathered the packs and left Fuentes and Miguel alone. The omnipresent drone of radios and air conditioners filled the room.

Miguel waited patiently while Fuentes examined his notes on a yellow pad then tapped out a message on his phone. Finally, he placed the phone on the desk and looked at Miguel. He considered him a long moment before he spoke.

"We have delivered a message to the second American. He will assume that the message was the extent of our actions against him. He will presume that if we were going to harm or kill him, we would not give him a warning as severe as this message."

"What message did you send?"

"We fire-bombed his vehicle."

"Ah."

"He will stay in his apartment – easy for you to take him."

Miguel nodded. He looked down at his hands in his lap.

"When should I begin?"

"Tonight, of course. With further thought, the American might react differently after a period of considered reason."

"I need a gun."

Fuentes opened a side drawer in his desk. He withdrew the revolver with which Miguel had killed the young man on the street. Miguel eyed the weapon fearfully. Fuentes held the pistol casually, pointing it in his general direction.

"If you again follow orders from Mexico without my knowledge, I will bury your mutilated remains in my back yard."

He laid the pistol on the desk top with a heavy clank.

Miguel remained still in the chair for a moment. Finally, Fuentes leaned back in his seat. Miguel rose and approached the desk. He collected the weapon and hid it in his clothes.

Fuentes wrote something on the bottom of one of the yellow lined pages littering his desk top. He ripped the strip off the bottom and handed it to Miguel.

"This is his address. Do it tonight."

"*Si, Señor*", Miguel replied simply.

He turned and left through the kitchen as the three men had done moments before. Fuentes again picked up his phone and tapped out another message.

Miguel made his way along the walkway past the garage and into the alley. His white Toyota waited in the alley. All four windows were open. Miguel suffered no worry that the car would not be where he had left it. The windows were never rolled up during the hot summer months. Even at night the windows were ajar.

The vehicle had been in that spot for two days since he had traded it for his cartel-provided ride to and from the border. Miguel's disregard in securing his vehicle was justified in that he recognized that the worn auto held no allure for any would-be thief. The open windows demonstrated that the owner attached no value to the car and its worthless contents.

He entered the driver seat and turned the key. He backed the car away from the garage and accelerated down the alley. At the first intersection he turned the car from the crunching caliche of the alley onto smooth pavement.

He looked at the strip of yellow paper and read the address upon it. 12364 Brentwood, apartment 114: Rockledge Apartments. He had a general idea where the apartments were. He was a south side Mexican, but he knew a bit about the north side.

At the wheel, warm night air buffeted Miguel. Traffic was light on the freeway, but he forced himself to drive at the posted speed limit. If he was to succeed, he would have to avoid mistakes, including a police traffic stop.

He left behind the older houses and vast metal buildings of the south side for high rise office buildings and the neon lighted hotels of downtown.

The expressway wound through crowded urban areas and into a district of stately larger homes and vast green belts carpeting the more affluent neighborhoods of the near north side. He crossed the busy inner loop expressway and entered a region of strip shopping centers, illuminated with large signs and the brightly lighted windows of national retail stores and high-profile restaurants.

He left the expressway and followed the service road for a few blocks before he turned onto a four-lane boulevard. He soon made his way cautiously along a dark residential street upon which large apartment complexes lined both sides. The hour was late, and the parking lots were filled with the cars of sleeping residents.

He circled the neighborhood until he found the Rockledge Apartments. He parked his car in an available spot at the outer edge of the parking lot. He stepped out of the car and looked around him carefully. He was alone and unseen. He walked among the clustered buildings of the apartment complex, reading the large white numbers painted on the upper corners.

A light lit every doorway allowing him to easily read the apartment numbers at a distance. He found building one-hundred and soon located apartment 114. He circled the building and pushed through low shrubbery. Freshly mown grass cushioned his footsteps as he passed rear windows and small patios at the back of the apartment building.

He moved towards a dark window he determined to belong to apartment 114. He leaned against the brick exterior wall and listened for any noises within the unit. He doubted he would hear much, if anything, through the heavy insulated glass. He pressed his fingers against the nylon screen and carefully tested the window sash. Surprisingly, the sash moved under the pressure.

He pulled a lock blade from his pocket and cut the screen in a cross pattern. He pressed both hands against the top of the window sash and pushed it open. Cool air soothed his moist skin as the air conditioning fled the darkness of the apartment.

He again paused to listen. He heard no sound and detected no movement within the apartment.

The occupants must be asleep, he guessed.

He lifted a leg and slid slowly into the cool dark apartment. He entered a living room. He could make out dimly the furniture and a large flat screen TV. He closed the window cautiously. He straightened and withdrew the heavy pistol from his waistband.


Brand kissed Natalie deeply. Their naked bodies pressed urgently against one another. He could see only dim images of her in the darkened room. Occasionally the ambient light profiled her face and her body as she moved around him and over him.

He concentrated upon her with all his attention. Like a sprinter, running at full speed, he could maintain his concentration upon her only so long as his strength allowed. As it had many times since they had collapsed together onto the bed, his mind wandered, and his thoughts turned to his dead friend.

The memory caused him a most acute agony. His grief was not going to stay at a distance for much longer.

He again imagined a sprinter as his mind fled from Bert's memory. The image changed, suggesting the appearance of an exhausted and desperate runner. The runner cast terrified glances over his shoulder towards a terrible pursuer. The runner was Bert.

Brand felt tears burn his eyes. He wanted to return to the previous unimportant worries of his life before Mexico took his friend.

Natalie grabbed his neck with both hands and pulled him around and under her. She rose above him and pressed her breasts into his face. She brought all her weight down upon him.

The maneuver surprised him and, for a second, he recoiled from her impassioned violence.

"What is wrong with you?" she snarled with frustrated urgency.

Brand struggled to arrange his thoughts in an order where he could recover his composure. Natalie had once told him that when a relationship is good, sex is ten percent of the whole. When it is bad, it is ninety percent of the whole. He feared they were at the ninety percentile and he didn't want to sacrifice the one remaining thing they had together. Not yet.

Brand reached down low and grabbed her ass in a big hand. Without a word he joined her, and they rocked together.

Sometime later he sat at a little dinette table looking out the window upon neatly manicured grass and trim sidewalks, artistically illuminated by low voltage landscape lighting. Bert's memory had chased him from Natalie and their intimate warmth. It joined him now in a silent vigil.

Natalie's words came back to him. 'No one kills someone for flirting.'

What about chasing them all night, bringing a border officer in on the plan, killing Bert, and firebombing his truck? Does that seem extreme recompense for flirting?

Had he missed something about the dispute? Salazar was a man known to him for some three or four years. They were by no means friends, but he thought he had a good sense of the man. He was a typical tradesman. His crew was rarely made up of the same men from week to week. That was normal in the business.

What about the young Mexican who he had seen at the job site, and later at Arturo's bar? Was he the missing piece in the puzzle? From the casual attention due his position in the background, the kid seemed singularly unremarkable: no more than a skinny Mexican with shaggy black hair. He lacked the mien of someone who might set off alarm bells for Brand. Brand, however, had learned long ago that it was unwise to discount anyone when they were backed into a desperate situation. This kid, however, was not in a desperate situation. He seemed to act of his own volition and with alacrity. Brand doubted him the leader of the pursuit that night, but he seemed to be a key player, nonetheless.

He brooded on the matter for some minutes before his thoughts were distracted by a low rumble of thunder and the growing flicker of far off lightning. A storm was coming. He watched for the next flash of lightning, after which he counted the seconds. A dull rumble of thunder followed the flash some ten seconds behind.

His father once told him that for every second's interval after the flash there was a mile of distance. The storm was ten miles away. He didn't know if that was true, but since childhood he had embraced the theory as if it were. He gauged the progress of the storm in this way for some minutes. He eventually concluded that the storm was headed towards him. The lightning/thunder interval had shortened to five seconds - five miles away.

Brand was moved by a gnawing doubt. Something scratched at the back of his mind like a stray dog at the back door. He was missing something, and the missing piece troubled him greatly.

He sensed movement behind him in the darkness of the nearby living room. His neck prickled with the fearful sensations of his overly active imagination. He turned and waited for his eyes to pierce the darkness. He saw a small dark figure approaching.

He felt himself tense as the silhouette approached cautiously.

"Hey, Baby. Can't sleep?"

It was Natalie. She came near until he saw her clearly. She rubbed her eyes and laid a hand on his shoulder. She wore a thin night wrap. He pulled her towards him with a strong arm. She felt warm and inviting. He liked the feel of the smooth fabric of the wrap over her taut body. He leaned his head against her breast, and they hugged.

"I'm just thinking", he explained. After a moment more he added, "I can never sleep at your mom's house."

Natalie looked out the window but did not comment on his observation. She roughed up his hair, signaling her desire to return to the bedroom.

"Come back to bed and do your thinking next to me."

She backed from him, grabbing his hand. She pulled him to his feet, and he followed her to the bedroom.

# Chapter 19

Miguel left the darkened bedroom. The apartment was empty. He paused, the gun hanging in his right hand, as he considered what to do next. He opened the window by which he had entered the apartment and climbed out, lowering the window sash behind him. He pulled the screen off the window and carried it with him. He dropped it within a hedge row. A missing screen would draw less attention than a cut screen.

He crossed the distance between him and his car, seeing no one on the grounds or in the parking lot. Lightning flashed some miles away. He entered and started the car. Thunder rumbled at a distance as he drove casually through the lot and back onto the street. He returned to the service road flanking the expressway. He entered an on-ramp and pointed the old Toyota towards the south side.

He leaned over in the seat and withdrew his cell from his pocket. He pressed Fuentes' number from his recent calls screen. He waited as the phone rang. Fuentes answered on the second ring.

"Is it done?" He asked impatiently.

"The American wasn't there."

Fuentes frowned at the youth's reference to the 'American' when he himself was just as American.

"Did you get inside?"

"Of course."

"Does it look like he has moved out?"

"He still has clothes in the closet and in his drawers. A woman lives there also."

Fuentes was silent as he thought about this new information.

"Should I wait for them to return?"

"Unless you believe they will come to you."

It was Miguel's turn to frown at the older man's sarcasm.

# Chapter 20

Donna drained her second glass of Chablis as she might have drank cold water, had she been marooned in the middle of a desert for days. Her troubled brown eyes were darkened with smeared eye makeup. She poured another glass to the rim. She sat the empty bottle at her feet.

How do you package what she had learned in the last 48 hours in a way that two young girls could possibly accept that their father was dead? She scarcely understood what she knew.

The last four hours had been the most difficult of her life. The girls would soon arrive home from school and she had no idea how she would keep herself together. She had just returned from the morgue where the Eagle Pass police had left Robert's body.

The call from Eagle Pass police Saturday morning had been shocking in its unbelievable news of her husband's death. She had kept all of this from the girls, hoping that there was some mistake. It had been impossible to believe that Robert could be dead. She had kissed him goodbye only the day before.

A day of unanswered phone calls and one-way texts. She waited desperately for a reply or call from Robert that would straighten the whole mess and reveal the mistake of the police. Monday morning, she received a call from San Antonio police summoning her to the city morgue to identify the body.

The worst part had not been the moment in which she identified her husband's remains atop a cold stainless-steel table, beneath a thin green sheet. The worst part was less than an hour ago when she went through Bert's gym bag left outside her door Saturday night, found there when she returned from the movies with the girls.

There had been no note nor an explanation why it had been left. Robert was always busy, and she was accustomed to waiting for his explanations about his bizarre behavior. Sunday's call from the police made it probable that Brand had dropped off the bag.

The phone call from the police had come just after she had returned home from dropping the girls at school. At least once a week, it seemed, they missed the bus and she had to shuttle them herself. Sometimes it was because Megan and Marissa didn't get up when called. The preparation for school required a requisite amount of time no matter when the awakened. Often it was her own fault. She ran a from-home business and she had no set business hours. She worked as needed. Although she was afforded a bit more free time during the day than she would, had she kept regular office hours, her work schedule was such that she gave her time to it during all her waking hours.

The SAPD detective had given her the address to the city morgue. For some reason, she had felt no sense of urgency to go right away. She even loaded the dishwasher and picked up the house before leaving. Her reluctance wasn't dread. What was it?

She had left around noon. She had followed her GPS directions to the address provided. She had arrived and parked outside of a three-story red brick building of a design typical of government buildings built in the 60's.

Once inside, she had checked in with the officer at the front desk. He had her wait in a lounge area. From the dull green walls to the small nondescript urban-scape prints framed in black plastic, the waiting area looked to have been decorated by a sociopath with no idea for what the room would be used.

Some ten minutes passed before she was collected by a whipcord thin man who presented a badge for identification. She followed him down an olive-green hallway and into a small interview room. The thin man left her alone in the cold room. She took a seat at a long table and waited.

Two detectives appeared through the opposite door from which she had entered. Formal introductions prefaced an explanation that they had found her number in Bert's wallet. The contents of his wallet seemed to be intact. The detectives claimed to have come to that conclusion based upon the wallet containing several large bills, credit cards and a condom. The prophylactic was not a factor, but the presence of cash and credit cards led them to believe theft was not a motive.

They warned her that when she entered the viewing room to identify the body, she should prepare herself for what she would see. The victim had died as a result of extreme head trauma. Several stab wounds were apparent on the torso. They seemed particularly uncomfortable as they told her that he had been disemboweled.

Finally, they asked if they might pose a few routine questions before moving to the viewing area.

She had agreed, thinking, 'You mean while I am still calm.'

She had endured nearly a half hour of interrogation where she was questioned on every aspect of her personal life with Bert. Several of the questions included Brand and his relationship with Robert. She answered as best she could, considering the ever-present dread of the task ahead dominated her thoughts. As the interview continued, she felt her body quake. She was unsure whether she shivered from the cold of the air conditioning, or if she was reacting to the fear of what she would see.

Finally, the interview came to a close and she followed the detectives to a narrow room. A thick pane of glass separated her from a larger room which appeared to be a lab. Near the window was a steel gurney upon which lay a body covered with a green sheet. For a fleeting moment she one again hoped they were mistaken. Denial was late to the event.

One of the detectives asked if she was ready. She replied that she was, and he nodded to a man in scrubs across the glass.

The attendant pulled back the sheet revealing a battered and blood-caked face. She couldn't be sure if the face seemed flat due to the beating he had taken, or because of dead muscles, no longer taut with life and feeling.

He must have really suffered at the end, she thought, and the tears flowed. She had hunched forward as she fought shuddering sobs, trying to regain control of her emotions. The attendant pulled the green sheet back over the face. Donna didn't want to assign what she saw to her husband.

She hardly recalled the drive back home. Even now as she sat at the dining table, the event seemed surreal and dreamlike. Her wine glass sat on the dark wooden table beside Bert's phone. His blue gym bag lay on the floor near a table leg. Some of the contents sat piled beside the bag where she had dropped them after she found the phone.

She knew Bert's passcode for the phone from when he had asked her to order a pizza some weeks past. How brazen he was in giving her free access to something containing information as damning as did the phone.

Initially she had charged and powered up the phone to discover any clue to what had happened to him. Instead, his life was laid bare to her. His text messages were rife with infidelity and betrayal. His contacts consisted primarily of the names and numbers of women. She recognized few of those names.

The text messages were truly heartbreaking. The phone was filled with conversations dating from more than two years ago until the day he left for Mexico with Brand.

She grimaced at the thought of Brand. He obviously knew all about his best friend's infidelity. How many times had he sat at that very table with Bert, herself, and their daughters? Each time he had sat there eating impassively, all the while knowing every detail behind Bert's lies. It was no wonder he had left the bag on the front porch. The coward!

She lifted the wine glass and drained its contents.

# Chapter 21

Brand led Natalie into their apartment. She looked around suspiciously, as if she might find an attacker in waiting. Brand moved immediately to the bedroom where he quickly placed the Glock in his nightstand drawer. Natalie had not noticed the weapon. He thought it wise to avoid alarming her further. She had ardently resisted returning to the apartment. After some time, he had reasoned with her to do so. Knowledge that he was armed would likely undermine his solicitations.

He pulled off his shirt and pulled another from the second drawer in his chest of drawers. Natalie entered the bedroom carrying the clothing he had moved to the coffee table. She went to the dresser and placed the garments in a drawer. She closed the drawer and leaned against the dresser. She looked at Brand as he pulled the shirt over his head.

"This isn't working for me, Brand", she said evenly.

Brand watched her silently.

Here it is, he thought.

"I know you feel it too", she said with conviction.

Brand held his tongue. He had rehearsed this scene many times before, and he wanted to keep to the high road without antagonizing her with an air of superiority or vindication by agreeing with her.

She waited for him to respond.

"How do you want to do this?" He asked reluctantly.

He saw hurt darken her eyes. He winced inside. He knew that look. She would not handle this calmly for much longer. Hers was a brittle veneer when it came to matters of the heart. He believed her intentions genuine when beginning a discussion about their relationship. Her stamina was not great when her position was challenged.

"I'm not doing anything. You have put me in a position where I am in danger."

She turned fully towards him.

"How many people do you know can say their best friend was kidnapped and murdered by a drug cartel? Follow that with that same cartel firebombing their car?"

"You don't have to leave me", Brand reasoned. "Just stay at your mom's for a few days until I get this thing sorted out."

"How do you think you will be able to 'sort this out'?"

Brand stuffed his hands in his pockets. His temper was difficult to control. He inferred a patronizing undertone to her narrative. He considered her with a steady look of growing frustration.

"I'm not sure", he replied and walked past her, leaving her alone in the bedroom.

He went to the kitchen and opened the fridge. He wasn't sure what he was looking for other than something to occupy his thoughts in his need to remain in motion. He saw Natalie in his mind's eye, gathering herself for the next act in their break-up drama. He knew her. He also knew she had already made up her mind. She would need to establish "jilting kudos." It was easier to live with a break-up if you were the wielder of the axe instead of the recipient of the blow.

She emerged from the bedroom. She paused in the doorway, watching him impassively. His jaw tightened. She had regrouped and now she would fire both barrels at him.

"This isn't just about the past few days. You have been distant for the last couple of months. I don't have time to argue with you right now."

Natalie drew a deep breath as if the matter had been settled at great cost to her emotions. She moved to the bar top and collected her keys and her purse.

"You are leaving now?" Brand asked incredulously.

"Like I said, Brand, I don't want to argue."

"There is a distinct difference between arguing and discussing a decision that will affect everything we are."

She looked at him with genuine pity.

"I know this is hard for you. Talk will do nothing to change my mind. I'm leaving you."

"I am fine with you leaving me. What are we going to do about the apartment and all of your stuff?"

"You are fine with me leaving?" she cried with a gesture which indicated his betrayal.

Her expression softened a fraction as she grappled with the idea that her role of jilter was starting to look more like the less desirable role of the jilted.

"You are a dick", she cried.

She spun on her heel and moved towards the front door. She had gone only two steps when the door burst open. There stood Miguel, revolver raised in a firing position. His first shot struck Natalie in her chest, high up near her collar bone. She dropped to her knees with a muted cry. She pressed her hands to her chest as she tried to stop the spreading flow of blood from the fresh wound.

Miguel brought the pistol around in Brand's direction. Brand ducked behind the bar top as the pistol exploded a second time. The big slug splintered the cabinet behind the spot Brand had just vacated.

Miguel moved left, trying to get a clear shot at Brand behind the short line of cabinets below the bar top.

Brand moved back towards the kitchen wall cabinets looking for any kind of weapon. The Glock was in the bedroom and the gunman was between him and the bedroom.

His reflexes moved him as a quick movement at the end of the bar cabinets prefaced Miguel dashing into the center of the kitchen walkway. Brand moved with violent impetus but not before the heavy pistol barked and he felt the hot piercing burn of a bullet burrowing into his calf.

A combination of Adrenalin and rage darkened his vision. The pain would add its effect to his perception as soon as the initial shock no longer numbed the injury.

Brand moved towards the bedroom door with a mighty leap hindered by his wounded leg. He saw Natalie lying in a pool of blood. Her eyes stared up at the ceiling with the flat look of death. Brand groaned as he pushed off with his good leg, the bedroom door beckoned just beyond. He gathered himself for one last leap when the pistol belched flame and a large slug struck him in the center of his back. The impact knocked him flat.

Miguel approached the man cautiously for the kill shot. He paused at the sound of shouts and movement outside the open door of the apartment. He heard the unmistakable sounds of approaching police sirens. He drew a bead on the prostrate American and pulled back the hammer on the gun.

A gunshot exploded behind him and a bullet dug a furrow in the bedroom door frame. Miguel pivoted on his right foot and dropped low to the floor. A uniformed security guard stood in the doorway, a semi-automatic pistol in his hand. The guard brought the pistol on line to fire again. Miguel fired a snap shot, catching the guard in the stomach. The security guard grimaced and dropped to his knees.

Miguel rose. He ran towards the doorway. He dropped the security guard with a second shot to the head. His victim was silent as he fell on his side. Miguel jumped over the dead man and fled from the apartment.

# Chapter 22

Detective Hernandez walked the crime scene, careful to avoid the busy forensics team scouring the apartment for evidence.

He looked upon the two bodies with grim interest. In the living room was the female, attractive and young. The body of the uniformed security guard blocked the entryway, slumped against the door frame.

Hopkins, the lead forensics investigator on scene, filled in Hernandez as he worked.

"The male victim has been transported and is still alive, but his wounds are grave."

He indicated the two bodies with a gesture that admitted his next statement was unnecessary. "The security guard and the woman are deceased – cause of death: gunshot wounds. This appears to be gang-related."

Hernandez nodded and moved towards the kitchen. He was a decorated veteran of the SAPD. He was proud of his twenty-three years of service with the force. His work with the Gang Unit Task Force had elevated him to near-hero status. He drew no pleasure from his reputation. Like his father, he had joined the force to make San Antonio safer. He desired no additional thanks other than his paycheck and the opportunity to wear the uniform.

With every monumental bust he made, it was evident that there was no end to those who would take over for whomever he removed from the streets. The gangs were pervasive throughout the city.

Twenty years ago, gangs had limited the bulk of their activities to the familiar streets of the south side. Today gang activity was as common in the more affluent areas of San Antonio as in the poor neighborhoods.

The latest and most prevalent gang, *Tango Orejon*, seemed to control much of the organized crime in the city. The silly name translated 'Have Big Ears', belied a cruel and murderous organization comprised of young aggressive Latinos. *Tango Blast*, as many referred to it, was the largest in a list of more than a score of organized and dangerous gangs.

This shooting was bloody and ruthless, but something was different. The apartment was not marked in the usual ways, with gang graffiti or tell-tale ritualistic markings upon the victims.

A uniformed officer approached Hernandez, holding a notepad.

"Detective", he said, reading from the pad. "The two civilian victims have been identified as Carson Brand and his girlfriend Natalie Swanson. The security guard is Private Officer Rudy Cameron.

Witnesses say they heard multiple gunshots from within the apartment. The guard", he pointed towards the security guard lying in the entryway, "was in the middle of making a routine patrol of the property. He learned of the disturbance from a tenant who was walking her dog. He approached the apartment, then pulled his weapon and entered. More shots were heard, and a witness saw the guard go down, apparently from gunshot wounds inflicted by the perpetrator's weapon. Within seconds, a single Latino male was seen fleeing the scene."

The uniformed officer scanned his notes once more.

"No one we questioned saw where the shooter went, nor did anyone recognize him. We have a vague description: thin Latino male, about five-eight with dark hair, jeans, green hoodie, and 'a big gun'. That is a quote."

Hernandez grunted as he continued inspecting the living room/dining room area.

"Is Gold Cross en route?"

"Yes, sir."

"Canvas the surrounding neighborhoods for any other witnesses or someone who might have noticed anything out of the ordinary."

"Yes, sir", the officer repeated then turned on his heel to follow the directive.

Hernandez moved towards the blood stains where the male victim had fallen.

'Why did he run towards the bedroom instead of towards the front door?" He thought.

Hernandez entered the bedroom. There were no signs of struggle or anything in the room which might indicate the room was a part of the crime scene. He looked under the bed, then moved around the bed. A set of keys and a thumb worn western novel sat, face down and open, on the nightstand. He guessed the man slept on that side of the bed. He opened the nightstand drawer. A Glock pistol lay within the drawer.

"Going for your gun", Hernandez murmured under his breath. "Bet you wish you had kept it on you."

He lifted the pistol carefully by the hand grip and dropped it into an evidence bag. He returned to the living area as the coroner's staff collected the two bodies.

His mind returned to the killings. It was possible that the perp was interrupted before he could mark the kills. Hernandez shook his head. Something told him this was different.

# Chapter 23

Brand opened his eyes. His head swam from the morphine. He looked around him at the grays and tans of his hospital room. He struggled to gather his thoughts. Strange images and flashes of memories spun before him like a badly organized slide show. Finally, his recollections settled into a normal stream. He groaned as he recalled the attack - and Natalie.

He felt tears burn behind his eyes. He moved his hand to cover his face. An I.V. tube and a nagging stiffness in his back restricted his movements. Then he remembered being shot in the leg and the blow to his back, which must have been another shot. He moved gingerly, unsure how badly he was hurt. The drugs dulled his senses and, he presumed, the pain which would certainly have indicated the extent of his injuries.

"He's awake, sir."

Brand squinted in the direction from which the voice came. A uniformed police officer spoke into the walkie attached to his shoulder. He released the push-to-talk button and looked at him blandly.

"The nurse will be here momentarily", he said then moved outside the door. A nurse arrived some ten minutes later. She bustled about, taking note of the medical telemetry displayed on the numerous LED readouts of the monitoring equipment surrounding his bed.

"How are you feeling, Mr. Brand?" she asked crisply.

"Not sure yet", he replied honestly.

"Are you experiencing much pain, or a general discomfort?"

"Both, I guess."

"Well you are doing very well considering the gravity of your injuries."

Brand studied her carefully. She made no effort to exchange a look or engage him in any further conversation than she had already. Her manner was very business-like.

"Am I going to be okay?" he asked hesitantly.

She paused and looked at him with what he thought to be surprise.

"It seems you will be just fine, Mr. Brand."

She made a note on a chart attached to a Masonite clipboard.

"Some people would like a word with you if you are up to it."

"What people?"

"Law enforcement people, Mr. Brand."

"Can you cool the 'Mr. Brand' thing, please? I am well enough to talk with the police."

She frowned at him then turned to the door.

Brand lay alone for several minutes before a police detective arrived and showed his badge, taking a seat beside the bed.

"Mr. Brand, I am Detective Gabe Hernandez with the San Antonio Police Department. How do you feel?"

"A little stiff and woozy from the pain killers."

"Do you feel up to answering a couple of questions?"

"Sure. How can I help?"

"First off, let me convey my sympathies for your tragic loss. You have had quite a month."

Brand pursed his lips. He wasn't sure how things had changed so rapidly. The sting of loss seared him deep inside.

"I want to ask you about the break-in at your apartment."

Hernandez clicked a cheap ball point pen and folded his steno notebook over to a blank lined page.

"Let's start with the basics. Give me your full name, address, date of birth and what not for the record."

Brand thought about the request. Was this a test?

"Alright", he said slowly, trying to organize his thoughts. "My name is Carson Brand. I live at 12364 Brentwood Drive, apartment 114 in San Antonio. I am 34 years old and I was born on June 16th."

Hernandez jotted down the information and nodded as he did.

"Tell me about the events leading up to the attack."

"I was at my girlfriend's Mom's house the night prior. We went home, and a guy burst through the door and opened fire."

"Did you know the gunman?"

"Not by name, but I had seen him before."

Hernandez didn't look up as he asked, "Where?"

"On the job site where I have been working with my crew. He was a member of a concrete crew."

"Did you catch his name?"

"As I said, I didn't know him by name."

"I see. Let's leave that for now. Do you have any idea why he would want to harm you or your girlfriend?"

"None."

Brand felt a quiver of nervousness take root. How much did this Detective know? It might be time to come clean. He recalled the incident in Mexico with trepidation. How much should he reveal about a potential international incident? He focused on the Detective. The officer was looking straight at him, weighing something he saw in Brand's reaction.

"Do I need an attorney?"

"I don't know, Mr. Brand. Do you?"

Brand closed his eyes and gathered himself. There was too much to his story to pick and choose. He had never been much of a liar. He believed people lied for one of two reasons. Either they were afraid of the truth, or they were afraid of the person to whom they lied.

He wasn't comfortable with fear in any form. As a result, he generally faced his fears and acted in a genuine and fearless manner. He had to admit he was afraid now. His knowledge of the law was thin here.

"I'm pretty woozy with the drugs they are giving me. I want to make sure I am telling the truth and not offering some drug-induced fiction."

"Drug-induced fiction", Hernandez repeated as if the saying of it would emphasize the ridiculous nature of the statement. "Let's stick with what we know.

"A man broke into your apartment. He shot and killed your girlfriend, Natalie Swanson. He turned the gun on you and shot you twice: once in the leg and again in the back as you ran for the bedroom. Why did you try to get to the bedroom rather than escape out the front door? They were about the same distance away."

Brand nodded. They found his gun.

"My gun was in the nightstand in the bedroom."

"Your gun?"

The question sounded like an accusation.

"It's not registered to me because I bought it for cash from a guy I know. I have never fired it."

"Who did you buy it from?"

"I don't remember his name. We were having drinks at a bar when it came up in conversation that he had found the gun in a rental car and wasn't sure what to do with it. I offered to buy it and he agreed to the terms."

"How long ago was that?"

"Nearly a year ago, I believe."

"Have you been to Mexico recently?"

Here it comes, Brand thought with concern.

"Yes. I was in Eagle Pass Friday night. I crossed into Piedras Negras and had dinner and a couple of drinks."

"Did you go alone?"

Brand hesitated, trying to read the blank expression on Hernandez's face.

"No. I was there with a friend: Bert Gotardi."

"Where is he now?"

"He was killed in Mexico and his body was left in the Rio Grande."

Hernandez registered surprise at Brand's candor.

"And how do you know the details of his death?"

"I saw it on the local news."

"You crossed the border into Mexico, and he was with you?"

"Yes."

"Did he return to the U.S. when you did?"

"No. We got separated in Mexico."

"Why did you tell the border officials that you went into Mexico alone?"

"I was confused with everything that had happened."

Hernandez studied Brand for a long moment. He jotted down a note and again looked at Brand.

"What were the circumstances that separated the two of you?"

Brand sighed as he remembered the pursuit that night. He shook his head and recounted the story from the dispute over the Latina to the flight from Arturo's bar. He left out the gun fight and his assault on the border officer. As he wrapped up his story he glanced at Hernandez. The detective watched him with an expression of disbelief.

"Why didn't you report any of this to the border agents who screened you upon your return?"

"I didn't want to risk being returned to Mexico after attacking nearly a half dozen Mexican citizens."

"Mr. Brand, we don't turn American citizens over to foreign countries. You might have saved your friend's life if you had come clean with the border agents."

Brand closed his eyes to the burn of building tears. He had considered that fact over and over since Bert's murder.

"I figured Bert would get a little roughed up for flirting with the girl and he would return a little worse for wear, but with a lesson learned. I didn't believe they would kill him for flirting with a girl."

"Some friend."

Brand glowered at the detective. His eyes glimmered with regret, tears and anger.

"His wife identified the body. Have you spoken with her since your return?"

"I returned his overnight bag, but she wasn't at home, so I left it on the porch."

Hernandez perused his notes, tapping the pad with the pen.

"So, the gunman was at this 'Arturo's Bar' with three other men you thought to be locals?"

"That's right."

"It is your belief that Bert was killed because he flirted with a girl and this construction worker trailed you two into Mexico. He and his confederates abducted and killed your friend, firebombed your truck, then broke into your apartment and killed your girlfriend and tried to kill you?"

"That's what I know, Detective."

"How often did you travel with Mr. Gotardi into Mexico?"

"We went twice: last weekend and the weekend before that."

"Last weekend?"

"Yeah."

"Do you know what day it is, Mr. Brand?"

"I guess it must be Monday."

Detective Hernandez shook his head.

"It is about 10PM, Thursday the 22nd. You have been in the hospital for more than a week."

"What the fuck!"

"You have been in a coma since the day you were shot."

"I need to speak with my doctor."

"We will do that in time."

"We'll do it now, Detective. I must have nearly died to have dropped into a coma."

Detective Hernandez frowned at Brand. The interview wasn't going as he would have liked. He suspected the injured man was not being completely forthcoming. Hernandez decided to take a more direct approach.

"As I said, we will get to the doctor in time. I don't think you grasp the serious situation you find yourself in, Mr. Brand."

Brand's jaw worked as he tried to control his growing anger.

"What situation are you talking about?" He finally asked in a low controlled tone.

"I'm going to break this down for you as I see it. For the past year or so your friend, Robert Gotardi, AKA Bert, has made a small fortune smuggling illegal goods between Mexico and the United States. That is a matter for the feds, but my investigation requires I learn more about his involvement with certain parties on this side of the border.

"Your story is that he was kidnapped and murdered because of a girl. The girl you are referring to is a low-level lieutenant with the Juarez Cartel, a sub-set of the Gulf Cartel. She and Mr. Gotardi have met frequently, where she most likely gave him his marching orders, and probably delivered to him much of the illegal goods and cash he was to smuggle.

"We suspect he was skimming a small part of the drugs he was smuggling and selling the skim here in the states for a tidy profit. It stands to reason that the Cartel learned of his thefts and took care of him during your last visit. My question for you is how deeply are you involved?"

Brand was stunned. His mind struggled with the idea that his best friend could be involved in this kind of illegal enterprise without his knowing about it.

"I am not involved with any smuggling of any kind."

"So, the Cartel is gunning for you because they don't like your looks?"

"Up until a few seconds ago, I thought they were after me because I stood up for Bert when the concrete guys wanted to take him apart on the job site."

"You said yourself that this whole situation seems pretty extreme for flirting with a girl."

"Well that does seem pretty idiotic right now."

"It does indeed, Mr. Brand."

Hernandez leaned forward and his expression was hard as steel.

"You claim you knew nothing about any of Mr. Gotardi's activities, yet by your own admission you committed, assault and battery, possibly murder, assault of a law enforcement officer, you lied to federal officers and you were in possession of an illegal weapon. Two of your close personal group have been murdered in as many days. You seem pretty much a criminal to me. You had better tell me everything you know. Don't make the mistake of lying to me or holding anything back which might pertain to this case."

Brand returned a look of genuine surprise. He had to admit that Hernandez had a point.

"Your facts do explain the sports car and the new clothes. I just assumed he was buying on his wife's credit. He talked a lot about how he could repair anyone's credit. I figured he was working his magic. None of it made much sense to me but he was always a little deep for me. I am a carpenter, nothing more. I just reacted to the circumstances as they occurred."

Hernandez watched Brand silently as he considered his answer.

"Tell me about the girl and the construction guy."

"I only saw the girl once. She was at the job site the day Bert got into the altercation with the concrete guy. I didn't catch her name, but I remember she was hot and over-dressed for the job site. The concrete guy's name is Salazar. I've seen him on other jobs. We are regulars with a couple of the big G.C.'s in town."

"G.C.'s?"

"General Contractors."

"I see", Hernandez said slowly as he jotted down a note. "Do you know where I can find this Salazar?"

"Other than the job site, no."

"What is the connection between the girl and Salazar?"

"Salazar claimed she was his girlfriend."

Hernandez looked up from his notes with wide eyes.

"This Salazar must be quite the guy."

"That's the point. He isn't really. He is a regular guy who runs wetbacks on a construction crew. I was pretty surprised to hear that she was his."

Hernandez frowned at the negative reference to illegal immigrants. He tapped the pen on his pad, considering Brand with a black look.

"I suspect she is using him as a cover for some reason", Hernandez said, ending the short pause.

"For what?"

"Likely he is a smuggler as well."

Brand stretched with a grimace. His wounds were beginning to cause him discomfort beyond what the Morphine could mask.

"I'm ready to see my doctor now."

"I'll get the nurse."

Hernandez rose, folding his steno pad.

"We'll talk later."

Hernandez left Brand alone in the hospital room.

# Chapter 24

Miguel sat across from Fuentes. His manner was markedly different from his previous visits. He rested confidently in the steel chair. The whir of the air conditioners and radios possessed none of the sensory distraction it once held. He felt invincible. When you kill fourteen people in a month you gain a lot of self-worth.

He worked directly for the Cartel now. Fuentes was no longer a link in the chain between him and Mexico. The older man knew this, and Miguel sensed that Fuentes restrained himself with much effort. Miguel had ignored Fuentes' obvious disdain before, due to a respect for his station. The restraint expected of a neophyte no longer fettered him. He saw Fuentes as a relic of a bygone time. The present belonged to the strong and Miguel was the strong now.

Fuentes was an old man, bitter and headstrong in his antiquated beliefs. To the point, Miguel disliked the old man. His perception of the relationship between the Cartel and the *MuHa* leader was one of strained tolerance. Miguel thought he might serve the desires of Mexico if he eliminated Fuentes here and now. Only a small glimmer of a doubt stayed his hand. Even he understood the limits of his autonomy in these matters. He smiled slightly at the likelihood that his desire to kill the man would be satisfied soon enough.

Fuentes considered the deadly youth with a look of stern judgement. The boy was a dyed-in-the-wool mass murderer in the most literal sense. Fuentes knew of at least a dozen eliminations credited to the upstart killer. Fuentes fought the compelling urge to reach into his desk drawer, pull the heavy black Colt M1911, and kill the kid. The natural law in his line of work is, he who you bring to your world will invariably take you from that world at some point.

The arrogance of the killer was apparent in his disrespectful posture. His expression plainly displayed his disdain for the older man. He didn't have to express his desire to kill Fuentes. The old man saw it clearly. The urge to kill the young *Sicario* was nearly irresistible.

Both men suspended their thoughts of loathing for one another at the sound of the kitchen door opening then closing. The Latina from the job site entered the cold room. She looked around her as everyone did the first time they entered the loud room. She listened to the noise of the radios and the window units a moment as she acclimated herself to the din. The men took her in as they would have if she had been the President.

Her name was Christina and she was aware of the stir she caused when she walked into a room. Miguel, the younger man, averted his eyes like a school boy: the confidence of his murders forgotten for the moment. The elder, Fuentes, savored her as only the aged can. His wistful look faded in favor of an expression of kindly appreciation as the realization of his age and inadequacy overwhelmed his desire. He knew innately that he would fail at the test she would be if he tried for her.

Christina descended lightly onto the available steel chair, smoothing her skirt. She crossed her legs to the delight of both men. They looked her over, from her lustrous black hair, to the red undersides of her expensive pumps. She endured the appraisal with the aplomb of one accustomed to the constant scrutiny of desirous men.

"The American is conscious, and he is talking", she said simply.

Miguel's gaze hardened; Christina's legs forgotten.

"I will finish him."

"He is under police guard at all times. No matter. We may have to disband or move *MuHa*."

Fuentes leaned back in his chair and considered her words.

"What about Salazar?" Fuentes asked. "He knows little of our operation other than we provide wayward boys work and support. The police will eventually talk to him, but I believe he is under control."

"I had dinner with him last night", Christina said casually.

Fuentes smiled at the concrete man's naiveté. How could he believe a woman like Christina would give him a second thought? If it had been Fuentes instead, he would have been suspicious of her motives.

"He knows you", Fuentes pointed out critically.

"He knows nothing about me except a fake name and a fake story. Obviously, I can no longer see him. We will need a new anchor."

"Younger?"

Fuentes chuckled at his jest.

Christiana frowned.

"This is business, Fuentes. You would be wise to remember that. He knows you. That is a concern."

"My operation is clean. I am a small-time security specialist and that is all anyone will know. I stay active with local youth groups, but I pull none of my recruits from them."

"Salazar mentioned to me last night that he was curious about you. It was mentioned to him that you do more than provide labor."

She looked directly at Miguel but spoke to Fuentes.

"He said one of your 'boys' asked him if he knew what you really did, the day of the altercation with the smuggler and his partner."

Miguel struggled to meet Christina's gaze without success. His newly acquired confidence provided little support in the face of her accusations. He recalled his boast to Salazar with a twinge to his youthful pride.

Fuentes considered the young killer with a grim set to his face. The golden boy was not so perfect after all. Likely he had brought down the entire American side of the operation.

Christina continued to watch the boy expectantly. Fuentes was confused at her calm demeanor in the face of the danger they were discussing. Finally, Miguel looked up from his glowering thoughts. His face brightened.

"I will take care of Salazar myself."

Christina leaned back in her chair. She acted as if she had been waiting for those very words. Fuentes realized that she had been doing just that. He deduced that she wanted him to work out a solution himself.

"Go at once, before the police talk to him", she commanded.

Miguel stood quickly and rushed from the room. Fuentes peered at the beautiful woman, trying to understand her methods. She looked at him with a cold expression.

"Move *MuHa* tonight."

Fuentes wanted to protest but her steely gaze struck aside his words. Instead he nodded obediently.

# Chapter 25

Salazar ate the last cheese enchilada dinner of his life with large shoveled bites. The little *taqueria* was his favorite. He enjoyed the *pico de gallo* mixed with the rich cheese folded into the handmade corn tortillas. The flat oval of refried beans was made with an abundance of bacon grease, smoothing them into a creamy and delicious paste. His left hand grasped a fluffy home-made tortilla, poised to mop up tasty drippings from his huge bites.

He shoveled another large chunk of dripping enchilada into his mouth when his left eye disappeared into his skull, and the back of his head exploded as the wad-cutter .357 magnum round passed through. He heard the explosion of the gunshot as he fell and died on the twelve-inch VCT floor tiles.

Miguel shot the man once again to ensure he had not failed as he had with the American. He looked around, exaggerating his head movements to see fully through the narrow eye holes of the black ski mask. Salazar had been the only customer in the little taco shop. The usual patrons were likely on job sites or otherwise at work during the middle of the morning.

A terrified waitress covered her mouth with a hand, her eyes widened in fear. A cook in a greasy white tee shirt watched, transfixed by the horrific scene. Miguel considered eliminating these witnesses. He quickly rejected the idea. Although the day was warm, he wore a cold weather jacket turned inside out. That and the ski mask would make it difficult for the two to identify him with any accuracy.

Miguel turned on his heel and left the restaurant at a sprint. He ran along the front sidewalk of the strip mall past several storefronts of which the Mexican restaurant was one. A service alley created a narrow divide between two buildings in the strip mall. He turned down the alley, sprinting past the buildings into a vacant lot. The field was grown over with long grass and piles of junk, where locals had used the space to deposit loads of trash and debris they didn't want to pay to dump.

He crossed the lot and turned right along a residential street. He turned left at the first intersecting street, then entered an alley between the homes lining the streets to either side. The white Toyota sat behind a little garage. He stripped off the mask and jacket as he leaped into the driver seat and started the car. He checked the area around him and saw no witnesses. He put the car in gear and drove away as casually as his pumping adrenalin would allow.

# Chapter 26

Brand sat upright in his hospital bed. Beside him was a tray filled with dirty dishes. His appetite had returned, and he was full and restless. The uniformed cop head-checked him from time to time, confirming his continued presence in the room.

Hernandez had been by every day since the first day they had spoken. Brand guessed that he was no longer high on Hernandez's list of evildoers, based upon their recent conversations. Hernandez no longer grilled him, nor did he double down on questions meant to trip him up in his testimony. Most of what the detective asked had to do with additional details in respect to the Latina and his experience in Mexico.

Other than Detective Hernandez, only Karen had visited him. There was no one else to do so. His few friends were all dead. His parents had passed long ago. He was an only child so there were no siblings to make a begrudging visit. Bert had been his only friend. Natalie had been the closest thing to family he had. Brett and Lance had called about work then called no more.

Brand felt a familiar surge of heat. That little Mexican bastard had taken away everything that was important to him. He was consumed in the blaze of an internal rage he hadn't felt in some time.

When he was a kid in school, he never reacted well to bullies or even playful scuffling. One occasion surfaced in his memory. He had been in phys-ed class - it must have been his sophomore year. Class was ended, and he stood at his locker where he was changing from the navy-blue shorts and gray shirt of his P.E. uniform back into his street clothes. He stood there shirtless, digging through his pockets for the coins buried there. Lonnie White, the red headed, freckle-faced bully appeared suddenly and twisted one of his nipples.

He had yelled, "Texas Tittie Twister!"

Suddenly, with speed he did not realize he could achieve, Brand's fist had shot out and Lonnie dropped to the navy-blue utility grade carpet, out cold. The blow was automatic and instinctive. Neither he nor Lonnie saw the fist until it connected with the bully.

At the principal's office, minutes later, Brand had stood before the vice-principal with bowed head. The heavy man with the receding hairline and draggy Texas drawl asked him why he had hit Mr. White.

Brand's response had been short but accurate.

"I don't like being touched in a violent manner."

The mild tone of his response belied the aggression he had felt. His greatest desire was to have Lonnie White's throat under his thumbs. The urge had lasted months after his three-day suspension from school for fighting. His father had made him promise to avoid Lonnie White. Brand obeyed but his darkest desires centered around beating White mercilessly.

Brand felt an all-consuming desire to strike out for the loss he felt. He saw Bert's and Natalie's faces clearly. He gripped the sheet which lay over him. His eyes darkened as the violence he desired fought for control, like a rabid dog snapping and lunging against the chain.

Doctor Ross, his attending physician, entered the room. He beamed behind wire framed glasses. His smile faded a fraction as he beheld the black look on Brand's face. He slowed his gait, then stopped a distance from Brand's bed.

"We are releasing you this afternoon, Mr. Brand."

Dr. Ross cleared his throat as he regained his pleasant demeanor. He took a breath, smiled, then gathered Brand's chart.

He read the chart briefly, then looked over the top of his spectacles at the numerous LED read-outs from the nearby monitoring equipment.

"The wound in your calf is a small cut caused by the bullet grazing your calf. It is nearly healed. The back wound is more serious. There were no vital organs struck, only a broken bone which stopped the slug. You will need to take it easy for a few days, but you will be good as new with rest."

He retrieved a square note pad from his coat pocket. He tore off the top sheet and handed it to Brand. Brand glanced at it. The page was a prescription form. Indecipherable hieroglyphs apparently indicated a drug of some kind.

"Drop by the pharmacy on your way out. They will provide you with something to ease the pain. How do you feel?"

"I feel fine", Brand replied, stretching his neck and moving his head from side to side, as if the action demonstrated his recovery.

"Good", Dr. Ross said. "Do you have a ride home?"

"I'll call someone", Brand lied. There was no one to call.

"Well, that's it, Mr. Brand. Good luck."

Dr. Ross replaced the chart and left Brand alone.

The officer stood and entered the room.

"We'll give you a ride. Detective Hernandez wants you under guard for your own safety."

"For how long?"

"Until we locate the gunman who tried to kill you. Hernandez believes you are still a target."

"Why would he think that?"

"That guy, Salazar, you had that dispute with, was shot and killed this morning at a south side taco stand."

"It sounds like someone is tying up some loose ends."

"We believe you are right. You are a loose end, Mr. Brand."

"I need to go to my apartment, but I would rather stay in a hotel tonight, if that's okay with you."

"Fine by me", the cop said. "I'm not on your security detail."

Brand smiled politely. The cop was only doing his job, but he could have been a bit more sympathetic.

"Is Detective Hernandez coming by today?"

"He didn't mention it."

"Then I'll ask you. Can I get my Glock back?"

The cop gave him a hard look.

"You don't have a Glock. The gun you are referring to belongs to a former airline pilot. The gun is on its way to Florida as evidence in his murder trial."

"Wow. A gun with a history", Brand said without enthusiasm.

The officer nodded in agreement.

"The literal smoking gun in a case that was likely going to be dismissed without it. Lucky you never fired it. The suspect's prints were still on the bullets in the magazine."

"Lucky", Brand repeated without conviction. He had no way to defend himself. If what the officer said was true, he would need to be ready when the time came.

Since he had awakened, one thought had worked at the back of his mind. He was going to find Salazar and track down the Mexican kid.

The fire raged within him once again. He felt anger well up as he saw the kid in his mind's eye. He planned on killing him with the same cold indifference the bastard had shown when he killed Natalie, and likely felt when he mutilated and killed Bert. Now Salazar was dead. That would make the job more difficult.

Ignored, the officer returned to his chair.

The Latina was the key to this thing, Brand thought. If he found her, he would find the killer. The police security detail would be an impediment to an expedient search.

Brand was unclear whether he was still a person of interest or not. Hernandez rarely volunteered information. Although less confrontational in his questioning, he maintained a level of confidence with Brand that never stepped outside of the context of his usefulness in the investigation.

Brand was discharged mid-afternoon. He enjoyed the warmth of the summer sun on his shoulders. Two officers guided him into the back seat of an awaiting patrol car. They left the medical center and made their way across town to Brand's apartment. The officers accompanied Brand. He located his key as they walked to the front door.

To Brand's surprise, there was no obligatory crime scene tape or official notice on the front door proclaiming the site a crime scene. He unlocked the door and they entered the apartment.

The wide blood stain on the carpet where Natalie had died was arresting in its stark meaning. Involuntarily his eyes sought the other large stain where he had been shot.

His throat constricted with his sorrow and rage. He set his teeth against the rising emotions and went to the bedroom. The officers waited for him in the tiny tiled foyer.

Brand grabbed the gym bag. It was still loaded with clothing from his Mexico trip. He went to his dresser and packed several additional changes of clothing. He went to the bathroom and jammed toiletry supplies into available spaces in the overly stuffed gym bag.

Finally, he carried the bag into the dining room just off the little kitchen. A heavy wooden desk was against the far wall. He pulled the desk back and recovered a blue zippered bank bag. He pushed the pouch into the gym bag and shoved the desk back in place.

The officers watched him suspiciously as he returned to the front door.

"I run a framing crew. Many of my guys don't have bank accounts or I.D. I keep cash around for payroll."

Brand opened the bag, so they could see the blue pouch.

"Are you finished here?" One of the officers asked.

"I am."

They returned to the police car and drove to a nearby motel. Brand checked in and was soon sitting on the queen bed in his little room.

The loss of several days to the coma left him with a surreal sense of time passing. It was as if the world had moved on and left him behind. His small business was a tentative thing at best. A missed week at the apartment job site had left him replaced on the project. He was on foot since his truck was torched. All the money he possessed was a small balance in his bank account and the contents of the blue bank bag.

He opened a brown pill bottle and swallowed two tablets. His back was stiff and the ache in his calf was constant. He retrieved his phone from his bag and searched his past calls. He had called several dealerships after learning that the insurance company had totaled his truck and cut him a check. One of the calls had found a truck which interested him.

He called the dealership and waited as the phone rang. The salesman answered and Brand convinced him to pick him up. The departing police officers had assured him they would be around, but they weren't a taxi service. He doubted they would shuttle him to a west side dealership.

An hour passed before a knock sounded at the door. Brand went to the door and looked out the peep hole. A guy in a yellow golf shirt, a name tag, and a salesman's smile, presented his best image. Brand opened the door and left with the salesman. He didn't see the cops.

He guessed it wasn't like the movies where a car was stationed before the house at all times.

They drove to a small used car dealership on the West Side. After completing some paperwork, the salesman led Brand to the back of the lot where a late model blue Ford pickup waited. Brand walked around it then looked inside the cab.

"Do you want to test drive her?" The salesman asked brightly.

"No need. Let's do the paperwork."

The salesman shrugged and led Brand back to his office.

Brand signed over the insurance check and took the keys. He headed back to the motel, stopping on the way to grab a burger and fries. His wounds were beginning to ache, and the meds were back at the room.

He parked his new truck outside the door to his room. As he unlocked the room door, a black and white police car drove slowly past. Brand exchanged looks with the officer on the passenger side. They drove on without acknowledging him.

Brand closed and locked the door, then sat the bag of food on the round table next to the wall-mounted air conditioner. He laid his phone next to the bag then moved to the bed side stand where the TV remote lay. He turned on the TV and returned to the table. He ate his burger and fries, ignoring the commercials which appeared in quick succession on the screen. His mind worked on how he would find the Latina.

He needed a gun. Although he had never fired a weapon of any kind at anyone, he knew somehow, he would be equal to the task. He had seen firsthand of what these animals were capable. His was not a reaction born of desperate revenge. Rather, he felt an enlightened freedom to act as he wished without regard for the moral components associated with the killings he might commit.

A knock shook the door to his room. He stood and checked the peep hole. It was Detective Hernandez. He opened the door and Hernandez entered unbidden.

"Are you settled in, Mr. Brand?" he asked, looking around the room. He sat in the open chair at the table.

Brand returned to his seat opposite the detective. He stood uncomfortably across from the detective.

"I need a few days to get my bearings, Detective. I can't stay in my apartment right now."

"Yeah", he agreed looking over the room. "I wouldn't want to go back either if I was you."

Brand sat in his seat.

"What can I do for you, Detective?"

"Nothing. I just wanted to check on you."

Brand didn't believe him.

"Am I still under investigation as a smuggler?" Brand asked, watching Hernandez with a level gaze.

Hernandez considered Brand as he formulated a response. He grabbed a fry out of the shiny cardboard container and quickly tossed it into his mouth. Finally, he leaned back and took a breath.

"What are your plans, Mr. Brand?"

"I'm not sure yet", Brand responded a bit sharply as his impatience grew. "What should I do?"

"Once this thing is over, I would move if I were you."

"Move where", Brand asked inanely, attempting to maintain Hernandez's pace in the conversation.

"Away from here. Officer Holden told me he let you know about Salazar. We don't have the manpower to protect you. Your position is not one that would warrant you entering the witness protection program. You are kind of in a middle area not addressed by due process."

"So how long will Ying and Yang be on guard duty over me?"

"Unfortunately, they have never been on guard duty over you. My request for protection was downgraded to a drive-by order. You are on your own, Mr. Brand. You are no longer a person of interest in our investigation."

Brand watched Hernandez with a surprised look on his face.

"What about all of the crimes you said I might have committed in Mexico?"

"There have been no charges filed in Mexico. It is up to the feds if they are going to pursue charges of lying to an officer or obstruction of justice."

Hernandez stood and smoothed his suit coat.

"I like your new truck", he said as he moved towards the door.

"Thanks", Brand replied distantly. His thoughts whirled at this new information.

Hernandez took his reaction as shocked and scared.

"Mr. Brand, here is my card. Call me anytime if you feel like you are in danger or you think of something else which might help in our investigation."

He laid the card on the table next to Brand's phone.

"It's going to be okay."

Brand looked at Hernandez blankly. It took him a second to catch up with the conversation. Finally, his expression cleared, and he focused on the detective.

"I'm sure it will be. Thanks for stopping by."

Hernandez felt puzzled at Brand's reaction. The young man didn't seem frightened or in shock. He seemed preoccupied. Strange.

The detective left, closing the door behind him.

Brand drank a sip from the straw, his hand moist from the sweat beaded cardboard cup. He needed a gun and he knew right where to get it. The hardest part would be to try to talk her into letting him have it.

# Chapter 27

Donna dropped the girls off at school. Since their father's death, they had seemed more fragile and distant than before. It was all she could do to rouse them out of bed in the mornings. They refused to eat their breakfast and there was no way they would take the bus to school.

Megan was older than Marissa. She was having more trouble with Bert's death than her sister. Her mood swings were distinct and troubling. Marissa seemed more withdrawn than anything else. Separately, their reactions were vastly different from one another's, but they presented a united front in how they displayed their grief.

Donna turned into the driveway. An unfamiliar blue truck sat at the curb. Someone was behind the wheel though she could not identify the person through the tinted glass. She gathered her purse and opened the door. She stepped out, her eyes on the truck.

The truck door opened, and the driver stepped out onto the street. The truck blocked her view of the driver. She waited on the sidewalk leading to the front porch. The driver walked around the truck bed and into view. It was Brand. She felt a twinge of grief. Brand had been a fixture in their lives for many years. Her feelings battled for prominence. Seeing him was a comfort because of his familiar connection to her late husband. She struggled with the anger that welled up at his complicity in Bert's infidelity.

Brand approached with a hang-dog air about him. Donna frowned as her familiar regard gave way to anger and feelings of betrayal towards Bert's lifetime friend.

"Hi, Donna."

"Hello, Brand. Where have you been?"

"I was in the hospital."

"Are you sick?"

"Can we go inside? I need to talk to you about Bert."

"I think we have talked enough, Brand."

Brand halted and considered her with the look of someone seeing something for the first time. He obviously didn't expect this type of reaction from her. Donna felt her need for the familiar overcome her anger for the moment.

"Come in. I need a drink."

Brand watched her intently, trying to get a fix on what she was thinking. He felt uneasy with her. He had never been close to her, but he had always had a friendly relationship with her. He followed her into the house.

"How are you holding up?" he asked her back as they moved through the living room into the kitchen.

She opened a cupboard and withdrew a bottle of Bourbon. They always kept a bottle for Brand.

"A little early for me", he said as he eased himself stiffly into a chair at the round breakfast table. He looked out the large windows. The backyard needed a mowing.

"Coffee?" She offered.

"I'm fine for now", he replied.

Donna pulled a wine glass from another cabinet and filled it from a wine bottle on the counter. She joined Brand at the table.

"You've lost weight", Brand said with concern. "How are the girls?"

"This has been hard on us all", Donna said simply then drank from the wine glass.

Brand watched her for a long moment. Donna wasn't sure if his expression conveyed judgement at her early morning drinking or if she was crediting him with a judgement she felt because of her guilt at her weakness.

"Sorry for just leaving Bert's stuff on the porch. You weren't home, and I needed to be somewhere."

"I was at the movies with my girls."

She drank again from the wine glass.

Brand expected her eyes to shine from fresh tears. He was surprised that she didn't begin to cry.

"Are you okay, Donna?"

She sat the glass on the table and glared at him.

"You knew he was fucking around on me and you just sat there and laughed at me!"

Now her eyes reddened, and the tears welled up. Her brown eyes seemed to blaze with the heat of her anger.

Brand looked at her for a long moment. He felt a guilty relief that he no longer had to carry the secret.

She searched his face for any sign of remorse. She wasn't sure what she saw, but it didn't seem to be guilt.

Brand cleared his throat uncomfortably.

"It's true that I knew about some of it. I tried to tell him how wrong it was – how it would hurt you if you found out."

He looked at her with real regret.

"I am sorry, Donna. I didn't see any way to tell you, so I acted like I didn't know anything."

She said nothing for a long time. Finally, she spoke, her voice was weak with her emotions. Brand guessed she had not given herself the time to grieve – likely for the girls' sake.

"What happened, Brand? Why was he killed?"

The tone of her words and the simplicity of the question struck him dumb for a moment. Her question was like the title of the bizarre movie which had dominated his thoughts, consuming his every waking hour.

"The cops say he was smuggling drugs and money for the Cartel. He stole some of the drugs and sold them on the side. The Cartel found out about it and killed him."

Donna showed no reaction to the news. She sat there stock still looking at Brand. Tears rolled unheeded down her cheeks. She looked past him out the windows to the back yard. She lifted her glass and drank once more. She swallowed audibly. Brand suspected she swallowed wine and a lump in her throat.

"Did you know about that too?" She asked in the same low voice.

"I had no idea, Donna. I figured his frequent trips to Mexico were", he hesitated at the Implication, "a part of his playing around on you."

Donna continued her scrutiny of the world beyond the window. She didn't want to look at Brand. The tears had unnerved her to a degree, and she wanted to keep it together.

"Everything was on his phone: the women, the drugs, and the woman he met with to get the drugs, everything."

Brand registered surprise at her revelation.

Donna looked at him, her control somewhat restored.

"I knew the passcode to his phone. I ordered pizza with it once. He was so arrogant. His lies and deceit were right there. I never looked. It never occurred to me to look. Was I that naïve?"

Brand didn't respond. He was thinking about the Latina. Donna waited for a reaction to her question. Her expression softened as she focused on Brand.

"Brand, how are you doing?"

Brand looked at Donna as he placed his thoughts in order.

"I'm okay all things considered."

He leaned forward and looked into her eyes.

"You weren't naïve. You were loyal and trusting. We both were. I hate what you have been through. None of this is fair or right."

Donna looked at Brand with surprise. They had never spoken more deeply than the light fare of small talk, passing gossip or maybe a casual debate on politics. He had never shone a whit of interest in her outside of her role as a peripheral character in the world of Bert. This candor and plainly stated consideration left her speechless.

"May I use your restroom?" he asked.

"Sure. You know where it is."

He rose and made his way to the hall bath. He paused before the door to the bathroom and looked back towards the kitchen. Donna sat as he had left her, head down and thoughtful. He strode rapidly to the master bedroom. He went to Bert's side of the bed. He lifted the mattress and plunged his hand between the mattress and box springs. He fanned his arm until he located what he sought.

He withdrew a Sig Sauer, model 227, 9mm pistol. He hefted it in his hand. It was loaded. He pushed the gun into the band of his pants behind him and pulled his shirt over the exposed hand grip. He returned to the hall bathroom and closed the door. He flushed the toilet and washed his hands. He returned to the table. Donna had not moved. He was careful to keep his front to her, so she would not see a bulge from the weapon.

"Have you spoken with the cops yet?" he asked her.

"I answered some questions at the coroner's office, but not since. You?"

"At first they thought I was involved in the smuggling operation. I have been under considerable scrutiny."

"Are you still a suspect?"

"The detective told me I was off the most wanted list today."

Donna didn't laugh at his jest. She studied him with genuine concern.

"How is Natalie taking this whole thing?"

Brand swallowed and looked down at the table. He wanted to avoid talking about the incident at his apartment.

"She was shot at our apartment by the same guy who killed Bert."

"Oh my God! Brand! I can't believe it. You poor man. I'm so sorry."

Brand felt his eyes burn as he fought to control his emotions.

"I'd rather not talk about it, if that's okay with you."

Donna stood. She rounded the table and hugged him firmly. The pressure made his back ache.

"I didn't know. I never would have been so hard on you if I had."

Brand patted her on the back, hoping she would release him. He appreciated the concern, but the combination of his injuries and the invasion of his personal space caused him discomfort in her embrace. He doubted he would feel close to anyone for a long while.

Donna released him and returned to her chair. She looked at him, her mind racing to encompass this new information.

"How did it happen? Never mind. You don't want to talk about it. I wish..."

"Donna, someday we'll talk about it. I just can't right now."

His expression conveyed his sincerity.

"I do have a favor to ask of you."

"Name it", she said quickly.

"May I see Bert's phone? His contact is my only chance of tracking down the killer."

"Brand, you need to let the police handle this."

She studied Brand. He displayed no discernible emotional response to her advice.

"I know you. I know you are a tough guy. This whole thing sounds a little out of your depth. What do you plan to do if you find this killer?"

Brand pursed his lips. His jaw muscles worked as his will worked to master his anger.

"I really need to see the phone", he repeated in a controlled voice. "Just for a moment. "

Donna paused, trying to think of something to say that might dissuade him. Finally, she stood and went into the living room. She returned and slid the phone to him across the table.

"8-6-7-5-3-0-9 is the code", she said in a brittle tone.

"Really?" Brand said. "What a refugee from the eighties."

Brand typed in the code and opened the text message app. He searched through an embarrassing number of messages from numerous women. After a few long moments he found a message containing an address in Mexico. The sender's name was Christina. He opened the message string and read several of the texts. The individual messages were short and instructive. Mainly the messages consisted of meeting locations. Others seemed to be confirmations of appointments met, which he assumed were confirmations that goods had been delivered successfully. He scrolled down to older messages. He noticed a recurring text requesting a meeting "as usual."

'Meet me as usual at 9:30.'

Another read, 'Meet me as usual at 3pm.'

There were many with the same short instruction. He scrolled further down the string. He came to the first message, dated more than four months prior.

'Meet me at *La Casa Chapala*. In the bar. 10pm.'

Brand forwarded the message to his phone. He also texted Christina's number to his phone. He closed the display and handed the phone back to Donna.

"Thanks."

"Don't do anything stupid, Brand", Donna warned once again.

"Too late", Brand said only half joking. "It's going to be okay, Donna. I need to know the answers to a few questions I have. I'll leave police work to the cops."

They both stood. They looked at each other for a moment, grappling with their own thoughts. Finally, Brand went around the table and hugged Donna.

"Tell the girls I love them and that their daddy was a good man. It's important that they believe that."

Donna nodded. She couldn't commit to so big a lie.

Brand left her and went to the front door. He looked back. Donna stood where he had left her at the kitchen table. She watched him leave.

Once in the truck he did an internet search for *La Casa Chapala*. He found it immediately. It was a *"Restaurant y Cantina"* off Division on the South Side. It was before noon and likely too early to catch her there. He returned to his motel room. No cops drove by this time. He entered the room and pulled the Sig from his waist band.

Bert had been proud of the gun. He bought it soon after Brand had purchased the Glock. As with so many things in their lives, Bert was not going to allow Brand to have something he didn't.

Bert got into the construction business after he met Brand, who was a framing carpenter. If Brand dated a pretty girl, Bert would date a hotter one. They competed with one another in everything they did.

The day he bought it, Bert showed off the pistol to Brand outside the *Dog*. Brand remembered admiring the brand-new pistol in the black plastic case. Bert didn't appreciate his criticism of the caliber. Brand told him he preferred the knock-down power of a .45 caliber over the lighter load of the nine mil. Brand had asked him what Donna thought about his new toy. Bert had shushed him almost in a panic.

"Donna hates guns", he had said in a hushed urgent voice. "She can't find out. Good God she would have a litter if she knew! With the danger that the kids might find it, combined with her anti-gun beliefs, I'd be screwed."

"She's gonna see it around the house, Bert", Brand had warned him.

He remembered Bert's look of triumph.

"I'll hide it under the bed, between the mattress and box-springs. She won't find it and I will have quick access to it if I need it. The only way she will find out is when I pull it and take out a burglar or some home invading evil-doer."

"That doesn't make any sense, Bert. She'll find it the next time she makes the bed — and most certainly when she rotates the mattress every quarter", Brand pointed out.

"Not likely. The bed is a California King and I will shove the gun towards the middle of that big bad boy. Brother, she hasn't rotated a mattress in all the years we have been married."

His heart was a little sore as he dropped the pistol on the bed and moved to the bathroom. He filled one of the short glasses from the bathroom tap and took two pain pills.

His back was aching, so he lay down on the bed. Thoughts of Bert saw him off to sleep.

# Chapter 28

B rand parked the truck across the street from *La Casa Chapala*. He turned off the ignition and sat for a moment looking over the place. The building was a burnt orange stucco building with a façade front fashioned to look like an old-time hacienda. An elaborate neon sign flashed the name over a colorful background of animated *Señoritas* in various states of castanet dancing. Below the sign read 'Food and Beer *Aqui*.'

As it had been during his six-day vigil, the parking lot was full to the last parking space. There were a few older cars, as one would expect of a Mexican food place on the south side of San Antonio. Most of the other vehicles, however, were remarkable in that they were high end luxury sedans and expensive sports cars.

The patrons entering and leaving the establishment were dressed as if they were attending a Broadway musical rather than going out for Fajitas for two. The men wore expensive Italian cut suits. Most of them wore boots. Even from that distance, he recognized the distinctive cut of M.L. Leddy boots, custom made by the west Texas boot maker at a cost of six to ten thousand dollars and beyond.

The women were striking in their cocktail dresses, *Christian Louboutin* shoes, and sparkling jewelry. The two doormen were well-dressed in expensive black suits – no ties. Although the suits were tailored to hide their shoulder slung holsters, Brand could see the dim outlines of the armament they carried.

Brand was convinced of the reality of what he faced in this place. They should have called it *La Casa Cartel*. Donna was right on one count. He was out of his depth here. This was a giant step above beating on drunks in bars. He might be able to get into this place, but he likely would be unable to get out. Even at full strength, unhindered by two bullet wounds, he would have suffered misgivings at his survival chances.

A few years before, he had stumbled into a fight with three men. He learned a valuable lesson from the experience. He had little chance of defeating so many foes simultaneously without experiencing grievous injury to himself. That day he had been fortunate that the three assailants were more angry than skilled. A broken arm and a crushed larynx had allowed him time to escape unhurt.

The two doormen appeared more than able to take care of themselves in a fight. Likely, the restaurant was filled with men whose lives were geared towards conflict of every kind.

As he had during the last few nights, Brand entertained no ambition of entering the restaurant. Instead he relaxed as best he could and waited. His plan was to wait as long as he had to. Hopefully he would spot the Latina entering or leaving. He felt certain he would recognize her.

His memory of her was that she was a singularly beautiful woman. His taste generally ran toward blondes. He rarely dated outside of his race. It wasn't a rule, he just liked what he liked. He knew, under different circumstances he would have made an exception in her case.

'Yeah', he thought. 'He would know her if he saw her again.'

He settled down into the leather seat. He reclined the seat back a fraction until the ache at the bullet wound eased somewhat. The wound was healing remarkably by his estimation. He felt it wouldn't be long before he was at 100% strength again. The long vigil had given him time to heal. Nearly a week of immobility was frustrating but beneficial.

He had just reclined the seat when he sat forward, senses alert.

A black Escalade pulled up to the door and 'Christina the Latina' stepped out of the passenger seat. She shook her long hair and smoothed her skirt. She walked around the truck and stopped at the front doors. She exchanged a brief word with the guards and disappeared inside.

Brand relaxed in his seat. His course of action was clear. He would await her return from within the restaurant and follow her. Hopefully he would gain the opportunity to catch her alone. He felt a grim satisfaction in the fruits of his patience.

The driver moved the SUV away from the front door and out of sight behind the building. Brand didn't move from his current vantage point. Christina was not one to walk around back to catch her ride. The driver would pick her up at the front door when she was ready to leave.

Brand watched couples and small groups of well-dressed men come and go for nearly three hours before the black Escalade returned to the front of the restaurant. He raised his seat back to a level suitable for driving and waited for her to appear. She emerged from the restaurant, arms locked with an older man in a gray suit and cowboy hat. He wore sunglasses although it was after midnight. He smiled down at her. She looked to him with a merry laugh. They paused beside the black truck. The older man spoke to her, the cant of his head told Brand he was trying to convince her of something.

Likely, Brand thought, he was working her. He must be somebody important for her to yield so much time to him. A woman like her dispatched would-be suitors deftly and with an economy of effort. Christina seemed to be explaining her refusal in detail. Brand grew convinced this man was an important figure in the Cartel.

197

He watched intently as the sales pitch continued. If the cowboy hat succeeded, Brand would have a more difficult time getting to her. Christina leaned towards the cowboy hat and kissed him. ·

Brand nodded: kissed and dismissed.

Christina moved around the Escalade and entered the passenger seat, this time the door was attended by the driver. He closed the door carefully and surveyed the surrounding area as he returned to the driver seat.

Brand started the truck as the SUV moved smoothly out of the parking lot. He followed at a distance as the SUV entered the expressway headed north. Brand was invisible among the numerous vehicles on the freeway to even an alert driver. They drove for some time, leaving the *barrio* and entering the *King William District*.

The historical area was filled with homes dating from the 1800's. Most were historic structures: expansive estates carpeted with immaculate landscaping and protected behind wrought iron gates.

The Escalade entered the circular driveway of a smaller one-story stone house. Christina stepped out of the truck before the driver could move to open the door. She spoke briefly to the driver. She closed the door and moved around the front of the SUV. The driver waited until she had closed the front door to the house before he drove away. Brand ducked low as the Escalade passed his truck on the street.

Brand pulled the Sig from the console and stepped out of the truck. He looked around him for signs of any curious neighbors. He looked the truck over. It was a new enough vehicle that the neighbors would think it belonged to a neighbor's guest. He had done enough work in the area to know that workmen were not permitted in the neighborhood after 6pm. He didn't want to attract the attention of cops tonight.

Satisfied, he stepped onto the curb and ducked behind a hedgerow which marked the boundary of the property. He moved along the hedge until he came to the corner of the home. He looked around for security cameras and saw none. He continued down a narrow concrete walkway, looking into windows as he moved. He fought the nervousness warning him against his radical plan. Hernandez's litany of crimes he had already broken echoed in his head. The prospect of adding breaking and entering, home invasion, and possibly another assault charge was arresting in its gravity. A strong sense of emotion propelled him. Was it the familiar rage that typically drove his aggression or was he lost in a misguided vendetta? He shook his head to clear any doubts raised by his fears.

Towards the rear of the house he could see a single lighted window which looked in upon a large living room. The light came from the kitchen opposite him. Windows and a large accordion door covered the entirety of the back of the house. The curtains were open to the view of the backyard. Brand could see clearly in the semi-darkness via a faint illumination from ambient light emanating from surrounding houses. The backyard contained a kidney shaped pool and landscaping, featuring expansive colorful flowerbeds and topiary. There was little wonder the rear windows were uncovered.

Inside, he saw Christina go to the fridge and draw a glass of water from the dispenser. She drank the glass empty then sat it down on the granite countertop. She kicked off her shoes and dropped her watch and items of jewelry next to her purse on the countertop.

Christina left the kitchen and entered her bedroom. She changed into shorts and a comfy tee shirt. She gave her hair a twist and bound it with a hair elastic from her night stand. She returned to the living room where she stopped short. A man sat in the lounger near the TV. Her heart raced. She forced herself to appear calm.

"Hello, Christina", Brand said, a casual quality to his tone.

"Who are you?" She asked, matching his casual tone.

"My name is Carson Brand. I figured you already knew me."

"Ah", she said simply. "You are taking a dangerous risk being here."

Brand nodded his agreement.

"It's no more dangerous here than it is at my place."

Christina looked Brand over. At his surface, he was a cool character. After what he had been through, including breaking into her home, he didn't seem overwrought, nervous or afraid.

"Have a seat."

Brand indicated the sofa as he spoke.

Christina didn't see a gun, but she suspected part of his calm demeanor was due to his being armed. She obeyed.

"So, what now?" she asked, pulling her legs under her on the thick cushions of the sofa.

"Tell me about this Mexican hunting me."

"I don't know what you are talking about, Mr. Brand."

She saw a hard glint darken his expression. She knew he remembered her from the construction site.

"I'm a little pressed for time. More importantly, I am not in the mood to parlay. Who is he and where can I find him?"

"What do you want, Mr. Brand?"

Brand pulled the Sig from his pants.

"Careful with that thing, Mr. Brand. You don't want to hurt yourself."

Brand smiled in grim appreciation of her wit. He waited silently. He tightened his grip on the pistol grip to steady a slight tremor he felt at his core. He had to press from his thoughts the question of how far he would go with this.

Christina felt a twinge of fear at his reaction. She had expected a nervous construction worker on an aimless vendetta. This man handled himself like a pro. She suspected that his calm was not dependent upon his being armed after all. There was a strength about him rarely seen in amateurs in her line of work. Still she thought she detected a slight nervousness to him.

She applied her considerable powers of observation to the intruder. He was attractive, but not striking. From his seated posture she could determine little about him physically other than he seemed fit. He held the gun tightly, not desperately or menacingly. He presented himself as someone who was comfortable with the weapon and his ability to persuade with or without it.

"Mr. Brand..."

"Brand, please", he corrected her.

"Brand." She emphasized his name. "I am sorry for your loss, but you are in over your head. I will say nothing about this offense if you leave now."

"Christina", he said as he leaned forward slightly. "I am not here to negotiate with you. You will tell me how to find this Mexican. I am not afraid of your people, and right now, they are not here to help you."

Christina felt herself growing angry. This self-confident intruder apparently thought her no more than a weak woman whose strength rested in reliance upon the men who protected her.

"You would impress me with your foolish ignorance? Only a fool would not be afraid of us."

"The meet and greet is over, *Señorita*. Stand up."

Brand rose from the chair. He kept his distance from the beautiful woman. He suspected she hadn't reached her station with the Cartel without the ability to handle herself in hard situations. He did appreciate how she bristled when she felt marginalized.

Christina stood with a fluid movement. Brand held the pistol low and near his hip. He showed training: likely military rather than law enforcement, based upon his current vocation. She eased closer to him. She stopped the move when he steadied the weapon on her. He was prepared for an attack. She felt pleasure that he took her as a viable threat.

"Into the bedroom", he ordered.

She looked at him in alarm.

"Get over yourself", he assured her impatiently. "Do I look like I give a shit?"

She didn't reply, but instead moved to the bedroom. It was dark save for the lamp burning beside the bed.

"Get dressed", he said.

She moved towards the closet.

He shook his head.

He was cautious, she thought. He suspected she might have a weapon hidden among her clothes – and she did.

He indicated her discarded clothing laying on the bed.

"Get dressed", he repeated.

She hesitated. Where was he going to take her? She looked at him, weighing her options. Resigned to fate, she pulled her tee shirt over her head and dropped her shorts.

As expected, Brand looked her over with open appreciation. He was not a pro after all, she thought. She turned fully towards him.

"You don't have to go through with this, Brand", she said softly. "I know you weren't involved in your friend's misdeeds. All you have to do is let me go."

She moved a step forward.

Brand straightened as she grew nearer. She was stunning. He knew she was working him as she had other men. He also knew he wanted her badly.

"Get dressed", he again ordered, though without the conviction he possessed earlier.

She stepped forward.

He could smell her perfume. He could nearly feel her warmth.

She moved a hand slowly to his chest. She closed the remaining distance between them. He was tall.

His body stiffened as she moved her arms around him. She pressed her skin against his clothing. His breathing quickened in response. She lifted her face close to his. His lips met hers. She felt him harden at her waist. He kissed her deeply, not with the crushing force of urgent lust, but with the warmth of an intimate connection. She felt herself drawn to him. He was a really good kisser.

# Chapter 29

Miguel was growing tired of watching the apartment. It was apparent, to him at least, that the American was hiding out. Since his discharge from the hospital, he had not been seen at the job site, nor at the bar he frequented, and he definitely had not been to his apartment. Maybe he was afraid to return to where he had been shot and his woman had been killed.

The idea to finish the job on the American was Miguel's, but he perceived the organization would not tolerate failure. The futility of his prolonged vigil gnawed at him. His skill set was better served in motion. By his estimation, sitting for days in his crappy Toyota had reached its end. He pressed the display button on his phone. The time was 2:15am.

He exhaled audibly. His frustration would not end without action of some type. His sanctions were his worth. He had not killed anyone since the construction guy in the taco place. He should have finished the American instead of running after the security guard fell. He found no relief in the excuse of his inexperience. He was paying for poor judgement with his idleness and his time.

Thoughts of alternate methods for finding his target worked within his desperate thoughts. No one had told him to camp out at the apartment. He waited on his own account for the lack of any other viable plan. Even now he drew a blank. He was happier in the role of doer than he was in the role of planner.

He felt annoyed with the doubts he harbored. Resolve galvanized him in that moment. He started the Toyota with a deliberate motion. There was no use in spending another uncomfortable night in the car. He put the car in gear and made his way to the freeway.

He would give himself time to formulate a better plan. Besides, his bed called to him. He enjoyed his mornings with his uncle Raymond. There was always a hot breakfast and hot coffee.

As he neared downtown, a tickle of an urge scratched at his brain. He often experienced the irresistible sensation when he passed this way. He couldn't go an hour without thinking about her. Christina lived nearby. He didn't have the courage to approach her openly, so he watched her from a distance.

Since the day she had appeared at Fuentes' house, Christina's long legs and flowing hair had summoned his deepest desires. He had followed her from the job site two days after he had returned from Mexico via the tunnel. He had taken a chance that she would meet with Salazar, and it paid off. He tailed her most of the day until her driver dropped her at her house in an expensive neighborhood.

He battled his insecurities as he struggled to screw up the courage necessary to knock on her door. He could come up with no reason for a visit he thought she would buy. The last thing he wanted was to appear awkward to her. Instead, he contented himself to park outside her house and maintain a close proximity until he had gained enough notoriety within the Cartel to demand her attention.

He gave little resistance to the impulse as he took the exit near her house. He drove the dark tree-lined streets carefully. A late-night sentry with the local police department had sent him away the first night. Luckily the cop fell for it when he feigned ignorance and claimed to be lost. The officer offered him directions and warned him to avoid making the mistake again.

He never needed a long stay outside Christina's house. Entry into and exit from the neighborhood were the risky parts of his visits. He would be quick tonight. He was tired of the dirty car.

He parked across the street from her house and extinguished the lights. The front windows were illuminated dimly by a light somewhere deep within the home.

He surveyed the homes around him for any indication he had been noticed by a neighbor. Only one other vehicle was on the street, a Ford pickup. He was satisfied that he was unseen, at least for now. He adjusted his position in the seat. He unbuckled his belt and unbuttoned his pants.

# Chapter 30

Christina was atop him. She pressed herself down against him. Their rhythm varied its tempo depending upon their level of pleasure. Brand cupped her breasts and rose to meet her. She peaked, causing him to join her in climax. She collapsed upon his chest, her breathing rapid and labored. His arms fell to the mattress in spent surrender.

They lay like that for several minutes. The moments passed, leaving a void between them where their thoughts returned to the circumstances which had brought them to this point.

Christina rolled off him and burrowed under the bedding. She smoothed the covers around her then rested her head on her hand, supported at the elbow. She watched Brand with interest as he struggled to emerge from his cushion of satisfied pleasure.

"So where were we before we were interrupted?" She asked teasingly.

"I don't recall right now", he replied with a smile. "It will come to me."

"You can't stay here", she warned him with no real conviction to her words. She felt surprise at her attraction for him. Although sex was a part of her battery of weapons she used to get what she wanted, her giving herself to him was a spontaneous reaction rather than a ploy.

It had been some time since she had made love because she wanted to be with a man. She had nearly forgotten what it was like to have a man who made love to her. She had grown accustomed to sex based upon lust, power, domination, insecurity or the many other motivations which riddled the minds of evil men. Brand shared himself to the same degree that she gave of herself. He was generous and open to her. She couldn't deny her deep attraction for him physically.

She sensed he was good. She knew no one else who could make that claim. Her smile faded as she recognized the weakness she allowed herself with Brand. He had broken into her house and held her at gunpoint.

She stepped out of bed and went to the closet. She glanced at the hiding place where she kept her pistol. Instead of grabbing the gun, she pulled a light night robe from a hanger and pulled it around her.

Brand watched her appreciatively. He felt some guilt that he didn't miss Natalie in that moment. Had they been that far gone as a couple? He rose and pulled on his jeans. He slipped the Sig into his waist band. He blanched slightly as her gaze held the gun curiously. Instead of an awkward explanation, he pulled his tee shirt over his head and arranged the tail of the shirt over the exposed grip.

He raised his eyes to hers and they looked at one another, each unsure how to proceed.

Finally, Brand said, "I didn't plan this..."

"Don't." Christina interrupted.

"Let me finish", he said gently stopping her before she could push him away emotionally. "I figure this has put you in a difficult position. I didn't want to do that. I'm not sure what I expected but I am glad we are here together."

Christina watched him; a pleased smile pulled at her lips. She liked him too. She might have struggled to put her feelings into words if their roles were reversed. She waited for him to finish.

"This guy tried to kill me, and I don't believe he is going away without succeeding. Can you help me without jeopardizing yourself?"

Christina would have given Miguel to him gladly for several reasons, the least of which was that the *Sicario* was unpredictable and thoughtless in his sanctions. She was convinced he was the luckiest outlaw she had ever heard of. His kills were public and around witnesses, yet he remained at large.

He had become a favorite of Don Rafa Cantu. That very evening he had commented on "the ghost" as Miguel had become known. He claimed to have big plans for the young killer – if he lived long enough to participate.

"I can't help you, Brand. The stakes are too high for me."

Brand studied her, his mind searching for a solution. He was at a dead end. He knew he couldn't hurt her. He had intended only to frighten her before, and he no longer had the will to follow through with that.

"Okay", he said simply. "What would you do if you were me?"

"I would run", she said without heat. She was genuinely concerned. "The organization at the highest levels know who you are."

Brand shook his head.

"Christina, I didn't want this. I didn't start this. Whatever you think I am involved with, you are wrong."

"I believe you, Brand. My opinion doesn't count. The organization doesn't change a course once that course is decided."

Brand focused on Christina. His feelings warmed to her despite the danger he faced from her associates. He moved across the room. He pulled her close to him. He kissed her deeply. She responded to him, pulling him towards her.

# Chapter 31

Miguel collapsed against the back rest in the car seat. He fastened his pants and buckled his belt. He searched around him once more. The only car on the road, other than his, was the blue Ford truck. He started the Toyota, put it in gear and headed back to the freeway. His bed awaited. He would need his wits about him when he next spoke with Fuentes.

It took less than a half hour to make it to his uncle's house. The last ten minutes were torture. Sleep dogged him with a relentlessness that nearly overcame his refusal to pull over and rest. The eastern horizon showed the first hues of the dawn when he staggered into the house.

Inside, comfortable darkness and a seductive quiet beckoned. He heard the faint stirring of his uncle Raymond, his sleep troubled by the sounds of his nephew's early hour entry. Miguel fell wearily onto his bed fully dressed.

His final thoughts before drifting into a deep slumber were of Christina's face. He saw her in his mind's eye. She smiled at him with the unmistakable look of love and respect. He knew with a certainty another might perceive to be delusion; she would be his very soon. Once he killed the American, she would clearly understand his value to the Cartel and to her personally.

## Chapter 32

Christina slept soundly. Brand admired her as his mind worked over the problems he faced. His intention was to gain some information which might lead him to the kid. As much as he didn't want to involve Christina, he had to know how to find the killer.

Carefully, he slipped out of the sheets. He found his clothes and pulled them on quietly. He picked up his shoes and the pistol. He crept from the room and into the kitchen. Maybe he would find something that might help him.

Her purse and keys lay on the kitchen counter. He looked back towards the bedroom. He heard no sounds of movement. He carefully pulled the purse open and looked in. Her phone and, what looked like a notebook, lay on top. He pulled out the notebook. A loose sheet fell from the book onto the tile floor. He scooped it up and looked the sheet over. One side had a name and address written in a woman's hand – likely hers. It read: *MuHa - Fuentes – 1264 Sycamore. Rear Door*. The last was underlined twice.

Brand pocketed the note and replaced the notebook in her purse. He wasn't sure if it was pertinent to his search, but he was out of options. He again glanced back towards the bedroom: No change. He left through the rear French doors by which he had entered and closed them after him.

Christina peeked around the door jamb of the bedroom door. She watched Brand pass one of the backyard-facing windows in the living room. She suspected he might rifle through her purse for information. She remembered that she had left Fuentes' address in her notebook where she had left it prior to her visit with Fuentes and Miguel.

She went to her purse and pulled out the notebook. The slip of paper was gone. She frowned. She hoped she hadn't made a mistake. Her leaving the note was an uncharacteristic oversight. Mexico was going to end their affiliation with Fuentes sooner or later. With a little luck, Brand would get his revenge and take care of Fuentes and the *Sicario* for them. Win – Win.

Brand walked to his truck. He saw, with relief, that it was where he had left it. The hour was early, just before dawn. He had parked the truck before a large estate next door to Christina's house. It was likely, if he had arrived later, the owner might have had it towed. He retrieved his keys from his jeans and pushed the unlock button on the fob. The Ford awoke with a welcoming array of dome and parking lights.

He returned to his motel room, showered and went out for breakfast. When he returned, he flopped on the bed and turned on the TV. On the screen, two heavily made-up women sat at a table sipping wine and discussing politics. He fell asleep as they expressed their disdain for the president and his radical policies.

# Chapter 33

Brand turned onto Sycamore Street. He read the addresses, eventually finding the house indicated on the note. He turned down the next intersecting street and followed it until he arrived at a dirt alley. He entered the alley and drove slowly, counting houses back to the address he wanted. A dilapidated garage faced the alleyway. He parked the truck before the closed doors.

He chambered a round in the Sig and placed it in the front of his pants. He was committed to his course of action. This was the next level and he would act as necessary. His life depended on it. The same sense of nervousness he had felt outside Christina's rose gradually once more. He set his jaw against the weakness he suspected would grow if he allowed the fear to take root.

He grasped the gate at the corner of the garage. Although it looked as if it was overgrown and locked within climbing vines and long grass, he was able to open it easily. He moved cautiously along the side of the garage. His senses were alert for any sign of detection. He saw nothing that would indicate his approach had been discovered as he mounted the concrete stairs leading to a side door of the main house.

He tried the knob and the door gave easily. Cold air chilled his hand on the knob as it escaped from the darkness within the house. He looked up at the eaves of the house. He saw a closed-circuit security camera covering the entry. If anyone watched a monitor inside, they knew he was there. He listened for rushed footfalls or any noise which might indicate an attempt to repel him. He heard nothing save multiple air conditioners pumping cool air into the house.

He increased his pace. If he had the advantage of surprise, he doubted it would last. His best course was a swift advance. He moved silently through the kitchen and entered a dark living room. An older man sat at a desk like those he used to see in the admin offices of his old National Guard unit.

The man was busy with his phone. He looked up in genuine surprise as Brand entered. He hadn't been watching the bank of closed-circuit TV's behind him.

Brand brought the Sig up and pointed it at the startled man behind the desk. The older man froze with the phone held as it had been upon Brand's entry. By degrees, the old man recovered his composure and sat the phone on the desktop. He started to lower his hands below the desktop.

"Better not do that", Brand warned. "Stand up, Fuentes."

"How do you know my name? How did you come here?"

"Shut up. You obviously know me. Where is the kid who murdered my friend and my girl?"

With impressive comportment, Fuentes smiled slightly at the question.

"You are in over your head here, Mr. Brand."

"I am getting sick of hearing that. Answer my question, Mr. Fuentes." He emphasized Mister.

Fuentes watched him silently. Brand got the impression that Fuentes was testing him. It was likely that a bad man like Fuentes doubted a guy off the job site had it in him to back up his menacing entrance with meaningful violence.

"Come here", Brand ordered the older man, gesturing with the gun.

Fuentes raised his eyebrows and approached Brand with an amused expression. He opened his mouth to impart, what Brand predicted would be some pithy remark. Brand broke his nose with a hard left. Fuentes dropped straight to the ground, his nose a fountain of blood.

Brand moved around the desk and pulled the chair near the prostrate Fuentes. The old man stirred slightly and groaned as his senses returned. Brand stowed the gun and bent over. He grabbed Fuentes roughly and pushed him into the chair. On the table, beside the assortment of radios, he saw a roll of light gauge insulated wire. He picked it up and returned to Fuentes. The bleeding man was fully aware once more. His face no longer showed amusement. Instead, his eyes were wide, and his hands quivered with either fear or pain.

Brand bound his wrists to the arms of the chair. The restraint caused Fuentes to sit hunched down in the seat. Brand then bound his legs to the front chair legs. He wound the wire tightly, circling the strands several times, working the coils up the chair leg nearly to his knees. He bent the wire back and forth until it separated from the spool. Once finished, Brand stood and examined his handiwork. Satisfied, he tossed the wire roll back on the table, upsetting nearby electronic gear.

"I'm going to ask you a few questions. I will ask them once. You will answer promptly and honestly."

Brand leaned closer to Fuentes. He peered at him with a chilling look.

"You and your people have killed my family. One of your hit men shot me and nearly killed me. You are in a very dangerous situation. If you lie, deflect, mislead or give me any bullshit about how they will kill you if you talk, I will hurt you."

Brand straightened. Fuentes craned his neck to see his assailant. He opened his mouth to speak. Brand shook his head and grunted in warning.

"I predict a line of bullshit coming. I will pass this test. Think before you speak."

"I don't know where he is."

Brand pulled the pistol and pressed the barrel against Fuentes' leg just above the knee cap. He pulled the trigger. The muffled sound of the shot sent a slug into his leg.

Fuentes' scream was a shriek like Brand had never heard. Tears streamed from his eyes. Snot dripped from his broken nose. Brand felt surprise at how easy this was for him. He wasn't sure if he was hard-hearted, or if his dispassionate attitude was due to his sense of loss.

Fuentes continued to wail and blubber. Brand struck him across the face.

"Man up, old man. This ends when you tell me what I ask. Where is he?"

Fuentes spit blood and grimaced at the horrible pain in his leg.

"He lives with his uncle on the southwest side of town."

"I need an address."

"I don't have one."

Fuentes winced as Brand leaned closer.

"I don't know", the old man yelled.

Brand believed him. He thought about what Christina had said. "They know you all the way to the top of the organization."

"Who do you work for?"

Fuentes' battered face registered alarm. Brand gripped the Sig more tightly. The older man began to cry. Tears streamed down his cheeks. Brand fought his feelings of pity for the broken old man.

"Don Rafa Cantu. He runs the Juarez Cartel. He is here in town. I can tell you where he is if you let me go."

"I don't negotiate with killers", Brand said with a tight grit to his voice.

"I am not a killer. I am only a recruiter. I am a small fish in a big pond. What I have told you so far has ended my life if I can't escape the organization."

"Okay. I'm listening. Tell me about this Rafa guy."

Fuentes groaned from the pain. Brand suspected he would pass out before long. Finally, Fuentes took a ragged breath.

"Don Rafa is in town to make a deal with the gang called Tango Blast to transport and distribute his product here in the U.S.

"The DEA and ATF task forces have disabled much of our long-time networks. The *Sicario* who shot you is named Miguel. He has been eliminating those remaining elements of the network that have not been arrested. Your friend was one of those loose ends. We had information that you were involved with his theft from us. That made you a target."

Brand nodded. His mind whirled at the scope of what he was involved in.

"Where is this Miguel? If not an address, then something else."

Fuentes closed his eyes and shook his head helplessly.

# Chapter 34

Miguel entered the dusty alley behind Fuentes' house. He drove slowly. His attention was focused on the blue Ford pickup parked behind the garage. He was certain it was the same truck which had been parked near Christina's house the previous night. He parked beside the truck and got out of the Toyota, the heavy pistol in hand. He was unsure what the truck meant, but he suspected it was not good. He passed through the open gate beside the garage. Whoever entered last was not accompanied by Fuentes. He was strict about closing doors and gates.

Miguel felt his quickened blood flow warm his hands and his ears. He always experienced an odd warming of his extremities when he was near a killing.

He approached the side door carefully. The door was slightly ajar. This last inconsistency made it a certainty that the truck carried trouble: trouble for Fuentes and, likely, trouble for him. He pushed the door open enough to squeeze his lean frame through. The cold air chilled him.

Brand looked down at Fuentes. The older man was sweating, and his skin had faded to a pallor which lightened his swarthy skin. The outlaw was going into shock. Brand had received military training to identify and treat for shock in battlefield situations. He identified it, but he had no desire to treat for it.

His scrutiny of Fuentes occupied him, and he did not see the skulking figure of Miguel in one of the many TV screens to his right. However, his position did allow him to see movement at the kitchen door as Miguel peered cautiously around the frame. The Sicario aimed hastily and fired.

Brand spun on his left foot and the heavy slug meant for him struck Fuentes in the head. Bits of hair, brain and flesh mottled the TV screens. Brand sent two shots in the general direction of the shooter.

Although his view was brief, Miguel had seen enough of the scene inside the room to recognize that the American he sought stood over a bloody Fuentes. The bullets from the American's gun zipped through the doorway like angry hornets. They spatted against the back wall, knocking plaster onto the floor.

Miguel risked another quick look into the room. He saw the American jump for cover behind a metal filing cabinet near the right-hand wall. Miguel fired two more shots; both struck the steel filing cabinet behind which Brand had taken shelter.

Miguel fled out the kitchen door. He sprinted down the sidewalk and jumped into the Toyota. He turned the key and was moving down the alley before Brand made it to the end of the narrow sidewalk. He recognized the car as a white Toyota Corolla but nothing more. He returned to the house, grabbing a towel as he went through the kitchen. He quickly wiped his prints off the chair. He avoided looking at the mangled remains of Fuentes. As an afterthought he took the remaining roll of wire with him.

He looked around him for anything he might have missed. Two nine-millimeter shell casings caught his eye. The brass was an easy clue. The cops would be all over this place. He shouldn't leave any more evidence than the traces they might find that he couldn't remove. He pocketed the brass then looked for the expended casing from where he had shot Fuentes. He found it under the green steel desk. Returning to the kitchen, he wiped the doorknob, closing the door behind him.

He wiped the rough metal of the gate, though he doubted the uneven surface would yield a decent print. He started his truck and drove away.

Although he searched closely, he saw no sign that anyone had heard the gun fight inside a house only a few doors away. He made his way towards the freeway, alert for any sign of the Toyota.

# Chapter 35

Miguel drove with abandon. His thoughts whirled in a manner he could not control. He had gone from hunter to hunted in an instant. His was not an intellect which pounced upon an idea like a cat on a darting mouse. His way was meandering and plodding.

His immediate reaction was blank surprise. How did the American find Fuentes? What was he missing, where this construction worker could truss Fuentes and beat him? Fuentes was a veteran in the service of the cartel. He was armed at his desk and he had numerous security cameras at his disposal.

The truck! That blue Ford pick-up was significant. The truck was near Christina's house, though some distance down the block. Was the American stalking her house? How long had he been there prior to Miguel's arrival? How long was he there after?

Grim thoughts crowded Miguel's mind, vying for dominance. One dark image fought to the forefront like a manic fan at a crowded concert. The American had been in Christina's house. Why? His first conclusion was too uncomfortable to readily accept. He rejected the image which flashed within his pained imagination. He fought the sight of Christina and the American together, coiled with one another. Christina was his alone. Time would see to that.

His slow reasoning searched elsewhere. He drew temporary solace from the content of his last meeting with her. Christina was certain of the need to eliminate the associate of the bearded smuggler. Although Miguel had arrived at the decision to finish him, she seemed well behind the idea. It was her resolve which had endorsed his actions thus far.

Miguel gripped the steering wheel until his knuckles showed white. How else would the American have known the identity and location of Fuentes? Had he tortured her for information? Had she volunteered what she knew?

Miguel's inner conflict fell away from him, leaving him clear and purposeful. He didn't trouble himself with motive or the search for a corroborating rationale. Christina would tell him what he wanted to know. If she was unharmed, she had volunteered information and was no longer a prize in his estimation. She was an enemy to the Cartel and to him also.

He reached for his phone. He pulled a number from his contacts and hit 'call.' The other end picked up on the first ring.

"*Coma*?" said the voice on the phone.

Miguel spoke Spanish in reply.

("Fuentes is dead, killed by the American. Christina told him how to find him.")

("And Christina?")

("She is dead also"), Miguel lied. He felt no qualms with the lie, being that he would make the statement true in a very few minutes.

("The American killed her?")

Miguel thought he detected anger – possibly hurt – in the voice. Miguel suspected he might not receive the accolades he imagined if it was learned he had killed her. He would confess once emotions had run their course.

("*Si, Don Rafa*. The American got the information he needed and killed her.")

("Do not stop until you have brought me the head of this American.")

The phone went dead.

Miguel had concocted a story he believed was likely without any hard evidence. He had no choice now but to kill Christina. He sensed he would need to act quickly before Don Rafa sent men to confirm Miguel's report.

He stepped on the gas, moving from lane to lane, weaving along the four-lane expressway. He would no longer sit outside of the little stone house. He felt an eagerness rooted as much in desire as it was in curiosity.

# Chapter 36

Christina glistened with tanning oils. She wore large sunglasses and a small two-piece swimsuit. She paced around a chaise lounge next to the sparkling waters of her backyard pool. She held her phone to her ear. She looked vacantly at the pool as she listening to the voice on the phone.

"*Si.* Everything is arranged on this end. Product is already in place. The courier service is confirmed."

She listened to a similarly vague style of conversation from the other end of the call. Their way was simple but effective. Speak in English always. Use terms common to any business operation. One never knows who is listening.

"I will notify you if there is a change. Have fun."

She ended the call and set the phone on the pebbled concrete in the shade of her lounger. Her thoughts returned to the pleasant memory of last night. Brand was a growing preoccupation with her. No matter how she reasoned away the pleasantness of her impression of him, she found undeniable comfort in the idea she would see him again. After much deliberation and self-deprecation, she had allowed herself the luxury of him in her busy mind.

A small twinge of worry darkened the horizon of her busy thoughts. He would act on the note he had found. What were the ramifications? Her position within the organization was strong, but how would he carry out his part in the actions she had initiated through the careless note? Would his activities lead back to her?

She maintained her belief that the loss of Fuentes and, with luck, Miguel would be a benefit to the cartel and Don Rafa. The Don didn't know it, nor did he believe it, but Christina understood the workings of a man's mind. Men are always enthralled with the daring. Good business rendered the sentiment counterintuitive for the continued success of a risky enterprise.

Her thoughts paused at the sensation of an errant trickle of perspiration. The droplet ran down her neck and slid between her shoulder blades. She wound her hair in a knot and stepped into the cool waters of the pool. She smiled at the sensation of the water receiving her heated flesh. She lowered herself until only her head remained above the water.

She floated slowly towards the deeper end of the pool, eyes closed. A faint pleasant smile arched her lips. She languished for some time in this manner before the water began to feel chilly and she once more desired the heat of the sun on her skin.

She returned to the shallow end and the arched stairs. She stepped from the pool, water beading and dripping from her lean body. She stopped at the pool's edge.

Before her stood the *Sicario*, Miguel. He gawked at her body with an unabashed openness. His brazen leering appraisal troubled her. He was somehow different since their last meeting. Her intuition buzzed its low but firm warning. She was immediately on guard, though she did not yet know why.

"Miguel", she said evenly. "Why are you here at my home?"

"Fuentes is dead", he replied.

She perceived that he was watching her closely. He seemed to be gauging her reaction to the news. With a shock she knew Brand had killed him. She covered her thoughts with a measured query.

"How?"

"The American killed him", Miguel lied.

"You have not eliminated him yet?"

Christina suspected that Miguel knew something he wasn't telling her.

"He never came back to his apartment. I found him at Fuentes' house. He had him tied to a chair and was torturing him when I arrived."

"You didn't kill him there?"

"I tried. He fired back. He had the advantage. I will kill him soon enough."

Miguel recounted the events confidently. She could see that he was certain in the inevitability of his victory.

"So why are you here? This is inappropriate. My home is not open to you."

Miguel frowned. Christina felt a twinge of fear growing slowly. Where was the shyness? Where was the boy who averted his eyes when she entered a room? Who was this leering character with the confidence of...? What did he know?"

"The pool is nice", he observed. "It is a shame there is no one to share it with you."

"I prefer it this way", she said sternly. "Shouldn't you find the American and finish the job?"

Miguel laughed lightly. His eyes looked over every inch of her. His lust was openly displayed. His recklessness was an important detail. He demonstrated no restraint with her. Dread chilled her despite the summer heat. He knew the truth. She felt blood drain from her ears leaving cold fear.

"Don Rafa may come by at any moment. He would not be pleased to see you here."

"Don Rafa is not coming here", Miguel assured her softly. "We should go inside. It is hot out here."

Christina leveled at him a look of disapproval. She moved to the lounger and retrieved her phone.

"We will see what he says about your impertinence and your leering disrespect."

She activated the phone and opened her phone call app.

"Put down the phone, Christina", he said in a low but threatening tone. She looked up from the phone. He held the big revolver. The dark cavernous barrel covered her steadily. "Inside."

She led the way up the stairs and through the opened spacious accordion doors leading into the living room. Miguel paused long enough to close the doors. He looked around the room.

"Nice house", he said. Where is your bedroom?"

"You are an animal", Christina spat at him. "No woman would give you a second thought. Is this how you get what you want?"

Miguel bared his teeth as his anger grew.

"You will do what I want", he assured her. His tone held a growl which seemed unnatural given the thin timbre of his voice. "Move!"

She turned towards her bedroom. Her heart and her thoughts raced desperately. Of the few things she knew about the young man, she knew he was a merciless killer. She knew she was in mortal peril. She also knew that her life depended upon her decisions over the next few minutes. She halted before the bed and turned to face him. She felt terribly exposed in the wet bikini.

"Undress", he commanded in a breathless voice.

She fought the weakness rising within her. Her tears burned the back of her eyes. She fought for control. She needed her wits about her. As casually as she could, she drifted towards the closet, loosening the ties at her swimsuit.

"Where are you going?" He demanded.

"Just to the closet. I have a wrap."

"You don't need a wrap", he said firmly. His eyes were wide, and his breathing rushed with his desire. Perhaps she could use his discomfiture against him.

"I know I can't stop you, so might I not at least make it as comfortable as I can."

Miguel seemed confused by her acquiescence. Christina reached the closet and slid the door open. She removed her top. Her exposed breasts occupied all his attention. The heavy revolver sagged slightly in his hand as his attention focused upon her nakedness. She pushed her bikini bottoms to the floor. He stood stock still, taking her in.

He moved the pistol to his left hand and worked to unfasten his belt. She bent over, into the closet showing him everything he desired.

She grasped the black nine-mil in the shoe box on the floor. She looked back over her shoulder. His focus was completely on her naked back side. He fumbled at the button and zipper on his pants.

She straightened, spinning around. She brought the little automatic up rapidly. Too late, he stepped back a half step and hurriedly tried to cover her with the revolver. She fired first but the bullet went wide, breaking the mirror over her dresser. She saw his pistol rise in his left hand as if in slow motion. Although his motion seemed slow, she could not force herself to react as quickly as she felt she should have.

The big gun bucked and belched fire. He wasn't experienced firing with his left hand and the bullet went wide and splintered several louvres on the closet door.

She fired again – a snap shot in panic due to the near impact of his shot. Her bullet went wide over his shoulder, causing him to duck. He moved the gun to his right hand and raised it on line to fire. He closed one eye as he took careful aim.

Two gunshots sounded in quick succession from beyond the bedroom. Miguel jolted sideways, colliding with the chest of drawers.

Blood spread from the bullet wounds in his side. He crumpled to the tile floor. The pistol clattered a distance from him. His eyes squinted in pain as he searched for the shooter.

Brand entered the room, his Sig at the ready. He kicked the big revolver out of reach and moved to the cowering, naked figure of Christina. He helped her upright.

She threw her arms around his neck and pulled him close. She shuddered, and tears filled her eyes with the release of the terror at how close death had come to her. Her mouth sought his. She kissed him over and over. His face grew wet from her tears and her kisses. He held her tightly, letting her work past her impassioned state. After several moments where her desperate kisses slowed and she held to him weakly, she leaned back and gazed into his eyes.

"Thank you", she said in a voice husky with spent emotion. "He would have killed me."

Brand looked down at her and nodded grimly. His own emotions were frazzled. He had never shot nor killed anyone before this. The finality of the act was dawning on him. The adrenalin and the heat of the moment were giving way to the dire reality of the dead body across the room.

"Get dressed, Christina. We have to leave this place."

"What about him?" she asked, nodding at Miguel's corpse.

"Do you own this house?"

"The organization owns it."

"They can deal with it. He probably told them about me which means they will figure out who told me how to find the old man."

"You killed Fuentes?" she asked incredulously. She was again surprised at his self-possession in the dispensing of violence and death.

"No. This shithead kid missed me and hit him."

Christina nodded as she moved from him. She pulled clothing from the closet. Although they had been together intimately mere hours earlier, he averted his eyes and left her alone in the bedroom. From the living room he wondered if he should have stayed with her rather than leave her alone with a dead body. He reasoned that she had likely seen more dead men than he had.

In moments she emerged from the bedroom dressed in jeans, a black tee shirt and high heeled boots. She carried a leather tote bag.

"I'm ready", she announced.

# Chapter 37

B rand packed his things into the blue gym bag. Christina sat at the little table next to the air conditioner. The motel room was dark save for slanting rays of sunlight spilling through a gap between the heavy drapes. They did not speak, lost in the troubles of their own thoughts.

Brand marveled that he felt no guilt in killing the young Mexican. He searched his heart for any sense of remorse, or whatever he might feel about the killing. Maybe he was numbed by the salve provided by revenge. He reasoned that vengeance might involve an accompanying sense of dark accomplishment. Perhaps he might have reveled in the grisly victory, his grief sated at the cost of the killer's life. He found no misplaced elation. Nor did he feel his thoughts receding into the darkness of the murder he had committed. Murder? The word seemed unrelated to what he had done. He had done what was required to accomplish an end.

"Are you okay", Christina asked, her voice drawing him from his brown study.

He looked at her. He was surprised by her intent scrutiny.

Christina searched his face and his manner for some sense of his mental state resulting from the killing of Miguel. She was no stranger to death. Rarely was it in such proximity, but the presence of it permeated the business of which she was a part. She had observed its effects on many who had taken a life. Everyone processed it differently. Those who dealt best with killing rarely hailed from the innocent public. There was a glimmer of despair in the makeup of those who could abide with the responsibility of the deed.

She was in grave danger and she had to know if she could count on Brand. He had surprised her in his acceptance of his role in this violent situation as a matter of course. Killing Miguel was the singular step he, or anyone, could take which tested one to the breaking point. Would he break?

Brand didn't answer her question right away. He explored his resolve with a deliberate provocation of his feelings. He forced himself to relive the killing in his mind. He recalled every detail, even the crack of breaking ribs as his slugs splintered bone as it entered the boy's body. He felt nothing.

He focused on Christina.

"I am fine", he said with a casual steadiness that roughened her skin with goose flesh.

She believed him.

Brand zipped his gym bag.

"Come on", he said and headed for the door.

She rose and followed him obediently out the door and to his truck.

"Where are we going now?" She asked, opening the passenger door.

Brand didn't reply until they were seated, and the truck was running.

"This Don Rafa, is he the kind of guy who lets things go?"

Christina smiled doubtfully in spite of herself.

"His way is to finish every job, one way or the other."

"Fuentes told me he is the head of the Juarez Cartel."

"Not even close", Christina said with a firm shake of her head. "The *Cabeza de la Serpiente* would never risk crossing the border for the sake of making a deal. Every law enforcement organization in America, from the local Sheriff to the FBI, is continually on alert on the long chance that he would be that stupid. Rafa works for Don Rojas."

"You're saying, killing Rafa won't get these guys off my tail?"

"We are both dead, *Mejo*. We may escape for a while, but our fates are sealed."

Brand put the truck in reverse without speaking. He resented her verdict of death. He felt within himself a strength which ensured his doubtful suspicions were only a possibility rather than a certainty. He had almost everything he needed to control his destiny. He required one more thing. He needed more ammo.

# Chapter 38

Detective Hernandez squatted low to see the victim's face. The deceased was an older man, possibly in his fifties. He was bound to a steel chair with some type of light gauge wire. His head was broken like a thrown melon. His brains were sprayed upon a bank of closed-circuit TV's on the wall, apparently the result of a large caliber gunshot wound. A smaller caliber gunshot wound, possibly a nine-millimeter, was apparent in the right leg, just above the knee.

Hernandez straightened stiffly. He surveyed the room. The living room was filled with electronic communications and surveillance equipment. A tall black filing cabinet showed two dents. Again, the damage appeared to be the result of two large caliber slugs.

Four investigators pored over every detail of the crime scene. Hernandez watched them as his mind worked. He knew of this man. His name was Obduleo Fuentes, a security services and alarm vendor.

His name had come up on occasion in a number of his investigations related to gangs and drug activities. Although he was known, there had been no evidence to tie him to any of the crimes. The sight of Fuentes bound to a chair, tortured, and murdered might indicate his involvement despite the lack of evidence.

Hernandez went to the file cabinet and cast his gaze along the line he determined to be the path of the bullets. He looked beyond the kitchen door. The back wall showed two ragged holes, below which lay a small pile of white dust and wall board.

Hernandez turned to one of the busy investigators.

"Joseph", he called. "Take a look in the kitchen with me."

Joseph, a youngish man in a crime scene Sani-suit followed Hernandez into the kitchen.

Hernandez pointed at the bullet holes.

"We have a second gunman - smaller caliber weapon. It looks like the killer interrupted a meeting and the two gunmen had it out."

Joseph glanced at Hernandez with a wry grin.

"Some meeting", he grunted. "I'll process it."

Joseph turned on his heel and returned to the living room.

Hernandez walked slowly to the side door. He inspected the door for clues. It was slightly ajar. A uniformed officer stood sentry outside. He stepped aside as Hernandez descended the stairs.

From the narrow sidewalk he looked both directions along the fence line which marked the property boundary. He saw nothing out of the ordinary besides the police cars on the street before and in the alley behind the house.

He walked the sidewalk towards the alley. Passing through the rear gate, he looked around at the small group of spectators outside the yellow crime scene tape. A photographer snapped pictures of tire tracks. A uniformed officer held up a note pad and Detective. Hernandez nodded him over. He stepped towards the garage and waited for the officer.

"No one seems to have heard anything: no gunshots or anything out of the ordinary."

The officer indicated an elderly woman standing to the side, talking with a female police officer.

"Mrs. Maria Machado found the body. She visited him regularly, bringing him meals and homemade *tamales*. She says he lived alone but received many house guests daily. From her descriptions, most were Hispanic males in their late teens to early twenties. She claims that Fuentes was active in the community. Mainly he ran an impromptu youth outreach program where he helped troubled youths get jobs, primarily in the construction sector. He told her that he gave the boys an alternative to gang violence and drugs."

Hernandez watched the old lady and the female officer as he listened.

"Anything else?" he asked.

"I asked her if there were any cars or persons she saw visit regularly. She claimed that it was common to see a large black SUV parked here behind the garage. Otherwise, she rarely saw the same car or people twice. She mentioned that lately she had noticed a beat-up white sedan a couple of times, driven by a thin, young, Latin male. Her description was pretty general."

"Thanks Tim."

"No problem" Tim replied as he turned his pad to a blank page. "We are canvassing the neighborhood. I'll drop a copy of my report on your desk."

Hernandez crossed the yellow tape and walked the alley. He turned onto the paved street and continued along until he reached his unmarked Ford in front of Fuentes' house. He started the car and drove slowly through the neighborhood.

He suspected that ballistics would confirm that the slug that killed the victim and dented the file cabinet would be a soft tipped .357 magnum – the same as the weapon used in the Brand apartment killings and the murder at the taco restaurant.

Nine-millimeter was the most common caliber among pistols. The .357 Magnum was the common weapon in these crimes. Based on eyewitness reports, and the slugs recovered from the apartment and restaurant victims, the murder weapon had been a heavy revolver. The extreme trauma to Fuentes' head would indicate a large caliber soft tipped slug, probably a .357 magnum.

Hernandez needed to talk with Carson Brand again. He radioed dispatch, asking for uniformed officers to meet him at the motel where he had last seen Carson Brand.

He arrived at the motel within a half hour of departing the Fuentes crime scene. Brand's room door stood open; a uniformed police officer waited just inside the room.

Hernandez shoved the shifter into park, and he stepped from the unmarked sedan.

"He's not here", the officer reported, nodding over his shoulder towards the empty room.

Hernandez shouldered past him and made a quick search of the room. The officer watched him, wearing a grim smile at the pointless search.

'Perhaps', the cop thought, 'the Detective suspected he hadn't looked under the bed.'

Hernandez returned to face the officer. He read his name tag.

"Officer Perez", he said sharply. "You were on the monitoring detail for Carson Brand?"

"Yes sir", Perez replied unsure of where this was going.

"When was the last time you saw him or any sign of his presence here?"

The officer looked down as he worked to remember details.

"His truck hasn't been parked in the parking lot since yesterday evening. We followed the monitoring routine to the letter."

"And you didn't feel it was worth reporting?"

"I didn't feel what was worth reporting?" Perez challenged.

"The prolonged absence of a person of interest in an ongoing investigation."

Officer Perez opened his mouth to speak. Frustrated with the accusation, his teeth clicked together in mute defiance.

"Put an APB out for the apprehension of Carson Brand."

"Yes, sir", was the simple reply and the officer left the room.

Hernandez slammed the motel room door as he returned to his car.

"Incompetence", he muttered turning the key.

He maneuvered the unmarked car out of the parking lot and headed back to the police station. He had plenty of paperwork to keep him occupied until they caught up with Brand.

# Chapter 39

Brand left the motel office holding a key on a yellow plastic oval key chain. The motel was straight out of an episode of *77 Sunset Strip*. It was a perfect place for them to hide out. It was off the beaten path and the management accepted cash.

Christina watched him dubiously as he settled in behind the wheel.

"Some gangster you are", he said with a grin. "You are used to five-star treatment. This is how the victims and the fugitives live."

Christina frowned at his deprecating humor. He was right, she admitted, she had come a long way from her roots in Juarez only to again plunge to the bottom so abruptly. Her pride struggled with the reality of her situation.

Brand drove around the central courtyard of the motel property. The tidy green square contained manicured flower beds and a rectangular concrete swimming pool. Christina's thoughts conjured images of the pool behind her house. The dream had been so brief.

Brand parked in a slot before a room door identified with a painted number eight. She followed Brand into the dark room. She set her bag on the queen size bed and sat beside it.

Brand dropped his bag on the floor and faced Christina. He stood silently for a long moment. He looked at her, but hardly saw her through his busily churning thoughts. Finally, he reached into his pocket and withdrew a crumpled slip of paper. Christina recognized it as the note he had found in her notebook. He sat next to her and looked at the note. Finally, he turned slightly towards her.

"I need your help", he said, gesturing with the crumpled paper.

Christina knew his meaning. She had been willing to be the casual recipient of his actions before, why not continue to aid in that regard? Her resistance to the idea surprised her. Loyalty was a guiding principle in her character, but she was as much in danger as he. No amount of continued allegiance to the organization would close the rift between she and the cartel. She looked at the note as if it were a physical manifestation of her weakness: maybe it was.

"What can I tell you?" Christina asked with a shake of her head. Her fear harbored doubt. Her doubt bred a crippling despair at the futility of any effort to resist the forces that would be brought to bear against them.

"Tell me everything you know about the people you work for ", he said gently. "You may know something that you think is unimportant but might be a key to our survival."

Christina laughed hollowly.

"Survival", she repeated bitterly. "We are dead already."

"Give that shit a break for a minute."

His words were harsh, but his tone was gentle. She looked into his eyes. Somehow, she drew a small measure of comfort from his strength of will. With that relief came a reluctance to admit the horrible role she had played in the organization. His friend and his girl were dead largely because of her actions and decisions in the affair. She could not bring herself to dwell on her participation. If Brand suspected what she had done, he would react in a manner she was certain would be unpleasant for her. She re-examined her situation, hoping to find some way to salvage any aspect of her life from the ruins she imagined.

With a conscious effort she swallowed her shame. Her resolve could not bolster her confidence to a degree that she might hold his gaze. Her eyes dropped to her hands in her lap. She drew a deep breath before she spoke.

"The organization generates revenue in two ways: drugs and human trafficking. We...they smuggle drugs into the U.S. - mostly it is Cocaine. Marijuana is not as profitable as it used to be now that many states have legalized it. We smuggle immigrants in, and on occasion we transport girls. "

She looked at Brand. His eyes shone with a hardness she had not seen before. Her heart fell under his disapproving scrutiny. She looked away. She fought the warm discomfort behind her eyes where tears formed.

"Fuentes was one of our anchors on this side. He ran a security company that installed alarms and contracted security guards for local businesses. Most of the guards were non-commissioned making it easier for him to plant operatives. These operatives aided us in distribution and transport of our goods and services. On occasion, Fuentes would recruit young, underprivileged boys as *Sicarios*. These are hitmen for the organization. We prefer American Latinos because they are free to move back and forth across the border where a Mexican national could not.

"Over the last few years we constructed tunnels under the river at points where we purchased American ranches. Couriers shuttle our goods and passengers into holding areas, then we transport them around the country in smaller quantities and groups. If we were to release large groups of people into the population centers along the border, it wouldn't be long before authorities pinpointed our entry points.

"With the arrest of many of the leaders of what you call 'the Mexican Mafia', much of our old infrastructure was exposed. After a rash of seizures of large overland shipments by American officials, we had to bring our tunnel operations on line sooner than expected. Miguel and other cells in Laredo, Eagle Pass and Del Rio, took out any remaining assets with knowledge of our new distribution network.

"Don Rafa Cantu is here to tie the new distribution chain into the larger gangs in metropolitan areas near the border crossings.  He is responsible for the success of all operations north of the border. He is second only to *Cabeza de la Serpiento*, Pablo Rojas."

"I've heard of him", Brand muttered grimly. "Where do you fit into this whole thing?"

"I do little involving the operation of the cartel", she said earnestly. "I am a liaison for highly placed visitors and officials."

Christina darkened with embarrassment.

"I ensure they feel welcome."

# Chapter 40

**B**rand pursed his lips, nodding his understanding. Her eyes flashed anger at his immediate rush to judgement of her.

"You know nothing about me", she spat, her shame disguised as anger.

Brand put a hand on her shoulder.

"Calm down. We all have to make a living. I've done things I'm not proud of too. Let's focus on those things that matter."

Christina eyed him suspiciously. She had only done what she had to do! She had arrived here with one of those shipments of girls. Her fate would have been much more dire if she had not caught the eye of a highly placed distributor here in the states.

"Is Cantu the older guy I saw you with in the cowboy hat?"

Christina looked at him in surprise.

"Yes. How...?"

"I watched you at the Mexican restaurant last night."

She nodded her understanding.

"If you are only the entertainment on this cruise, why do you seem to be in charge at some level? You weren't at the job site to entertain high ranking officials. You didn't take Cantu up on his offer last night. Frankly, I get a sense that you are more than you say you are."

Christina studied Brand for a long moment. He was sharp.

"I have been with the organization for a long time, in cartel years."

Brand nodded at the dark humor of her statement.

"It is convenient for me to handle certain matters rather than expose others to the risk and expense of handling those matters themselves."

Brand studied her carefully. She inferred from his manner that he was re-evaluating her, considering her newly revealed role within the organization.

"So, Hernandez was right about you", he said thoughtfully.

"Who is Hernandez?" she asked.

"Detective Gabe Hernandez, San Antonio PD."

"I see", she said softly. Her problems were growing.

"He grilled me pretty hard too. We are in this thing together, as I see it."

"What is your plan, now that you know what I know?"

"My understanding is that we are in danger from Cantu and his goons, the local gangs here, and the cops at every level of the government."

Christina eyed him expectantly. He was only confirming her doubts about their situation.

"Let's start with Cantu. Where is he?"

Christina shook her head.

Brand rose from the bed. He went to his bag, unzipping it as he moved to the bathroom vanity. He withdrew the Sig and checked the clip. He was down to eight rounds. He replaced the clip and returned it to the bag.

He turned back to Christina, leaning against the vanity. She sat on the bed, her legs crossed. She was a beautiful woman in Brand's view. He wasn't sure exactly what she meant to him, but he was certain he wanted to keep her safe. Under her calm façade, he sensed she was shaken to her core. More than anyone, she knew what they faced, and he thought he saw clear signs that it terrified her.

"Tell me what you want to do", he demanded with slight heat.

He was in a situation for which he had no basis of experience nor training. Her short comments of dread and fatality helped him none. She had been in the organization long enough that she should have some idea what to do next.

Christina watched him mildly. An overpowering sense of fatigue weighed upon her like wet clothes. She wanted nothing more than to get under the blankets and hide in the dark room. She had heard of many who had tried to escape the grip of the cartel. None of those succeeded. Without exception, they had all died.

Brand waited for a response. She continued to look at him even as her eyes reddened and filled with tears. By degrees, her posture wilted. Finally, she collapsed on the bed. She snaked upward until her head rested upon a pillow. She pulled the gold floral print bedspread over her and turned her body towards the wall, away from Brand. She shuddered visibly under the covers.

Brand assumed she was weeping. He watched her for a long time before he finally joined her on the bed. Christina lay with her back to him. Her breathing was not rhythmic as when one was asleep. She was awake, plagued by her own thoughts. He settled deeper into the pillow. Outside he heard voices as others passed the door headed to their own rooms. The passersby laughed softly as they spoke together in low tones.

Brand thought back upon his daily troubles of less than a month ago. His life had seemed stressful. Worries about obtaining construction jobs, making payroll, and struggling with Bert's irregular hours had seemed difficult. He realized dejectedly that he would gladly trade his old troubles for these new deadly problems in an instant.

He laughed with a short grunt filled with pathos. He crossed his arms defiantly. He knew with certainty he would never be the same. The evolution had already begun. He had tortured one man and killed another that very day. What a thing to say. He scarcely believed the reality of it.

Christina moved slightly; a small groan escaped her. Her breathing and the noises she made told him she had drifted into a troubled sleep.

His thoughts drew him back to his musings of a strange self-analysis. How long would he feel this fascination with his new role as a...what was he now? The mantle murderer seemed to fit presently.

Hadn't he acted in defense of another person? The kid, what did she call him? A *Sicario* – killer – is what he was. Killing him was justified and necessary. In his view, that didn't mark him as a murderer.

Once more, he marveled at the distance he was able to maintain from feelings of fear, regret and guilt. He hadn't asked for any of this. He was drawn into a world peopled by the lowest class of society who dwelled in the dirt and filth of life's dark maw.

His face flushed as raw anger worked within him. The idea that people could be so imbued with a lust for money, that they would stoop to any act to obtain it, infuriated him. Moreover, their fervor had spilled outside of the pages of newspapers, the monotone reporting of disconnected television anchors, and the dark minds of movie-makers. The unbelievable stories of those unfortunate few had seemed sad but distant. He was now one of those hapless victims about whom he had read in the news stories. His life was forever changed, and for what?

The irresistible quality of his life's path frustrated him. The helplessness of his situation infuriated him. The feeling was a palpable thing to him. He drew comfort from its innate power.

This feeling of rage and desire! Black dog is what he used to call it. The description was innately accurate. Its call was more that of a wolf than a dog – a wolf with a hunger for violence that would not ever be satisfied. At its strongest, he felt an ache. He tasted a metallic emptiness in his mouth. If he gave into it, he might surrender with a frustrated whine like a wolf on a heavy chain.

He felt embarrassment. He was trying too hard to define a baser instinct he had frequently harnessed since he was old enough to experience conflict.

In elementary school he was a small skinny kid. Joe Dove had shoved him down in an alley on his way home from school. Later, Gary Bitner had punched him in the face.

He remembered the words of his father as he had looked at Brand's young bloodied face. He had held out his hand before the small boy.

"Hit my hand", his father had commanded softly.

Brand had punched the hand, the blow hardened by fresh humiliation.

His father leaned in close to Brand.

"That punch would have knocked me down, son."

Brand remembered the glory of hope and the possibilities hinted at within the lesson. His heart sang with an eagerness to use this newly discovered power.

Later that day his father had called Brand into the living room. When he arrived, his mother stood behind his father, her face set in stern judgement. His father stood in the center of the room, head down. He placed his hands upon Brand's shoulders.

"Car", he had said gently. "Your mother and I talked it over, and we think I was wrong to encourage you to fight these bullies."

Brand had looked at him with confusion.

"The Bible says we should turn the other cheek. Let the Lord deal with these boys in his way. It is not our place to do God's work."

Brand's looked at his mother, just behind his father, nodding her confirmation at his father's reversal.

Brand remembered the sinking feeling of heart-breaking betrayal. Did King David turn the other cheek when Goliath threatened? Didn't Sampson ask for one last burst of strength to bring down the palace atop his enemies? Didn't Jesus cast out the money changers and the Pharisees?

His father and mother didn't live to see the bullies fall before his toughness and resolve. His father, he was certain, would have been secretly proud of the man he had become. Brand never sought trouble, but he never ran – and he certainly never turned the other cheek. Sorry God.

Brand's thoughts focused once more on the present. Beside him, Christina dozed, her breathing rhythmic and calm. The room was dark, save a glimmer of light finding access around the edge of the heavy drapery.

He saw Bert in his mind's eye. Sorrow tightened around his heart like a slowly constricting belt. He missed his friend. The beautiful Christina provided no comfort from Natalie's memory. No matter their difficulties, he knew he loved Natalie somewhere deep inside him. It may not have been a love which prevailed over hurt feelings or misunderstandings, but it was love, nonetheless.

Like a slowly rising warmth, sleep pulled him from his waking troubles. One moment he was awake surrounded by his worries, the next he was submerged in pleasant but bizarre dreams of Bert, Natalie and his mother and father. It seemed only a moment later that he plunged from a cliff in his old pickup. The ground rushed up to meet him. He awoke with a start, bolt upright.

He moved his hand across the rough bedspread. The covers were flat across the mattress. Christina was gone. He rubbed his dream weary eyes and looked around him. A shaft of bright sunlight sliced into the room. He listened for a moment. There was no sound of movement within the room or the adjoining bathroom. He was alone.

Somehow, he knew Christina hadn't gone out for coffee, leaving him to speculate why she had left him behind. He felt, with a nagging certainty, that she was gone for good. How did he know that?

# Chapter 41

Christina waited at a busy intersection near downtown. She had left Brand at dawn. She had settled upon a course of action the previous night, only half listening to Brand's entreaty for her insight on how to best escape their harrowing situation. Years of experience with the cartel had taught her many things. Chief among those was that the key to survival was sacrifice. Sometimes the sacrificed was of oneself. Other times it required the sacrificing of another. This was a situation involving the latter. Brand was a singularly fascinating man, but her life and her position were a more important consideration.

As for her fears of Rafa: all of this could be explained credibly with the surrender of her knowledge of Brand. He had found the address when he went through her things. She hadn't betrayed anything. She refused to throw away her life's experiences and her hard-won station within the organization for an infatuation.

Although her intentions were justified and calculated, something caused her to take a cab far enough away from the motel room so that the team sent to collect her would not happen upon Brand once she was secured.

She had phoned Rafa directly. His voice, although heavy with disappointment, held an encouraging tone of hope and faith in her doubtful loyalty.

She frowned at her lingering feelings for Brand. Her protective measures were no more than futile delays of the inevitable. His death was her only salvation. She knew the truth, but she couldn't commit to it yet.

A sleek red Corvette stopped at the curb, and the passenger window slid down silently. A burly, tattooed Latino grinned at her with a mouthful of gold teeth.

"Get in, *Mamasota*", he said with a gesture of his well-muscled, colorfully tattooed arm.

Christina turned her head, rejecting the offer. These gang-bangers were coarse and arrogant. An unescorted woman was irresistible to these animals.

"Don Rafa sent me, Christina."

She looked at him in disbelief. Reluctantly, she opened the door and settled into the passenger seat, under the weight of the driver's greedy stare. The Corvette's engine growled as it accelerated into the heavy traffic of the busy street.

# Chapter 42

Don Rafa Cantu was less than pleased with the report from his new friend in Tango Blast. His concern for Christina had resulted in the discovery of an inaccuracy with Miguel's earlier report. After the *Sicario* had reported her dead, Rafa had sent two men to clean the King William house. There, they found no sign of Christina as reported. Instead, they found a dead Miguel.

Cantu felt, with certainty, that the American was involved. He wasn't sure yet how much of what Miguel had told him was accurate, but it was likely that Brand was a danger to them.

It was reasonable that the American had killed "The Ghost" and fled with Christina. Her reported involvement with the American could no longer be doubted. If the authorities were to capture them, her knowledge of the organization could be catastrophic if shared with the police.

Cantu looked up from his pondering. Before him stood a remarkably muscular Hispanic. He was covered in tattoos from below his chin to his hands. Baggy jeans concealed his lower extremities, certain to be as tattooed. The man grinned cruelly. Gold, silver and black filled his mouth where one would expect a smile consisting of teeth.

"You have her?" Rafa asked the leering gangster.

"She is here. My men have her in the study."

"Bring her to me."

The burly man left silently. Moments later he returned, Christina in tow. He pulled her forward and shoved her towards Rafa. The leader restrained a protest at the rough treatment of the beautiful woman. Instead he gestured to him.

"Leave us, Blocks."

The thug shrugged and turned on his heel. He closed the door as he left.

Rafa pointed to a leather overstuffed chair. Christina obediently sat in the chair.

"Why have you betrayed me?" He asked simply.

Christina looked at him with surprise.

Rafa watched the woman. To her credit, she didn't show discomfort, nor did she deny the accusation. She merely looked at the Don with a patient countenance. Rafa waited another moment for her to react. His suspicions were still just that, suspicions. He had no hard evidence against her. His experience told him that her perfidy would ultimately be revealed. Others in her position had betrayed themselves, no matter how clever they were. Secretly, he hoped she would reveal only those facts which would clear her name in this ugly matter.

She was a prize he had coveted for many years. Younger members of the organization had enjoyed her company. Most of those were dead now. He alone controlled the cartel north of the border. He alone held the yolk of authority. She was his or she would no longer belong to anyone.

"Miguel was a liability", she said simply. "His recklessness was a danger to everything you are working towards, Don Rafa."

Rafa nodded. She admitted to the charge of aiding in the death of the *Sicario*.

"Fuentes was all but in the grasp of the authorities. Miguel killed him as the American tortured him for information. Miguel broke into my house and tried to rape and kill me. The American shot him before he succeeded. I acted as if I was enamored with the American. He held me captive until I saw a chance to escape. I fled and called you immediately."

Rafa moved to the leather Devan across from Christina. He sat, crossing his leg over his knee. He smoothed his pants leg, arranging the crease carefully.

"Tell me how you met Mr. Brand", Rafa instructed her.

Although he spoke to her, he examined the seam of his trousers.

"He broke into my house and questioned me at gunpoint."

Rafa looked up with surprise plainly visible on his face.

"At gunpoint", he repeated. "And what did you tell him while he held you at gunpoint?"

Christina didn't like where the conversation was going. She sensed that danger lurked beneath the casual manner of the Don.

"I told him nothing. He searched my things and found Fuentes' address. He returned after Miguel killed Fuentes and killed Miguel as he was about to kill me."

She paused to measure Rafa's reaction. His eyes had returned to his pants once more.

"I saw that he had found the address, but I knew he would kill them both for killing his friend and his girlfriend. I believed the two would act as payment for his loss."

Rafa nodded absently. Finally, he looked at her.

"What led you to believe this construction worker was a killer?"

"There was something about him that made me feel like he was desperate and would resort to any means to avenge his loved ones."

"Wouldn't it seem more likely that a typical blue-collar *Americano* would go to the police rather than go on a killing spree?"

Christina grimaced in reaction to Rafa's sound logic.

"But he did not go to the police. He did capture Fuentes and kill Miguel."

"Yes, he did", Rafa agreed. Now two of my organization have fallen at the hands of a construction worker. One of my highly placed people helped him do it."

Rafa looked up. He watched her with an unpleasant glint in his eyes.

"It is not my place to say, Don Rafa, but both were liabilities to our organization. I believe them better dead than arrested."

"You are right, Christina. It is not your place to say."

Rafa called out loudly, "Blocks."

The tattoo-covered, muscular gangster opened the door and entered the room, followed by two large *cholos*.

"Take her", Rafa said and looked away as they obeyed.

"Don Rafa", Christina protested.

Her words were cut short by a hard slap across the face from one of the two gangsters who flanked her on either side.

They dragged her roughly across the rich wood flooring of the finely decorated hallway. Blocks opened a door to the right and led her and her captors down a dark flight of cold concrete stairs. The air smelled dank with mildew and stale dirt. They shoved her against a concrete wall and shackled her with heavy manacles fastened to the cold wall.

Blocks tore her clothing from her body. She writhed wildly, trying to prevent him from removing her undergarments. Blocks grasped her neck in a heavily veined grip and tore her bra and panties from her body. She wept, her remaining strength gone with her clothing.

The three men passed their lustful eyes over every inch of her body. Her vulnerability and her helplessness terrified her. Blocks grabbed her left breast and squeezed it painfully. All three laughed at her cry of discomfort.

"We are all going to fuck you, *Mamasota*", Blocks promised her. "One by one, over and over, until there is nothing left of you to take."

Blocks spit in her face. He turned on his heel.

"Fucking *Puta*", he muttered as he led the *cholos* to the stairs.

She heard the loud click of the light switch and the door slammed shut at the top of the stairs. She was immersed in total darkness.

Her body shook, and she felt the humiliating warmth of her bladder releasing down her leg.

"What have I done", she wailed.

Brand was her one hope, and she had tossed him away in favor of a foolish idea that she could bargain with the cartel.

# Chapter 43

Detective Hernandez read the report for the second time. As with so much of this case, he had little hard evidence upon which to base his theories. Something told him that the key to this entire investigation was Carson Brand.

He doubted that even Brand realized his relevance. Hernandez was convinced that Brand was no more than a peripheral character, uninvolved directly with the actions at work around him. Still, there was a deliberate and concerted effort to eliminate him by highly placed forces in the cartel.

Brand was an oddity to Hernandez. He had interviewed many people in his career. Few showed a combination of honest concern and carefully crafted subterfuge simultaneously. Brand answered with candor, but he seemed disconnected from any investment of emotional currency with his testimony.

Victims, particularly, were easily moved with strategic questioning. Their raw reactions were easily manipulated in their weakened emotional state. Perpetrators established a firm boundary beyond which they would not cross when questioned.

Carson Brand seemed open and honest about what he knew, but Hernandez felt distinctly that the man was hiding key details about his experience in Mexico. Hernandez believed Brand was masking strong emotions. Was he intending to go vigilante? Hernandez believed the answer was yes. Were the nine-millimeter slugs from a gun Brand had managed to obtain?

Hernandez suspected Brand was in the middle of a vengeful tirade, to account for the deaths of his loved ones. If what he suspected was true, Brand was a highly functional sociopath. Was he a killer?

The gunshot to Fuentes' knee was inflicted to extract information in a torture interrogation. The two slugs in the kitchen wall were return fire at the killer who had shot Fuentes, maybe by mistake, and took two shots at the interrogator hiding behind the file cabinet. If Brand was the man who tortured Fuentes, what did he learn and what were his goals?

What did they know about Fuentes? Outside of his security business he seemed to have little interest in anything besides his impromptu youth outreach program. Was the killer – the 5-8 Latino - one of his troubled youth? Hernandez leaned back in his chair.

Of course, he thought as it became clear to him. Fuentes was a recruiter for the Cartel. It was possible that the shooter who killed Brand's girlfriend, Salazar in the taco stand, and likely Robert Gotardi, was a *Sicario* recruited by Fuentes. Brand was interrogating him for information about the killer. The *Sicario* had interrupted them and killed Fuentes.

Hernandez picked up the phone on his desk. He dialed the extension to his boss.

"Captain, we need to talk."

# Chapter 44

Brand drove slowly through the strip center. He found the gun store and pulled into an available parking space close by. He entered the store, returning a few minutes later with a box of 9mm ammunition and two large capacity clips for the Sig.

He pulled on a pair of latex gloves and opened the ammo box. He wiped clean each bullet before carefully inserting them into the clips.

With the insight provided by Christina had come a sense of caution. His earlier trip to the grocery store had yielded personal items necessary for his time away from his apartment, and a box of latex gloves. He was unsure of his path forward, but he was going to practice as much caution as he was able.

His thoughts wandered as he performed the mundane task. He shook his head in wonder. Christina was gone. He felt confusion at her disappearance, but he held to the belief that she had returned to the Cartel. The kid would have killed her if Brand hadn't intervened. What if the kid was acting on orders from the cartel? If that were true, Christina was in grave danger if she had indeed made it back to Rafa.

He recalled the older man in the cowboy hat who had accompanied Christina at the restaurant that night. Rafa had seemed almost a father figure in his demeanor towards her. Brand suspected that was an act. Brand believed some men did what was required to get a woman in the sack. Christina was a valuable prize for any man within whom blood flowed. If she had returned to Rafa thinking his feelings for her would stay his hand, she might have walked into a dire situation.

Natalie crossed his mind. He saw her face in his imagination. She was lovely and smiling. Immediately, he felt a pang of sadness. With the emotion came his memory of her face as she fell to the floor, shot dead. Killing the *Sicario* had done nothing to alleviate his pain. The kid had acted on orders from the Cartel. Likely, those orders came directly from Rafa.

Brand backed out of the parking space and made his way onto the busy street. He entered the light traffic with locating the Cartel leader his primary intention. He had no lead other than *La Casa Chapala*. It seemed to be a Cartel hangout, based upon the armed sentries and the grease balls who patronized the place.

Despite Christina's apparent betrayal, Brand held no malice towards her. She was vulnerable as long as they were together. She may have felt she had nothing else but her position with the Cartel. What future did she imagine with Brand? Apparently, she imagined nothing that was better than a risky return to an evil organization. The decision was likely to get her killed.

Brand ground his teeth. He couldn't save Natalie. He would not lose Christina. He made his way south towards the restaurant. He hoped some opportunity would present itself. He doubted anyone would expect him to assume the mantle of aggressor. He hoped to take advantage of the presumption if it was assumed he would run away rather than fight for her.

Just after nightfall he found himself parked across the street from *La Casa Chapala*. His truck occupied the same parking spot it had previously. The restaurant was busy with the comings and goings of well-dressed gangsters and their comely companions. As before, two menacing-looking guards stood sentry at the front doors.

He waited no more than an hour before he watched a black SUV stop before the restaurant's double doors. From the vehicle emerged Rafa, accompanied by three tattooed men in shiny suits. They wore heavy gold jewelry, visible anywhere skin protruded from their clothing. One of the group, a heavily muscled man, grinned at Rafa. His mouth shone with a jeweled and gold 'grill.' In Brand's opinion, without the suits they would have appeared as no more than gangbangers from the South Side.

Brand rubbed his eyes and sat lower in his seat. He vowed to end this nightmare tonight. He was tired of running. His thoughts were not occupied with the thoughts of fighting a powerful cartel. His conflict was with men, not a criminal enterprise. He refused to be intimidated by a reputation or the fear of future reprisal by unseen forces. Rafa, and now the three gangsters in his company, represented a definable and measurable enemy. Let the future bring what it may. To Brand, his course was clear. He blocked all else from his mind.

Several hours later, the four reappeared through the double doors of the restaurant. Rafa seemed no different than he had appeared upon entering the restaurant. His three companions, however, displayed signs of the effects of many cocktails.

The black SUV rolled to a stop before the passengers, obscuring Brand's view of them. He watched as Rafa and the bulky gang leader rounded the front of the vehicle and entered the passenger doors. The SUV pulled away only to halt just beyond the pick-up point. Another shiny SUV stopped before the restaurant and two large suited men entered the back seat. Both SUV's pulled away from the restaurant. They turned onto the street and sped away.

Brand followed at a distance. Rafa's guard had grown to five. Three was a logistical possibility in a fight. Five reduced his odds for victory by half.

He was a veteran of many fights. He could defeat two adversaries in hand to hand conflict. Three doubled the threat. In an armed conflict, three was difficult but manageable. He was presuming Rafa would play a small role if he participated at all. Brand believed that a man committed to his own resources in the face of violence would not require so many guards for an evening of dinner and drinks. Something was happening beyond a meeting with colleagues for cocktails.

Brand felt a gnawing worry for Christina. Although he had no idea whether or not she was in Rafa's control, his instincts told him she was. The entourage he followed might easily be normal operations for a cartel boss, but he had seen Rafa alone with Christina that first night. He rallied a force for some good reason.

Brand followed at a distance for several miles. The drive took Brand north of the city and into a region of rough wooded hill country. The freeway gave way to a smooth divided highway which wound its way into a sparsely populated region of bedroom communities. Some were developed tract housing sub-divisions. Others were larger acreage estates with sprawling homes. The black trucks turned from the highway onto a narrow, paved road leading into one of these larger estate communities.

Brand recognized it as a sub-division in which he had framed several houses. He killed his headlights and followed the tail lights before him. With the aid of the leading vehicles and a dim glow from the rising moon, he was able to stay on the roadway, close behind the cartel vehicles. Brand increased his following distance as brake lights shone and the trucks slowed before turning into a driveway. They waited for the automatic gate to open fully before they passed through. Brand pulled his pick-up to the road side and waited.

Beyond the shielding trees at the road, motion sensor lighting snapped on as the trucks approached a large house. The home was typical of many in that community. It was a two-story stucco structure with large swooping arches and Cantera columns.

Brand referred to the style as *Faux Mediterranean* due to its similarity to the coastal houses of Italy.

Brand watched the steel gate close. He opened the door and stepped out of the truck. He pocketed the two extra mags and the Sig. The homes in the vicinity sat on large lots. He saw no houses or lights of houses nearby. He took comfort that he could use the bordering property for access to Rafa's house without alarming the neighbors. He chose a route to the left of the big house. He jumped the short pig wire fence bordering the neighbor's property and followed the property line until he passed behind the rear line of Rafa's house.

The rear of the house was cast in darkness other than the casual glow of light spilling from the rear windows. Brand climbed the high wrought iron fence protecting the Don's property line. The climb was hazardous in that the balusters terminated in twisted points some inches above the top rail of the fence. By suspending himself above the fence on stiff arms, he was able to plant a foot on the top rail before jumping to the ground on the other side.

Brand squatted low, listening for any sound of an alarm set off by unseen motion sensors. From his position in the darkness of the native foliage, the house remained quiet. The property was landscaped near the house, but more primitively appointed farther away.

Native Dwarf Juniper and sparse grasses covered most of the property. Brand rose and moved cautiously towards the back of the house, carefully avoiding clumps of prickly pear cactus.

He moved stealthily, ready to bolt if his movements activated security lights on the house. He reached the rear corner of the house without setting off an alarm or activating any motion sensor security lighting. The rear of the house was heavily landscaped with cactus and intricate flower beds. Most of the rear windows were aproned by darkly mulched plant beds.

Brand stayed low as he mounted the long porch at the rear of the house. Long arches supporting dozens of hanging flowerpots made up the edges of the porch. The entire back wall was comprised of floor to ceiling windows with large accordion doors in the center.

Brand peeked around one of the arched columns. He saw the six cartel members standing in a loose circle, speaking earnestly. Brand gathered from their body language that they discussed a serious matter.

Rafa listened impassively as the muscular gangster spoke with violent gestures. Rafa's face registered no reaction to the exclamations of the tattooed man. The two large men who had followed in the second SUV crossed their arms and watched Rafa.

Although Brand could not make out the specifics of their conversation, it was obvious that the muscular man was arguing to have his way in the matter they discussed.

Looking quickly around, Brand backed into the darkness beyond the porch and moved towards the side of the house. The sound of a window sash sliding open caused Brand to leap to the ground. He lay flat, in the open lawn just beyond the window. He moved his head slightly until he could see the window. The muscular man stood there. He placed a cigarette in his mouth and scratched a match against the window frame and lit it.

Brand waited anxiously for the man to see him lying in plain sight and sound an alarm. The gangster didn't see him. Brand surmised that his position was in comparative darkness and the man's eyes were not adjusted to see beyond the bright lights of the room. A voice sounded from within inside. Brand heard him clearly.

"He didn't say you couldn't have the whore, *Vato*."

The tattooed man glanced behind him.

"The old man is a fool for the bitch."

There was a pause as the unseen speaker considered his next words.

"She is alone in the cellar. No one would know if we tried a little taste of her."

The smoker inhaled deeply of the cigarette. He exhaled a large cloud of smoke, baring his shining grill.

"True", he said to the night. He flicked the cigarette out the window and pulled it closed. He turned from the window and left the room with his unseen companion.

Brand jumped to his feet and went to the window. He tried the window sash and it opened easily. He pulled himself up and into the room. He drew the Sig from his belt band and checked the breach for a round in the chamber. Satisfied, he moved carefully to the door and peered around the corner. The tattooed man disappeared into a side entrance down the hall. Brand looked in both directions before he moved towards the door through which the gangsters had disappeared.

The door was ajar. Beyond the door, Brand saw a staircase leading below the level of the first floor. Ornate wall mounted lighting fixtures illuminated the stairwell with a dim glow. Brand heard voices raised beyond the stairwell. He heard the faint sound of a woman's voice raised in protest. Brand carefully pulled the door closed then crept silently down the stairs. As he descended the stairs, he could make out what was being said.

"Rafa will kill you if you touch me."

Brand recognized Christina's voice.

"I promised you we would all fuck you. We are the first."

That was the voice of the tattooed man.

There was a period of silence followed by a cry of fear from Christina.

Brand moved beyond the stairwell and into a broad rectangular room. He saw the two men groping a naked Christina. Her mouth was contorted in shame and her eyes were red with tears. Brand trained the Sig on the tattooed man.

"Hey", he called.

The men turned towards his voice.

Brand shot each man in the head. They fell to the concrete floor like sacks of meat.

Brand moved to Christina and examined the shackles. The cuffs were locked. He searched the men for a key. He found none. Christina wept helplessly, turning her body away from him to hide her shame. He tested the anchors attaching the chains to the wall. They held firmly.

Brand shook his head, looking Christina in the eye.

"I need a key", he said simply.

"Rafa has the key", she responded in a weak voice. Her eyes widened at the portent of his words. "Can't you shoot them off?"

Brand looked at her for a moment, weighing his options.

"That only works in movies. Bullets will only dent them at best. Likely, the impact would hurt you. We need the key."

Christina bowed her head, surrendering to the despair she felt.

"Somebody might have heard me shoot these two. We don't have much time."

Brand looked around the cellar. Against one wall, racks filled with wine bottles extended from one side to the other and from floor to ceiling. At the far end was a narrow door. Brand went to the door and opened it. He turned on the light. The room was filled with wiring, security boxes, phone blocks and a large electrical panel. He searched for anything he might use to break the cuffs. He found nothing. He turned off the light and returned to a shivering Christina.

"Is that a way out?" she asked, her voice a whine.

"No", Brand replied. "It is a home run."

She looked at him blankly.

"Sorry", he said. "It's a construction term. It is an electrical utility closet."

Brand leaned over the tattooed man's dead body. He pulled his shiny suit coat off him and wrapped it around Christina. It was large enough that it covered much of her even with her arms spread wide by her restraints.

"I need to find Rafa."

"Don't leave me Brand", she cried desperately.

"I can't wait here, Christina. I have to get the key, or bolt cutters or a hammer and chisel. Everyone knows you are down here. It is only a matter of time before they do whatever they have decided to do with you."

Christina made no comment. Her head was bowed in utter surrender. Her spirit was broken. Brand felt badly for her. Her world as she had known it had ended.

He brushed her hair from her face and lifted her chin until he could look in her eyes.

"I will be back. Don't give up."

Her eyes showed only dull despair.

Brand turned to the stairs. He climbed them two at a time. Pausing at the door, he listened for any sounds of approaching footfalls. The hall was silent. He carefully turned the knob and pulled the door slowly open. After a few seconds of listening, he ventured a look each way down the hallway.

Where were the remaining three thugs? Where was Rafa? Brand turned to his left away from the small room by which he had entered the house. He came to the end of the hallway. It ended in a short vestibule where two flights of stairs rose to the second floor in opposite directions. He took the left flight, climbing the stairs, Sig at the ready.

From the top of the stairs Brand entered a large room with vaulted ceilings and roughhewn exposed beams. Heavy wrought iron chandeliers hung on thick black chains from the high ceilings. Under the chandeliers sat a long table amidst rustic furniture and large canvas paintings on the walls. Opposite him were three doorways. The first two doors were closed. The third was open. He heard voices somewhere beyond the open door.

Brand moved swiftly but silently towards the voices. He leaned lightly against the wall next to the open door.

"I am giving the girl to Blocks and his men. She betrayed us with the American, Brand. "

The voice was that of an older man. Brand assumed it was Rafa's.

"And what of the American?"

The speaker had a heavy accent.

"Kill him. This has gone on long enough. Miguel failed because he lacked resolve. I expect success from two of my best *Sicarios*."

Brand set his jaw. The two men who had joined Rafa were Cartel hit men. He had the drop on them. He acted quickly. Moving through the doorway he had only an instant to survey the room. Three men stood together, and one man sat in a chair to the left of the other three. The two large *Sicarios* had their backs to him. Rafa faced the door and the remaining gang banger from the restaurant sat casually on a leather lounger.

Brand placed his first two rounds center mass in the backs of the hit men. The third shot bored a ragged hole in the seated gangster's neck. Rafa leaped for cover. Brand pursued, kicking the gun he pulled from his clothing. He brought the Sig down hard across Rafa's temple. The old man sagged under the blow. Brand pulled Rafa upright, shoving him roughly against the wall.

One of the *Sicarios* groaned and struggled to rise. Brand shot him again. He ceased his struggles. The seated gangster clasped the wound in his neck and gurgled his last. Brand again gave his full attention to Rafa.

"Give me the key", he demanded without preamble.

Rafa looked at Brand with undisguised interest.

"So, you are the American we have been looking for", he said, his words strained with the pain of his head wound.

"Shut up and give me the key."

"The hero", Rafa commented sarcastically. "You risk everything for a Juarez whore. Typical American sentiment."

"You are a real dumbass, talking shit when I'm holding a gun and a bad case of the red ass. No more small talk: you give me the key, or I go to work on you."

Rafa looked at the dying men in the room.

"Your fate is sealed. You will not see another dawn."

Brand grabbed Rafa by the neck and lifted him off the floor. He struck him twice, hard across the face with the Sig. He slid the pistol into his waistband and frisked the Don quickly. He found no key on his person.

"The key", Brand repeated, pulling his pistol from his waist band.

Rafa 's eyes rolled as he lingered in a place between consciousness and black oblivion. Brand shook him roughly.

"The top drawer in my desk."

Rafa's battered face turned blankly in the direction of a large ornate desk opposite them in the room.

Brand dragged Rafa to the desk. He opened the narrow drawer under the desk top. A silver handcuff key lay in the narrow pen holder among pens, pencils and paper clips. Brand took the key and dropped Rafa into the high-backed chair behind the desk.

Brand turned away towards the door. Behind him he heard rushed movements and a low grunt. He turned to see Rafa pulling a large nickel-plated pistol from a hiding place under the desk. Brand wheeled and took a snap shot. The bullet flew wide and struck a leather-bound tome in the bookshelf behind the Don. Rafa took a hurried shot in return. Brand heard the hiss of the bullet and felt his hair pulled as the bullet narrowly missed him. He pulled the trigger twice more. Rafa grunted as the slugs burrowed into his chest. Brand fired two more shots, finding their mark center mass. Rafa sagged back into the chair making moist hick-up sounds as he tried to breath his last.

Brand turned to the door.

Christina waiting for him in a basement naked and alone, with two dead men, seemed a nightmare. Her anguish, in addition to the possibility that the reports of multiple gunshots might have drawn the attention of neighbors, caused him to sprint back to the cellar. There he found Christina as he had left her. The *cholo's* coat lay below her on the cold floor. Her head sagged atop her naked shaking body. Brand guessed she had been shackled to the wall for some time.

Christina looked up slowly. She peered at him intently for long seconds before she believed her eyes. The possibility that he would return after so much gunfire had seemed an impossibility to her. Her thoughts since his departure had been only to gather about her the last of her strength and dread desperation for what her short future would hold. She knew what was to be her fate. Her final moments would be horrible before they killed her. She fought her retreating sensibilities, disbelieving her eyes. Carson Brand stood before her. She must have suffered a shock so great that she was imagining things.

"Christina."

He spoke her name urgently as he unlocked the shackles. She collapsed into his arms with grateful relief and the exhaustion of insensate limbs.

"How are you still alive?" she murmured, her tormented eyes flooded with tears.

She had no strength to stand. Brand held her upright. He retrieved the dead man's suit coat and wrapped it tightly around her and lifted her. He carried her to the stairs. He took them two at a time as if she weighed no more than a child.

Her comfort in his arms was a stark change from her hours against the cold concrete wall. She sobbed and pressed her face against his chest and neck.

Brand moved rapidly, but he maintained his vigilance in case others hid somewhere in the house. Rafa did not have a garrison of armed guards patrolling the grounds. This was nothing like what he had seen in movies. Rafa lived as his neighbors did. His neighbors probably had no idea they lived next door to a drug kingpin.

Brand opened the front door cautiously. The front of the house was cloaked in darkness. The only light was from low voltage landscape lighting and two ornate gas lamps to either side of the broad parking area.

He carried Christina through the parking area towards the narrow driveway leading to the street. The motion sensor lighting suddenly turned the front of the house into a false midday. The abrupt flood of bright light hurried his steps. He moved as quickly as he was able, carrying Christina's sagging weight.

He stopped at the gate. The gate did not swing open on its electric motor. His bulk was not enough to break the beam that activated the opener. He went to the keypad on the left of the driveway. A round button below the narrow keypad was either an intercom button or a switch for manual opening. He pressed it. The gate opened slowly, the electric motor whirring confidently.

Brand slipped through the opening gate and hurried to his truck. He moved to the passenger door and placed Christina in the seat. He buckled her in then moved around the truck to the driver side. He cranked the truck and turned it around towards the highway. At the highway intersection, he waited for traffic to pass from both directions. He glanced at Christina. She watched him with wide eyes.

The dash board lights cast her in an eerie hue. With her matted hair, make-up smudged face, and dreadful expression of exhaustion and retreating horror, she appeared more a wraith than a living woman.

"Are you okay?" He asked.

She didn't reply immediately. Her dark eyes searched him in an unsettling gaze. Finally, she spoke.

"How can you be alive? Who do you work for? How did you find me?"

Her last question faded into wracking sobs. She covered her face with her dirty hands. She sagged against the seat belt.

Brand wanted to pause long enough to comfort her. Instead, he pressed the accelerator. Rather than heading south, back to San Antonio, he turned north. He knew the area well. He had grown up nearby. He hoped they would be beyond the notice of the authorities and the cartel if they hid outside of the city.

He was wrong.

# Chapter 45

Christina dried her hair slowly. Her shoulders and wrists ached from the chains and the long hours against the cold wall. She wasn't yet herself, but her appreciation that she still lived, and had escaped the cruel lust of the Tango Blast leader, bolstered her mood.

She paused, a thick strand of her long dark hair grasped within the folds of a puffy white towel. She looked at herself in the mirror. The slight green hue of the fluorescent vanity lighting illuminated her haggard visage with an unflattering pall. Her eyes seemed strange to her. The horrors she had endured remained within their fathomless depths, hidden in deep shadows. Her lips trembled with her rising emotion. She realized in that moment how much of her pain was bottled up behind a brittle veneer of skin-deep strength.

With a guilty glance, she saw that Brand was under the covers of the King bed behind her. It hadn't taken him long to shed his clothes and collapse into an exhausted sleep.

Little conversation had passed between them during their trek through the dark country of south Texas. They had driven for just over two hours before Brand had decided on a ramshackle motel near a small country town.

She had waited while he checked in at the night clerk's window. He had returned, looking her over for a moment before he drove to the rear of the horseshoe shaped building and stopped inside the dull lines of a parking spot at the outside edge of the parking lot. He had explained that he didn't want to park directly in front of their room in case they were discovered. He had helped her out of the truck, her movements stiff from her long hours chained in the dark cellar.

Brand snored lightly in the darkness beyond the bathroom light. Christina finished drying her hair and pulled the rough bath robe tightly around her. She turned off the light and moved to the far side of the bed. She kept the robe on as she curled up under the blankets.

Brand's snoring paused briefly at the disturbance. She remained still in her place at the far edge of the bed, her mind whirling in confusion. Contrary to how she thought she would feel, she yearned to be close to Brand. She moved until her back was firmly against him. She pressed her body into Brand's, his warmth a comfort even through the thick robe.

He didn't gather her close with an embrace, yet he didn't move away from her. She felt instinctively that little of his fondness for her remained. At least not to the degree it had before she betrayed him. She knew enough about men to know that he still found her attractive. At some level, he still wanted her. She suspected he was not as distant as he was acting. He wouldn't have risked his life rescuing her if he did not have feelings for her still.

Despite the desperate grip with which she held to her treasured self-reliance, Christina basked in the relief she felt under his protection. He had displayed a remarkable strength of courage and resolve in the short time she had known him. They hadn't discussed the specifics of her liberation, but she suspected Brand had done in a night, what opposing cartels and law enforcement had failed to accomplish over many months. In her mind, her future was as uncertain as ever. Even so, she felt an unreasonable optimism which she unquestioningly attributed to Brand's role in her interests.

It occurred to her that Brand was the most honest specimen of a man she had ever known. His motivations seemed rooted in a sense of practicality no matter the forces opposing him. He worked at problems in a linear manner. Although his procedures seemed derived from the most fundamental solutions to complex problems, he appeared to automatically take subterfuge, and elements from unexpected quarters, in stride. How much of his success was purely luck was uncertain.

A small twinge of worry tickled her thoughts just beyond the edge of her contentment. She felt uneasy at the idea that luck played a part in his success. Luck never holds. Fate always prevails.

Sleep finally drew her from her pain and worried thoughts. Her dreams, however, remained troubled with images of violent thugs and danger. Strangely, Brand did not appear in the nick of time to save her from those who would do her unspeakable harm in her nightmares.

# Chapter 46

He was known as Goliath because he had been the state powerlifting champ in high school. He was no longer built like a spike as he had been in school, although his beer gut was as taut as his barrel chest and powerful arms.

His given name was Jose, but he had introduced himself as Joe growing up. The Anglicization of his name had been his parents' idea.

Comfort, Texas was a sleepy town with little to offer its residents other than isolation and a solid dose of *bucalism*, as the mayor used to say in his weekly newspaper column. Joe had never read the Mayor's weekly Op-ed, but the term had been embraced by many of the older residents in town. Joe had heard the word often but did not really know the meaning. He had overheard a white guy in line at the store tell his friend that it meant being *countryfied* – another strange term.

Joe didn't give a shit about any of that anymore. He drove a nicer truck than the whites who outnumbered the Hispanics in the community three to one. He made more money than anyone in the little town. Although the mayor still wrote his little piece for the newspaper every week, Joe controlled Comfort with an invisible hand of fear and intimidation.

The three-man local police force worked for him. After only one of the city councilmen's houses burned to the ground, the call to "do something about the scourge which haunts the city" died away quickly. Whenever a state trooper visited Comfort, Texas, it was only to eat a hot home-cooked meal at McIntyre's Café at the Comfort exit on Interstate Ten.

Joe's secret was kept from all outsiders. In return, he allowed the town to operate as it saw fit, providing it saw fit to turn a blind eye to the entrepreneurial endeavors he managed for the cartel.

Joe drove his jacked-up GMC slowly along the two-lane service road beside the interstate. At this hour, traffic was light on the highway. The occasional long-haul rig blasted by with yellow and red lights like a high-speed carnival. The trucks passed with a roar of Diesel engines and humming tires, leaving in their wake soothing quiet.

Joe drove slowly, his window opened so he could see clearly without the dark tint impeding his vision. He was not enjoying his late-night drive. He preferred his bed, which even now was warmed by two lovely *senoritas*. Joe ran things here, but Mexico controlled the enterprise which kept Joe in a nice truck and smuggled girls. So, when they instructed him to look for a blue Ford four-wheel drive, guess what he did?

Joe didn't know Don Rafa, but he knew who he was. He had been mid-blowjob when the phone rang. He had answered, pressing the girl's face back into his crotch. The voice on the phone told him that Don Rafa had been killed earlier that night by a white dude in a blue Ford truck. He was supposed to be some kind of badass and he was accompanied by a hot Latina. She had been somebody in the cartel before she had betrayed Rafa. Now she would share the American's fate. That was a quote from the Mexican on the phone.

Joe shook his head with a wry grin. We are all Americans here, *Mojado*, he thought. They hated Americans in Mexico. That was a distinctly Mexican thing.

A wildly successful American business would never hate its biggest customer. The drug trade was viewed as a birth-rite amongst those who participated in it. Drugs were Mexico's largest export to America. It was bigger than even the growing oil trade between the two countries.

The sense of entitlement was pervasive within the cartel. They operated their business with the confidence of the righteous. They hadn't created the product, nor had they hooked millions of Americans on it. They merely serviced both. When something or someone threatened the natural order of things, it or they were dealt with quickly and summarily.

Joe's phone lit as a silent call came in. He pressed the blue tooth button on his dash.

"*Si.*"

"We found it, Goliath. West of town at the Palisades Inn."

"I'm on my way. Don't do anything until I get there."

Joe ended the call and rolled up his window. The big tires on his truck spit gravel as he accelerated along the service road.

# Chapter 47

Christina awoke with a low groan. Her body ached. She moved her hand slowly across the bed. Brand was no longer there. The empty mattress was still warm from his body heat. She lifted her head and looked around the dark motel room. She saw only darkness. A small shaft of light entered the room as the window drape was pulled slightly from the edge of the window frame. She could see Brand dimly by the yellow light.

He didn't turn from his scrutiny of whatever he saw outside their room.

"Get dressed. We have trouble."

Christina felt her heart race. She struggled to shake from her the sluggishness of sleep. With a silent grimace of pain, she pushed herself out of the bed. She still wore the bathrobe. She had only the gangster's suit coat for clothing. She pulled on the coat over the bath robe. She moved to Brand and stood next to him at the window.

"Ready", she said in a small voice.

Brand glanced down at her. His mouth compressed in a grim mirthless smile at her attire. The plan was to buy her clothing first thing that morning. She was stuck in a bathrobe and a dead man's suit coat for now.

His attention returned to his truck. A shiny *vatomobile* sat in the space beside the pick-up. Within the shiny red car, the cherries of two cigarettes glowed in turn like distant signal fires on a mountaintop. Brand looked around the room. He quickly gathered his gym bag with all his possessions packed within. He moved to the bathroom, searching as well as he could in the dark.

"There is no window in the back", Christina informed him in a measured tone.

She felt fear rising despite her efforts to remain calm. The nightmare seemed to never end. How did they find them?

A noise of Brand breaking something in the bathroom drew her away from the window. Although the bathroom was dark, her eyes were adjusted to the dim conditions and she could see him working at the wall beside the toilet.

Brand had yanked the towel bar from its mount next to the vanity. He used it to break a hole in the Sheetrock beside the toilet. He inserted his fingers into the ragged hole and tugged. A chunk of drywall came away. He continued pulling at the Sheetrock until he managed finally to open a hole large enough for them to squeeze between the wall studs. The siding on the outside of the wall was a pressboard material, manufactured to look like wood.

Brand kicked at the siding. As he suspected, much of the old siding was rotten from years of rain and neglect. After several kicks he opened a hole to the back of the motel. He pushed the remaining siding away with his hands. He tossed his bag outside and squeezed through after. He held his hand out to Christina who easily fit in the hole.

"Wait here for me", Brand instructed her.

He pulled the Sig from his tote and left the bag on the ground. He moved quickly towards the end of the motel building. He doubted the men in the car had heard the sounds of the wall breaking at the back of the motel. Most of the noise had occurred within the room, and the back of the motel was likely beyond earshot.

At the front facing corner of the building he peeked around it towards the smoking men in the low rider. He couldn't see the occupants past his truck but there was no activity that would indicate they suspected anything was amiss.

His truck provided welcome cover as he crossed the parking lot, headed towards the waiting men. As he approached, he could hear music emanating from their car. He recognized Tejano music similar to what he was accustomed to hearing on the job site.

Brand circled to the back of his truck, sneaking up on the men from between their car and his truck. The driver's side window was open. A cloud of cigarette smoke wafted lazily onto the still night air. The men chatted in Spanish, laughing quietly in their comfortable seats.

Brand eased the pistol into the window and pressed it against the driver's temple.

"Hey dip shit", he said in a low even tone. "Either of you moves, you die."

Both men froze for a moment before extending their hands towards the dashboard, demonstrating they would cooperate.

"Passenger, get out and come around the front of the car." To the driver he said, "Stay perfectly still."

The driver nodded slowly.

The passenger opened the door and the dome light cast a stark glow in the car's interior. He moved around the front of the car with his hands raised.

Brand backed away from the driver's window, keeping the Sig on his man.

"Now you get out and move to the front of the car. Slowly", he warned.

When both were standing together before the car, Brand reached in and removed the keys from the ignition. He moved forward, covering them carefully.

"Both of you move to the back of the car."

Brand indicated a route around the open passenger side of the car. He followed slowly, giving his captives a wide berth. He tossed the keys on the ground near the rear bumper.

"Open the trunk."

They looked at Brand then at one another. Their minds worked furiously, trying to formulate an escape plan.

"Do it", Brand urged sharply.

The driver bent over and gathered the keys. He unlocked the trunk and it swung open. The trunk was full of miscellaneous junk. A spare tire took up most of the space in the center of the trunk. The remainder was filled with trash, clothing and nondescript bric a brac.

Brand laughed aloud.

"It's gonna be tight in there *Vatos*", he said with genuine humor.

"This is bullshit", the passenger complained. One look at Brand locked his teeth together in fear.

After a moment Brand said, "I'll tell you what. If you tell me how you found me, I won't lock you in the trunk. Deal?"

"Hell yeah", the driver replied. "No harm there, white man. We know your truck. Everyone knows your truck. Even the cops know your truck, you *pinche volio*."

Brand's eyes narrowed at the insult.

"Get in", he commanded with a gesture of the Sig.

Passenger's face contorted in anger.

"You are a fucking liar, *pinche gringo*."

"You are a loud mouth wet back. Get your ass in the trunk before I shoot you and stuff you in there."

Passenger considered his options for a moment longer than Brand liked. He aimed the gun at the man's chest. His arm stiffened in readiness for the shot. The angry gangster's face contorted in confusion and fear. He quickly climbed into the trunk. The driver didn't hesitate as he followed suit.

Brand pressed down on the men, shoving them lower into the messy trunk space as if they were baggage in an overhead compartment. He slammed the trunk lid. He heard the occupants grunt in pain.

Brand ducked between the car and his truck as a pair of headlights turned into the motel parking lot. The truck behind the headlights was a muscular looking four-wheel drive with at least a six-inch lift and aggressive off-road tires. The truck approached slowly, the driver surveying the area. Brand suspected the driver was connected with the two greaseballs in the trunk.


Joe's headlights shone on Manny's car and the blue Ford. He didn't see anyone in the car. This concerned him greatly. Manny was obedient and predictable.

He halted the big truck in front of the two parked vehicles. He shifted into park and opened the truck door. He stepped down cautiously, eyeing the darkness around him suspiciously.

Brand remained where he was, Sig at the ready.

Muffled voices and the sounds of the two men in the trunk struggling in their confined quarters drew Joe's attention.

"What the fuck", Joe muttered and moved towards the rear of the low rider, his caution momentarily displaced by dismay.

Too late, vigilant suspicion returned to him as his reason caught up with him. Two of his men were in the trunk of their own car. Someone would have had to put them there. Suddenly a dark figure was before him. He dimly saw the automatic pistol held low and ready.

Joe was known for his quickness. When he wrestled for the school team, he won every match in which he had ever competed. Much of that was his innate unconquerable strength. Second only to his might, was his ability to move around an opponent with lighting reactions when a hold was taken. His reflexes kicked in now. He leaped directly at the man holding the gun. Before Brand could react, Joe was on him, his gun hand gripped in a vice of muscle and sinew.

Brand's initial impression of his assailant was that he was big and fast. He had crossed a considerable distance of ten to twelve feet in a fraction of a second. Brand saw a bright flash and a mottled pattern of speckles of light as the big man's first blow struck him on the side of his head. Brand brought a knee up sharply.

Joe took it on the meaty part of his left leg, bludgeoning the smaller man again in the head. Joe was surprised. The smaller man seemed unhurt by two powerful blows to the head. Joe squeezed the man's gun hand, crushing the bones of his hand and fingers into the rigid steel and plastic of the gun. He pulled the hand towards him and around, bringing his victim in a position where he coiled his right arm around his neck.

Brand felt himself crushed against the bigger man. Somehow, the man had maneuvered himself into a strong position behind him. The bigger man tightened a huge arm around his neck, cutting off his breathing. Brand knew he had little time to break the hold before he passed out. He lifted his right leg and stomped down hard on the big man's foot, high up near the ankle.

Although he wore sturdy cowboy boots, Joe felt a sharp pain where the move violently compressed the long thin bones atop his foot. Joe moved his foot back to avoid a second stomp and leaned back. The maneuver was meant to lift the smaller man off the ground, eliminating any leverage his opponent might gain.

Brand felt himself lifted easily. His back arched as the big man leaned back, supporting all of Brand's weight. Brand bent his right leg up between the Joe's legs.

Brand couldn't kick high enough to go for his crotch and Joe knew it. Instead, Brand rotated his hips and used Joe's base against him. He pressed violently with his right leg, opening a small gap between he and the bigger man. Brand struck a hard left hand to Joe's lower abdomen, just right of center. He struck him three more times in quick succession. Each blow found the same spot.

Joe's grip weakened on Brand's gun hand.

Brand dropped the gun as he jerked his right hand out of Joe's grip. He brought both his fists up on either side of his body, the fists impacted at Joe's temples.

Joe released Brand and shoved him away from him. His vision clouded red from the temple blows.

Brand was on him in an instant, raining a flurry of head punches around Joe's eyes.

Joe knew his adversary was trying to blind him and possibly incapacitate him. A big fist struck out and Joe felt Brand reel backwards, struck full in the face. Joe moved forward to press his advantage.

Brand kicked him in the balls.

His vision hindered, Joe didn't see the kick until it struck his crotch. Joe had been racked before and was able to continue his attack through the growing pain. Unless one was kicked firmly and fully in the testicles, the pain took moments to convey the impact. This was one of those "deciders" as Joe like to call it. His balls hadn't decided whether they had been injured or just threatened. Joe didn't hesitate while his nuts decided whether or not to register sharp pain.

Brand sidestepped the bull attack. He punched at the man's exposed neck. Joe lowered his chin instinctively and the impact bounced off his jaw, supported against his shoulder. Joe swung a big fist up and around. Brand caught the punch in his chest. With a jolt, he feared his heart would stop from the impact. The man punched like he was swinging a bag of bricks.

Joe saw that his last punch had jarred the man. He followed the chest shot with a solid left to the face.

Brand stepped back to reduce the ferocity of the left, but it still hurt him. With a grim understanding, Brand noted that the big man was as dangerous with his fists as he was when grappling at close range. He had the advantage in straight up fighting. Brand looked for any opening in which he could deal a blow which might slow the building momentum of the big man. The man was well-trained. It was like fighting a Rhino.

Joe recognized the doubt in his enemy. He had seen it many times in his opponents. The next step was dreadful and sure. Joe moved in to finish his man. He slammed Brand against the side of his truck, knocking the wind from his body. A hard right ensured Brand would not catch his breath. Joe threw Brand to the pavement and pinned him with his weight. He grasped the smaller man's neck in two bearish hands and squeezed down on his throat.

This is the end, Joe thought. A cruel smile tightened his lips into a pale line of triumph.

Brand clawed at the huge hands with no effect. He pressed with all his strength, trying to move the man off him. His efforts bore no result. Brand struggled desperately as his strength diminished from a lack of oxygen and fatigue. He felt his body convulse as it tried to draw a breath that would never come. His muscles burned with his effort and the exhaustion of life-giving oxygen. His vision darkened, suffocation shutting down critical body systems.

Joe felt the life leaving the man beneath him. Soon the man stopped struggling. Joe would maintain his grip long after life had left the man's body. He would take no chances. Joe drew a deep breath, an involuntary reaction to his victim's inability to do so.

A sharp, heavy impact crushed in his skull. Joe collapsed on top of Brand's unconscious body. Another impact closed Joe's eyes, blood spread across his scalp and onto the parking lot tarmac.

Christina dropped the heavy iron pipe and grunted as she pulled the heavy Mexican off Brand. She dropped to her knees beside him, cradling his head in her hands. She placed her ear close to his mouth. She felt relief at the slight sound of shallow breathing. He was still alive.

She stood, looking around her. No cars passed along the highway beyond the parking lot. The two remaining cars in the lot confirmed that few of the rooms were occupied. She couldn't see any lights flipped on nor did she see curtains moved by guests disturbed by the life and death conflict which had just ensued.

With a glance at Brand, she determined he would live until she returned, she walked towards the motel. She lifted her pace as she crossed the middle of the pavement. Her bare feet slapped softly as she ran. She arrived at the hole by which they had escaped their room.

She collected Brand's bag and returned to the truck. She dug around the bottom of the tote until she found his keys. Peering at the fob, she located the unlock button. Two quick presses of the button caused the truck's lights to rise in a welcoming glow.

Christina opened the truck's rear passenger door and helped Brand into the back seat. She made him as comfortable as she could before closing the door and moving to the driver's seat. She started the truck and drove away from the motel, headed West.

Brand groaned. His throat hurt as if it had been crushed with a steel press. His breathing was restricted by the swelling. He knew that over the next few hours, he would feel every sledgehammer blow from the big Mexican. Damn he was strong. He remembered nothing beyond passing out under the big man. His next memories were of him lying in the back seat of his truck, moving at speed. He lacked the strength to sit up.

Christina glanced into the back seat.

"Are you okay", she asked with real concern.

"Just a little beat up", he said faintly. "How did you stop him from killing me?"

"You had a big pipe in the back of your truck. I hit him with that."

"That was my jack handle. Thanks for saving my life."

Christina smiled. Brand was not a proud man. He was, as usual, practical.

Brand closed his eyes and touched his face with a tentative hand. He would have a big bruise on his face.

"How long have I been out?"

"A couple of hours. He almost killed you."

"Where are we?"

"We are on the interstate headed West."

Brand opened his eyes, realization pressing hard into his scattered thoughts.

"What time is it?" He asked.

Christina glanced at the clock on the radio.

"Just before six", she replied. "The sun is about to rise."

"Pull into the next big truck stop you see."

"I think we should keep moving until we get a lot of miles between us and the motel."

I agree", he groaned as a throbbing pain grew in his head. "The cops have an APB on this truck, and the Cartel knows what we are driving. We need a new car."

The sun peaked over the eastern hills as Christina entered the vast parking lot of a truck stop under a sign bearing a cartoon beaver.

Brand raised himself upright in the back seat.

"Park around back with the employees."

Christina was uncertain how she would differentiate between employee and customer vehicles, but she drove in the direction indicated. As Brand had predicted, Christina found a cluster of a dozen or so older dilapidated cars and trucks. They had the look of autos that would likely not be used on a long trek for fear of mechanical failure. She parked the blue truck in an available space among them.

Brand opened the rear door and stepped gingerly onto the ground. He set his teeth against the pain he was enduring. Leaning against the truck, he waited for Christina to join him. When she didn't immediately open the driver-side door, he moved forward in front of the window. She pressed the button and the window opened smoothly. Brand nodded as he was reminded that she wore only a bath robe and a shiny suit coat.

Brand opened the rear door and grabbed his tote. He unzipped the blue bank bag and withdrew a handful of cash.

"I'll be back. They sell some clothes here. What size shoe do you wear?"

Christina considered his bruised face for a moment quelling the protests rising within her.

Finally, she replied.

"Six."

Brand limped the hundred or so yards to the store entrance. Keeping his head down, he made his way to the famously clean bathrooms inside.

He stood before a mirror at one end of a line of sinks covering an entire wall. His appearance surprised him. He looked like hammered shit. His left eye was nearly closed. A large purple bruise painted the swelling near the eye. His right cheek was a swollen mass.

He placed his hands under the faucet, actuating the hands-free valve. He rinsed his hands and face. The cold water soothed his hot damaged flesh. He drew soap from the automatic dispenser and washed spots of blood from his face and hair. He worked his tangled hair into a semblance of order with a thorough soaking and a poked combing with his fingers. He dried himself with handfuls of paper towels.

Satisfied that he had done all he could with his appearance, he returned to the vast market lobby. He limped along the main aisle until he arrived at a clothing rack alcove containing a minimal selection of clothing. Most items bore the beaver logo with clever slogans beneath.

He found a rack containing clothing embellished with Texas-themed slogans and trite graphics. He selected the least audacious shirt in Christina's size, and a pair of sturdy shorts. He selected a pair of white sneakers in size six. He grabbed two sandwiches and two bottles of water then paid at the cash register. The cashier eyed him with a mixture of curiosity and alarm.

"You ought to see the other guy", Brand commented with a friendly grin.

The cashier thought about his comment until she finally understood the humor. A smile displaced the alarm and she wished him a nice day, handing him the change for his purchase.

Christina watched Brand limp the long distance back to the truck. He handed her the bag.

"Sorry. This is the best I could do." He explained.

She withdrew the simple garments, holding them aloft to inspect each item. She tried her best to conceal her displeasure at the tourist slogans and the quality of her new wardrobe.

Brand turned away so she could change privately. He cast his gaze around him, taking in the stark terrain and the passing traffic carrying busy travelers to destinations unknown.

The sun rose brightly in a cloudless sky. Traffic roared along the interstate, and a steady procession of cars and trucks moved in and out of the expansive truck stop parking lot.

Many of his favorite memories as a boy were the frequent road trips his parents brought him on. Long hours in the back seat of their big sedan never bored him. He loved watching the passing countryside. There was something about travel that incited his adventurous spirit.

His father travelled often for work. His mother was a stay at home mom and was free to accompany him on many of his business trips. Many of his summers were spent on the road with his mom and dad. He had wanted to be a truck driver at one point in his early teens. There was no finer life he could imagine than the life on the road, seeing the nation slip by while driving a big rig.

Practicality intervened and he found himself working construction through his high school years. He had an affinity for the craft, and it paid better than most jobs for a kid with no college degree in a tight economy.

He turned his head towards the sound of the driver side truck door opening. Christina stepped out of the truck. She wore a white tee warning anyone who might admire her bosom, 'Don't mess with Texas.' The tee shirt was tucked into tan shorts. Her white tennies sparkled with rhinestones. It was obvious she didn't like the new clothing, but Brand had to admit she looked good in anything she wore.

Brand gathered his gym bag from the truck and led Christina towards the trucker side of the parking lot. Dozens of long-haul rigs were parked in a tight grouping behind two long rows of covered Diesel pumps.

Soon, Brand and Christina were able to catch a ride with a trucker headed west. After fielding a few curious questions regarding their appearance and situation, they climbed into the tall cab and watched as the truck stop dropped behind them. Brand had captured one last glimpse of his new truck before the big rig accelerated slowly as it merged into traffic on the interstate. He felt as though he were abandoning a friend. The truck was new to him, but he had already developed a bond with the trusty vehicle.

The truck driver drove them as far as Sonora before he announced that he had to divert north. It was late afternoon when he dropped them at a Walmart. They watched the truck move away along the dusty main street. The truck turned onto the interstate service road and was gone. Brand turned to Christina. Her gaze held the direction from which the truck had disappeared. She slowly averted her eyes until they met Brand's. A mist shone in her brown eyes. Brand tried to think of something to say, but instead took her hand in his.

"Let's get you something to wear", he said, then led the way to the store with stiff strides.

# Chapter 48

Matthew Kilgore watched as Texas State Troopers tore the blue F-150 pickup apart looking for clues. He sat comfortably in the air-conditioned gray sedan bearing U.S. Government plates. The truck stop was crowded with patrons' vehicles and a loose ring of on-lookers, craning their necks to watch the officers work the scene.

His position with the DEA afforded Kilgore a considerable world view of the strange and unusual. Nothing in his career could have prepared him for the journey of an average joe, from blue collar working drone to Cartel buster overnight. With little or no training, and absolutely no plan he could discern, Brand had succeeded where so many had failed.

His department had been abuzz over the past two weeks with the intel of an intensive manhunt for a U.S. citizen, Carson Brand. Their imbedded assets reported him killing several cartel operatives including the head of the border operations, Rafa Cantu.

For months prior the DEA had been unable to locate the highly placed cartel strongman, even after months of thorough searches and digital surveillance. The break in the case had come when a neighbor had dialed 911, reporting gunshots heard at a residence just north of San Antonio. The responding Bexar county sheriff's deputies reported discovering six dead in the home, of which Rafa Cantu was one.

According to San Antonio police investigators, Brand was suspected in the killings of at least one more cartel member, a *Sicario*, prior to that. The resulting APB had led to the discovery of the blue Ford F-150 at a west Texas truck stop. Kilgore had been in the area on a related case when the call came in.

Kilgore's phone rang. He tapped to answer.

"Understood. Where?"

He listened to the man on the other end of the call.

"I'm on scene at the truck stop near Junction. I'm on my way."

He ended the call and turned the key. Three more cartel goons had been attacked in Comfort.

He drove east.

He made the trip to Comfort in under an hour. When he arrived on the scene, Kendal county sheriff's deputies and DPS troopers had cordoned off the parking lot of an old motel. Two *cholos* were cuffed, leaning against a red low rider. Kilgore parked his sedan at the perimeter barrier and entered the investigation cordon.

A DPS trooper nodded at his ID.

"What do we have here, trooper?", Kilgore asked.

"We haven't had the chance to fully process the scene, but it seems a Caucasian male fitting the description of one Carson Brand got the drop on these two guys who were watching his room while they waited for their boss to arrive. The Caucasian male locked them in the trunk of the car and engaged in a hand to hand altercation with one Jose Reta - the dead guy under the sheet."

The trooper indicated a body under a sheet on the opposite side of the car.

"Mr. Reta succumbed to two hard blows to the back of the head, presumably caused by a heavy blunt object, that big pipe there."

Kilgore craned his neck to see around the red car. He nodded his acknowledgement of the information.

"The Caucasian was holed up in room 14 directly across the parking lot. He broke through the back wall of the room and circled around these guys. He may have had an associate with him. We found some evidence of a second occupant in the room. Long hairs may indicate a woman."

Kilgore nodded.

"Interestingly", the trooper continued, "These two guys have been very forthcoming with useful information. We will confirm this, but apparently Jose Reta is the guy running a number of human trafficking safe houses and several warehouses of drugs, guns and cash. The Mexican cartels have set up a considerable base of operations here."

"These two told you all of this?" Kilgore asked with surprise.

"We have Wixson", the trooper said significantly. "He offered them some kind of deal if they cooperated. They really want the deal."

Kilgore had heard of Wixson. He was a Texas Ranger known for his ability to extract information from even the most unwilling perpetrator.

"Is Wixson here?"

The trooper pointed at the motel office with his Bic pen.

"He's questioning the manager."

"Thanks, trooper."

Kilgore walked to the office. He entered, announced by the ringing of a little brass bell over the door. A tall man in Wranglers, a long sleeve pearl snap shirt, and cowboy hat, looked up from his conversation with an Indian man in slacks and shirt sleeves.

"Kilgore, DEA", he said simply.

Wixson shrugged and returned his attention to the manager.

"He said his name was Harold Wilberforce", the manager explained with a thick accent,

Wixson nodded wearily. "And he didn't have any ID?"

"He paid in cash, too. Have I committed a crime officer?" The manager asked testily.

"I don't know, Mr. Patel. Have you?"

"You are the cop, not me."

"It would be wise for you to remember that", Wixson warned him. "Was he alone?"

"He checked in alone. He arrived late and checked in at the night window. I could not see inside his vehicle."

"Do you have video recording equipment attached to the security cameras out front?"

"They have never worked since I bought the place", the manager complained.

"You have my card", Wixson said, folding his note pad. "Call me if you remember something."

Wixson turned on his heel and walked past Kilgore without acknowledging him. Kilgore followed him out the door.

"Ranger Wixson", he said to the Ranger's back.

Wixson stopped and faced Kilgore.

"Do you have any idea where Carson Brand is headed?"

"Since when did the DEA pick up the man hunt?"

"I could ask why the Texas Rangers are involved?"

Wixson looked around him as if Kilgore would gain an explanation from their surroundings.

"The suspects have crossed one or more local jurisdictions in this case", he explained with a weary teacher to dense pupil air." It is customary for the state police to fill in the jurisdictional gap."

"I understand that part. Why the Texas Rangers instead of DPS?"

Wixson considered the fed for a moment.

"We think he is headed to Juarez", Wixson said, turning from the DEA agent. He moved towards the state officers processing the crime scene.

"Juarez? Why?"

"The girl is from Juarez", Wixson said without facing Kilgore. "He's taking her home."

"His associate is a woman? Who is she?"

Wixson halted and faced the Federal agent. He sized up Kilgore critically.

"You Feds work at an awfully high altitude for law enforcement experts", Wixson observed, his squinting lids compressed over hard gray eyes.

He watched the agent react to the criticism for a long moment as he decided what he wanted to share with him.

"Alright, I'll do your job for you. Her name is Christina Villarreal. She was originally trafficked here as a working girl. Because of her looks, she was held, then passed around a handful of cartel movers, each ending with the death of the bad guy. Most recently she has operated as a mid-level lieutenant under the late Carlos Rafael Cantu. It is unknown why she is now in the company of an American construction worker on a seemingly unprecedented killing spree of cartel bad guys."

"Maybe he likes her looks."

"I'm sure he does. I don't know yet why he is committed to her. It is also unclear how he is thwarting both the cartel and local authorities with little or no apparent training or experience. Does the DEA have any insight on our fugitive?"

Without hesitation Kilgore nodded as he replied.

"He served in a Texas Army National Guard unit for six years. He has the reputation of a hard-working entrepreneur and is known to be a hard ass when pressed. His parents died when he was a teen – killed in a flood. He moved in with his friend Robert Gotardi's divorced mother where he graduated high school and joined the Guard. He has no immediate or extended family and few friends."

Wixson pursed his lips as he thought about what he heard.

"You guys have worked up quite the dossier on this guy. What's your interest?"

"We have no interest outside of monitoring the situation as it progresses."

Wixson smiled without mirth or good humor.

"Right." He shook his head finally. "Will there be anything else?"

"Thank you for your input", Kilgore replied with equal ambivalence.

Wixson turned on his heel and continued to the crime scene.

# Chapter 49

Brand hefted the keys to a '96 Toyota Camry. The Hispanic man pocketed a handful of cash and watched as Brand started the car and drove away. Brand drove a block before turning onto a side street. He collected Christina where she sat on a bus stop bench. Her appearance was much improved by her new shorts, peach blouse and white tennies. She carried a plastic shopping bag with two more changes of clothes and fresh undergarments. She rose and approached the car, eyeing it critically. She took her place in the passenger seat and pulled the door closed.

"Ready?" Brand asked before pulling away from the curb.

She nodded and gave the road her attention. Her thoughts whirled about her as the little car picked up speed. Soon they were back onto the interstate driving west. The Sun slowly approached the flat horizon ahead of them. Christina pulled a pair of sunglasses from the bag. She peeled the stickers from the lenses and put them on. She watched as they passed a sign reading 'El Paso 360 miles.' Her gaze moved to Brand. His right wrist rested atop the steering wheel. His attention stayed on the road.

"We will need to get off the interstate just after Van Horn", she informed him.

"Why", Brand asked with a glance at her.

"There is a mandatory Border Patrol check point a few miles beyond that. If what they told you is true, we won't get past the check point."

Brand looked at her once more.

"Any ideas how we get you home?"

"There is a tunnel under the river south of Van Horn. We will have to cross there."

"Van Horn is a long way from Juarez", Brand warned her. "I don't imagine the car will fit in the tunnel. Do we walk the remainder of the way in Mexico?"

"A car will be there. We will have to take it."

"Take it", Brand repeated with meaning. "Take it from whom?"

Christina made no reply. She merely looked at Brand with a blank expression.

Brand returned his attention to the road. He had to remind himself of his promise to keep Christina safe. Entering Mexico seemed like a bad idea. He had barely gotten out alive the last time. The cartel was looking for him now. Delivering himself to their door was a frightening thought. Using one of their smuggling tunnels was suicide.

"There has to be another way across", he insisted doggedly. "I have been to El Paso before – when I was a kid. My memory of it is essentially Las Vegas without the strip. Juarez bumps right up against the border in several places. If we can find a way around the check point, surely we can figure out a way to get you across."

"We found the El Paso / Juarez boundary to be one of the most highly protected regions anywhere on the border. There is no way across anywhere in the city: maybe in New Mexico, but not in El Paso. Besides, there is no way around the check point."

Brand noted the 'we' reference, referring to her former role in the cartel, with interest. Her lingering attachment to the organization rankled him. He couldn't help that his regard for her diminished with the association. As a result, his desire to continue with her on this fool's mission waned also.

Christina seemed to sense the change.

"I owe you my life, Brand. I would not find fault with you if you decided to leave me."

Brand kept his eyes on the road. He made no reply.

"I wouldn't blame you if you stopped right now and left me beside the road."

Brand considered her intently as his thoughts worked at the dilemma. His eyes remained upon her for a long enough period that she glanced ahead of them, hoping he would take the hint and again focus on the road. Finally, he returned his attention to his driving.

Behind his calm countenance raged an internal debate. The temptation of so easy an escape from the dangers ahead was seductive. The promise he had made to himself to keep Christina safe resisted strongly, but with little compelling reason to back it. He was no knight, nor did he consider himself a hero. She was beautiful, but her loyalty was not returned – at least not considering her ill-advised flight to Don Rafa and his goons. She apparently continued her affiliation with the cartel. The near-tragic result of her betrayal had not been enough to change the context by which she defined her relationship with the organization. She still said 'we' when referring to the cartel.

Brand's jaw worked as his mind struggled with his doubts. Was he questioning her allegiance or was he searching for any reason to quit? Was his quandary a product of fear? He shook his head as if to clear the mist of uncertainty with a physical manifestation of his returning resolve. He was as deeply involved as she. If the two men outside the motel were to be believed, both the cartel and the police were after him. His instincts rang within him with the certainty that he was the primary target of both entities, not her. He again marveled at the singularly bizarre path his life had taken. What could he expect to be the outcome? How does a fugitive's flight end?

He grimaced. The future held nothing other than heartache and death. Brand restricted his thoughts from any contemplation of tomorrow. Grim understanding made his decision without his help. In many ways, he had no choice. Perhaps he might achieve some positive result from the finality he believed waited at the end of their journey.

Brand looked at Christina once more. This time his expression was strained, but warm. She saw in his eyes a light like a faraway tongue of flame, beckoning her to gather close to its comfort and warmth. She leaned her head back in the seat and watched him. She experienced a release of her growing tension, her fears temporarily eased despite his lack of assurance. She closed her eyes and allowed herself a moment of relief. She knew he would not leave her.

Brand sensed the change within her. Christina's confidence in him and her reliance upon him dashed any remaining doubts.

Dusk settled upon them with a coppery gloom. Clouds converged in the west, masking a brilliant sunset with the promise of foul weather. Round sandy hills dotted with the stubble of sage and greasewood crowded around the small town of Van Horn.

Under Christina's guidance, he left the interstate for a narrow two-lane highway. The road was straight and stretched for several miles before them. Brand wondered at the open aspect of the terrain. Where would a tunnel be hidden in such a wide-open vista? How far away was the Mexico border?

They drove for nearly an hour before Christina directed Brand onto a dusty trail of a road. Night was dark around them and their headlights seemed inadequate in illuminating the road ahead.

"Drive slowly. Keep the dust down", she warned.

Brand reduced his speed and peered around him in a pointless scrutiny of their dark surroundings. He glanced at Christina. The blue and green dash lights cast her in a ghostly glow. He saw something in her expression which hinted at a deep emotional upheaval.

"Are you okay?" he asked gently.

She replied with unexpected candor.

"This is where we crossed when I was brought here."

Brand returned a look of bland acceptance.

"I was kidnapped from my home and brought here with several other girls. I was lucky to survive."

Brand gripped the steering wheel more tightly. He understood her reaction to the place. She had been a victim of Human Traffickers. Everyone heard the stories. He had never truly bought into the idea. How could someone allow themselves to be kidnapped and whored? How hard could it be to escape once on the American side? He didn't know the answers, but what he knew of Christina caused him doubt in his understanding.

"There" she said pointing at a rusted stove resting on its back in the dust. "Park here and turn off the lights."

Brand obeyed. They sat in the quiet car for a moment. The desert air buzzed with the din of insects and the warm breezes of the night. Christina opened her door and stepped out of the car. Brand followed suit, closing the door after him.

He reached into the back seat and withdrew the gym bag. Inside he found the bank bag containing his remaining cash. He checked for the nine mil. He moved clothing aside to see the weapon despite the weight causing the bag to sag where the gun lay.

Christina moved around the front of the car and stepped off the hard pan of the road and into the silty desert floor. She carried her few belongings in a plastic merchandise bag.

Brand followed carefully.

Lightning sparked threateningly in the west but provided no illumination by which to choose his steps. In the darkness ahead,

Christina moved smoothly along despite the unseen rocks and dark brittle vegetation upon which Brand stumbled frequently. After a particularly abrupt crash, Christina stopped, giving him a look of warning. He could not see her clearly in the dark, but he felt embarrassment at his clumsiness compared to her silent progress.

Brand almost ran into Christina as she halted at the edge of a gulch. It was impossible to tell how deep the ravine was below them. Christina peered into the darkness. She seemed to locate a route down and descended into the defilade with only a soft sliding sound. Brand searched the black ravine below but saw nothing more than darkness.

Blindly, he committed himself to follow. He reached for the ground to support his descent. A thorny bush caused him to shift his weight onto his feet. He slid to the bottom with much noise and several scratches to his arms and torso. He cursed himself for his clumsiness. Christina moved silently until she was close enough to lay a warning hand on his arm.

"Stay close", she whispered in his ear.

She held his hand, walking carefully until they halted before a steep bank. Brand strained his eyes until he could make out a round object centered in the embankment. Christina grasped the edges of the object. Brand heard metal rubbing metal. He reached out and felt the lid of a 55-gallon barrel. He helped Christina, and soon the lid came away in their hands. A perfect circle of black appeared where the lid had been. Brand suspected this was the mouth of the tunnel.

Christina hesitated for a moment before she committed herself to the opening. She climbed into the hole, leaving Brand alone. He stepped into the hole, pushing his gym bag ahead of him.

Inside, he moved on his hands and knees. He crawled downward the length of eight barrels before stepping onto the compacted dirt of the tunnel bottom.

He was surrounded by the darkness of a tomb. He sensed the warmth of Christina next to him. They were absolutely blind there.

"The smugglers use NVG's", she whispered. "We won't be able to see, but the tunnel is straight."

Brand nodded before he realized she couldn't see his reaction. Their progress was slow as they felt their way along the rough right wall of the tunnel. At regular intervals they encountered a heavy wooden post against the wall. Brand reasoned that the post supported a heavy beam above them.

They moved for some time like that until he felt the wall begin to feel damp then wet. They must be near the Rio Grande. He felt a rising fear of the tunnel collapsing under the weight of the river. He assuaged his doubts with the thought that the tunnel was used often and likely would hold until they reached the other end.

Christina halted abruptly and Brand bumped into her.

"There is water on the floor here", she whispered.

"We are under the river", he assured her. "It's to be expected."

"We are not under the river yet.", she told him. "We are still going downhill. Under the river the tunnel levels out. The tunnel may be flooded. This one is seldom used anymore."

Brand waited for her decision. He was out of his depth here.

"Let's turn back", she said finally.

"And go where?" He asked. "Maybe the tunnel is still passable. We have to try."

Christina found his hand and held it in a quavering grip. She said nothing, but he sensed panic building in her. He was uncertain why she was so afraid, but he felt they needed to try after coming this far.

"I'll move ahead", he offered. "Let's go a little farther before we turn back."

He shouldered his gym bag and moved around her, stepping into ankle deep water. Christina resisted for a moment before he finally drew her along behind him. The sound of sloshing water filled the dark tunnel as they descended. The water grew deeper with every step. Soon they were hip deep, and the tunnel floor continued to drop away from them.

Christina again pulled against Brand's forward movement. Brand paused at her resistance.

"I can't swim", she said in a tense voice. "I can't go any deeper."

"Give me your bag", he directed her.

She handed him the merchandise bag containing her newly purchased clothing. He emptied the contents into his gym bag. He wrapped the pistol inside the plastic bag, tying the bag at the top. He replaced the wrapped gun in the bag and zippered the gym bag closed.

"Christina, you are going to have to be brave. You won't have to swim. If the water goes as high as the tunnel roof we will turn back. I promise."

"Stay close to me. Here, hold my hand."

Brand slung the bag and grasped her hand. She groaned in fear and he pulled her along with a firm grip. The water level reached his chest and he slowed, doubtful of their continued progress.

Christina grabbed his shoulder with her free hand and pulled herself up and onto his back. She shuddered as she clung desperately to his neck and shoulders.

Brand realized that the deepening water was nearly over her head at that depth. He was at least eight inches taller than she. He released her hand. She renewed her grip with both arms.

"We'll go a little farther", he said carefully. Her face was close to his ear. He felt her body tremble against him. The cold water was probably a lesser contributor to her shaking than the fear of drowning in the black, cold, muddy water within the small confines of the tunnel.

Brand moved forward carefully, feeling the tunnel floor for any sign of leveling out. Level floor meant they were at the bottom of the tunnel's descent and would gradually rise once more on the other side. With alarm he realized that the tunnel floor continued its downward slope as it fell away beneath the cold water below them.

"I can't go any further", Christina cried in his ear. Her courage had abandoned her.

Brand paused. He feared she would fall into a desperate state which could drown them both. He had to admit that the dark wet cave was horrible in its embodiment of the perfect nightmare scenario for anyone who was frightened of drowning. He had spent countless hours SCUBA diving. His experiences included running out of air at depth and, once, even a mild case of Nitrogen Narcosis. He was uncomfortable in this environment, but decidedly not incapacitated by fear.

He turned, pulling Christina around to a position in front of him. She hugged her body tightly against his. He wrapped his arms around her.

"It's okay", Brand said confidently. "I've got you. It's scary down here, but we have to try."

Brand reached over his head into the darkness. He could just touch the moist ceiling above him.

"I need you to hang onto my back. We are going to swim a ways. You stay on my back."

Christina groaned and her body shook violently.

"The ceiling is a few feet above our heads. We will go as far as we can until the ceiling gets close to our heads. If we can go no farther, we will turn around and find some other way across."

"I want to get out of here", she whispered urgently.

"Me too", he agreed. "Hang onto me. I'll help you."

Christina pulled him close. He felt her body shudder with her sobs.

Brand turned to move on. Christina pulled her body around and behind him, clinging tightly. Brand pushed off the bottom and committed to floating on the surface, treading water and moving forward carefully along the right wall. He could not see the ceiling, nor could he feel for the top of the tunnel for fear of sinking into the cold black water. He suspected that even a brief submersion under the cold water would set Christina into a dangerous panic.

He pulled water smoothly for some time before his head grazed the tunnel ceiling. He felt along the wall until he grabbed one of the heavy wooden support columns.

"Christina, grab this post", he said.

"Why?" she asked in a voice which sounded as if she was nearly frantic.

"I need to check the tunnel floor to see if we are at the bottom yet."

"God no", she said loudly. "You are not leaving me, Brand."

"Christina", he said, bringing his face close to hers. "I will be right here. I just have to touch the bottom for a second. I'm not going anywhere."

He heard her crying in the dark. Her sobs came helplessly. Brand guided one of her hands to the post. She found a hold on a rough bolt protruding from the post where it met the beam overhead. She released him with her other hand and gripped the post. He pulled the gym bag over his head, looping it over her arm. The bag was heavy with drenched clothing and the pistol. Christina shrugged the strap onto her shoulder and renewed her grip on the post and the rough bolt.

Brand pulled a deep breath and dropped below the surface of the black water. He pulled himself down with strong pulls of his arms. His feet touched the bottom of the tunnel. He exhaled until his weight settled onto the bottom. He used his arms to aid in moving his feet along the bottom of the tunnel. He slid along the tunnel floor in this way some half a dozen feet. He thought the floor felt level. He pulled himself along a few more feet through the water. He felt not only level ground, he sensed the tunnel floor rising beneath him as he moved.

His lungs began to ache from the exertion without the benefit of fresh oxygen to his muscles. He forced himself to move further along the floor until he was certain the tunnel was rising towards the other side of the river.

He rose to the surface, pulling air in deep gulps. He was a short distance ahead of where he had left Christina. He found the ceiling close to the water's surface, but he still had room to breathe.

Christina was easy to locate in the dark. Her breathing was audible as she pulled short staggered breaths. Brand returned to her. He spoke softly to her before reaching out for her.

"I'm back", he announced in the dark.

He heard her start then immediately grasp him and pull him close.

"Can we get through?" she asked, in tears.

"Yes", he replied. "We are at the middle. The ceiling gets close to the water's surface, but we can breathe easily. We are going to back stroke until we can touch again."

"Why?"

"It is the only way we can both breathe and stay together. You float and I'll pull you along with me."

"Brand", she moaned. "I want to get out of here."

"We are almost there, sugar. You have been very brave so far. Keep it together for a few more minutes and we will be out of this."

Brand took the bag off her shoulder and wrapped it once more around his shoulders and neck. He felt concern that the added ballast combined with supporting her might sink him. He set his jaw resolutely and faced their back trail. He turned her back towards his chest. Her body was stiff with fear and the cold.

"You have to relax to float", he warned her. "Try to relax your body. I'll do the work."

She relaxed with a monumental effort. He pulled her gently along, careful to keep her face above the water. The deep water and limited air space created the most likely scenario for her to panic, and the most dangerous if she did.

He kicked with his legs and pulled water with his free arm. Although he struggled to manage her weight with the gym bag pulling down on him, they made good progress. He sensed that the ceiling was rising above them. He took a deep breath to inflate his lungs and create additional buoyancy. He quickly lifted an arm towards the ceiling. He touched nothing above them. He moved both arms to Christina and allowed his feet to straighten under them. To his relief, he touched the floor of the tunnel. He stood and pulled Christina along until the depth was such that she could walk comfortably.

Walking in the dark water along the tunnel was a relief for them after the harrowing swim and the doubts of their success. Soon they climbed higher onto dry ground. Soon after, they reached the barrel exit and climbed the metal tube into Mexico.

# Chapter 50

**B**rand helped Christina out of the metal mouth of the tunnel. He was chilled from his time in the cold water. He was certain she was as cold if not more so. She was smaller and lacked body fat. The gym bag streamed water onto the dust of the desert floor. Their extra clothing would be of no help with their chilled flesh.

As on the U.S. side, he could see nothing in the deep gloom of the starless night. Clouds covered the night sky. Luckily, the lightning had not delivered on the promise of a storm. However, the wind had risen significantly. The rising turbulence whipped their wet flesh, causing them to suffer with the chill.

"You mentioned a car before", Brand said in a low voice which shuddered with the cold.

"I don't think this tunnel is used anymore because of the rising water", Christina said through chattering teeth. "There likely is no car waiting here."

"If it were, where would it be hidden?"

Christina looked around her to gather her bearings. Her memory was vague, but she knew approximately from which direction she had been led to the tunnel so long ago. In the years since, she had been party to other shipments bought through this tunnel. She kept that fact to herself. Brand would probably disapprove.

"There", she said, pointing southeast.

"Come on", he said, picking up the bag as he turned towards the indicated direction.

The ordeal in the tunnel had taxed much of Christina's strength and consumed her will. She trudged behind Brand with the movements of an automaton. She focused solely on keeping up, staying just behind him. The cold wind tore at her cruelly. She depended upon his strength to get them to the next phase of their journey, no matter what that phase might be.

They followed a winding draw for several yards until it issued onto a flatter region of sage and caliche.

Brand grunted his relief.

He could just make out the dark silhouette of a car at the edge of the flat area. They moved quickly towards the auto.

In the dark, details were difficult to discern. They could see that the car was an older sedan of American make. Brand grabbed the driver side handle and pulled the door open. The hinges protested at the action with a creaking groan.

Christina moved around to the passenger side and pulled the unwilling door open. She fell into the dusty seat and quickly shut the door to the chilly night air. They felt immediate relief in the car, sheltered from the freshening wind.

Brand felt the ignition for a key. There was none. He felt under the seat. He clenched his teeth against the discomfort of reaching blindly under the old seat. He opened the glove box. It was empty save for some glass fuses and a cellophane wrapper.

Frustrated, he tried the ignition tumblers without a key. To his surprise the switch turned but no dash lights lit, and the motor made no sound of starting. The battery was dead.

As the urgency of flight action dissipated from him, a growing awareness of the unpleasant conditions within the forgotten car grew. The close air stifled them with the sourness of aged sweat and the rancid rancor of rot.

Brand steeled himself with an invisible barrier of reasoned acceptance as he inventoried the likely sources of the rancid stench. With a muttered curse, he wondered why someone would have preferred to defecate within the cramped confines of the car rather than avail themselves of the vast spaces outside.

As if providing an example of a condition which might encourage such a decision, the light tapping of big raindrops struck the car, increasing in intensity until the car roared under the heavy pelting of a crushing deluge.

Lightning blinded them, and immediately they felt the deafening concussion of thunder exploding directly over their heads.

The little car shook beneath the assault. Brand gave Christina a sidelong glance meant to convey wry humor at their continuing hard luck. His grin froze at the look of misery and doubt on her face. The dim light of the flashing lightning storm provided enough illumination to plainly see her misery.

Brand slid over to the passenger side of the car. The brittle vinyl upholstery cracked under his weight as he sidled up beside her. He wrapped his arm around her shoulders and pulled her close to him.

She found some comfort in the warmth of his body heat and the gesture. As before, her resolve was exhausted. It seemed to her that every small triumph was rewarded with a larger obstacle. There seemed to be a powerful vengeful force at work here. Why was their journey so difficult and rife with hardship? There were any number of travelers on either side of the border who travelled hundreds of miles easily and without incident. They had faced mortal danger countless times in the last few days. Considering the difficulties they faced in their journey to Juarez, they could have more easily swam the Atlantic to some far away European city than cross the state for a few hundred miles.

She appreciated Brand's consideration. He was doing his best to comfort her. He was probably as miserable and doubtful in their prospects as she.

A blinding flash and a clap of thunder, like a bomb, caused her to jump in his arms.

"Goddam it!" She shrieked in fear and frustration.

Brand said nothing. He wrapped his other arm around her and held her close to him. Their combined body heat was helping greatly.

Within minutes after the terrifying ferocity of the last thunderclap, the din of the pelting rain diminished atop the old car. Soon only spare taps of widely spread raindrops struck the car. The interval between drops lengthened until the only sound of falling water were the drips of remaining moisture falling from the car to the ground.

A light breeze rushed through the surrounding stiff underbrush as the storm moved away. Lightning flashed intermittently, the thunder lagged at a greater and greater interval, indicating a growing distance as the storm moved away from them. Soon the loitering breeze followed the receding storm, and they sat within a silent car in a still night.

Brand released Christina and gathered the gym bag. He looked to the condition of the pistol. The plastic retail bag had done little to keep the weapon dry. The Sig was soaked. Brand shook the pistol, and water dripped from the seams and from between the moving parts of the pistol. He pulled the slide and locked it open. He withdrew the clip and shook as much water from the mechanism as he could.

He pulled a soaked heavy tee shirt from the wet contents within the gym bag. He squeezed with all his strength. He realized he would not be able to achieve any level of dryness which might absorb the moisture from the weapon's mechanism. He blew on the gun uselessly. He again shook the weapon, resulting in a cascade of additional droplets escaping from within the cold pistol.

"I think we ruined the Sig", he commented absently, shaking and wiping at the wet weapon.

Christina watched his efforts to dry the pistol, her thoughts far away, occupied by the futility of their efforts. Her outlook to the future was dark. The obstacles against them seemed to never end. Her mind fought her for control, and that control would lead to a place of despair and probably death.

As if to confirm her doubts, the night was suddenly alight with a bright white artificial illumination. Brand looked behind them through the rear window. He squinted against the multiple beams of bar-mounted lights atop an unseen off-road vehicle. Another set of lights came around the first and lighted them from a quartering angle.

Dark figures hustled from the trucks and towards them, creating strobe-like shadows as they surrounded the old car. Fully illuminated, Brand saw some half-dozen men wielding automatic weapons converge upon the car and yank open both front doors. Brand and Christina were pulled roughly from the car and thrown upon the ground. Dust coated their wet clothing and skin.

Doubled white pull-tie cuffs locked their wrists behind their backs. Brand was pulled off the ground and onto his feet. He stood there, head down. His mind worked wildly at the hopelessness of their predicament. He glanced at Christina as she in turn was lifted to her feet. The faces of their captors registered only stern purpose. He saw no emotion, neither victorious nor gloating, on the faces of these grim men.

A lone figure appeared around the perimeter of armed men and moved towards the captives. He was not tall, perhaps eight inches above five feet. He was inappropriately well-dressed considering the environment. The gleam of his highly shined black shoes dulled in the dust. He looked Brand in the eye with a stern expression of interest, as if he was studying a strange and fascinating creature.

Finally, he spoke. His precise tones framed his accented English. In the back of his mind, Brand guessed this man appeared to be highly educated in American schools.

"We always disconnect the batteries. It extends the charge life."

Brand nodded as though he was receiving valuable information from a friend.

The well-dressed man turned to Christina.

"Do you know me, Christina?"

"*Si, patron*", she replied. Her voice quavered with her emotion.

He turned to Brand.

"I am Pablo Rojas. I hear I am called *Cabeza de la Serpiento* by the American authorities."

He ended his explanation with an eloquent gesture which dismissed the *nom de guerre*.

"It is significant that I had to apprehend you myself with my personal mercenary guard."

Brand looked at the men surrounding them. He was disheartened at the easily recognizable level of will and training apparent in the deliberate actions of their captors. There wasn't a man there he would not have been reluctant to fight individually. Combined, he believed, they represented an impossible foe.

For the first time in his life, Brand felt a certainty that he would not live through what followed.

"Take them", Rojas ordered.

Their heads were shrouded in black hoods, and they were spirited to separate vehicles. Brand listened for Christina in the darkness of the hood. She made no sound of protest nor did she make any cry of fear or anger. Her silence was more disturbing to Brand than if she had raged against her captors. He remembered her surrender to the cold dark confines of the tunnel. She had been at her breaking point. He suspected all hope had fled her, leaving only resignation and bitter terror.

Rough hands guided him until he was pushed forcefully into the back seat of one of the trucks. He felt himself pressed between two captors, one on either side. The truck lurched forward, making a tight circle until it moved along a bumpy road. His captors uttered no word as they travelled for what seemed like hours.

At first, he had attempted to keep an internal record of how long they drove the dirt road. After he recognized the sensation of smoother pavement grinding under the truck's heavy tires, they travelled along a paved road with no change in direction for a long enough time that he lost count of the seconds and minutes.

He was sure, based upon their turning left onto the pavement, that they travelled in a southerly direction. He was not familiar enough with the geography of Mexico to know of any nearby towns, so he rode along blindly in fact and in understanding.

Finally, he felt the truck slow and turn right onto another paved street. They drove only a short distance until the truck swerved left and came to a stop. He heard truck doors open. Strong hands gripped his clothing, and he was pulled from the seat. He managed to get his legs under him, remaining precariously upright under the careless handling of his captors. He found himself stumbling upstairs until the night sounds fell away as he was guided into a building. The door was closed behind them.

Brand was pressed into a hard chair, the hood yanked from his head. Across a folding card table sat Rojas. His men lined the stone and adobe walls of the low-ceilinged white room. The obligatory bare light bulb hung over the table casting its dingy glow.

The man who held the dark hood carried a vicious looking machete in his right hand. He moved to a position behind Rojas.

Rojas leaned towards Brand with a look of open interest on his face.

"I feel like I am meeting a celebrity", he said with genuine awe.

His lack of sarcasm or guile surprised Brand.

Rojas registered candid fascination with his captive.

"Is it true you are a construction worker with no formal training in combat or law enforcement?"

Brand controlled himself, holding back a number of possible retorts. His instincts warned him that his next words were critical to keeping him alive, even if only for a few extra moments.

"Who would have believed such a thing?" Rojas exclaimed with obvious disbelief.

Rojas gestured to one of his men.

Brand's gym bag was placed before the drug lord. Rojas slowly opened the zipper. He did this without looking down, watching Brand as though he might disappear if he looked away.

From the wet gym bag Rojas removed all of the contents, arranging them in separate piles in an order he alone understood. When the bag was empty, before Rojas sat four piles. The one nearest Brand was a wrinkled pile, consisting of Christina's newly purchased clothing. The panties and bras seemed too intimate for the setting. Brand felt embarrassment for her in the careless display of her most private things in plain view for that rabble of thugs and criminals.

He knew innately that his feelings were ridiculous and wasteful. The next pile were his clothing items. Inappropriately, his sense of humor struck him as he thought that they would find no underwear in his pile. He never wore any. He swallowed a helpless grin.

Rojas noticed the brief spark of humor and the immediate wash of self-discipline which covered the change. Brand saw that the keen scrutiny of his captor had seen through his cover. The king pin seemed to make a mental note.

The third pile was a stack of moist currency, Brand's cash reserves, remaining from his original stash taken from his apartment.

The final stack consisted of his wallet and the Sig. Small spots of trace rust had begun to mottle the blue steel of the pistol. The box of ammunition lay near the pistol.

Rojas sat the gym bag on the floor at his feet. He opened Brand's wallet and removed his driver's license. He read the information on the card then arranged it neatly before him. Rojas removed each item from Brand's wallet one by one, noting the information contained in his social security card, bank cards, the delicate remains of old business cards, and finally the soggy photo of his mom and dad he kept in an inner pocket of the leather bill fold.

"Very clever, Carson Brand. Your cover is quite complete. Most anyone would never believe you anything other than an ordinary American blue-collar worker."

Rojas shook his head meaningfully.

"I am not just anyone. My gift is that of the seer of truths. I have ascended to my station because I never rely on those things presented to me. Your accomplishments give you away."

Brand felt confusion at the direction the interview was taking. His experiences since just before Bert's death seemed to him an unlikely string of bizarre events, occurring at random and survived with the help of no small amount of luck. Rojas seemed to place great credence upon the random outcomes of his encounters with the cartel.

"You have obviously had extensive training and experience. I am troubled that I have never heard of you. My sources go deep within your country's protectorate. Never have I heard of you, a deep cover rogue operative. Who do you work for, Mr. Brand?"

Brand shook his head. The dirt on his face was beginning to itch. He brought his shoulder to his cheek and tried to brush away some of the grime from his face.

"Where is Christina?" He finally asked. His voice was calm and level but for the strain upon him which hardened his words.

"She is beyond your concern, Mr. Brand. Christina is again in the role within which she should have remained from the start. My American operatives are – were – too accommodating. She is a whore who got in too deep. She is no longer in too deep."

Brand set his jaw against the reality of what she faced. He knew that any further protests on her behalf would do nothing for either of them. His chief concern must be focused on himself.

"So, what do we do now?" Brand asked with the same tone of quiet strain.

"Down to business: I like that. You and I have a few things to discuss before I handle your problem."

Brand nodded. He fought fear and doubt. His was not a lingering hope. He wanted nothing more than to live these final moments as a man. Rojas apparently thought him an agent in the service of the government.

"I am not who you think I am", Brand said simply. "I am not a rogue anything. I am lucky to have survived until now."

Rojas shook his head.

"That explanation will not work anymore. You will tell me who you work for. You may not realize it yet, but you have no choice."

Rojas searched Brand's face for a moment. He smiled cruelly as he gauged Brand's fear.

"You do realize it after all", he said as if the revelation was remarkable.

Rojas leaned back in his folding chair.

"I have had many encounters such as this one, Mr. Brand. Each one follows a distinct pattern. There is an established psychological process all captives adopt: false cooperation - hoping they can deceive me; resistance - they test my resolve; deception - they say what they think I will believe; and finally, acceptance - they know that their fates are set. It is at that point that I learn what I wanted to know from the outset.

"Mr. Brand, save us both time and tell me who you work for."

Brand looked vacantly at the piles on the table as his mind worked to create an acceptable answer. After a short assessment of his thoughts, he looked at Rojas. His plan was desperate, but he determined that he had nothing to lose.

"Before we begin" Brand said, his demeanor changing from a fearful captive to what he deemed would be perceived as a professional agent, "would you mind telling me what gave it away?"

Rojas smiled slightly. His eyebrow arched with interest at the candid acquiescence of his prisoner. He took his own moment to assess Brand's motives before he finally spoke.

"A teachable moment is what you are looking for? Unfortunately, whatever you learn from this encounter will not help you. There will be no opportunity to refine your technique. You are not leaving this room alive, Mr. Brand."

Brand swallowed hard. Rojas smiled his recognition of Brand's fear. The men around them shifted as they too saw the signs of Brand's dread.

"I will indulge you", Rojas agreed with a tone which nearly smacked of genuine pity.

"Over the past few weeks you have single-handedly killed a number of my most skilled *Sicarios,* and many highly trained members of my control and management team in Texas.

"You see, Mr. Brand, we run our organization as any other big corporation. We hire only highly qualified candidates with proven abilities and quantifiable track records. The men you have killed were veterans in their craft. You moved through them easily. No mere construction worker could have managed it. You turned one of our loyal operatives with ease.

"You escaped a local, state and federal dragnet with little effort. There is only one answer - they allowed one of their own to slip through in order to enter Mexico and find me.

"You are exhibiting none of the classic reactions of one facing certain torture and death. As I mentioned, I have been here many times. I have sat before every type of captive. I have seen those who cry and beg. I have heard the blubbering and begging pleas of the common dog. Your self-discipline and comportment, in a situation which you are showing signs you recognize as dire, indicates training.

"Finally, you have told many about your military service in the middle east. Alcohol seems to be your weakness, Mr. Brand. You talk too much when you drink."

Brand shook his head in disbelief. This stranger knew of his exaggerations of his military service. Those stories were never meant to accomplish more than to embellish a lack-luster part-time military career in the company of real warriors. He felt a keen sense of humiliation that his lies were so widely known. His ruse was forgotten, dashed to pieces by the embarrassment of his manufactured tales at the bar.

"I was in the national guard." He said. His false confidence abandoned him for desperation and fear. "I have never served outside of stateside military installations. That was just bar talk."

"Are you claiming that you are guilty of Stolen Valor? Not likely Mr. Brand. Your skillful actions back your claims of extraordinary ability and training. Your government does not recruit construction workers into their ranks. They recruit heroes with a requisite training and aptitude to serve."

Brand searched Rojas' face for any doubt upon which he could reason. He saw none. His gaze dropped to the table. He reflected upon his exaggerations of his military service. He thought about Mr. Muscles and Gwen. They seemed so far away. If Karen were here, she would have given him a professional look of disapproval with a dismissive shake of her dark head.

Rojas nodded to the man with the hood and machete. The man approached Brand with a black look. Two others grabbed Brand and held him motionless as Machete man cut the plastic slip ties and grabbed Brand's left hand roughly. He slammed the hand on the table and lifted the machete high for a hard-descending blow.

"Alright, alright!", Brand said abruptly.

He felt fear and rage boiling up from deep within him. He set his jaw as he watched the deadly raised blade. As if a shade was lifted from his mind, he acted with a clarity of purpose he would not have expected of himself in his dire position.

"I am a part of a secret anti-drug interdiction task force. We work at the edges of the law in order to protect American lives. My job was to find you and get close to you. You don't have much time before that door is knocked in and you and your men will be killed."

Brand held Rojas with a look which could have easily been interpreted as that of a mad man. Rojas froze in his seat. A disbelieving smile fought to discredit Brand's words. The machete man looked at Rojas for the sign to complete his task. Rojas shook his head at him. The blade lowered slowly.

Brand eyed the Cartel boss steadily. Lies got him here, maybe lies could save him. He forced himself to hold the Don with an unflinching stare. He knew any quavering or false impression would give him away.

Although they apparently spoke little English, the surrounding mercenaries shifted in their places nervously. The prisoner's sudden change from cowering wretch to authority figure was easily perceived despite language barriers. Rojas studied Brand, searching his face for deception.

"They implanted a chip in my head", Brand cried with false triumph. "My reason for being here is purely to locate you. I knew I would die for it. My country is worth my life."

Brand leaned into his captors as he shifted his weight onto the balls of his feet.

"Finally,", he said with a victorious set to his face. "We have you Pablo Rojas!"

Rojas rose. His fists were clenched beside him.

"*Pinche Volio!*"

He pointed at his men.

"*llegar a los camiones que cabrones!*"

The mercenaries stumbled over themselves as they hurried to obey their boss.

Brand stood in one quick movement. His chair shot away behind him as he flexed his legs to a standing position. The two men restraining him moved quickly to strengthen their hold on him. Brand jerked his body around bringing his elbows up violently. The smaller men fell backwards, struck violently by the move. Brand kicked Machete man in the groin. The long blade dropped towards the ground. Brand caught the weapon on its way down. He brought the machete up violently, slicing the man deeply along his bulging stomach.

Two of the mercenaries tripped over the hurtling chair and fell in a heap, blocking the doorway to the room. The others struggled to right themselves as they tripped over the fallen men.

Brand spun around as another mercenary took a wild shot at him. The bullet narrowly missed Brand and struck a man next to Rojas. The drug lord leapt to his left as Brand jumped towards the table, toppling it with his weight. He leaned back until he was able to grasp the Sig. He thumbed the hammer back and leaned forward. He held little hope that the sodden pistol would fire, but he had only a small chance that any part of his desperate ploy would work. He turned his head in time to see that Rojas watched him, frozen in place.

Recognizing the trap in which he had fallen, Rojas reached into his coat and withdrew a gold plated automatic from its holster and grinned in fear as he tried to bring the weapon to bear on Brand.

Brand bent at the waist and turned the barrel of the weapon as best he could, in the direction of Rojas. Brand pulled the trigger, firing two rounds in rapid succession. Surprisingly, the weapon belched fire and the first bullet struck one of Rojas' henchmen. Brand shifted slightly and fired again. Rojas grunted as a slug struck him low and deep. He involuntarily squeezed off a shot which struck another of his henchmen beyond Brand.

In response to the sudden gunfire, the remaining startled mercenaries reached for their weapons. Only a few of the men managed to raise their weapons as Brand turned in a tight semi-circle, squeezing the trigger again and again.

Mercenaries fell under the fusillade. Few of the gunmen had time to bring their weapons into a position where they might deliver an accurate shot. Those who managed to get off a shot fired wildly and with little accuracy. Brand steadied his concentration upon performing a systematic arc, hopeful that he could maximize the fifteen rounds in the Sig's magazine.

Soon the room was littered with the still and writhing bodies of the dead and wounded men. Among them was Rojas, who lay upon the floor in a growing puddle of blood.

Brand rose and stepped over him. He squatted low until he was able to pick up the machete which lay where he had dropped it next to the dead man of the hood. He returned to Rojas. He looked down at him. The drug lord watched him silently as his body shook with the shock of his wound.

"That was luck", Brand told him, his voice husky with his effort and the dawning reality of his narrow escape from death.

Brand watched the Don die. He looked around the room. He believed at least two of the other half dozen men in the room were dead. Others groaned and struggled with their wounds. Brand shot a man who reached for his weapon.

Three are dead, Brand thought.

He dropped the machete and gathered his wallet and money and shoved them into his pockets. He pulled the clip from the Sig and loaded it from the ammo box on the table. He bent down and used

Rojas' shirt to dry the weapon as well as he could. Brand inserted the filled clip and chambered a round.

He walked slowly around the room, searching for any man who might understand English. Near the door a mustached Mexican struggled to lift himself into a seated position. His expression transformed into an evil grimace when he saw Brand approach. Brand squatted before the man.

"Do you speak English", Brand asked him, bringing the pistol on line with the man's face.

"*No se. No habla Engles*", was the reply.

"Right. You better pick up some English quick or I will start putting holes in you."

Brand pressed the pistol against the man's forehead. His expression was equally menacing.

"Where did you take the *senora*?"

The wounded man appeared to ready himself to deflect with a claim of ignorance once more.

Brand pulled the hammer back on the pistol and pressed it harder against the man's forehead.

The mercenary grimaced at the pain of the muzzle pressing into the skin of his forehead. He seemed to reconsider his reply.

"She is gone", he replied in broken English. "The *Caravan LaVaca* leaves early. The whore is halfway to Houston by now."

Brand ground his teeth at the insult.

"Where will they cross into America?"

The wounded man seemed genuinely confused by the question.

"*No se, gringo.*"

"Where – *donde* – is she now?" Brand hissed through bared teeth.

"She is in hell, gringo."

It took all of Brand's self-control to restrain himself from pulling the trigger. Instead, he struck the Mexican across the temple with enough strength to knock-out the man. Brand rose and again fought the urge to kill the man.

He mastered himself and returned to the overturned table and fallen chairs. He recovered the clothing and other items from the floor and placed them in the gym bag.

With a last look around, Brand left the room. Outside, the morning was dawning with a thin gray line at the eastern horizon. The air was cool and damp from the recent rains.

He went to the nearest pick-up and opened the driver side door. He saw that a key was inserted in the ignition switch. He slid behind the wheel and started the engine. His plan was aggressive and risky.

He was in a small village of tiny dingy houses and forlorn looking retail shops. Few cars were on the streets. He backed the truck out of the crude dirt drive before the small house.

He had no idea how to find the tunnel. He was lost in Mexico. He decided on a more direct plan. He followed the narrow road until it ended at the wider paved road of the main thoroughfare, upon which they had arrived. He turned west and left the little village. He continued west until he came across a paved road leading north. He turned onto the road and drove until it ended at another cross roads.

This, a graded dirt road, appeared to be frequently used. He again turned west and drove until he found another road headed north. In this way, he drove in a zig zag pattern towards the border.

Finally, one of the northern roads ended at a low fence and a broad pasture. Beyond the clearing, at about a quarter mile's distance, he saw the green massed foliage of a dense tree line. The trees were willows. He knew that willows typically grew near water. He guessed that beyond the screen of wispy trees flowed the Rio Grande.

He left the truck in the middle of the road and hopped the fence, his gym bag slung over his shoulder. He jogged the distance until he entered the tree line. As he suspected, the muddy waters of the river flowed languidly beyond. The American side beckoned.

Brand lifted the gym bag above his head and waded into the river. He was able to walk the width of the river, at its deepest reaching his armpits, until he stepped onto American soil.

He had expected to find himself crushed under an onslaught of border patrol agents descending upon him after his easy illegal crossing. Instead, he heard only the songs of distant birds and the slight morning breeze rustling the yellow grasses around him.

Brand continued his northerly trek. He hoped to come upon a highway or perhaps a ranch house where he could arrange transportation. His only clue as to Christina's whereabouts was the mercenary's mention of Houston.

He was far from Houston, no matter where he had crossed. The complication of an ongoing statewide manhunt would make the journey much more difficult.

Brand paused within the cover of a low clump of bushes. At a short distance he saw a shiny pick-up truck pass upon a two-lane highway. He approached the road cautiously, alert for law enforcement vehicles. He found a hiding spot near the road and waited for the next car to approach.

He finally saw an approaching eighteen-wheeler. He moved to a clear place at the road side and waved at the approaching truck. To his relief, he heard the air brakes and the truck slowed until it stopped beside him.

Brand stepped onto the stairs and opened the passenger door. A big man in a yellow logo shirt and shorts grinned at him.

"You look a little worse for wear, pardner. Where you headed?"

"Houston", Brand replied simply.

"Well I can get you most of the way there. I gotta make a stop in Refugio."

"I appreciate the ride", Brand said with genuine relief. "I'll even buy lunch if you're hungry."

The truck driver laughed and patted his round stomach.

"Friend", he said with a jolly booming voice. "You can't maintain this build and not eat."

Brand took his place in the seat and pulled the door closed. The truck pulled away from the roadside and soon they were headed smoothly east.

"Why you are soaked, son? Did you swim the Rio Grande to get here?"

The truck driver laughed at his jest. His passenger was clearly white and American.

"It's a long story, sir. Do you have a towel I can sit on until I dry?"

"Reach back into the sleeper and grab that blue towel hanging on the hook."

Brand did as he was instructed. He toweled himself and his clothes off as best he could. Finally, he folded the towel under him and sat back heavily with a sigh.

Brand looked at his feet as he thought about Christina.

The driver glanced at him, but after seeing Brand's expression, decided to wait a while before he engaged him in conversation.

Brand noticed the deference with silent gratitude. The strain and exertion of the last few days was catching up with him. He felt an all-encompassing fatigue.

His last thoughts before he fell into a deep sleep were of those he had lost. He would never again laugh at Bert's antics. He would no longer worry whether Natalie was loyal or not. He was alone once more, as he hadn't been since the death of his parents.

# Epilogue

They called it *Gladiator Floor*. Harris county lock-up was a nightmare at any rate. Poor living conditions and inadequate numbers of guards made the typical day a hazardous one for inmates. The Houston newspapers had run opinion pieces featuring the shoddy conditions and the rising fatalities within the jail.

The 7th floor of the Harris County Lock up was one of Houston's best-kept dirty secrets and Brand was now a part of that secret hell.

Carson Brand was housed with the hardest gang bangers in the pod. The guards staged the fights and bet on the outcomes. Every tattooed hard case there was trying to make his bones.

Brand was new, which made him a target. His introduction was short but compelling. A fellow inmate broke down the details for him moments before he was singled out to participate. You fought when the guards told you to. There was no refusal. Those who refused to fight were raped.

His bare feet felt raw on the concrete floor. The lean, sinewy black man across from him glared fiercely. His tattooed skin shone with sweat. Corded muscles moved beneath slick skin like angry pythons within a shining sack   Tattoos covered him from the top of his bald head, down his torso and into the black and white striped jumpsuit, draped low where it was tied off at his waist.

From their cells, inmates yelled as they craned their necks to get a view of the combatants through rough gray bars.

Three guards grinned cruelly.

The white boy was going down.

Walker was their longest reigning champion. Of all the inmates, he seemed to enjoy the fights most. The others fought because combat was preferable to the alternative if they refused. Walker thrived on the conflict. He reveled in the notoriety and the stench of fear that ran down his opponents' legs.

The new guy was no match for Walker.

Brand saw the guards but could only guess at their thoughts. His sole preoccupation was the fierce black man before him. Brand quartered his body slightly away from his opponent. He flexed his knees in a ready position. He had no idea how the attack would come, but he knew it would happen soon. He felt himself growing angry. He disliked being pressed into a fight he hadn't started. He certainly resented the obvious opinion that he was an easy victim for the tattooed black criminal.

Walker approached Brand casually, his hands hanging low along his sides.

The guards chuckled. They had seen this technique before. The white guy was toast.

Walker continued his forward movement until he saw the smallest movement as Brand prepared to create space between them. With incredible speed, his right hand shot towards Brand's face. Brand turned his head and caught the blow as it glanced harmlessly off his jaw.

Just as blindingly quick was his return shot. Walker caught the blow fully in the center of his face. He felt his nose break and his teeth rattle loose. Brand pressed his weight onto his left foot and collapsed Walker's throat with a sharp left.

Walker fell, holding his throat as he tried to clear his airway. Brand stepped in and delivered a rapid flurry of rights and lefts to Walker's face.

The guards found themselves frozen in disbelief. Their champ was being dismantled before their eyes. The white guy was fast, and he hit hard. The sound of fists on face were sodden chunky sounding blows.

As one, they emerged from their stupor and rushed to pull Brand from atop Walker. The latter was out cold. His face was a tattered and bloodied mess.

Brand struggled to shake off the guards' restraining holds in his frenzy to get at Walker.


Brand was in solitary confinement when he was collected and led to the visitor's hold. He entered the room bound at wrists and ankles with heavy shackles.

Alone in the room stood a tall thin man in a suit holding a red folder. He nodded to the guards and they sat Brand at the center table. They used a spare set of cuffs to shackle him to the table. The guards hesitated over Brand.

The man in the suit waited for them to leave. Finally, he spoke with the authority of a federal officer.

"Give us the room gentlemen."

Reluctantly, the guards retreated behind the heavy door and bullet-proof glass enclosing the visitor's hold.

Brand considered the man in the suit with a disinterested expression.

The man in the suit noticed the look.

"So, you are a hard case now", he observed dubiously.

Brand said nothing. He merely watched the man.

"I am Matthew Kilgore, DEA. You are in a lot of trouble Mr. Brand."

Kilgore approached the round steel table and sat across from Brand. He lay the red folder on the table before him.

"What would you say if I offered to get you out of here today – right now?"

"I would say yes", Brand replied immediately.

"We'll get to that. Right now, I want to ask you a few questions."

Brand was silent once more. He waited for Kilgore to get to the point.

"Your recent activities have drawn a lot of attention from highly placed individuals on both sides of the law. I don't believe you will last long in here once it is known that you single-handedly wiped out the Gulf Cartel."

Brand watched Kilgore with an impassive eye. He remembered Detective Hernandez's list of crimes he had committed. He had since added many more.

"What's in the folder?"

"This is a dossier on you Mr. Brand. We dug deep on you. Some of what we thought was just luck and timing turns out to be a combination of genetics and plain old toughness."

Brand looked at the red folder curiously. He had no idea what the federal agent was talking about.

Kilgore opened the file at the center. Notes and official-looking forms were clasped to both flaps of the folder.

"Have you ever heard of *Berserker Blind Rage Syndrome*?"

Brand snorted and laughed at the term.

"Not until now", he replied.

"Initial sampling of your behavior indicates that you likely have it. Do you ever feel an uncontrollable rage that you just can't keep inside?"

Brand looked at the agent with surprise.

"Black Dog", Brand replied in a low voice.

"Pardon me?"

"I call it 'Black Dog' when it happens."

"This syndrome is rare these days. It is written about in great detail in ancient Norse and Viking texts. They believed that their greatest warriors were possessed by ferocious animals that bestowed a ferocity and strength that was otherwise unexplainable. Symptoms include greatly increased strength, targeted violence, quickened reaction time, and in some cases, amnesia after the event."

Kilgore considered Brand for a long moment before he continued.

"Do you drink?"

Brand nodded.

"I enjoy a bourbon from time to time."

"Copious alcohol consumption is considered a major contributor."

Kilgore closed the file without reading it.

"You are accused of every crime known to man including, but not limited to, murder, aiding and abetting, grand larceny, assault and battery, smuggling, obstruction of justice, several weapons charges and crossing international borders illegally. Based on your impressively speedy creation of a very considerable rap sheet, the law will imprison you for the rest of your life. How do you feel about that, Mr. Brand?"

"It sounds like I am in a tight spot. What do you recommend we do about it so that I can leave here right now?"

"I want you to go to work for me", Kilgore replied simply. "As a private citizen everything you have done over the past months are

351

criminal offenses. As a federal asset, all of those things are done in the line of duty and would likely warrant some type of award or citation."

Brand shook his head at the irony. He wasn't being given many options.

"Join me and walk away from this mess clean. Allow yourself to be appropriately rewarded for a job we have been trying to do for a long time now. We will train you and help you channel your inner 'Black Dog'."

"It sounds like I have no other choice."

"You don't — at least not a choice that ends well for you."

Brand looked down at his chains.

"I'm ready to go."

**Look for Carson Brand's next novel:**

# Bert's Tale of Booze

A grey sky hovered low upon the wet roofs and bundled masses heaving along the streets of the village. Cloaks clung tightly around chilled shoulders. Peace tied swords weighed heavily, ankle bells tinkled with each step, and ponderous chain mail shifted and tinkled with their haste. The scarred double doors of the great hall resisted the large crowd entering to receive a small amount of warmth and a large amount of ale or Meade.

At the center of the roiling throng stood a large bearded man in stiff leathers, broad gauntlets and grieves. His arms spread dramatically as his deep voice boomed. All present knew of him and his tale. No matter the frequency of the telling, his ode was welcomed as a mainstay of the festival.

"Settle in with me now. Join me in a moment which will come only once. We will never be here again!"

Like a blanket, silence fell upon the large hall.

The large bearded man looked about critically, as if he searched for any single member who might be unworthy of the coming tale. Reluctantly his eyes turned from the crowd and to the broad beams and thick rafters of the great hall.

A methodical chant began with a single voice but was picked up by the throng until it thundered. A single word chanted in slow but irresistible rhythm.

"Bert! Bert! Bert!"

One large raised hand silenced the crowd. He shook his head as if in denial of any credit for himself personally. His tale was not his to own. He was merely a container, sharing its contents with those who would benefit from the gift.

With one last long panoramic look he began:

*In the days of the warring tribes of the highlands, only a handful of hardy nomads travelled a strange and forbidding land. One of these, a battle-hardened band of travelers, made their way into a vast wilderness. They searched for a place in which to settle, where the weather allowed for farming and the waters were suitable upon which to sail and fish. Finally, weary and near despair from the hardships of their journey, the weary band gained the summit of a windy hill. Below them, they beheld a valley of unrivaled beauty. Rolling grasses and the feathered greenery of generous trees gave way to the gentle azure waters of a protected bay.*

*The leader, O'levre, surveyed the new and beautiful land with a satisfied eye. This wise leader was a large and powerfully built man. His countenance was broad with high cheekbones and a powerful jaw. His piercing blue eyes gleamed their approval at their good fortune. Finally, he proclaimed this valley their new home.*

*A small settlement grew on the shores of the protected bay's welcoming waters. The bounty guessed at was well exceeded by the harvest reaped from the fertile land. The sea teemed with fish. Their nets, many times, were too heavy with fish to recover without releasing a portion of their catch.*

As the seasons passed gently and without incident, their lives obtained a peace previously unknown since their flight from a troubled homeland.

O'levre, the warrior, grew calm in this tranquil place. His hawkish eyes soon lost their sharpness of war. The peace within him opened his awareness to those things of beauty around him. Among them, he noticed the interest for him of a lovely maiden.

To his battle-weary eyes, she was cornflower and goldenrod. Often, he found himself in a state of unconscious rapture. His senses were immersed in his preoccupation of her. The very parting of her generous lips when she spoke caused him a start and filled him with the most exquisite sense of pleasant warmth.

Her name was V'rona. She was aware of his affection for her. She had grown up with the stories of his ferocity in battle: the same stories who's very telling served as a primary deterrent for ambitious enemy attacks. Her fear gradually became curiosity, then finally attraction. The idea of so ferocious and infamous a lion becoming a warm and loving companion was irresistible.

Their love was just beginning to bloom when the enemy arrived. The skies grew dark and the seas grew black with his rage. This land was his refuge from the rigors of his life as a god above.

O'levre and his clan gathered in the center of their small village. They watched the threatening skies with the stern mien of a people accustomed to facing the threat of a powerful and strange adversary. A lightning bolt struck near them and from the blast appeared a golden being. He was magnificent to behold. He was beautiful and terrible at the same time. His voice opened like the heavens.

"My name is Ba'acus. You are strangers to this place and unwelcome here. I will allow you one opportunity to leave before loosing my almighty rage upon you."

O'levre stepped forward. His jingoism, recently dormant, once again possessed him. He felt, as before, at home in his sense of impending conflict. Ba'acus eyed him with grim interest.

Even to a god, O'levre was an impressive specimen of manhood. The god looked the warrior up and down. His gaze then surveyed the others in the circle. Inevitably, his keen eyes settled upon the lovely V'rona. He took in her beauty with obvious relish. O'levre was not pleased with the god's interest paid V'rona.

"This place is our home", the leader proclaimed with a menacing tone. "We will not leave."

Surprising to all present, the god did not grow angry at O'levre's challenge. Rather, he appeared amused at the temerity of the fierce leader.

"Very well", the golden god said, "I will allow you to stay in my paradise. The levied price for your new homeland is this lovely maiden."

He pointed a stiff arm at V'rona. Deliver her to me at the top of the northern promontory at sunrise tomorrow, or I will visit upon you my Devine wrath."

With this dire proclamation, the being rose from the ground with a whirling storm of wind and rain. In an instant he was gone, and the sky was cloudless as before.

The elders gathered before O'levre. There was no talk of delivering one of their own to this vengeful being. The talk was of war and how it should be waged against so ominous a foe. As they had their entire lives, they donned armor and gathered to them the weapons and shields so recently traded for nets and plow shares.

The next morning the villagers gathered at the central square, dressed and equipped for fierce and final battle. The pleasant morning sun rose as it had every day since their arrival. Today, however, it dawned upon grim battle-hardened faces and the dull chink of armor and weaponry. Every eye searched the skies for sign of the imminent threat they would face in battle. Although fear was a part of every battle, none was exhibited by these veterans of a lifetime of armed conflict.

The Sun rose as it always had. The minutes passed, yet no mighty foe appeared. There was no darkening of the horizon or tossing of the seas. Minutes grew to hours with no difference to that day's advance than any other. Suspicious of a plot of attrition, the fighters maintained their ready positions as the day waned then darkened as the evening grew nigh.

O'levre finally looked about him with no small sense of pride. His men had lost none of their discipline nor a whit of their military bearing in the softness of their new gentler lives. He tapped his spear on the hard ground three times: the traditional signal. The company of soldiers relaxed their vigilance as one.

After a short conversation, it was decided that a cautious and alert withdrawal to their homes was warranted. Bright torches were lighted throughout the village and guards were posted at the village's edges in all four directions. The remaining force would rest during the night then resume their watch the following day.

O'levre had slept only a few moments when a deafening screech brought him bolt upright. The air whooshed as if pressed by powerful forces. The village roused with a cry of women and the angry roar of the men.

O'levre grabbed his spear and emerged from his warren. The sentry torches shone upon the shining scaled coils of a giant flying beast. It was more than twice the size of their largest fishing vessel. As the beast rose, O'levre recognized the destroyed remains of V'rona's small warren.

O'levre moved towards the rising beast. Fear for his new love gripped his strong heart. Below the flying behemoth was clutched *lovely V'rona in a large clawed grip. Beast and prey were soon lost to the inky blackness of night. The men ran in pursuit of the beast but were soon left hopelessly far behind. In defeat, they returned to the small village. They pledged to take up the hunt at first light.*

*O'levre returned to his warren, heavy of heart. Dread at what might befall his love at the whim of so awful a creature filled his imagination. It was a credit to his strength of will that he found the ability to sleep for the few hours left to him that night.*

*For the second day, the men were up with the dawn. They again gathered in the village center to muster their forces for the day's work. To their surprise, the vengeful god awaited them. He stood with arms crossed. His mighty chest heaved with the strength of his emotion.*

*Before the men could act upon their rage and rush the being, he pointed a large accusing finger at them.*

*"You have lost her!" he boomed. "My bride is lost to me...and to you!"*

*This last he leveled directly at mighty O'levre.*

*The leader was confused at the god's senseless accusation. He was unaccustomed to the unfamiliar emotions he felt, and he struggled to regain his comfiture.*

*"You are responsible for this!" O'levre retorted impotently. We shall recover V'rona."*

*"No", the golden god shouted. "Only one of you may face the beast!"*

*From the folds of his tunic he withdrew a jeweled bottle. He held the heavy vessel in a single sinewy hand.*

*"All shall drink from the Nectar of the Gods. Only he who does not succumb to its pleasures shall be fit to confront the beast in battle. It is written that only one may defeat the beast where a host would fall."*

*O'levre approached the golden god. He took the heavy, ornate vessel from him and hefted it in one mighty hand.*

"There is hardly enough in this container for a single thirsty man. How shall it provide for a host such as us?"

The god shook his head.

"He who passes the test shall confront the beast and defeat him alone."

With that, he vanished as he had previously, in a violent storm of wind and rain.

O'levre moved to the center point of the square. He pulled the heavy stopper from the bottle's spout. He sniffed the contents suspiciously. Finally, he instructed his men bring goblets and flagons, so they might begin the test.

Soon all returned to the village center, equipped as commanded by their leader. The bottle was passed among them, each man filling his vessel to the rim. As one, they lifted their cups and drank deeply. They waited, looking at one another for some tell-tale sign of change or transformation. Instead, they felt only a lightening of their thoughts and moods.

They refilled their cups and again drained them. Soon they felt a strangeness growing behind their eyes. A lightness of spirit affected each of them to a man. The gravity of the situation faded from dire consideration to a topic of lighter concern. It seemed, in some way, even a bit humorous that a mythical beast would appear and spirit one from among them, as in some fabled tale.

The third time the jeweled vessel made its round, a general sense of increased camaraderie gripped them in a warm fraternal embrace. Their conversation went to the long-time friendships and brotherhood linking each man to the other.

This ritual continued through the remainder of the day and far into the night. The decorative container failed to grow empty. For that matter, it seemed never to drop below full. The effect upon the warriors was remarkable.

*Finally, as morning arrived, preceded by a dull thin gray line on the horizon, only one man stood. O'levre looked about him in the dim light of the infant day. His fellow warriors lay upon the ground and against trees, snoring and blubbering their helpless condition caused by the Nectar of the Gods. The answer was clear and not surprising to those few women awake at so early an hour. O'levre once again would be their champion.*

*Although wobbly from the effects of the nectar, he made ready to set out upon the trail of the beast. He paused once more to survey his countrymen. Amidst the prostrate sat the ornate vessel, innocently awaiting its next victim. O'levre boldly collected the bottle and took one more long draught from its wide mouth. He felt no fear of the contents within.*

*He strode from the village, bottle in hand. His shield was slung over his shoulders and his spear was gripped tightly in his free hand.*

*Surprisingly, he found the beast's lair within less than a half day's walk from the village. To his relief, V'rona stood amongst a half circle of tall stones, the front guarded by the wary beast. She appeared unharmed. The large creature surveyed the approaching man warily.*

*O'levre halted mere yards from the monster. He pulled the cork from the jeweled vessel once more. From it he drew a long pull. The pleasant warmth of the liquid provided him a comforting glow from his throat to deep within him. He once more, felt the pleasant sensation, as the nectar again affected him. His head swam slightly, but his courage was bolstered.*

*He placed the bottle gently upon the ground and gripped his spear in his right hand. He brought his heavy shield into proper position for battle. He lowered his huge head and rushed the scaled creature with his war cry: the same cry which had demoralized the enemy on countless occasions. The beast watched him with dull red eyes.*

With an incredibly quick movement the beast whirled his entire body and struck at O'levre with a maw of razor-sharp teeth.

O'levre saw the attack in plenty of time to react. However, for the first time in his life, his reactions were not rapid enough to avoid the move. O'levre disappeared within the creature's mouth with a loud crunch.

V'rona screamed her surprise.

Without a pause, the beast lifted on its large scaly wings and flew towards the distant mountains.

As if by magic, the golden god stood just outside the circle of tall stones. He considered his beautiful prize with great relish.

Surrendering to her inevitable fate, V'rona approached the god with lowered sad eyes.

The god took her in his powerful embrace. As he turned towards the azure sea, just visible in the distance, V'rona looked into the god's face.

"Will you leave the jeweled bottle and the magic nectar within?"

The golden god looked down upon her with surprise.

In his booming voice he replied. "I never touch the stuff."


Deafening cheers from the grateful crowd made the welkin ring. Bert bowed his head. His work here was done.

CRAIG RAINEY

*Craig Rainey (1962 - ) is an American film actor and author. He was born in San Angelo, Texas and now lives in Austin. He cowboyed professionally in south Texas. He was an NCO with the Texas Army National Guard. One of his first published works was the award-winning screenplay, Massacre at Aqua Caliente, soon to be a major motion picture. He wrote the full-length novel by the same name based upon the script.*

Made in the USA
Las Vegas, NV
25 June 2022

50710149R10213